PRAISE FOR *SHEEPISH*

"A sun-kissed beach-read set on the magical island of Martha's Vineyard, where baby lambs frolic in the salty sea air and lovers seem destined to misunderstand each other."

--Elizabeth Shick, author of *The Golden Land,* Winner of the AWP Prize for the Novel

"The perfect literary rom-com, rich with Vineyard charm and unforgettable characters."

--Elisa Speranza, author *of The Italian Prisoner*

"A delightful romp in both the quiet off-season and the lively summer months, *Sheepish* will have you craving a steaming bowl of chowder, a hot lobster roll, and a scenic drive up-island while you cheer on Aly as she navigates the winding path of love—and finds herself in the process."

--Emily Cavanagh, author of *Her Guilty Secret*

"Set against the stunning backdrop of Martha's Vineyard, *Sheepish* is a lighthearted, beautifully drawn story of friendship, identity, and the quiet magic of starting over."

--Dianne C. Braley, award-winning author of *The Silence in the Sound* and *The Summer Before*

"With the perfect blend of suspense, sweetness and sizzle, T. Elizabeth Bell delivers another delightful story rooted in her signature 'Vineyard Bliss.'"

--Alice Early, author of *Moon Always Rising*

"Bell has done it again with a delicious Martha's Vineyard love story, this time between a city girl and a salty island fisherman. *Sheepish* is a beautiful ride through some of the island's most iconic beaches, trails, and neighborhoods—it will transport you to the Vineyard no matter where you are! Toss it in your beach bag and enjoy the escape."

--Julia Spiro, bestselling author of *Such a Good Mom, Full,* and *Someone Else's Secret*

PRAISE FOR *COUNTING CHICKENS*

"Bell paints a lovely, vivid picture of the vibrant, year-round island community...Remy is compelling, beautiful inside and out...a stunning protagonist." --Kirkus Reviews

"A charming tale...Counting Chickens takes you deep into the real Martha's Vineyard. You'll finish loving the characters, longing for the scenery...an infinitely fun read for anyone who wants to escape.... I was on vacation from beginning to end."

--Brooke Lea Foster, bestselling author of *All the Summers in Between*

PRAISE FOR *GOATS IN THE TIME OF LOVE*

"A delightful romp of a novel that will transport you to summertime island life, complete with sandy beaches, sun-warmed skin, briny oysters and tangy blueberries, ocean sunsets, and, of course, romance."

--Kathleen McCleary, author of *Leaving Haven, House & Home,* and *A Simple Thing*

SHEEPISH

A Martha's Vineyard Novel by

T. ELIZABETH BELL

PABODIE PRESS

Sheepish is a work of fiction. Names, characters, places, and incidents are the product of the author's imagination or are used fictitiously. Any resemblance to actual events, locales, or persons, living or dead, is entirely coincidental.

Copyright © 2025 by T. Elizabeth Bell.

All rights reserved.

No part of this book may be used or reproduced in any form or by any electronic or mechanical means without written permission, except for quotations of brief passages inserted in reviews or critical articles by a reviewer. Scanning, uploading, and uploading of this book, or facilitation of such without the permission of the publisher is prohibited. Please purchase only electronic editions, and do not participate or encourage electronic piracy of copyrighted materials.

Pabodie Press books may be purchased for educational, sales, or business promotional use.

Printed in the United States of America.
First Pabodie Press edition 2025

ISBN: 978-1-7330851-3-7
eISBN: 978-1-7330851-4-4

Library of Congress Cataloguing-in-Publication data not available at this time.

Cover design by Tilden Biss8ell
Poem printed permission of D.B.M.
Author photo: C.C. McIsaac

10 9 8 7 6 5 4 3 2 1

For Mama and Dadad, with love

🐑 🐑 🐑

A year ago, I was just a lamb
But look at me now, my fleece is glam
My gals tell me I shall be shorn
But on this topic, I am torn
They say my wool needs collection
But why change shear perfection?

--D.B.M.

🐑 🐑 🐑

PART 1 — SPRING

This was not what Aly had planned for her vacation.

Shivering in her raincoat and wet socks, she looked down at her new boots, soaked and ruined by the muck, then over to the damp, wooly shape that was doing a weird up-and-down thing that Aly sincerely hoped was normal. Or at least normal for a sheep in labor.

The cold drizzle condensed into fog. Across the muddy pasture, Tisbury Great Pond dropped behind a pale scrim in the early morning light. This wasn't like San Francisco. There, the fog (nicknamed Karl by the locals) rolled in like a comfortable blanket and made everything soft and misty. This was pea soup fog: thick, cold, and wet, with a tinge of rotting seaweed and salt. Somewhere out on the water, a flock of geese honked, laughing at her.

Across the pasture, the rest of the small flock huddled together under a shelter. "Where is he?" Aly asked Beau, Hannah's border collie. Once again, she scanned for headlights on the road that ran by the pasture. Still no sign of Whit, the guy Hannah told her to call if she needed help. Like now.

Where are you? Aly texted again. But there had been only the one response ("On my way") to her five earlier texts, two voicemail messages, and several futile shouts into the misty, breaking dawn.

She wiped a drop off her nose with a cold finger. No use feeling sorry for herself. Still, this was not the surprise trip that she'd planned for Hannah's thirtieth birthday: four glorious days in

Virgin Gorda, lounging under palm trees on a beach as tropical breezes rustled the fronds. They would hike lush jungle paths through the hills and snorkel with the sea turtles in the warm, crystalline water. In the evenings, she and Hannah would take one of the crazy open-air jitney taxis into town for fruity cocktails and as much seafood as they could eat. It would have been perfect, exactly what Hannah deserved for her birthday.

But March was lambing season on Martha's Vineyard, and Hannah couldn't leave the Island. So instead of bikinis and turquoise water, Aly had been lured to the Vineyard with promises of long walks down beautiful, empty beaches and cozy evenings in front of the fireplace, and the chance to catch up—really catch up—with each other's lives. What mattered, of course, was spending time with her dearest, oldest friend.

It was just fate blowing a big raspberry that sent Hannah racing off to Vermont when her mom fell, just hours after Aly stepped off the plane.

The sheep bleated, low and sad. Beau gave a muffled woof and looked at Aly. He was eerily smart, as if he knew what he'd do if he had something more useful than paws. Should she Google wikiHow on how to deliver a lamb? Watch a video on YouTube? Aly blew out a puff of air, tucking a lock of wet auburn hair behind her ear as she gathered her courage. "OK. I'll take a look. But," she warned, "I'm a web designer, not a vet."

Aly walked over and peered at the rear end of the sheep, which was about as useful as diagnosing a car's engine trouble by looking under the hood. The ewe rolled her big black eyes and gave another sad bleat.

Aly patted the sheep's wet, spongy wool. "I can't help you. I would if I could," she said as a thick band of fog rolled in, shrinking Aly's world to a tiny globe of girl, dog, and a very pregnant, very unhappy sheep.

🐑 🐑 🐑

Beau's ears perked up, and he barked twice before dashing across the field to disappear into the mist. "Come back! Don't leave me here! Beau! Beau!" Aly shouted. The dog circled back, panting, then sped off again. "Beau!!"

"Aly?" a man's voice called. "Beau, stop running off. I can't see where you're going."

"Here!" Aly shouted.

A tall, broad-shouldered figure slowly emerged from the fog, wearing a wet canvas jacket, jeans, and muddy work boots. Beau ran another circuit, yipping excitedly at his heels.

"Whit? What took you so long?"

Whit crouched next to the sheep. "Take it easy, girl. Everything'll be fine," he murmured. "Got here as fast as I could. I was looking in the other pasture. You didn't tell me where you were."

"Thank you for coming. But you could've called. I left a ton of messages." In some irrational part of Aly's brain, Whit was to blame for her being soaked, worried, and cold.

"Phone died." Whit looked up at Aly with weary, heavily lashed eyes. His black hair was wet and mussed as if he'd just gotten out of bed. She caught a whiff of stale beer. "How long has Maisy been like this?"

"I'm not sure." She glanced at her watch. "Beau woke me up maybe an hour and a half ago?"

Whit frowned and moved around to the rear of the sheep. The ewe shuddered, and as if she'd been waiting for a competent midwife, bleated to tell Whit what was wrong.

Aly gasped as Whit took off his jacket and rolled up one shirt sleeve to the elbow. "Please tell me you're not going to do what I think you are going to do."

"Got no choice."

Aly turned her back to Whit and the sheep. "I cannot believe this is happening."

"I've got to turn the lamb. Hold on, Maisy-girl. Let me just push here and..."

A sucking sound made Aly cringe. Squeezing her eyes closed, Aly tried to envision herself warm and dry under a palm tree, sipping a rum punch with a tiny paper umbrella.

"Getting there," he said, looking up at her pinched face. "Are you squeamish?"

"Yes," she snapped as another cold trickle of rain dripped down her neck. "Who wouldn't be?" she muttered to herself. Aly had grown up in rural Vermont, but that didn't mean she knew anything about farm animals. She breathed deeply and took a sip of her imaginary cocktail through a long paper straw. *Tiny pink umbrella, pineapple and coconut juice, a double shot of rum, and a sprinkling of freshly grated nutmeg on top. Lime. She'd forgotten the lime. Or maybe passion fruit juice...*

Whit grunted. "Almost there," he said. "Just a little more. You got it, Maisy!"

Aly glanced over her shoulder. Whit was crouched beside the ewe, who was licking a lifeless-looking shape. "Oh no, is it...?"

"Very much alive. Baby lamb chop here'll be up and around in no time," he said, patting the mother's damp wool. "It's hard work, being born."

Whit stood up, stretched his arms overhead, and yawned. The fog, now glowing pink with the dawn light, began to lift, allowing a glimpse of water through the mist. Like a miracle, the newborn lamb struggled to its feet, wobbled, and bleated.

"That's amazing," Aly said with a rush of excitement.

"Look, he—or she—is trying to find breakfast already. Now let's see what else we got going on in there," Whit said. "Maisy looks big enough to be carrying twins, maybe triplets. Hopefully the next one'll slide right out. Shouldn't take long."

Beau, pleased with his role in the morning's adventure, shook himself, spraying muddy water over Aly's pants.

"Oh, Beau, did you really need to do that?" she asked. Hannah's warm house—and a set of dry clothes—beckoned. Aly started to pull a boot out of the muck and stopped. Hannah had trusted her to keep an eye on things. Whit or the lamb might need...something. Aly drew her soggy raincoat tighter around her. She might be incompetent as a midwife, but she'd see this through.

Whit looked up and smiled. "Go inside and get warmed up," he said. "No worries, I got this."

🐑 🐑 🐑

Aly put the copy of the *MV Times* on the coffee table and smoothed the wool blanket across her lap. Headline stories about the Steamship Authority's new ferry reservation system and the latest West Tisbury town hall meeting made for less than riveting reading. Winter clothes scrounged from Hannah's closets and drawers had taken the chill out of her bones, but Aly's attempt to start a fire in the huge fireplace had been less successful, sending a plume of smoke into the living room instead of up the chimney.

Beau barked at the sound of the kitchen door opening. "I need to use the sink," Whit called. Aly heard the groan of the spigot, followed by the sound of gushing water.

She unwrapped herself from the blanket, pulled off her ski hat, and shuffled into the kitchen. In addition to the hat, she had on huge, Hannah-sized gray sweatpants, thick wool socks, and an enormous moth-nibbled sweater that looked like it came from a Goodwill bin. (Which, knowing Hannah, it probably had.) Her friends in San Francisco would laugh if they could see her—her Type A, perfectionist boyfriend, Kevin, most of all. But she was finally warm.

"It smells smoky in here." Whit stood at the sink in a plaid flannel shirt rolled up above his elbows, lathering his hands and forearms with a bar of soap.

"I tried to light a fire in the fireplace," Aly said.

"Did you open the flue?"

"Oh. Maybe not," Aly said, annoyed that years of using a remote control to flick on her gas fireplace had caused her to forget that first basic and critical step.

"That's usually the problem," Whit said. "Good news—old Maisy had triplets. Second slid right out. But a bit touch-and-go there for a while with the last one, I had to…"

"Would you like some coffee?" Aly interrupted, not needing the details of Whit's obstetrical interventions.

"Sure. Thanks." He dried his hands on a dish towel and turned around with a grin. "Long night, but we've got three new healthy baby lambkins to show for it."

Whit's lopsided smile hit Aly like a shockwave. It deepened the crinkles in the corners of his mouth and cheeks and set his eyes, cat's eye gold, alight, warming Aly in a way that all the layers of wool had not. Straight white teeth and curved lips were paired above a lean jaw shadowed with stubble. He filled the small kitchen, even taller and more broad-shouldered than he'd looked in the field.

"Glad I finally showed up?" Whit said, raising an eyebrow.

Aly blushed, realizing she'd been staring—and that he'd noticed. She felt a twinge of guilt about noticing Whit's good looks. She was, after all, happy with Kevin. Mostly. All relationships had issues, and theirs were nothing fatal. Just…stuff that they needed to work out. And they would. Then it dawned on her. Hannah had been dropping oblique hints about a new man in her life. All she would say is that he was tall, dark, and handsome. Aly wasn't really into the lumberjack look—she'd had enough of that growing up with Hannah in Vermont—but if Whit was the new boyfriend, she got it.

"Yes, of course. Thank you for coming out here in the middle of the night," Aly said, with a rush of gratitude.

"No problem. When's Hannah getting back?"

"Soon, I hope. I'm just visiting for a few days from San Francisco."

"So Hannah said. City girl, huh? I'll come back to check on the new lambs tomorrow afternoon." Whit's eyes slid past Aly to look out the window. In the distance, tendrils of fog fairy-danced across the field, and the dawn light skimmed Tisbury Great Pond with a rose-gold glow. "One of the prettiest views on the Island, I think." He glanced at his watch. "On second thought, I'll pass on the coffee." He pulled his wet jacket off a peg by the door. "Do you need me to check out the fireplace?"

"I can do it." Aly might not be able to midwife a sheep, but she could open a flue.

🐑 🐑 🐑

Half an hour later, Whit pulled his truck to the curb on North Water Street, the toniest street in tony Edgartown. He stepped out, knocked the mud off his boots, and took his guitar case from the passenger seat. Yawning broadly, he walked up the steps to the impressive front entrance, a deep front porch framed by fluted white columns.

What a day—and night. First, the meeting with his lawyer and the trip to the courthouse, then the late gig playing at the Ritz, topped off with the long drive out to Hannah's in the predawn light to search in the rain and fog for a poor mama sheep.

With no heat or water in his summer cottage, he was grateful to be staying at his friend Chas's grandmother's house. Whit fumbled with the key and opened the front door. Bone-tired, the expression went. That's what he was: wet, cold, bone tired, and feeling decades older than his thirty-one years. He needed sleep. A very long, very deep sleep.

"Good morning, Prince Charming," called Chas from the top of the stairs. "Convince Cinderella to invite you to stay the night?"

Whit looked up from untying his boot laces. "You're up early," he yawned.

"And you were out all night." Chas wore a pair of striped pajamas with his initials embroidered on the pocket, his sleep-mussed blond hair sticking up in a cowlick in the back. He ran his eyes over Whit. "So, who was she? Looks like you didn't get much sleep," he said approvingly.

"I was with Maisy. And, yeah, I'm beat."

Chas's eyebrows shot up. "Maisy? Do tell."

Whit was too tired to string Chas along. "One of Hannah's sheep." He stretched his arms and yawned. "Hannah had to go off-Island. Her mom had a bad fall and is in the hospital. Hannah had some friend staying with her who freaked out and called me when Maisy went into labor. I had to turn one of the lambs."

Chas made a face. "I suppose you still remember what to do after working at that sheep farm down in New Zealand."

"Sheep station."

"Sheep whatever." Chas pursed his lips, looking disappointed. "Here I was imagining you having a wild night—well, Martha's Vineyard-in-March wild—ending with a lovely fluff-the-pillows with some local hottie." He looked Whit over from head to toe and sighed. "All that gorgeousness—well, you need a shower—going to waste. If I find you a date, will you go?"

"Probably not."

"Whit Dias, you need to get out and have some fun. Get over that Petty-Patty-Petra girl, whatever her name was. Too bad, she seemed like your type. Boaty. Fishy," Chas said. "But it's been, what? Over a year?"

"Eleven months."

Only a week before Whit had returned to the Vineyard from his winter gig in St. John, Petra had shown up in the harbor on her

Eurotrash boyfriend's 75-foot yacht. Seeing her lounging on the deck in her bikini, laughing and drinking wine, stabbed a fishing knife into his heart. Back when they were together, he'd let himself fall into a hazy dream of forever. It had been hard—harder than Chas knew. But he'd learned his lesson. You couldn't ever really know what someone was hiding in her past or was up to when you weren't around. He'd believed Petra when she'd said she loved him and wanted to be with him, never suspecting she was only using him to get back—and back at—her wealthy ex. Whit should have known: he'd watched his bored, unhappy, unfaithful mother play similar games with his father, deserving as that asshole might have been. But Whit had been played for a fool, a mere boy toy until Petra could reel in a bigger, richer catch.

"More than long enough." Chas crossed his arms and mock-scowled at Whit. "Your only flaw is that you don't listen to me. I'm asking you to date, not be a boy whore."

"Fine." What Whit wanted was food, a shower, and bed, in that order. He did not need a lecture from Charles George Parkerson IV. He opened the hall closet to put away his guitar. "You said you were going to come hear me play."

Chas leaned against the banister. "Just wasn't feeling the Ritz last night. Not my scene."

"Yeah. I guess not." A very un-Chas-like crowd frequented the Island's best (and only) dive bar in winter. But for Whit, it felt like home. And the gig put a few welcome dollars in his pocket.

Chas brightened. "You need coffee. And something to eat."

Whit followed Chas into an enormous, spotless kitchen. A big bay window overlooked a formal garden, winter-brown and tidy, the clipped roses and mulched beds waiting for spring.

"Speaking of dating," Chas said. "My choices are extremely limited here in the off-season. I've looked," he said, pushing the button on the coffee maker.

"Not like August, huh?"

"Not in the least. But somebody had to keep an eye on the house while the workmen were here."

"And you are both a dutiful grandson and unemployed."

"I prefer to think of it as being on sabbatical," he said. "I'll make us breakfast."

Whit yawned. "So, what did you do last night instead of the Ritz?"

"Binge-watched *Queer Eye* and drank a bottle of Granny's good Bordeaux." Chas pulled a carton of eggs from the refrigerator. "I was feeling sorry for myself with you leaving tomorrow to go back to St. John."

"I'd better stay until Hannah gets back," he said. "That friend of hers seems clueless. She—or the sheep—might need me again."

Chas beamed. "As do I. You know, we haven't properly celebrated your big win in the courts of justice," he added. "How about I make a reservation at Atria tonight? Champagne, oysters, a nice steak?"

"Hardly anything to celebrate, Chas." He still couldn't believe that he'd been sued. And all because an idiot client on one of his fishing charters last September had lost her diamond bracelet overboard while reeling in a bluefish. It took the judge—an avid fisherman—all of thirty seconds to dismiss the case. But still, it meant Whit had been dragged up from the Caribbean to Martha's Vineyard in the middle of his busiest month.

"But if you're paying, Mr. Moneybags, count me in."

🐑 🐑 🐑

Beau watched Aly's every move like she was under some sort of doggy surveillance as she set a fire, flopped on the squashy sofa, got up, sat back down, got up again. Spats of rain and a chill wind had replaced the fog, rattling the panes in the windows and seeping carpets of cold under the doors. Outside the windows, gusts chased shadow cloud-shapes across the field and churned whitecaps on the pond, as the small flock of sheep huddled together in the pasture. Growing up in Vermont, Aly knew what early spring was like in New England and had sworn never to come back. But here she was on a wet, windy island in the middle of the cold Atlantic.

The cottage was decorated in Early Yard Sale, with a hodgepodge of sofas and chairs grouped in front of the huge brick fireplace. Stacks of mail and magazines cluttered every surface. No books, Hannah wasn't a reader. The windows were small, the ceilings low, the beams massive. There was even an old-fashioned spinning wheel sitting in a corner next to a bag of yarn. Hannah had told her that her house was old, but Aly hadn't realized how old. This wasn't faux *Dwell Magazine* old. This was wide-plank-floorboards-and-rippled-glass old. And, for all Aly knew, Colonial-era ghosts hiding in the closets.

But Hannah's messy house felt comfortable and homey, especially with a nice big fire blazing. Aly breathed in the familiar, calming scent of woodsmoke. So different from the straight-from-the-West-Elm-catalogue look of the place she shared with Kevin, with its sadly scentless gas fireplace. Hannah's reminded her of her beloved first apartment in a Victorian rowhouse in the Mission, a third-floor studio walkup that she'd furnished with thrift store finds and a futon bed for a sofa.

Aly put another log onto the fire and made herself a cup of tea. The kitchen felt empty without Whit. He had to be Hannah's new mystery boyfriend. She'd done good: handsome and a nice guy to boot. Settling down at the table, Aly turned on her laptop and, briefly reassured by the glow, logged into Wi-Fi using the password ("Sheepish") taped to the refrigerator. Ten minutes later, the network-connection-lost message flashed onto the screen. One bar of service on her cellphone. Hannah even had a landline. Aly shook her head. This place wasn't just old; it was positively prehistoric.

Sipping her tea, Aly stared at the pan of maple-cinnamon rolls that Hannah had left. They had everything she'd banished on her current "eat healthy" diet: refined sugar, white flour, and gobs of butter. She caught Beau staring at her as she stuck her finger into the glaze.

"No judging," she told him. "I get enough of that at home." She pulled out a gooey roll and took a bite. Then another.

Aly debated eating a second roll. She should feel guilty or sick or something, but instead a warm, happy spot sat underneath her belly button. Aly ate slowly, first unrolling the treat, and then savoring the crisp outside before nibbling her way into the soft, pillowy center edged with cinnamon swirl. As she licked her fingers, she found herself back in Hannah's mom's kitchen, helping Hannah's mother mix and shape what she called her Cinna-Love Buns. The Watsons had taken Aly into their warm embrace when she was a child, giving her everything that her own troubled teenage mother could—or would—not. For which Aly would be forever and eternally grateful.

Hannah's mother, Jo, had smooth pink cheeks and a ready laugh. She wore soft cardigans and jeans, with her frizzy gray-brown hair pulled back in a rubber band bun. Hazel eyes shone bright behind gold-rimmed glasses. Jo's grandma-in-training appearance hid a brilliant academic mind. Aly loved her. She hoped that Jo's fall was just that, tripping over a rug or something, and not more serious.

She picked up her cell to text Hannah. *How's your mom? What do the doctors say? Can you talk?*

Her phone rang. "Hey Aly. Thanks for checking in," Hannah said. "The doctors don't seem super worried, but Mom's still having dizzy spells and her something-something levels are all off, so they're running more tests. And she looks awful—two black eyes and cuts all around where her glasses pressed into her face. Nine stitches in her chin. And she's concussed, so she's having these terrible headaches. But it could've been so much worse."

"Doctors are always super cautious."

"I guess," Hannah sighed. "How are things there?"

"All under control," Aly said. "Big news. One of the sheep—Maisy, Whit said—had triplets last night. Beau woke me up like you said, and I called Whit, and he took care of everything." Hannah didn't need to hear about her cold, wet night or the details of Whit's heroic veterinary efforts.

"Thanks for holding down the fort. And thank Whit too."

Aly wrapped her fingers around her mug to warm them. "He'll be by later to check on the lambs." It felt good to talk, to hear Hannah's familiar voice. "So, anything you want to tell me about Whit?"

"What?"

"Tall, dark, and handsome, you said. Very handsome, I couldn't help but notice."

"Yeah, so?" Hannah said, sounding confused.

"He's not the mystery boyfriend?"

"Whit?" Hannah laughed. "No—he's a good friend. And a very good guy. He'd do anything for anybody. But let's just say that any girl who's interested in dating him is going to end up disappointed," she added. "Got to go—the doctor's coming. I'll call you later."

Aly scooped up another bit of the frosting and covered the pan. She'd get Hannah to divulge the identity of her new boyfriend later. Speaking of boyfriends, Aly looked at her watch, calculated the time difference, and dialed Kevin. He'd be up. Or if he wasn't, he should be.

"Miss me yet?" Aly asked.

"Of course," Kevin replied in a groggy voice.

"And Miso?"

"Definitely. Heartbroken. He hasn't ralphed up a hairball since you left," Kevin said with an audible yawn.

"I bet he's happy having you all to himself."

"Probably. He's taken over your side of the bed. Having fun?"

"I wouldn't exactly call it fun, but...." Over the sounds of Kevin's morning routine, Aly recounted a passably amusing version of her lambing adventure. It was a pretty good story, now that it was all over, the lambs were fine, and Aly was inside, warm and dry.

She could picture Kevin in their sleek, white kitchen. With a six-burner Viking range and a built-in refrigerator hidden in a wall of glossy cabinets, the kitchen had sold him on the apartment. When he asked her to move in with him, Aly was sad to leave her cozy place in the Mission, but she loved living in a building with a roof deck and a doorman to keep the porch pirates away. With La Boulangerie around the corner and a short Uber ride to Ripple, Kevin's soon-to-open restaurant, it was everything they wanted.

"So, not exactly reliving your bucolic Vermont childhood? I never pictured you as a midwife to a pregnant sheep," Kevin chuckled, the coffee grinder whirring in the background. "I can't imagine you were a very good one."

"Hannah's friend Whit was. Me, I was cold and wet and kind of scared," Aly said. She stared out the window at the gloomy rain and brown, leafless branches moving in the wind. "I miss you."

"I miss you too. But you wouldn't see much of me even if you were here. That guy I found to fabricate the hood for the grill? He just told me it'll be another month. And dealing with the city on the permitting is driving me nuts. I can't get them to call me back."

"So, you don't *really* miss me," Aly said.

"Of course I do," he added absently. Aly could tell he was back to thinking about the restaurant. As usual.

Kevin had been dreaming about opening his own restaurant since he'd been in culinary school. He fit all Aly's requirements in a boyfriend to a T: he had ambition and passion, a sense of humor, boyish good looks with straight black eyebrows, and a shock of thick hair. And, on the rare occasion when he wasn't too tired, he was nearly as good in bed as he was in the kitchen. He wasn't perfect, of course. Kevin had a chef's ego and was more than a bit of a control freak. But Aly didn't mind, not really, that he was a perfectionist. She was used to it. Besides, he was almost always right.

"So, what are you doing, other than birthing sheep?"

"It's called lambing."

"Other than lambing."

"Nothing. The weather's been horrible. And Hannah's Wi-Fi is lousy. I can't even stream anything."

"You spend too much time on screens."

Aly sighed. "And what should I do instead?"

"Read that book I gave you. The Marie Kondo—you did take it, didn't you?"

"It's in my backpack."

"You know your closet and drawers are out of control. That can be your project when you get back," Kevin said.

As usual, he was correct. Her stuff was a mess. Aly hated throwing things away, no matter how old: the washed-thin blue corduroy shirt she'd had since her freshman year, the ratty straw beach bag with the big purple flowers from a college trip with friends to Hawaii, her collection of silly animal-shaped tea infusers that Hannah had given her as birthday gifts over the years that cluttered up a drawer in Kevin's kitchen. He called her sentimental. It wasn't a compliment.

"Did Hannah leave you anything to eat?"

"Homemade cinnamon rolls—I don't want to think about the calories." She opened the fridge and freezer. "Not much. I'll probably nuke up a frozen Stouffer's for dinner."

"Aly, love, you can cook for yourself. I've spoiled you."

She could hear Kevin's smile. "I like being spoiled." A longing to be back home, drinking coffee with Kevin out of her favorite octopus mug, displaced the warmth from the Cinna-Love Bun. With Kevin so distracted and working like crazy to get Ripple open, Aly treasured their ritual of a first morning coffee together.

"You should go out and buy some of those little bay scallops. Do up a couple of tablespoons of brown butter, but be careful not to overcook them. Add a tiny squeeze of lemon at the end. You'll thank me."

"Yes, Chef."

Aly could hear the faucet running. "The property manager is coming this morning to check out that leak in the bathroom."

"Finally," Aly said. "I'm tired of putting towels on the floor."

The apartment buzzer rang in the background. "That's probably him. Gotta go. Love you."

"Love you too."

🐑 🐑 🐑

Beau padded over and laid his head in Aly's lap. "It's good for me to be unplugged. Right, doggy?" she said, stroking the long, soft fur on his ears. Aly settled herself on the sofa and opened her book. But reading about organizing her drawers into rows of tidy little t-shirt soldiers felt like a guilt trip. Instinctively, she reached for her laptop. The network-connection-lost message popped up again. Aly stared at the screen, groaned, and stood up. "Where's the router, Beau?"

She paused at the open basement door. She'd looked everywhere else. It must be down there, where it smelled of mold and mice. Aly flicked the light switch. A lightbulb hanging from a wire barely illuminated the gloom. Gripping the banister, she made her way down the steep, narrow staircase into what must have been the old root cellar, now filled with stacks of moldy boxes and old furniture. She pushed the reset button on the router, ran back upstairs, and sat waiting with her laptop for the little lights on the black box to do their magic. Nothing. She rebooted her computer. Still no signal. Mustering her courage, Aly dashed down again into the creepy basement and did a full reset of the router, unplugging it, waiting a full minute, and trying not to scream when she heard a scurrying, scratching noise from the corner.

No Wi-Fi. Cut off from the world.

Back upstairs, Aly leaned her head against the sofa. If she were at home, she could walk down the street to her favorite coffee shop, chat with the baristas, and set herself up with her laptop in a cozy corner. But here, finding an open café with Wi-Fi meant driving Hannah's truck eight miles into town, part over unmarked, rutted dirt roads, in the pouring rain. And maybe finding her way back.

Or Aly could make the best of it. There was a cozy fire and Beau for company. Frozen mac and cheese for dinner and cinnamon rolls for dessert—she didn't have to buy scallops. Acres of fields and a big old barn to explore if she felt like going outside.

And a real bathtub.

Aly was pleased to discover the clawfoot tub in the upstairs bathroom. Her city apartment had a shower but no tub, and she hadn't taken a long, leisurely bath in ages. She turned on the taps, hot as she could stand it, and stripped off her layers of clothes. With goosebumps puckering her naked skin, Aly stepped over the edge and lowered herself into the steaming water, sighing as the warmth seeped inside her body. Her next apartment, Aly vowed, would have a bathtub.

She closed her eyes and adjusted her washcloth as a pillow. She was, she knew, very lucky. She had a job as a web designer that she loved and was good at, and an income that meant she didn't need to worry about money. A sleek apartment in a good neighborhood in a spectacularly beautiful and fascinating city. An almost-fiancé who was charming, talented, and brilliant. She even loved Karl-the-Fog. Her life had everything she'd ever dreamed of, everything she'd ever wanted. A few dark, lonely days in Martha's Vineyard would only make her appreciate it even more.

As Aly lounged in the tub, letting the heat warm her bones, she thought of Whit's cute smile, how he'd stepped in to help that poor sheep. Such a nice guy—and very good-looking to boot. Too bad Hannah wasn't dating him.

She lathered her wet hair, breathing in the familiar floral scent of her favorite Japanese shampoo. As a treat for Hannah (and herself), she'd splurged on a day spa's worth of lotions, serums, and scrubs. When Hannah arrived, they'd play "beauty parlor" like they used to (except for the major upgrade from Suave shampoo and Jergens lotion), then sit snuggled in front of a blazing fire, sipping wine, and chatting about everything and anything.

Aly dipped her hair under the water, feeling the silky auburn strands float around her face and shoulders. Hannah would come back soon, and everything would be perfect, just like she'd planned.

🐑 🐑 🐑

"Hey, Beau. How are you and Aly making out?" Whit asked the dog as he walked across the muddy field. Beau gave him a look. "That good, eh?"

Turning his collar up against the wind, he scanned the property, marveling again at Hannah's luck in landing a gig as the Hutchinson's caretaker, housing in the old cottage included. The property, twenty-two acres of forest, fields, and rare sandplain habitat on Tisbury Great Pond, had set the owners back millions. And that was before they built their vacation home, an enormous modern glass-and-wood architectural "statement" at the pond's edge. The design was supposed to suggest the upside-down hull of a wooden sailing ship. Rolling her eyes, Hannah had nicknamed it the Dinghy.

The small flock of sheep watched Whit's approach with wary eyes. Buried within their thick winter fleece, the Corriedales looked like shaggy balls of off-white yarn. This wasn't a real sheep farm, of course. The owners had bought the sheep to add to the "bucolic air" of their new vacation place. (And to qualify as a "small family farm" and save a bundle on taxes.) Lawn ornament sheep, Hannah called them. Whit shook his head. Summer people. Go figure.

"Hey there, Maisy," Whit called, cautiously approaching the new mother. He watched as two of the lambs nursed, the smallest waiting its turn at the milk bar. After a few minutes, Whit gently placed the third little lamb next to the others to feed, but the ewe turned her head and pushed the newborn away.

"Maisy. Come on. Everybody gets a turn."

Whit tried again, this time pulling off one of the nursing lambs. Maisy pushed the tiny lamb away again, this time knocking it off its feet. The newborn looked at Whit and bleated. Whit gave it one more try, this time distracting the mother with a handful of hay. But the ewe had made up her mind.

"I'm disappointed in you, Maisy." Whit scooped up the newborn in his arms. "Looks like the bottle for you, lamb chop."

Whit carried the lamb back to the house and let himself in. "Hannah? Are you here?" he called.

"She's still in Vermont," Aly replied from upstairs. "I'm in the bath."

"Damn," Whit muttered. The lamb gave a tiny bleat. "One of the new lambs got rejected," he called up the stairs. "I need your help."

Water splashed. Aly padded down the stairs in bare feet and a huge, white, terrycloth robe. Her skin was rosy, and her hair hung in wet strings. "What do you mean, rejected?"

"Maisy won't let one of the triplets nurse." Now that he wasn't half asleep, Whit could see that Hannah's friend was more than a panicky city girl knee-deep in sheep muck. She was downright pretty. He shook his head, scattering away the thought. "It happens sometimes. This one'll need to be bottle-fed."

The baby lamb looked at Aly and gave another weak bleat. "Bottle-fed?" Aly tightened the belt on her robe. "Shouldn't you try again with mother?"

"Once the mother rejects the newborn, she doesn't change her mind." The lamb wriggled in his arms. "Little lambkins here will need to eat every two hours. After the first day, you can stretch it to three or four."

"Every two hours?" Aly asked, eyes wide.

"You hold her while I go look for the supplies," he said, gently placing the lamb in Aly's arms. Whit paused as he opened the door. "It's easy. Even for a city girl."

🐑 🐑 🐑

"Don't look at me like that, Beau," Whit said to the dog as he carried the box of feeding supplies back from the barn. "She can handle this."

Whit set the box on the kitchen counter. He glanced over at Aly, who was gently petting the tiny lamb in her lap. "Hannah only had a little colostrum formula. They probably carry it at the feed store. If not, I'll call over to Ned at Allen Farm."

"It's trying to suck my finger," Aly said, stroking the newborn's white fleece. "Poor little lamb, rejected by your mom. I guess that mother sheep thought twins were enough trouble," she said, carefully setting the baby lamb on its feet. As Aly bent over, Whit caught a glimpse of her cleavage along with a whiff of something flowery and feminine. She straightened up and smiled at Whit.

Whit realized with a jolt that his first assessment had been inaccurate. Aly wasn't pretty, exactly. Striking. High cheekbones, pale skin with a sprinkle of freckles across her nose, and full lips. But what arrested him were Aly's deep blue eyes, framed with long lashes under dark, wing-like brows. The giant robe made her seem small and fragile, as if she were wrapped in a roll of cotton wool. Whit felt his neck flush as a droplet of water slipped down her bare skin. Maybe Chas was right. It was time to start dating. Not this citified girl, obviously, but someone.

The lamb looked up at Aly, then Whit, and bleated piteously. "I'd better get that bottle ready," Whit said, pulling his eyes away from Aly. He put a pot of water on to boil and started searching the kitchen cabinet. "The directions for the formula are right on the package," he said, setting a bowl and measuring cup on the counter.

The lamb toddled over to Beau and lay down next to him on the dog bed. Beau lifted his head, looked confused, and settled his chin back to stare at Aly. "He? She? Is a cutie," Aly said. "Where did you learn to do that? Deliver lambs?"

"She. New Zealand," he said, measuring out the formula.

Aly's eyes lit up. "What were you doing there?"

"Backpacking. It was a long time ago," he said. "Decided to stay a while. Ended up as a roustabout on a big sheep station on the South Island. Probably the most beautiful place I've ever been," he said. "That's where I learned about sheep. Lambing, shearing, the whole thing."

Using a pair of tongs, Whit pulled the bottles from the boiling water and put them on a kitchen towel. "You have to sterilize everything first and warm the formula too, like for a baby." He filled a bottle, screwed on the top, and set it back into the water to heat up. "When's Hannah coming back?"

Aly sighed. "I don't know. Before her birthday, I hope. That's the reason I'm here. But they're still running tests on her mom."

"I'm sorry to hear that."

"Me too." Aly looked around and sighed again. "Gross weather. No Hannah, no Wi-Fi."

"Well, you didn't pick the best time to visit. On the Vineyard, we joke that the months go January, February, March, March, March, June."

"Haha," Aly said. "I'll take San Francisco's fog over this. I got a fire started, though."

Whit checked the temperature of the bottle. "This is ready." He turned to Aly. "Hold the bottle at udder height." Whit handed the bottle to Aly, scooped the lamb off the dog bed, and set it on its feet. "Hold tight."

Aly's eyes opened wide as the lamb, like a tiny sucking machine, took the bottle, her head bobbing up and down as she tugged on the nipple. "Oh my gosh," Aly laughed as she stood up to avoid having the bottle pulled from her hand.

"Told you."

"Should we make another?" Aly asked, trying to get the empty bottle away from the lamb.

"One at a time. We don't want to overfeed her."

Fortified by her first real meal, the lamb took two bounding leaps, startling Beau. Aly laughed, low and resonant, nothing like Petra's high-pitched giggle. "Look at that! She's like a stuffed animal come to life."

"Nothing much cuter than a newborn lamb," Whit said, picking up his jacket. "Remember, a bottle every two hours. We want to get baby lamb chop here off to a good start." He opened the door.

"Wait. I'm not sure I...." Worry crossed Aly's face, dimming her bright eyes. She took a deep breath through her nose and another and looked up at Whit. "I don't think I can do this."

"Aw, Aly, it's easy," Whit said. "Any problems, just give me a call."

"Can't you take the lamb and feed it, and bring it back? Just for tonight?" She glanced at the lamb and back up at Whit. "I'll pay you?"

Whit stared at Aly. There, for a moment, he'd thought that Hannah's friend was OK. But no, anything that might inconvenience her—sheep giving birth, a poor tiny lamb who needed to be fed—was too much trouble. City girl, and a useless one at that, feeling sorry for herself about the weather and the Wi-Fi. Just like the other summer people, paying to have others do their dirty work.

Whit pressed his lips together. "I'll take the lamb nights until Hannah gets back. As a favor—to Hannah."

🐑 🐑 🐑

The next morning, Aly woke up and stared at the beams over her head, disoriented for a moment. *Oh, right, Hannah's house on Martha's Vineyard.* She turned her face to look outside the window. The pond shone metallic gray, and the weather threatened rain again, but the tiny bedroom was cozy and warm. Aly snuggled beneath the down comforter, pulling it up to her chin, and yawned. She had slept a deep, dreamless sleep, the first in months. Rolling onto her side, she picked up her phone to check her messages. Nothing from Hannah. Or Kevin.

Wrapped in her robe, Aly padded into the kitchen. "Oh!" she exclaimed, spotting the lamb curled up asleep on a towel in Hannah's laundry basket. "I guess Whit just let himself in," she said, taken aback. How many people knew Hannah hid the house key in the outdoor shower?

Aly leaned over and ran her hand over the lamb's white fleece, soft as a baby blanket. "I hope Whit's not upset with me." She shouldn't have made him take the lamb. But the idea of being left responsible for the newborn alone in an empty house had unleashed a wave of anxiety. What if the lamb wouldn't drink from the bottle? Or she got the formula wrong, or fed her too much? Or, in her exhaustion and jet lag, didn't wake up and forgot to feed her at all? Whit must have realized it would've been a terrible idea to have left her in charge. It wasn't like her to slough off responsibility like that. At least not under normal circumstances. But yesterday was anything but normal.

She picked up the note he'd left beneath a new bag of lamb formula. "Whit says you're eating well, and I only have to feed you every three hours, a full bottle, starting at…." Aly glanced at her watch. "9:00 a.m. That's not bad." She looked at her watch and yawned again.

Aly mixed the formula while her coffee brewed, remembering how gentle Whit had been with the lamb, how small it looked cradled against his chest. "Ready for breakfast? Well, your second breakfast." The lamb opened her eyes, and Aly bent down to lift her from the basket. "Oh, you are a baby, aren't you," she crooned, nuzzling the soft, warm fleece, as fresh and fragrant as newly cut grass.

Aly set the lamb on the floor, took the milk bottle from the saucepan, and tested it. The lamb, seeing the bottle, tottered over and bleated, such a loud noise for something so small. "Hungry again, are you?" Aly crouched down, and the lamb latched on, again nearly pulling the bottle from her hand. "Whoa, you do have the hang of this!" she said, grinning as she watched the little lamb drain the bottle.

She lifted the lamb onto her lap. Whit didn't say anything about burping her, even if that was a thing with sheep. Aly traced a finger along the lamb's small, perfect ears, as delicate as a flower petal. "You need a name," Aly said, giving her pink nose a gentle boop as she searched her brain for famous sheep. "There's Dolly, the cloned sheep. And Shaun the Sheep. And there's some sheep Pokémon—Mareep and Flaaffy and Wooloo," she added. "Or something springtime-like, maybe." Aly could feel the lamb's heartbeat underneath her fingertips. It was so tiny and fragile, so utterly dependent on her. "Buttercup? Daisy? Dandelion?" The lamb looked up at her, and Aly felt her heart expand, as if, like the Grinch in the Christmas cartoon, it grew three times its size.

"Dandelion it is," she smiled. "Don't you worry, little Dandelion. I'll take care of you."

PART 2 – SUMMER

Aly stirred her Bloody Mary and took a sip. She wasn't sure what they put in it, but Kevin thought Hog Island Oyster Co. made the best Bloody in San Francisco. Tongue tingling, she took another sip as she marshalled her thoughts. If she and Kevin took a trip together, maybe things would be better between them. He was under pressure. Aly got that. He wanted the restaurant to be perfect. He wasn't neglecting her on purpose. She wanted to be supportive and understanding. She was trying. She really was.

"I think you'll love the inn I booked. I get that you can't take off the Fourth of July weekend, but we'd just be gone a night," she said. "One, we both love Monterey. Two, it was going to be a surprise, but I booked us a behind-the-scenes otter visit at the aquarium. And three, there's that new hot chef at the Sardine Factory—Jodi something? It took some doing, but I managed to get us a reservation for dinner," she said, tapping her fingers one-two-three on the table. "And if you need to get back, we're only a couple of hours away. Please. You need a break. You know you do. I've barely seen you in months." And Aly hadn't been away either, not since her cold, wet trip to Martha's Vineyard.

If it were up to her, she would have booked a whale-watching trip too, but Kevin didn't like small boats. And this trip would be about reconnecting as a couple. Aly loved scrolling through hotel and Airbnb listings on her laptop, looking at photos of all the places she and Kevin could go. If he had the time. She'd picture them staying in incredible hotels and eating amazing food, and she'd pretend that the imaginary trips on her computer screen were almost as good as going for real.

Kevin's eyes slid past Aly to watch the ferry crossing the bay to Oakland. "I'm still too busy, Aly. Even if I could take time off, I don't want to spend it in the car and in some museum full of kids," he said with a frown. "Last night, Bex—the new sous chef—nearly had a breakdown. I had to help her at her station all night."

Kevin had been planning every detail of Ripple for years, not just the menu and assembling one of the best wine lists in the city, but making sure that everything was perfect down to the table flowers, a single huge white moth orchid in a handmade glass vase. Although the early reviews were almost uniformly positive, Kevin obsessed over every tiny criticism. For his mental health—and their relationship—he needed to get away.

"You only opened last month," Aly said. "You're still working the kinks out."

Kevin stared at her. "So why are you even asking me to go out of town?" he snapped. He ran his fingers through his black hair, badly in need of a trim. "You're always trying too hard. Just stop." He took another bite of his geoduck ceviche and chewed slowly, his mouth ever so slightly open and nostrils flared. Kevin claimed it was the only way to get the full flavor of the food, something about the retronasal smell modality and flavor being created by molecules going up into the nasal passages. Knowing the science behind it didn't make his habit any more appealing.

"I hope you can get your deposit back," he said, finally swallowing. "Remember last time?"

Kevin's criticisms, justified or not, twanged an ugly chord inside Aly. "Refundable," she said, stirring her Bloody. She faked a smile. "We'll do the trip some other time." It would do no good to nag. He would get even more annoyed, and it would ruin their brunch. Someday, she'd have the old Kevin back, the one who was fun and charming. Aly took a bite of her grilled oyster. "Remember our Singapore trip?" she asked, hoping to restore Kevin's good mood.

He relaxed, seemingly relieved that they weren't going to get into an argument again. "That was pretty incredible. I could eat the food at the hawker stalls every day for a year. And the chili crab at the place along the boat quay. Amazing."

"And you got some awesome ideas for the menu." Aly's *Crazy Rich Asians*-inspired trip had been a big splurge, but it had been worth it. "Remember the Marina Bay Sands Hotel? With the infinity pool on the roof?"

"No way I could forget that." Kevin jabbed his fork into a bite of the clam ceviche. "Here, try this." She leaned across the table so Kevin could put the morsel in her mouth. "What do you think?"

"Good. Sweet and salty. A little chewy," she said. "Geoducks are disgusting, though, with that big, long, nasty phallic-looking neck or leg or whatever it is. Have you seen that TikTok of the girl biting into it raw, and it squirts? Yuck," she said, making a face.

"It's the siphon." He took another bite, focusing on chewing the clam. "Hmm. I could sauté them with oyster mushrooms and a soy-butter beurre blanc. I'll check with my seafood guy."

Aly knew that look. He'd just left the table, once again going into obsessing-about-the-restaurant mode. "I know, let's go for a walk along the Embarcadero after this," she suggested. "Or, even better, drive up the coast. We haven't done that for ages. It's a beautiful day for a change. We should take advantage of it," she said. "We could go up to Point Reyes and get back before the dinner service. And there's a sheep ranch where we can stop and visit the lambs. Wouldn't that be fun?" Aly missed little Dandelion, despite all the pictures and videos Hannah sent.

Kevin shook his head. "I'm meeting with the guy about the exhaust system."

"On a Sunday?"

"I had to twist his arm to get him to come. I've got to get that sorted out. I need to be able to do smoke infusions."

Aly frowned, tamping down her resentment. Kevin had promised they'd spend the day together. A promise he'd broken time and time again. "After that?"

"I don't know how long it's going to take." He patted her hand. "Aly, you know how it goes."

🐑 🐑 🐑

Aly spent the afternoon on her laptop, cancelling reservations and trying to get over her disappointment. Counting her blessings. Aly had reinvented herself in San Francisco, first in college, then with Kevin, leaving her Vermont nerd-who-never-fit-in persona behind. She'd studied hard at college and found a career that she loved. And Kevin. He was a big part of her transformation, teaching her about wine and fine food, introducing her to new people and places, and encouraging her to upgrade her wardrobe and jewelry. His restaurant would be a success, and he'd eventually stop working so hard. They'd get engaged, then married, and then maybe start thinking about kids.

Aly leaned across the sofa to pet Miso, who stood up to avoid her hand and strolled away, waving his tail like a middle finger. "Ungrateful beast," Aly grumbled. Miso was still Kevin's cat despite Aly's feeding him. Too bad his good looks, all soft, silky white and gray fur, were paired with a cat-snob personality.

Her cell rang, and Aly answered. "Jo, good to hear from you," she said, leaning back and putting her feet up on the coffee table. She was always happy to chat with Hannah's mom. "Everything going OK? No more dizzy spells?" Both Hannah and Aly had been relieved when the doctors finally diagnosed Hannah's mother with vertigo, and nothing more serious.

"That procedure, where they flipped me over and upside down to reset the crystals in my ear, worked like magic," said Jo. "But I wanted to check in, dear, to see how you are."

"Work's going great. I was a little worried with the merger and everything, but so far, so good." Aly had been working with her team at Spire on 4-D website design for educational clients, the three dimensions of space, with the fourth being time. "We're on schedule to launch in six months."

"Wonderful. And you still like your boss?"

"Elisa's is the best." Aly and Jo spent the next half hour chatting, with Jo cheering her on as always, better than any real mom.

It had been a mistake to bring Kevin to Nonna's.

Decidedly untrendy, the Italian restaurant in San Francisco's North Beach neighborhood had been run by the Menditto family for generations. The décor featured red flocked wallpaper, heavy dark wooden chairs, and white paper over the tablecloths. Decades of candle wax coated the raffia-wrapped Chianti-bottle candlesticks. The entrees were as heavy, old-fashioned, and enormous as the oval plates they were served on. But Nonna's always had an empty table on those nights when Aly couldn't stand another evening by herself while Kevin worked. When it was slow, Nonna would take a break from the kitchen and visit with Aly, bringing a plate of cannoli. Her bright, old eyes flashing, she'd quiz Aly about her life—especially her love life—and dispense advice seasoned by age and experience.

Aly thought that if Kevin would eat the food hot and fresh (not reheated leftovers), he'd appreciate the restaurant's good, basic homestyle Italian cuisine, a change of pace from trendy coulis-of-this and fusion-of-that. But now, she saw the restaurant through his eyes—faded, shabby, and tacky.

Kevin waved down a server. The portly waiter, Nonna's son, strolled over. "Menus?" Kevin asked.

"Of course." The waiter's face lit up when he saw Aly. "Aly!" he exclaimed, bending over to kiss her on both cheeks. "Nonna's in back rolling the gnocchi. I'll tell her you're here."

Kevin rolled his eyes. "How often do you eat here?"

"Often enough."

"He left without bringing us the menus."

Understandably, Kevin had zero tolerance for sloppy service. "Here, eat a breadstick," she said, pushing the basket across the table. "He'll be back."

Nonna flung open the kitchen door and hobbled over to the table. "Mia Aly!" Aly stood and hugged her. Nonna's gray head barely reached Aly's shoulders, and her ample bosom squished against Aly's midsection. She looked over at Kevin. "And this is?"

"Kevin. My boyfriend." Nonna had warned Aly about marrying a chef, that she'd end up like her, either at home by herself with the babies or stirring pots in the kitchen. *You want to see your husband? The restaurant must become your life. And for the bambinos too!*

"Oh, Kevin-the-sexy-chef, who is opening his own restaurant. You finally brought him to meet me!" Nonna exclaimed.

Kevin flashed her his boyish grin, the one that had melted Aly's heart the first time they'd met. "Nonna, I've heard so much about you," he said, laying on the charm. "You have to give me the recipe for the *grissini*. They're perfect," he said, waving a pencil-thin breadstick.

"Ask the Alessi Company," Nonna laughed. "Those, they're out of the box. But look at you two, no wine, no menus! Enzio, get over here," she called to her son with a snap of her fingers, "And a carafe of Chianti, on the house." She kissed Aly's cheek. "You two have a nice romantic dinner. Next time, we will have a chat, just us girls."

Enzio returned with the wine and menus. "Any specials this evening?" Kevin asked.

"Everything is special," he replied and turned to Aly. "Let me guess, Sunday gravy and meatballs over spaghetti, small Caesar, garlic bread?"

"You remembered," Aly said, pleased. She sipped the wine. Far from the best, but it tasted like home.

"And for you?" he asked Kevin.

Kevin pursed his lips. "Veal *piccata*, *caprese* salad to start," he ordered. "Anyone should be able to cook that," he said after the waiter had left. "I've had enough gummy gnocchi and poorly cooked pasta to last a lifetime."

Aly bristled. "I like the food. And Nonna's gnocchi isn't gummy." Aly grew up eating store-brand boxed mac and cheese that her mother used to buy on sale, but Hannah's family cooked Italian—well, Italian-ish. Aly's favorite was something called a million-dollar casserole with a glob of cream cheese in the middle. It was like a Betty Crocker version of a *pasta alla burrata*, baked until it was all hot and melty and creamy with spaghetti noodles well past al dente. It wasn't that Aly didn't appreciate fine cuisine; Kevin (and San Francisco) had turned her into a foodie. But after a long day of work, she wanted comfort food and a place that felt like home.

She watched Kevin look around the room, taking in the candlesticks, the faded photos of C-list celebrities on the walls, and the threadbare maroon carpet. "And I like the décor. This isn't Ripple. And it doesn't want to be."

"To each his own," Kevin said. "You know, I really couldn't do it—open Ripple—without you." He reached out to trace his fingertips over the back of Aly's hand. "It's been hard on us both, but things will get better. I promise."

Aly's mood softened a bit. Kevin worked to the point of obsession, but he always let her know how much he loved and valued her. And she loved him.

"Aly," called a loud voice. "And the soon-to-be famous chef Kevin Wang."

Both turned to see a couple approaching the table. "Hi Mitchell, Hi Sarah," Aly said. "I haven't seen you in months." The pair, incognito tech millionaires, had founded their own startup: he in a t-shirt, joggers, and gray dad sneakers, she in a beachy cotton sundress. The three had been in the same freshman dorm at Berkeley, the sort of friends you make more by proximity than affinity.

"I thought you'd moved out to Marin," Kevin said, looking less than pleased at the interruption.

"We did. But we're fans of Nonna's cooking. Like Aly here," Mitchell said, kissing Aly on the cheek.

"I hope you ordered the gnocchi. And the meatballs. I could eat Nonna's meatballs every day," Sarah said. "Kevin, we heard you just opened a restaurant in Noe Valley. So exciting."

"Would you like to join us?" Aly watched the irritation on Kevin's face be replaced with a warm, welcoming smile. Of course, Aly thought, potential investors.

Aly tuned out as Kevin went into his selling-the-restaurant-concept mode, responding to Sarah and Mitchell's suggestions for the menu and decor (both of which she knew Kevin had no interest in changing) as if they were the most brilliant ideas ever.

"And what about you, Aly? How have you been keeping yourself busy?" asked Sarah.

"Work mostly…"

"Aly went to Martha's Vineyard," Kevin said. "And birthed a lamb, if you can believe it!"

"A what?" asked Mitchell. Aly had gotten used to how Kevin would answer for her, talk over her, as if whatever she said couldn't possibly be as interesting or important as what he was saying. Granted, Kevin was the better storyteller. But she felt disrespected. Every time he spoke, the spotlight turned on him, leaving her in the shadows.

Aly leaned back in her chair, listening to Kevin tell her story and sipping her wine, waiting for the moment when she might jump into the conversation, even though she knew she'd be interrupted and overridden again, the topic changing to what Kevin wanted to talk about. Like always.

🐑 🐑 🐑

The office espresso machine whirred and hissed. Through the window, the view from the Forty-first floor was spectacular: the iconic Transamerica Pyramid, the bay sweeping around the city, the iron-red Golden Gate Bridge in the distance. Sometimes she'd sit back, amazed at the path her life was taking. If she hadn't become best friends with Hannah in second grade and been welcomed into the family like a second daughter, and if Hannah's professor parents hadn't noticed Aly's brilliance in math, helped her with her SATs and scholarship applications, and paid for all the testing and fees, she could've ended up.... Aly didn't want to think about it.

Aly added a splash of oat milk to her espresso, carried her cup back to her workstation, and logged back in. Three new meeting requests. An email announcing the latest employee departure, another software engineer off to greener pastures. It seemed as if everyone else in the tech world moved from job to job, looking for new challenges, a promotion, a bigger paycheck. But not Aly. She liked her job as a web designer at Spire, loved her project, her boss, and her team, a group of brilliant goofballs. Despite all the chaos of Spire's acquisition by CaptiveZone, her 4-D web design project had emerged from first-level beta testing with flying colors.

A message from her boss flashed in the corner of her screen. *Aly, please stop by my office as soon as possible. E. On my way,* she replied, wondering what Elisa wanted with her early on a Monday morning. Then a light bulb came on in her head. Rumors were that the new management had approved awarding on-the-spot bonuses to top performers. Could she be getting one?

Aly arrived at her boss's office to find Elisa sitting with a man Aly didn't recognize. "This is Dillon, the new head of product development," Elisa said, looking grim.

Aly introduced herself, shook the man's hand, and sat down. This wasn't a meeting to give her a bonus. She hoped she wasn't being reassigned. "You've done some nice work here on your project," the man said. Aly glanced at Elisa. She wouldn't meet her eyes. "Unfortunately, I've got some bad news," he continued. "We've been looking at how to streamline the company and eliminate redundancies. At CaptiveZone, you know, we have a team working on something very similar to what you're doing. I appreciate your hard work, but it doesn't make sense for us to keep both teams on."

Aly blinked, unable to believe what she'd just heard. "But the other project. It's not nearly as far along."

"The marketing group thinks the other project has more potential," the man said. "I'm sorry."

"I'm... I'm being let go?" Aly stammered. "And the rest of the team too?" Poor Chris, with his new condo and huge mortgage. Aqsa, barely a month on the job. And Peter, just back from paternity leave.

"The whole team." Elisa looked miserable. "It should be easy for you to find a new job. Even in this market. You know I'll give you a fantastic recommendation. And you'll get a generous exit package, of course."

"I can't believe this is happening," Aly said.

"We've found it's better to do these things quickly." The man stood up. "You'll need to visit HR and have your workstation cleared out by the end of the day."

"Today?"

"Today," he replied, turning the doorknob. "And best of luck. I'm sure you'll land on your feet."

🐑 🐑 🐑

Aly stretched out on the sofa next to Miso, who gave her a side-eye, stood up, and walked away. It was just more bad luck that, after months of waiting, the plumbers had shown up this week to fix the leak behind the bathroom sink. She turned up the volume on her headphones to drown out the banging. An incipient headache lurked at the edges of her brain.

It was getting harder to fake going to work. The first day, Kevin had unexpectedly come home to find her in bed, hung over from a night out drinking with her now ex-colleagues and still reeling from the news that she'd been fired. She'd cobbled together a semi-plausible lie about getting a bad headache (that part was true) and coming back to take an Advil and work from home. Aly went for a run, then spent the rest of the second day in a coffee shop in Berkeley—she didn't want to see anyone she knew—leaving her lonely, depressed, and jittery from caffeine.

She had to tell Kevin she'd been fired. But she didn't want to add her problems on top of his. Aly wasn't going to be her mother, hiding for weeks the fact that she'd been fired from yet another job. What difference did a few days make?

In truth, Aly was afraid Kevin would see her as less than perfect. He admired her professional success, her ability to make it in the male-dominated tech world. He was so proud whenever Aly got a promotion or raise. Without saying anything, Kevin would let her know he thought it was her fault, that the real reason she was fired was that she wasn't good enough.

Aly closed her laptop as hot tears filled her eyes. Maybe she wasn't a superstar. The project that she and the team had worked on so hard for the past year had been tossed into the dumpster. Like Aly.

Despite her severance pay, Kevin would want her to start job hunting right away. The idea made her want to crawl under her bed and curl up in a ball. Her resume was seven years out of date. The tech market had softened. Even if she did find a suitable opening, the five-step interview process would be agonizing. Screening interviews, behavior interviews, a portfolio panel review, and, worst of all, the whiteboard interview: Aly would be given a design problem and be required to work out a solution on the fly while being watched and scored. Whiteboarding, waterboarding. It was all torture. But even that wasn't the end. Final-round candidates would be invited for an entire day of intensive on-site interviews with top management. After which, maybe she'd get an offer. Or not.

She didn't want to join a new company. She wanted to keep working with Elisa, her awesome boss and mentor. She didn't want a new challenge—she wanted to finish her project. Aly pressed her hands against her eyes. The interview process filled her with dread. She didn't interview well. She hated talking about herself, having to come up with strengths and weaknesses-that-weren't-weaknesses, talking with strangers who were going to reduce her to ticks on a score sheet. Despite her skills and experience, she was sure she'd blank out under pressure. Most of all, Aly hated being judged. And being found lacking.

Aly groaned and pulled the sofa pillow over her head. The banging from the bathroom had stopped, but a new noise, like a dentist's drill crossed with a circular saw, bored into her brain. There was nowhere in the apartment to escape the racket, and her fancy noise-cancelling headphones didn't cancel construction noise. She'd already gone for a long jog over to the Twin Peaks only to get back and realize she couldn't use the shower.

Buzz buzz. A video popped up on Aly's phone of a lamb frolicking in a bright-green field to the tune of *Hello Sunshine*. The sky was cornflower blue, and the lamb looked as white and soft as a baby's stuffed animal. The caption read *Dandelion of the Week! Baaa!! We miss you!!!* Aly felt a pang. If Hannah were there, she'd make everything right.

Aly clicked on three red hearts and started to type *miss you too* and stopped. That was her answer. If she took the redeye, she could be on Hannah's doorstep by tomorrow morning. Hannah would be ecstatic; she'd been as bummed as Aly about their abbreviated March visit. And Kevin was so busy, he wouldn't care.

Dear Hannah. It was inexcusable that Aly had only visited once since Hannah had moved to the Vineyard. True, Aly had been busy at work and was saving up all her vacation days to (in theory) travel with Kevin, but that wasn't a *real* excuse. Plus, she had promised Hannah she'd come back again, this time for a real visit.

Hannah always made Aly feel good about herself. And Aly could see dear little Dandelion in person. In sheep? Whatever. Her fingers sped over the keyboard. Five minutes later, she booked seat 22A on JetBlue on the redeye to Boston, connecting to the short Cape Air flight to the Island.

Aly clicked "buy" and leaned back on the sofa. She barely registered when the metallic screeching hit a new, even whinier pitch. It was time to start packing.

Taking a deep breath of fresh air, Aly climbed out of the cab at Hannah's. It was like someone had taken a pencil sketch of dreary Martha's Vineyard in March and started to paint, coloring the fields in with a lush, vivid green, with swaths of clear cerulean blue for the sky, and dots of pure white for the sheep and their lambs. Beyond the pasture, Tisbury Great Pond, bounded to the south by the distant edge of dunes and beach, sparkled with shards of light. The white sail of a catboat bellied with the breeze as it skimmed across the water. It was almost too beautiful for words.

Beau ran up to the fence with Dandelion at his heels, baa-ing like crazy. "Oh my gosh, Dandelion, you got so big!" Aly exclaimed. "You remember me? And Beau too!" She opened the gate and dropped to her knees to hug the lamb. Beau nosed under her arm to be petted.

"Nice place you got here. What a view," the cabbie said in a heavy southeastern Massachusetts accent as he deposited Aly's bags on the flagstone walk. "That'll be thirty-five bucks."

Aly paid the cabbie, and with a big grin on her face and the lamb at her heels, lugged her bags into the house. Since her last visit, Hannah had painted the front door—unlocked, as always—a cheerful shade of blue to match the sky.

For the first time since she'd lost her job, Aly felt optimistic. Yes, this was a good idea. And thankfully, Kevin thought so too. Aly had been nervous about telling him; he never liked her taking trips without him. She reminded him of their cancelled Monterey weekend, and he didn't argue (asking only *can you get away from work?*) and offered to pack a cooler with a to-go dinner from Ripple: tea-smoked duck confit, a quart of his amazing star anise-thyme oxtail ragout, and miso-roasted potatoes. With a stop at the Dandelion Chocolate Factory (but of course!) for a box of signature chocolates, and a week's worth of summer clothes in her duffel bag, she was ready to go.

Hannah's house was bright and cheery, with wide-open windows letting in the fresh air and a bunch of daisies in a mason jar on the table. After unpacking, Aly sat down on the floor with Dandelion and Beau. She inspected the lamb from the tip of her pinkish nose to the end of her fleecy tail. "You're even bigger than Beau. You must be eating well," she said, wrapping her arms around the baby sheep's chubby midsection. She pressed her cheek against Dandelion's thick coat, clean and white and soft with lanolin, and breathed in the scent of fresh grass and warm wool. "I wonder if you'll still follow me around like you used to?" Beau rolled on his back and wriggled, asking for a belly rub as Dandelion tried to climb into Aly's lap. So different from Miso, who hid his cat-self half the time when she came home from work, deigning to come out only when Aly had filled his food bowl. She laughed as she petted the lamb with one hand and stroked Beau's soft black and white fur with the other. San Francisco and her job woes felt far away.

Aly heard tires on the gravel drive. Giddy with anticipation, she got up and hid in the dining room. Dandelion ran over baa-ing as the kitchen door opened. "Hey, how did you get inside?" said a man's voice that Aly recognized: Whit. "You're an outdoor sheep now, Dandelion. You know that. Beau, you fell down on the job, buddy."

"Whit, hi," she said, coming out from her hiding place. "Dandelion's not allowed inside anymore?" Still baa-ing, the lamb romped around Whit's feet like a wooly bouncing ball.

Whit looked startled. "Hannah didn't tell me you were coming back."

"She doesn't know." Aly felt her breath catch seeing him again, taller and broader and more handsome than she'd remembered. He wore a Larsen's Fish Market t-shirt, ragged Carhartt work shorts, and broken-down leather boat shoes. Whit's black hair was longer and his arms and face darker, with pale crow's feet radiating from the corners of his gold-brown eyes.

Whit raised an eyebrow. "A surprise, huh?"

"I can't wait to see her face."

Dandelion looked up at Whit and bleated until he bent to rub her ears. Aly had barely laid eyes on Whit during the remainder of her March trip. He'd come by late those first few nights to get

Dandelion but barely speak two words to Aly and drop the lamb off in the mornings before she woke. Aly got the distinct impression that Whit didn't like her.

And still didn't.

"Um, thank you again for everything you did. You know, with Dandelion and everything."

"No biggie. Always happy to do Hannah a favor." Whit walked into the living room. "I'll be out of your way in a minute. Just picking up my guitar. Hannah fixed the bridge for me."

"You play?"

"Here and there, with different folks." He lifted the guitar out of its case to examine the repair. "Dang! Hannah did a really nice job on this," he said, deftly finger-picking a quick riff. "I got a gig with the Flying Elbows at the Grange tomorrow night. Old timey stuff. Hannah said she wanted to come." Whit looked up and paused, as if debating whether to say anything. "You know, she's really busy with work. She's got a big job in Oak Bluffs that's got to be finished before the Fourth of July."

"I know that," Aly lied. "I'm perfectly happy reading a book at the beach while Hannah works. Or maybe I can help her paint."

"Right," he said, sounding skeptical. He put his guitar back into its case. "You might want to tell her you're here."

"And ruin the surprise? No way!" Aly said, suddenly getting annoyed. Like Whit knew Hannah better than she did.

"Suit yourself," he said and picked up his guitar case. "Now, out with you, Dandelion," he said, shooing the lamb outside. "See you around, city girl."

🐑 🐑 🐑

Whit poured a fresh cup of coffee into his favorite blue Chilmark Pottery mug and walked out to the deck. As always, the view across the water slowed his pulse and lifted his spirits. Lucky, he thought for the umpteenth time. So lucky to have this place.

He'd been coming to the summer cottage on Tisbury Great Pond with his Grandpop since he'd been a little boy. It had been the best part of his summers. Of his whole childhood, really. His parents would drop him off for a day or two. Longer if he'd been getting on their nerves. Whit and his grandfather would catch crabs, fish for stripers and bluefish, and dig for soft-shell clams. Most afternoons, they'd canoe across to the beach to swim and hang out, Whit reading a book, his grandfather taking a nap. Evenings were for card games, reading, or working on whatever jigsaw puzzle Grandpop had laid out. It had been Whit's refuge—and his grandfather's—from the rest of the family, especially Whit's wound-too-tight mother, the martini-drenched doyenne of Edgartown. The cottage was more or less the 1940s version of a man cave. Now, thanks to his Grandpop's generous bequest, it was Whit's summer home.

The house was one of several pond-front houses (more shacks than proper homes) built by a clique of Harvard and MIT professors and their families wanting to go rustic for the summer. The cottages—camps, as they were called—didn't even have power until the mid-1980s, relying instead on propane generators and oil lamps. There were two bedrooms off the living room, a tiny galley kitchen with a scarred linoleum countertop, and a dining table facing the view. Sagging bookcases held dozens of history books and mildew-spotted boxes of games and puzzles. Chas nagged Whit to paint the old water-stained cedar paneling white, redo the kitchen, and replace the shabby furniture and faded rugs. But Whit had no interest in changing a thing. The cottage was just the way he liked it: simple and comfortable, a place to hang out, read, relax, and play his guitar.

His heart broke to see the old camps being torn down, one by one, and replaced by posh vacation houses like the Dinghy, trophy homes for people who "needed" five thousand square feet, fully equipped exercise gyms, and saltwater swimming pools, despite having the pond and the ocean on their doorstep. The days of wanting a simple retreat for the summer, an escape into nature as different as possible from the rest of the year, sadly appeared to be passé.

Sipping from his mug, Whit watched a catamaran skim across Tisbury Great Pond toward the beach. An osprey circled and dived above Big Sandy, emerging from the water grasping a thrashing fish in its talons. On the far side of the pond, a half mile away, he could barely pick out the shape of the Dinghy and tiny white dots of sheep.

Whit shook his head. That Aly. Clueless, just showing up and probably expecting Hannah to drop everything to entertain her. A houseguest was the last thing Hannah needed, already so stressed-out about getting Constellation Cottage painted before the owner's big Fourth of July bash. But Hannah had such a big heart, she'd never say a thing. Or maybe Whit was wrong. Maybe Hannah would be happy to see her. Either way, Aly would be gone in a few days, back to San Francisco with a few envy-inducing vacation photos for her Instagram account.

Whit leaned back and closed his eyes. He had a blissful few hours between his morning fishing charter—no stripers, but the clients caught a mess of bluefish—and his afternoon booking with a hopefully-not-too obnoxious family from New York City. With luck, they'd have such a good time they'd tip well and tell all their friends. It was a good day, two trips out. He'd been trying to bring in more business, but he needed a hook, something to drive customers his way.

Money. Whit had never thought about money when he was growing up. But now he had to. Buddy Vanderhoop had a new charter fishing boat, and the bookings on Whit's boat were down. Gigs playing music were both tough to land and didn't pay much. Bartending at the Ritz was always an option, but that held zero appeal, even if he had the energy to pull late shifts at the bar and get up a few hours later to run early-morning fishing charters.

Whit sighed and closed his eyes. The sensible thing would be to rent the camp and live on his boat. His neighbor, Alice, knew someone who was desperate for an August pond-front rental—and, if he fixed the place up a bit, it would pay out the wazoo. It would solve his money problems for the year. And break his heart.

🐑 🐑 🐑

Gravel crunched under tires. Whit, stretched out for a nap, kept his eyes closed. Probably the UPS guy delivering the solar cellphone charger he'd ordered for the boat.

"Halloo!" Not UPS. Chas.

Whit got up and walked to the front door. "Hey buddy, what's up?" he asked, leaning against the jamb. Seeing Chas always made Whit smile. The relationship appeared improbable to anyone looking in: the fisherman/musician and his Club Monaco-tailored, trust-funded friend. But the roots of their friendship went deep, the bonds strengthened by loyalty through the adversity that was their respective upbringings, featuring parental selfishness, profligacy, narcissism, greed, alcohol, infidelity—and, in Whit's case, the shitstorm that was his father's divorce from Whit's mother.

Although Whit wouldn't touch a penny even if offered, his family was not quite, but nearly, Forbes-list rich. His arrogant, self-centered father "managed their investments" while his beautiful blond mother shopped and partied, self-medicating her unhappiness with drinking and having affairs. He had an older brother, a carbon copy of his father, and a much younger sister who was an Instagram influencer or something in LA. He never talked to any of them, which was fine with him. Whit had Chas, and that was enough.

Whit watched Chas unload two big shopping bags from the back seat of his blue Mini Cooper convertible, setting them down next to a leather duffel and a big YETI cooler. "You really need to get the road scraped," Chas said, reaching through the passenger-side window to grab a paper bag. "My poor Mooch kept bottoming out on the potholes." He launched the paper bag at Whit with surprisingly good aim.

"What's in here?" Whit asked, catching the bag.

"Sandwiches from 7a. Knowing you, you haven't eaten."

Whit shook the bag. "Let me guess. A Liz Lemon?"

"Two. And peanut butter cookies," Chas said. "I woke up in a mothering mood. The second sandwich is for me, so don't go inhaling everything."

Whit's stomach growled a thank you. "What's with all the other stuff?"

"Oh. Dear Granny was getting on my case again. I told her I was going off-Island. But then I thought I'd stay a few days with you instead," he said with a charming grin. "You don't mind, do you? I've hardly seen you in weeks."

"You know you're welcome anytime," Whit replied. "But I thought the accommodations weren't up to your standards."

"Which is why I've brought you some presents. New sheets, pillows, and towels for the house," Chas said, carrying the shopping bags inside. "Nice ones, for both of us, from that new store in Edgartown. And some new cushions for your outdoor chairs. So we can enjoy your gorgeous view in comfort."

"My stuff isn't that bad," Whit said, picking up the cooler.

"Oh yes, it is. You've had this place, what, three years? And your sheets are still some horrible no-iron polyester from the 1960s," he accused. "I can't believe you sleep on them. And your towels have holes. I'm taking those to the animal shelter."

Whit knew it would be no use trying to refuse the gifts. "Why was Granny on your case? About getting a job? You could use one, you know."

"She's given up on that. Besides, my talents are much better put to use working on the Possible Dreams auction. Did I tell you we've got Seth Meyers hosting again?" Chas asked. He pulled a set of creamy Sferra sheets from his duffel to show Whit. "Aren't these nice? No, not a job. Granny keeps hinting that I need a girlfriend."

"You're never going to have a girlfriend," Whit said, unloading a package of strip steaks from the cooler.

"Of course not." Chas set two bottles of Bordeaux on the counter. "I snitched the green peppercorn sauce for the steaks—that's the stuff in the jar—from Granny's cook. You remember Laura?"

"Are you going to tell her?" Whit asked.

"Oh, Laura won't care," Chas said blithely. "It's leftover."

"Tell Granny, you doofus," Whit said, playfully punching Chas's arm. "When are you going to tell Granny you're gay? I bet she knows anyway. She's a sharp old bird."

"Never."

"Afraid you'll jeopardize your position as her favorite grandchild? And your chance of inheriting her house?"

Chas gave him a hurt look. "I am her favorite, but that's not it. We had tea together the other day. Granny is very worried about what will happen to the house after she dies. She desperately wants great-grandchildren running around it. And for them to leave it to their children. My brother and sister are both married. And want kids." He turned to Whit. "Do you know what my siblings would do if they got their hands on it? They lie and tell Granny that they wouldn't change a thing. But I've heard them talk when she's not around. My brother would sell it and cash out. My sister would bring in her atrocious decorator to 'update it' and rent it for tens of thousands of dollars a week," he said, looking horrified.

"Have you told Granny their plans?"

"I tried. She doesn't believe me. Both my brother and my sister are very good liars, and Granny can't imagine anyone wanting either to sell or to rent the place. She wants to see the house used for fundraisers like those she used to host. And she knows that I do like throwing a party for a good cause. It's a beautiful venue—the gardens, all those lovely antiques and paintings. And so much wonderful family history," he said with a sigh. "But the great-grandchildren thing. That's key."

"You don't need a wife to have kids, Chas."

Chas shook his head. "Granny is very, very old-fashioned. Especially about things like that. Even if I could convince her, she'd be devastated if she found out that I'm gay."

"You don't know that."

Chas sighed. "Trust me. I do. Remember that Halloween when I wore the inflatable pink ballerina costume around Edgartown? I had you film me, and we uploaded it to YouTube?"

Whit laughed. "Unforgettable. That was hilarious. That guy in the Vineyard Vines store who walked up and squeezed your boob? What were we, twelve?"

"But what came after wasn't so funny. My father was furious that I'd dressed like a girl with makeup and a tiara and everything. I'd embarrassed him. I ran over to Granny's for sympathy." Chas leaned against the counter. "But she told me that my father was right and that I didn't want people to think I was one of 'those boys.' I was devastated."

"That was years ago, Chas."

"I know. But I've heard her say other things. About 'gay cousin Mathew.' She was apoplectic when he married Benedict in that big wedding at the Harborview."

"That makes her old-fashioned, like you said. It doesn't make her a homophobe," Whit countered. "And isn't Benedict sort of a sleazy gold digger? Maybe she was just mad about that, not that her cousin was marrying a guy."

"Well, I'm not telling her that I'm gay. And that's that." Chas pulled two beers from the refrigerator. He made a face at the can. "Narragansett? Really?"

"My house, my beer." Whit unwrapped his sandwich and put it on a paper plate. Once Chas got stubborn, it was no use continuing to argue. "If you're going to be around, I've got a fishing charter client tomorrow afternoon. No mate. You want to come along?"

"Hmm," Chas mused. "Do I have to bait hooks? Stab large fish in the eye?"

"Your job would be to help chat up the clients and keep the boat going straight while I do the rest. No hard lifting required."

"Can I pretend my great-great-great-grandfather was the whaling captain?"

Whit grinned. "Only if I get to pretend my great-great-great-grandfather was the robber baron."

"Deal."

Now that he was here, Whit was looking forward to Chas's lively company for a while, so long as he respected Ben Franklin's saying about houseguests and fish stinking after three days. They carried their sandwiches onto the deck and sat down. Whit took a bite of his Liz Lemon, crunching through the potato chips and coleslaw into the pastrami.

Chas wiped a drop of Russian dressing from his chin. "I need a beard."

"What? I thought you hated beards."

"No, not that kind of beard. The solution to my predicament: a fake girlfriend to take to Granny's. Someone she can imagine me having those babies with."

Whit nearly choked on his sandwich. "You've got to be kidding."

Chas took another bite, thinking. "But there would have to be some reason I haven't brought her around before. And, obviously, she'd need to meet Granny's standards. Beauty, manners, education, pedigree…"

Whit set down his sandwich. "Please don't tell me you're serious."

"Oh, I'm serious." Chas sipped his beer and made a face. "And we need to find a real girlfriend for you. One who likes bad beer."

Tired from her overnight flight, Aly flopped down into an Adirondack chair in Hannah's backyard. Overhead, the breeze rustled the leaves of the lichen-furred pear tree. In the distance, she could hear the ocean, so relaxing after the city's constant clamor of cars and people. No sign of Hannah yet, but that didn't matter. It was lovely just to sit there and do nothing, simply breathe in the fresh, clean Vineyard air, deliciously green with a hint of ocean salt.

Dandelion bounded over with a small, happy bleat. "I missed you," Aly said, reaching down to stroke the lamb's soft ear. "You've grown so much. We owe Whit, don't we?"

Whit. She hadn't given him a thought while she'd been in San Francisco. She'd forgotten how he filled up a room, as if there were more of him than whatever cubic feet his physical body took up, how his lopsided smile transformed his face, etching warm, appealing creases in the corners of his eyes and mouth. He made her feel unsettled. And a bit guilty for noticing how attractive he was.

Unfortunately, Whit *was* right: she hadn't factored Hannah's work schedule into her plans for the week. Her vision of the two of them starting their day with a morning class at the Yoga Barn, followed by a day at the beach or exploring the Island, with some shopping and eating out thrown in here and there, had gone poof. But it was OK. She'd use the time to be the best houseguest ever: running errands, doing the dishes and laundry, vacuuming up the dog hair. Whatever Hannah needed her to do. They'd have evenings together, and that would be enough.

Dandelion wandered off to graze under Beau's watchful eye. It was so quiet that Aly could hear the lamb nibbling the blades of grass. On the other side of the pasture, a swan paddled slowly across the pond, followed by three chubby gray cygnets. Aly could see why Hannah had fallen in love with the Island.

Her cell buzzed. *Did you make it? You promised you'd let me know.* Kevin. Oh shoot. He always worried when she forgot to check in. Her fingers flew over her phone. *Sorry! Yes, I'm here,* she texted back. *Hope it was an easy trip,* he replied. *Did you get to everything on the list before you left?* Aly tensed, trying to remember what was on

Kevin's list. *I hope so,* she answered, not certain that, in the rush of packing, she had. She watched the dots on the screen turn into words. *I hope so too. I'll call you when I have time. Have fun.*

Aly leaned her head back and looked up at the puffy sheep-shaped clouds in the clear blue sky, trying to visualize what was on the list that she might have forgotten. Kevin could keep a thousand details in his head, but not her. So, Kevin had bought her a to-do list notepad with little boxes to tick off. If something was on the notepad, Aly had no excuse not to do it. The list helped keep the little details of their life together under control.

Aly hated the list.

Absentmindedly, Aly peeled a strip of paint from the arm of the chair. Kevin. She hoped that distance and time apart would give her perspective on their relationship. So far as Hannah—or anyone else—knew, Kevin was the perfect boyfriend, the ideal partner for the life Aly had constructed in San Francisco. But things weren't perfect. And she didn't know how to fix them.

Aly worked another fleck of paint loose with her fingernail. She needed to talk to Hannah. But that would somehow make the problems... real. They weren't that bad, she told herself. All couples had to make compromises. But, to her, it felt as if all the compromises had been on her side of the ledger. Things would get better when Kevin wasn't so busy and stressed. His criticisms of her were intended to be constructive, not mean. Kevin was a perfectionist. That was just who he was. He truly loved her. And she loved him.

Aly and Kevin were the perfect couple. Everyone said so. She couldn't lose both her job and her boyfriend. That would be too much.

She stood up and meandered over to Hannah's vegetable garden to escape her thoughts, Dandelion and Beau trailing behind like a game of follow-the-leader. "Not for you, you sweet little Velcro sheep. You might eat something," she said, opening the gate. Hannah's green thumb put Aly's gardening attempts at the apartment (which consisted of plonking some succulents into containers on the deck and forgetting about them) to shame. The garden was framed with rustic posts wrapped in wire deer fencing. Rows of herbs, flowers, and vegetables flourished in raised cedar box beds. Cucumber plants climbed up the fencing, early cherry tomatoes ripened on their vines, and baby lettuces were lined up like shaggy pompoms in tidy bright-green rows, all asking to be made into a salad to go with Kevin's oxtail ragout. Hannah would be back for dinner—and, Aly hoped, a very happy surprise.

Whit groaned as the sightseeing bus he was following stopped in front of West Tisbury's charming white-steepled church. The bus—and if he were really unlucky, tourists on mopeds—would slow his drive up-Island to a meander. Whit checked his watch, hoping Chas would show up as promised to help with the afternoon's charter. Chas wasn't the most reliable of crew members. But with the shortage of summer help on the Island, Whit would take what he could get. Regardless, it was looking to be a gorgeous day out on the water and another eight hundred in his pocket, more if the clients tipped well. And having Chas on the boat was always entertaining, if nothing else.

Lost in thought, Whit was oblivious to the charms of the drive up-Island. The road, bordered by ancient stone walls, curved up rolling hills past gray-shingled farmhouses and open pastures, occasionally opening to offer a glimpse of the ocean. After stopping at the Chilmark Store for a roll of paper towels, he took a left at Beetlebung Corner, past the new fire station and the Chilmark Church, and down the hill into Menemsha.

Whit spotted Chas's Mini Cooper in front of the Copperworks Gallery and shook his head. Chas was going to get himself towed again. Tiny Menemsha, with its quaint, gray-shingled boat houses and fishing shacks, was still a working harbor and a favorite stop for visitors. Whit had been spending time there his whole life, first as a kid fishing off Dutcher Dock with his grandfather, then talking his way onto whatever fishing boat would take him out. Sleepy for most of the year, come summer, the town overflowed with vacationers looking for photo ops, the best fresh fish, lobster rolls, chowder, spectacular sunsets—and parking spots.

Pulling into his own spot, Whit stopped to pick up an extra bag of ice from the Co-op and walked to the dock. His boat, a converted Maine lobster boat, gleamed like a princess among the rust-bucket commercial fishing boats. He'd named her *Noepe*, the

Wampanoag name for Martha's Vineyard, to honor the Island and a distant Wampanoag forebear.

And there was his mate-for-the-day lounging in one of the fishing chairs. "Chas, tell me you're not really wearing that," Whit said as he dropped the ice into the boat. "You look like a cross between the Skipper and that rich dude from *Gilligan's Island.*"

Chas tipped his captain's hat to a jaunty angle, flicked an imaginary speck from his navy double-breasted blazer, and adjusted his cravat. "I thought it might add a note of class to this old tub. Too much?"

"Much too much," Whit said, trying not to laugh. "Where did you get that outfit?"

"One of Daddy's closets. Back when he was the commodore."

"…of the Edgartown Yacht Club," Whit said, locking his jaw to affect a Boston Brahmin accent. "I remember. His ego blew up like a blimp. Hold on." Whit ducked down into the cabin and came back out with a baby blue windbreaker and baseball cap, both embroidered with *Noepe* in white script.

Chas unbuttoned his blazer. "Now I'm going to look like the help on a Carnival cruise."

"You are the help," Whit said. "Off with the blazer, Gilligan."

Reluctantly, Chase changed into the jacket and baseball cap. "Happy?"

"Much better," Whit said, looking up as he stowed the cooler.

"Hmph," Chas sniffed as he adjusted the cap to better showcase his hair and put on a pair of Ray-Ban sunglasses. He rolled up the jacket's sleeves to his forearms and then proceeded to fold the cuffs of his pants. Satisfied, he turned to Whit.

"What do you think?"

Whit nodded slowly. Chas smiled, pleased. "Now you." Whit sighed but let Chas fuss over details he would not even think of—a flip of hair here, a tuck of shirt there—until he too looked boating-magazine-worthy.

"You know," Chas said. "My father could get you a mooring in Edgartown harbor. Steer the yachting types your way. I'll even lend you the blazer."

"I like Menemsha."

"But it's, um, a little scruffy, don't you think?" Chas wrinkled his nose as a whiff of chum wafted in the breeze.

"It's a fishing village. It's supposed to be a little scruffy. And hey, you'd better move the Mooch. You're going to get towed."

"I sweet-talked Annette into letting me park there. Cute blue car in front of their cute little gallery to bring in the customers."

"How do you always do that?"

"My innate charm. Now, I was thinking how you could make more money off this tub." Whit groaned. "Just listen. You could run *Jaws* cruises. Repaint your boat to look like the *Orca*—you could rename it too—and show the customers where Quint's house was down there next to The Galley. Then, pretend to go looking for sharks for half an hour. No stinky bait and fish guts to deal with. You could run a cruise every hour and take out, what, a dozen people at a time?"

Whit glowered. "I don't need a bunch of day trippers with their bratty kids chanting *duuunn dun duuunn dun* and whining when they don't see a shark."

"Hmmm," Chas murmured. "You're right. That would be ghastly. I'll have to come up with a better idea." He looked down at the fish logo on his windbreaker and made a face. "You really need some decent branding. Did you draw this fish?"

"What's wrong with it?" Whit took off his hat and looked at it.

"It looks like one of my guppies. After it died," Chas said.

"It's supposed to be a striper," Whit frowned at his logo. Chas was right. It did look like a dead guppy. He put his cap back on.

"And you need a social-media presence. And a website. With all the new visitors to the Island, you can't rely on word of mouth."

"I know. But I hate doing that stuff," Whit said. "We need to get set up here. Can you dump the ice into the coolers?"

"Aye aye, Captain." Chas ripped open the plastic bag. "Oh, by the way. We're invited to dinner next Friday. It's Granny's birthday. Command performance. The whole family will be there."

"But I'm not family."

"Close enough. Granny adores you. You're the black sheep of your family, not mine," Chas said, lifting the next bag. "I need you to keep me from saying something I'll regret to dear old Dad." He gave Whit a pleading look. "Please? Granny's cook is pulling out all the stops. Oysters, vichyssoise, Beef Wellington, asparagus,

Pommes Anna," he wheedled. "And Pavlova for dessert—your favorite."

As he listed each dish, a vision of Granny Marguerite's long mahogany table laden with food set Whit's mouth to watering. "You got me at vichyssoise," Whit said. "And I haven't seen Granny all summer."

"Wonderful," Chas grinned. "But you have to sing for your supper, so bring your guitar. Granny expects to be serenaded as a birthday gift."

"Anything for Granny." Chas was right. The evening would be more pleasant for Chas—and Granny—with Whit there as a buffer. "Here come the clients, I think," he said, watching a group make their way down Dutcher Dock.

Whit scanned his boat to make sure everything was shipshape. He was proud of *Noepe*. Not only did she look good, with her high flared bow swooping back in a graceful line to a low freeboard at the spacious stern, but she could handle the heavy New England seas with ease. Her conversion from a ratty lobster boat had taken Whit two years and had been the most satisfying thing he'd ever done.

"Welcome to *Noepe*," Whit said as he helped the three couples aboard, members of a fancy rod-and-gun club near Boston. "I hope you're in the mood to catch some fish!" he added, slipping into his charm-the-rich-clients mode. "It might be a bit rough going with the wind today, but that never stopped a real fisherman," Whit chuckled. "Let me introduce you to my first mate, Chuck. But he also answers to Gilligan." Chas shot Whit a look from under the brim of his baseball cap. "Our three-hour tour will take you to a deserted island, but I promise not to shipwreck us there."

"Deserted island?" asked the leader of the group, outfitted in full Orvis from the top of her bucket hat to her canvas boat shoes.

"We'll be going to the lee side of Nomans Land. It sounds like 'no man's land', but the island is named after Tequenomans. He was a Wampanoag chief," Whit explained as he untied the line.

"Has anyone ever lived there?" asked Bucket Hat's husband, settling his bulk into one of the fishing chairs. "I'm a history buff."

"As am I," said Whit, pleased to have a client who shared his interest. His own family members could trace their heritage back to the late 18th century when his great-great-something grandfather, Joseph Dias, arrived on Martha's Vineyard from the Azores as a deckhand on a whaling ship, eventually working his way up to captain after several successful voyages. Ambergris and whale oil gave him the means to build a grand house on Edgartown's North Water Street, claiming his place next to all the stiff-necked Yankee captains.

Whit untied a line from the stern. "The Wampanoags lived there, of course, then fishermen and sheep farmers in the 18th and 19th centuries. After that, it was a private game preserve until the 1940s," he said. "The island was used as a target range by the U.S. Air Force until 1996, but it's a wildlife refuge now. The government never bothered to finish cleaning up the unexploded bombs, so no visitors are allowed." Whit turned to Chas. "Chuck, get the bow lines, please?"

"Aye aye, Skipper."

Whit steered the boat out of the small harbor, past the Coast Guard boathouse, and through the breakwater into Vineyard Sound. He pushed the throttle forward to accelerate, feeling, as he always did, the exhilaration of being out on the water, cresting the swells as he set course for the fishing grounds.

🐑 🐑 🐑

10:00 p.m., and Hannah still wasn't home. Aly sat staring at the wine bottle, debating whether to pour one more half-glass. Annoyingly, Whit was right. Surprising Hannah wasn't such a good idea. At 7:00, Aly had warmed up the ragout, made the salad from the garden, and opened the wine to breathe. By 8:00, she was starving, so she ate a few bites and put the rest into the refrigerator. Now the wine bottle was half empty, and Aly, semi-tipsy, was sitting in the near dark to not give away the surprise.

At last, headlights appeared on the road, and Beau barked and ran to the front door. Aly stood up with a grin on her face, anticipating Hannah's happy, astonished look when she turned on the light. Two car doors slammed. Hannah wasn't alone. The kitchen door opened, and Aly heard the unmistakable sound of passionate kissing.

"Oh, ummm," Hannah moaned. "Let me get that off you."

Aly stood frozen in the dark, trying not to laugh. Shit. If she didn't say something right now, Hannah and her unknown lover could be naked in seconds, which would make an incredibly awkward situation even worse. But on the plus side, at least she'd finally meet Hannah's mystery man.

"Surprise," Aly called, turning on a light and walking into the kitchen. There was Hannah with her shirt unbuttoned and her arms around what was objectively the most beautiful man Aly had ever seen. His shirt lay on the floor, and both—Hannah and the unknown hunk of gorgeousness—wore matching expressions of shock.

"Aly!" Hannah stammered. "You're here—why are you here?"

Not exactly the look of joy she'd expected. "I had some extra vacation," Aly said, shading the truth. "So, I thought I'd come for a surprise visit. Uh, surprise!"

Hannah finally blinked. "This is Lawrence. My um..." she said, looking sheepish as she buttoned up her shirt.

"Boyfriend," Lawrence said, walking toward Aly. His voice was cultured and deep, and Aly's eyes darted from his spectacularly sculpted chestnut-hued chest to his GQ-cover-worthy face. "Lawrence Hughes," he said, extending his hand.

"Aly Bennett," Aly said, shaking his warm hand. "I'm Hannah's friend from San Francisco."

"Pleased to meet you," Lawrence said, and looked at Hannah. "I should go, let the two of you catch up." He walked back over to Hannah and planted a gentle kiss on her lips. "Don't worry, I won't park your truck anywhere obvious. And I'll come back to pick you up tomorrow morning. Eight o'clock?"

🐑 🐑 🐑

"I still can't believe you're here!" Hannah grinned as she finished rebuttoning her paint-splattered work shirt. She wrapped her arms around Aly in a giant bear hug. "I'm so happy!" she said, squeezing Aly tight. Bronzed and brawny, Hannah had grown into her looks over the years, with big brown eyes, a mouth as generous as her smile, and a personality as exuberant as her dark gold hair.

Aly relaxed in her embrace. Hannah always gave the best hugs. "Me too."

"You nearly gave me a heart attack, turning the light on like that. You should've told me you were coming. You're on vacation? How long can you stay?" Hannah took a step back and looked at Aly. "OK. I don't think this is just a surprise visit. What's going on?"

Hannah and her intuition. "I'll tell you later. Important stuff first." Aly pulled the bottle of wine from the refrigerator and poured Hannah a glass. "You've been hiding that—that gorgeous man—from me?" she asked, in a teasing voice that hid her hurt from being left out of the secret. "Out with it. I want the whole story."

Hannah sat on a kitchen chair and twisted the end of one of her braids. "OK. OK. We met this spring. So, I'm painting this big old house—a beautiful Victorian in Oak Bluffs—and I'm up on a ladder outside one of the bedrooms. I saw him coming out of the bathroom after a shower. I almost fell off," she laughed. "It was the last thing I expected! No one is in those big vacation houses in the off-season."

"With good reason," Aly said, remembering the Island's March weather.

"Anyway, he saw me looking at him through the window and smiled. Oh my gosh, that smile was like…I don't know. I just kind of melted inside. And that was that," Hannah said. "Such a nice perk of working on that house." Aly knew that look: Hannah was smitten. "It was just sex at the beginning. We both agreed, but now…" She looked at Aly then away. "He's out of my league."

"Stop it. You're smart and talented and absolutely the best person I know," said Aly. "But why the secret?"

"We decided that would be best," she said, picking at a speck of yellow paint on her fingernail. She'd gotten a new tattoo on her forearm, a crescent moon. "His hoity-toity family wouldn't approve."

"That shouldn't matter. He's a grown man."

Hannah kicked off her tatty sneakers. "Trust me, it's easier this way. If I were a real painter, it would be one thing. But a housepainter?"

"You're a carpenter too," Aly interrupted. "And an artisan—remember that table lamp you made me for my birthday? It's amazing—so beautiful."

"Housepainter, carpenter, whatever. I don't fit," Hannah said and sipped her wine. "I'm not being insecure. Just realistic. Once the summer season really gets going over the Fourth, it's nonstop parties with the rich and famous. He won't have time for me." She played with the end of her ponytail. "He says he will, but I don't believe him. And he's got a deadline with a big show coming up."

"Show?"

"He's an artist. Like super-famous in artsy circles," Hannah said, eyes shining. "He's totally modest, but I looked him up. His paintings are in galleries in Soho and London—and the Granary here on the Island. He's gotten reviews in the *New Yorker* and all kinds of art magazines I've never heard of," she said. "And he's so kind and very sweet." She paused and sighed. "It's as if I'm in a romance novel, being wooed by the impossibly hunky hero."

Aly shook her head. A famous artist kissing Hannah in her dinky kitchen on Martha's Vineyard. "I'm sorry that was so...awkward. I kind of interrupted things."

"It would've been dessert after a full meal. We'll make up for it tomorrow," Hannah said with a wink. "But it's not only his parents and his social schedule. Once all the interesting people show up, why would he want to hang out with me?"

"Maybe because you're not like the rest of them?" Surprised to see confident, optimistic Hannah looking glum, Aly slid closer and squeezed her hand. "If he's got any sense at all, he'll make time to see you."

"Enough about me and Lawrence," Hannah said, fixing Aly with her eyes. "What is going on with you? How long can you stay?"

She took a deep breath, readying herself for the embarrassment of admitting she'd lost her job. If she couldn't confide in Hannah, who could she tell? "As long as I want. I got fired."

Hannah's eyebrows shot up. "What? You? No way."

Aly briefly recounted how she and her team were canned after Spire's post-takeover reorganization. "So that's the story. I'm officially 'redundant.'" She leaned back in her chair. Telling Hannah both made her feel better—and made it all too real. "Moneywise, I'm OK for a while. I got severance, and I'll be eligible for unemployment."

"That's not really being fired, Aly." Hannah pressed her lips together. "That's just—I don't know, companies being horrible. After you'd been so loyal and worked so hard for them. What did Kevin say?"

"Oh, he's supportive, of course," Aly lied, not ready to dump her relationship problems on Hannah just yet. "He thought it was a good idea for me to come visit," she added truthfully. "And it is."

Hannah's brown eyes oozed empathy. "How are you doing? Really?"

Aly felt tears prick her eyelids. "OK-ish, I guess. I feel as if a big part of my life—and I don't know, my identity?—has disappeared. It's just not fair. My project was going really well. And I really don't want people to know I was let go."

"Don't worry about that. It's nothing to be ashamed of."

"I know," Aly sighed. "But I can't help feeling that somehow it was my fault. And I'm dreading having to look for a new job."

"You don't need to think about that right now. Take some time for yourself, figure out what you really want to do," Hannah said in an encouraging tone. "A job is just a job, it's not who you are. Besides, there's more to life than hobnobbing with all the tech billionaires in Silicon Valley," she teased.

"I don't know a single billionaire," Aly said.

"Millionaires then."

Aly managed a smile, thinking of Mitchell and Sarah. Thanks to Berkeley, she did know a couple of millionaires.

"And on the bright side," Hannah continued, "you get to take a summer vacation here on the Vineyard, you lucky duck. You didn't get to see anything in March." She rested her chin in her hand. "First, you've got to go to the beach and walk down to Quansoo and Black Point Pond. You've probably gotten all California-snooty about your beaches, but ours are beautiful here. And tomorrow is Saturday, so the farmers' market is at the Ag Hall. And the Chilmark Flea Market is awesome; a couple of my friends have booths there. Oh, and you'll have to see Menemsha, and the Gay Head Cliffs, and the campground at Oak Bluffs, which is a bunch of cute little Victorian cottages. And Edgartown is really pretty with old whaling captains' houses and the lighthouse. You're going to love the hiking trails, and there's this secret kettle pond you can swim in. I'll make you a list."

"That all sounds great," Aly said, buoyed by Hannah's enthusiasm.

"I just wish I weren't so busy right now," Hannah said. "But I've got to finish Lawrence's house. I'll try to work faster. I want to play a little too!"

🐑 🐑 🐑

Catching up on sleep after her redeye, Aly woke at noon to a warm breeze fluttering the curtains by her bed and the sound of distant ocean waves. A glass of wild daisies and a note from Hannah sat on her bedside table. Pushing through the dense blanket of dreamless sleep, Aly stretched, yawned, and stood to look out the window. Bright sun and a bluebird sky promised a perfect beach day. Below her, Dandelion grazed in the yard, and the rippled surface of Tisbury Great Pond sparkled sequins in the sunlight. Aly gazed at the line of dunes and distant pale crests of the waves—her destination for the afternoon.

After a cup of coffee and an English muffin topped with wild blueberry jam, Aly rubbed a thick coat of sunscreen onto her pale skin, found her hat and sunglasses, and loaded up a tote bag. With a beach chair over one shoulder and the bag over the other, she wobbled and bumped Hannah's old bicycle a mile down the rutted dirt road. She skirted the locked gate (per Hannah's instructions) with its "No Trespassing/Private Beach" sign, left the bike in the small parking lot, and climbed the path through the dunes.

Aly paused at the crest to take in the view with a rush of awe. Stretching twenty miles from Chappaquiddick in the east to Squibnocket Point in the west was one continuous line of sand bounded by dunes, unmarred by a single beach house or condo. It was wild and timeless, and drop-dead gorgeous.

"Wow," Aly said aloud, the breeze blowing strands of hair across her face. Carrying her bag and chair, she walked a little way down the beach to where the dunes flattened into a wide expanse of sand separating the ocean on one side from Tisbury Great Pond on the other, so flat that a high tide could wash over. On the pond side, two small aluminum boats and a Sunfish had been pulled onto the sandy shore. Children, their bright blond hair reflecting the sun, splashed in the shallows under the watchful eyes of their parents in their beach chairs. Further down the beach, a young couple threw a tennis ball to an enthusiastic spotted dog as a smaller, black dog ran barking after seagulls. On the ocean side, a pair of swimmers bobbed in the waves.

Aly unfolded her chair and sat down. Digging her toes into the sand, she closed her eyes, feeling the childlike joy of going to the beach. The warm, salty breeze swept over her, carrying the sound of seagulls and children playing. She'd never grown accustomed to San Francisco's frigid and foggy summer weather. Hot sun, sand, sea. This was how summertime was supposed to feel. Opening her eyes, she fished out her novel—the latest Emily Henry, no Marie Kondo this time—from the beach bag. Not far from shore, a seal, with big round eyes and long whiskers, popped his head up to watch Aly with a curious gaze. She'd grown up going to lovely Lake Champlain with Hannah and her family, but the ocean had a special draw. What would it be like to be a seal, breathing air but living life underwater? As if refusing to answer her question, the seal ducked under the surface and, unseen, glided away.

"Mmm," Aly murmured as the sunshine's warmth settled inside her, gradually melting away something hard and tight that had lodged like a stone weight since the day she was fired. Hannah was right. A job *was* just a job. It wasn't who she was. The box of expectations and deadlines and worry thinned to tissue and, shredded by the wind, floated out to sea.

"Phineas, come here!" a woman's voice called, interrupting her reverie. A moment later, a small, wet, furry, and very sand-covered black dog launched himself into Aly's lap. "Phineas!" the woman cried, running up to Aly. "I'm so sorry! He's just a puppy, and not a very well-trained one."

"I love dogs," Aly said as Phineas tried to lick her ear.

The woman lifted the wet puppy from Aly's lap and clipped him onto a leash. "Probably not this one. Phineas, you're a bad dog," she scolded the pup, who happily wagged his tail in reply.

Aly laughed, wiping wet sand off her legs. "I was about to take a swim."

"I really am sorry." The puppy started barking and biting at the leash. "I'll keep him tied up. Phineas, stop it!"

Aly watched her drag the puppy down the beach and stood up, brushing more sand from her body. Sand was the main reason Kevin didn't like going to the beach. It was…sandy. Got into everything, he complained. If you want to swim or sunbathe, he reasoned, you go to a pool. Salt water made him sticky. Add a little sand, and he was affirmatively grouchy. Despite her best efforts, she had made no progress in converting him to enjoy the pleasures of vacationing at the beach. It was just one of those little things that they'd agreed to disagree about. Aly sighed. Should she be missing Kevin? At least a little? Or wishing he were there too? But she didn't.

Aly set her hat and sunglasses on the chair. A swim, a little reading, and a beach nap. A perfect afternoon, doing exactly what she wanted.

🐑 🐑 🐑

Hannah pushed her chair back from the kitchen table. "I met Lawrence's family today," she said, taking a second helping of warmed-up ragout. "He didn't expect them until tomorrow. So of course, we're up in Lawrence's bedroom, um, taking a little break…"

"No wonder you haven't finished painting their house yet," Aly teased.

"Shush," Hannah said. "So, we both throw on our clothes and run downstairs. Of course, Lawrence's mother looks like she's stepped out of a society magazine, and there I am in my filthy overalls." She rolled her eyes. "I made up something about being in Lawrence's room to unstick a window, not that it mattered. It was weird—I was like the invisible woman. I mean, I guess I get it. I'm just their house painter. But still."

"That'll put a crimp in your style—no more going up a ladder and sneaking in his bedroom window."

"Haha," Hannah said. "But how was your day? I haven't had time to go to the beach since the weather got nice." She pressed her finger into Aly's shrimp-colored arm. "You look like you got some sun."

"I put on a ton of sunscreen," Aly said, watching the white mark on her arm disappear. "I wish you could've come."

"Me too," Hannah said. "But it stays light so late, we could go down after work for the sunset someday."

"And we could take a picnic dinner. That would be fun," Aly said, eating a cherry tomato out of the salad. "I didn't expect the beach to be so empty—and wild. I saw like ten people, total."

"It's mostly private beaches here on the Island," Hannah said. "But around the pond, only the Quansoo people—that's the stretch of beach to the west of where you were—are fussy about trespassers," she said. "Not all of them, of course. But you were on Tississa. The people there are very chill. Did you swim?"

"Both in the ocean and the pond. I didn't expect the pond to be so warm! That's one thing I don't like about California. The Pacific is freezing. And I hate wearing a wetsuit." She sipped her wine. "But I've always loved the beach. Remember that place in Chatham your parents rented once when we were little?"

Hannah laughed. "I'd forgotten about that. We had begged and begged them to go to the ocean so we could pretend we were Ariel from *The Little Mermaid*. We even brought our mermaid tail sleeping bags."

"Then it rained almost the whole week. And we were in our Disney karaoke song phase. We must've driven them nuts."

"At least you could carry a tune! I was just loud," Hannah chuckled. "I forgot about that. No wonder we never got to go again." She scraped the last of the sauce off her plate. "Mmm, this was delicious. You're so lucky that Kevin's a chef. Speaking of music, we should get going to the Grange. The Flying Elbows play old-fashioned jigs and reels—don't make a face—you're going to love it. And Whit."

Hannah and Aly parked and joined the line of people waiting to go inside. The historic, gray-shingled post-and-beam barn was quickly becoming Aly's favorite building in West Tisbury, so pretty and welcoming with its big front porch, white gingerbread trim, and large multipaned windows. They climbed the narrow staircase to the second-story theater and found a spot to stand at the back with a clear view of the stage.

Aly leaned against the wall and looked around. The Grange was as old and charming on the inside as the outside. Heavy, hand-hewn beams held up the rafters, and the setting sun lit the wavy glass in the windows aglow with orange light. The crowd trended older, dressed casually in t-shirts and shorts with a scattering of hippy-ish sundresses. Aly looked down at her outfit, feeling citified and overdressed in her black linen top and patent leather sandals.

Hannah had explained over dinner that the Island was grouped into locals, who had been born and raised on the Island, washashores, like Hannah, who had moved to the Vineyard from somewhere else, and summer people. The crowd looked mostly local to Aly's eyes, but (according to Hannah) the owners of some of the most expensive multimillion-dollar properties in Chilmark left their designer clothes behind and dressed like their handymen when they came to the Vineyard. While some people thought the clue was the hands—soft fingers and manicured fingernails—Hannah swore that hair (sleek, groomed) and boots (new, expensive) were the giveaways.

Whit walked onto the stage with his guitar and waved to the crowd. The spotlight brought out blue highlights in his black hair and deepened the creases around his smile. He wore a blue chambray work shirt, sleeves rolled to the elbow, and jeans. His scuffed, creased boots marked him, according to Hannah's clues, as a local. Aly had suffered stage fright ever since her disastrous performance as a singing sunflower in her second-grade play, but Whit looked relaxed and happy.

"Welcome, everyone, to the opening night of our summer season. We're going to have some fun tonight," Whit said, giving a slight wave to someone in the crowd. His eyes lit up when he spotted Aly and Hannah in the back. "The Flying Elbows have been playing here at the Grange since it was built. When was that? 1859?"

"Ah, come on, Whit," interrupted a voice from offstage. "We're old, but not that old!"

Whit grinned. "Easy to make that mistake. I mean, look at Dick there," Whit said, hooking a thumb at the banjo player standing at the side of the stage. The audience chuckled. "We'll start off with a song from William Litten's Fiddle Tunes playbook from 1802. But let me first introduce the players. Come on out, everybody." The band walked onto the stage, smiling and waving to the crowd. "We've got Joan on the fiddle, Scott on the mandolin, Dick on the banjo, Tom on bass, and I'm Whit. Ready, y'all?"

Whit picked out the tune on his guitar, and the rest of the musicians joined in. In the small open area by the stage, a white-haired couple stood up and began to dance, stiffly at first, then gracefully falling into step as movement and decades of partnering together loosened rusty joints. They were joined by a man and woman in their twenties who laughed and trod on each other's toes as they gamely tried to match their steps to the music.

Despite herself, Aly found herself swaying to the lively reel. At Kevin's urging, she'd adopted his taste in music—mostly jazz—but there was something about the purity of the centuries-old melody that resonated inside. She closed her eyes and saw a barn lit with candles and lanterns and dancers smiling as they paired off and danced figures on a sawdust floor. Aly could feel her feet light and hair flying as her partner's hands held hers together against the pull of centrifugal force. The image was so vivid that it felt like a flashback to an earlier life: she could almost feel her skirts swaying around her ankles, the ribbon that tied a locket around her neck, her breath coming quick and hard with exertion and excitement as she gripped the muscled forearm of her dance partner.

"So, you like this after all?" Hannah asked in a low voice.

Aly jumped, startled out of her dance with the imaginary partner, and nodded. "I didn't expect to."

"Told you they were good."

The song ended, and the crowd clapped enthusiastically, especially Aly. "That was Miss Flora McDonald's Reel. You could almost see her kicking up her heels, couldn't you? Next, we'll slow things down a bit with The Boatman."

The plaintive sounds of the fiddle nearly brought tears to Aly's eyes. Then Whit began to sing in a clear, gorgeous tenor. The lyrics were in Gaelic, but Aly could feel the loss and longing. It felt as if Whit were singing to her, and only to her. Without realizing it, Aly began to hum softly along with the refrain, harmonizing with Whit's voice.

The rest of the performance went by quickly. Aly was surprised and a bit shaken by how deeply the songs had affected her. It was strange. But not in a bad way. She could have listened to Whit singing all night.

"What do you think that song Whit sang in Gaelic was about?" Aly asked as they waited to go down the stairs. Faint notes of the melody still played in her head.

"No idea, but it was beautiful, wasn't it? The after-party is just around the corner off Panhandle Road. Let's go. You can ask him yourself."

🐑 🐑 🐑

Hannah parked next to two other Toyota pickup trucks in front of a decrepit shed. A green bike with a wicker basket leaned against one slanted wall, looking as if its weight alone would push the shed over. At the end of the driveway, music and voices came from a small, squat house covered in curled and cracked shingles. This was no quaint historic Cape or charming white clapboard Greek Revival like the homes they'd passed on Music Street. But the moonlight lit the field and a barn in the distance with a cool glow, and a fragrant pale-pink rose bush climbed a trellis around the front door.

"Teddy and Willow were lucky to find this place. An affordable year-round rental is like hitting the jackpot. So many locals have to leave the Vineyard because they can't find a place to live. And buying a house? Forget it," Hannah said as she opened the door to a small, crowded living room full of music and laughter.

Aly suddenly felt shy. One-on-one, she was OK meeting new people, but she'd always envied the way people were naturally drawn to Hannah's warmth and personality. "Do you know everyone here?"

"Pretty much. I'll introduce you around." A scruffy, somewhat dazed-looking man wearing a magic mushroom t-shirt walked up and wrapped Hannah in a huge bear hug.

"Dear Hannah, welcome!" he said as he gently rocked her back and forth before releasing her and kissing her cheek.

Hannah grinned. "Aly, this is Teddy. He's our host, grower of mushrooms, and bestower of fabulous hugs. Teddy, my friend Aly, visiting from San Francisco."

"Ah, cable cars, the Golden Gate Bridge, dim sum! Welcome to my humble abode," Teddy said and opened his arms. Aly wasn't much for being hugged by strangers, but her hesitation slipped away in his soft, warm, somewhat squishy embrace. It was a fabulous hug. He released Aly and gave her a beatific grin. "Make yourself at home, Aly. Drinks are in the kitchen, and Zeke's got weed of course, if you're so inclined."

"What's the latest with Choco-Teds?" Hannah asked. "Is that mushroom company really interested in making them?" She turned to Aly. "Teddy makes these chocolate-almond medicinal mushroom treats that actually taste good."

"And good for you," Teddy said. "Indeed, thanks to Batty, I'm selling the recipe and the name to Fungi Perfecti. Choco-Teds are going national! If you'll excuse me, I believe I need a beer."

"One of the sweetest and flakiest guys you'll ever meet," Hannah said as he wandered off. "Let's go talk to Nate and Sky. You'll like them," Hannah said, indicating a gorgeous couple standing by the fireplace. "He's a goatscaper and a cheesemaker, and she's a goat yoga instructor."

"Goatscaper? Goat yoga?"

"They'll explain. Hey, Nate!" Hannah called, pulling Aly by the hand and introducing her. "Aly wants to know what a goatscaper does."

"I don't do much," Nate said with a chuckle. "The goats do all the work."

"Goatscaping is using a herd of goats to clear brush," Sky explained. "They'll eat anything, even poison ivy. Nate sets up the pen and hopes they don't escape."

"Environmentally friendly. And cute," said Hannah. "And they put the baby goats to work in Sky's goat yoga classes. They like to hop up on you."

"If you're interested, the schedule's on my website," Sky said. "I'll comp you a class. Code's 'babygoat.' And guess what, Hannah. I almost forgot to tell you. Gaia's going to get a little sister!"

"Wow, congratulations!" Hannah exclaimed, hugging Sky then Nate. "That's so great."

"We're really excited," Sky said. "Gaia too." She looked at her watch. "Nate, we'd better get going. The babysitter needs to leave early tonight. Hope to see you in class, Aly."

"Sounds like fun," Aly said. She watched Nate and Sky say their goodbyes. "They seem really nice."

"They are," said Hannah. "A lot of people didn't think they'd stay together."

"Why's that?"

"Nate's a local guy—his family goes way, way back—and Sky was a summer person from this super-rich, snobby family," Hannah said. "Kind of a princess and frog thing."

"Nate's hardly a frog."

"So true." Hannah looked around the room. "Let's see, the scruffy-looking guy over there is Zeke. He's a budtender at the weed dispensary. Batty, in the red top, is his girlfriend," she said, pointing out a giant of a woman with impressive biceps. "She runs a kayaking operation over on Sengie—Sengekontacket Pond. And teaches kiteboarding. Remy and Jake should be here somewhere. She's a 'concierge' for rich summer people—including Lawrence's family," she added, rolling her eyes, "and does a bunch of other stuff. Her husband is a professor-writer type, you'd like them too. Let's see, Willow, in the purple over there, is a good friend. She makes fabric crafts for her booth at the Chilmark Flea Market. And she's a Reiki healer and reads auras—we'll have her do yours. I also saw Felicia and Duncan when I came in—she's a fancy caterer, and he raises alpacas. And Whit's over there by the window. I'll get us a couple of beers and start introducing you around."

Alpacas? Aly relaxed. This wasn't like the parties she went to with Kevin, where everyone was either in tech or the restaurant business. Maybe she'd take Sky up on her offer of a goat yoga class, why not? And she'd never met anyone who read auras. Aly leaned against the wall. What would her life have been like if she'd taken Hannah's freewheeling approach, trusting in serendipity? Would she be happier, or would she be the same Aly, just in a different place and job?

Scanning the room, Aly could see only one other person at the party who failed Hannah's hair-and-shoes locals test: a blond man lounging on the sofa in an immaculate button-down shirt, buttery-leather Italian loafers, and gorgeously wavy hair. Aly smiled at the thought that only she and the blond man had used hair mousse and a blow dryer today. He caught her eye and smiled back. Aly watched as the blond man called Whit over and patted the spot next to him. Putting a hand on Whit's knee, the man leaned close and whispered in Whit's ear. Both looked up at Aly.

A wave of awkwardness washed over Aly as they stood up and came over. "That was a great performance tonight," she said.

"Thanks. It was a good audience." Whit's stage charisma hadn't worn off. He gave off a vibrant energy, a magnetic, post-performance buzz. "So did Hannah like being surprised?" he asked, flashing that lopsided grin that had so charmed the audience—and Aly.

"I did surprise her. That's for sure," Aly said, recalling Hannah's look when Aly flipped on the kitchen light.

A man, carrying a case of beer with two bottles of wine balanced on top, bumped into Aly's back. "Oops, sorry," he said as Whit put out a hand to steady her.

His fingers on her bare shoulder felt warm and strong. Aly suddenly felt strange, in a sort of a butterflies-in-the-stomach way. "Um, that song in Gaelic, The Boatman? What's it about?"

"That's one of my favorites," Whit said, dropping his hand. "It's an old, old tune about two lovers separated by the sea, the boatman and his love, longing to be back together."

Aly still felt the imprint of his fingers on her skin. She willed the butterflies to stop flying around. "But how did you memorize all that Gaelic? Do you speak it?"

"A few words here and there. A while back, I was living with a family on the Isle of Skye—beautiful place. The grandad pretty much only spoke Gaelic. He taught me a few words—and that song."

"Ahem," Chas interrupted.

"We came over because my friend wanted to meet you," Whit said, slinging an arm over the shorter man's shoulders.

"Chas Parkerson," Chas said, extending his hand. "Whit tells me you're visiting from San Francisco." Chas's teeth, like his hair, were perfect. She shook his hand. Soft, with clean nails.

An older woman with a long, frizzy gray braid tapped Whit on the shoulder. "Can I grab you for a minute? Melissa and John are arguing again about the windmills. I need you to mediate," she said, and Whit excused himself.

"Aly. Aly Bennett. Are you visiting too?" she asked Chas. "You don't look like a local," she added and explained Hannah's "test."

Chas pushed back a lock of hair that had fallen across his forehead. "Ah, but Hannah's test only works up-Island. I live in Edgartown. We have lots of stores, and people wear new shoes. Even locals."

"It's kind of the reverse in San Francisco. There, you can pick out the zillionaires in the restaurant by looking to see who's wearing the crummiest t-shirt and sneakers."

Chas chuckled. "Good to know. I'll have to shop at the Dumptique before my next trip. By the way, I love your earrings. One gets so tired of seeing beads and wampum," he sighed.

"Thank you," Aly said as she put a hand to her earlobe. Her handcrafted gold hoops were a birthday gift from Kevin, though she'd picked them out. "What's the Dumptique?"

"It's the freecycle shed at the West Tisbury dump. Whit shops there," he added with a shudder. "I buy him nice things, but he won't wear them. Just puts them in the closet."

"Hannah probably shops at the Dumptique too," she said, wondering where Hannah was with their beers.

"How do you know her?"

"We were childhood friends in Vermont. I grew up near Middlebury—my parents are professors there." After so many years, the oft-repeated white lie came easily to Aly's lips. "But I went out to the Bay Area for college and stayed."

"Stanford? No. Berkeley, I think."

"Berkeley."

Chas cocked his head. "You're not a lawyer. Or a banker. Tech. Hmm..." he pondered. "Not a software engineer, they're all men. You're an account executive at Salesforce."

Aly smiled and shook her head. "You're only guessing that because it's the biggest employer in SF. Close though—I interned at Salesforce, but I'm in web design." Chatting with this attractive man felt like home. "The days when only geeky guys with a gaming obsession and poor personal hygiene went into computer science are long over. My turn." She made a show of inspecting Chas from head to toe. "Say 'I'm going to park the car in the parking lot.'"

"I'm going to park the Mooch in the parking lot," Chas said, faking a bland accent.

"The mooch?"

"My cah," Chas replied, sounding almost British.

This was fun. "Boston. New England prep school. Milton? Andover? Deerfield?" Aly guessed, listing all the New England prep schools she'd ever heard of.

"The first two," Chas replied.

"OK, college. Princeton, maybe, but I'm leaning toward Dartmouth."

Chas made a show of straightening his cuffs. "I'm a Princeton man, like all the Parkersons."

"You work on Wall Street or do private banking in Boston, and you're on vacation."

"Try again."

"Ok, you worked for a while, got bored, and decided you'd rather spend the summer on your sailboat or the golf course until something better comes up?"

"Daddy's sailboat. Farm Neck Golf Course, four handicap. Am I really so easy to figure out?"

"Maybe. What I can't figure out is what you're doing here," Aly said as she surveyed the sea of old t-shirts and well-worn jeans.

"Why, I'm here with Whit, of course."

A lightbulb came on. Whit and this charming blond man were an item. She'd seen stranger pairs in San Francisco. Whit was handsome enough to attract anybody, male or female. No wonder Hannah had said that any woman interested in dating Whit was going to end up disappointed. Aly did feel a little let down. Not so much for herself, but for womankind as a whole, she thought with a small smile.

"By the way, do you have dinner plans Thursday night?" Chas asked.

"I'm not sure. I'll have to check with Hannah. Why?"

"Check with me about what?" Hannah asked and handed Aly a Bud Light. "Sorry I took so long."

"I need Aly to do me an absolutely enormous favor for which I shall be forever in her debt. I need a date for my grandmother's birthday dinner. Will you lend her to me Thursday evening?"

"You want me to be your date?" Aly asked. Then she figured it out. Chas must still be in the closet, at least with his grandmother. "Oh. Are you asking me to be your beard?"

"Exactly. Brilliant girl, did you know she went to Berkeley?" Chas asked Hannah.

Hannah laughed. "You should go, Aly. Granny lives in one of those huge old captain's houses in Edgartown." She leaned over and whispered in Aly's ear. "I got a text from Lawrence. He's tied up all next week with family stuff but is free Thursday night. I was going to say no—I didn't want to leave you alone."

"Go," Aly whispered back and turned to Chas. "I'd be delighted to be your date. Now, what time, where—and what should I wear?"

🐑 🐑 🐑

"You did what?" Whit asked as he started his truck.

"Aly agreed to be my date. For Granny's birthday dinner," Chas said.

Whit shook his head. "Bad idea, buddy. Truly a bad idea."

"But why?" Chas turned to Whit and gave him a long look. "Ohhh, I get it. You're interested in Aly. Well, it's about time." He tapped Whit's shoulder. "And Granny won't approve if she's 'dating' both of us. But I'm a little surprised. I didn't think a city girl would be your type."

"She's not," Whit laughed. "And I'm not 'interested' in her."

Chas was hopeless, trying to fix Whit up with every unattached female he ran across. Sure, Aly was pretty enough, and he wouldn't have minded talking to her longer, but if—when—he started dating again, it wouldn't be some tech princess from San Francisco.

"Whatever you say, Whit, whatever you say. I saw the two of you together. Pretty cute."

"Stop it, Chas. I'm talking about you lying to Granny. She's going to find out, and she's not going to like it. Your family going to see right through it and fill her in."

"Oh, they won't. I've made sure they think I'm bi."

"I'm telling you. It's a bad idea." "

"I disagree. It's a brilliant idea. Just you wait and see."

🐑 🐑 🐑

Aly dipped a fried whole belly clam into tartar sauce. "Remember our summers when we were in high school?" she asked Hannah, savoring the clam's hot, crunchy, briny deliciousness. Outside the restaurant window, a lumbering ferry docked at the Oak Bluffs pier like an elephant executing a pirouette.

"I was so glad to get out of school. You, nerd brain, were like 'boohoo, no more homework,'" Hannah teased.

Aly swatted Hannah's arm. "That's not true."

"It *is* true. My parents would assign you stacks of books to read. You'd be all excited. I'd get a list of chores."

"Which I would help you with, as I recall."

Growing up, Hannah and her parents were the rock that had kept Aly from being swept away. Her childhood had otherwise been chaos with her mom partying and drinking and not being able to keep a job. Couch-surfing until her mother managed to save enough to rent another crummy apartment. The boyfriends. Aly, at sixteen, finally moved in with Hannah and her parents. Once Hannah's parents realized Aly had a shot at getting into an Ivy League college—something Hannah, with her severe dyslexia, would not—they made Aly their project, stuffing her schedule full of AP courses and getting her supplemental tutoring. Hannah professed to be glad to get her folks' attention off her academic shortcomings, but Aly always wondered if deep down she was jealous. Aly tried to make it right by surreptitiously helping Hannah with her schoolwork, reading her assigned reading out loud, acting as a scribe for her essays, and walking her step-by-step through her math homework, thus keeping Hannah's grades afloat without anyone knowing. In college, Hannah's grades tanked while Aly kept up her 4.0 average. Hannah's mom helped Aly pick her classes, steering her into a lucrative major that suited her talents, cheering her on through graduation and later as she launched into her career. For this and more, Aly would be forever grateful.

"OK, I admit I liked reading," Aly said, picking out another hot, crispy clam bit. "But I think my favorite thing was going out on Lake Champlain to all those pretty little coves," Aly said, dipping her clam into tartar sauce. "I still can't believe your mom and dad trusted us to take *Loona* out when we were in high school." Aly adored the antique Chris-Craft cruiser that Hannah's family had inherited from some rich relative, all gleaming mahogany deck and white leather seats. It made her feel like a star in a 1950s movie.

"Oh, she was a beauty, wasn't she?" Hannah agreed. "We used to think we were hot stuff, tooling around in that boat. Remember how we'd tie all the boats together, play music, and party?"

"And tubing? So much fun." Aly was always on the periphery of Hannah's boisterous gang of friends, too nerdy and awkward to be fully accepted. But Hannah wasn't going to let Aly waste her summer reading books.

"Then you disappeared on me. Went off to college and didn't come back. I mean, I understand why and all, with your mom moving away, but damn, I missed you."

"I'm here now." Aly's freshman year had been both the best and worst year of her life. The best because she had found a place where she felt she belonged with new friends who didn't know about her mom, the town drunk. It was the worst when her mother decided to "start her new life" and moved to Texas with her dirtbag boyfriend, making it clear that Aly had made her choice when she left Vermont to go to Berkeley, and now her mom was making hers—and it didn't include Aly.

"Took you long enough!"

"I was here in March."

"And before then? Never," Hannah mock-accused. "I've lived here almost five years."

"No excuses."

Hannah sipped her iced tea. "I know you were busy with your job and Kevin. It's not like I came to see you either."

"Yeah, but I could swing the plane ticket easier than you."

"Geez—you're so competitive. OK. You win the lousiest-friend award!" Hannah said, tossing her napkin at Aly. "Oh, before I forget, can you drop me off at Lawrence's extra early tomorrow? I'm running out of time to get the house finished." Lines of worry creased her brow. "I had a couple of guys working for me, but they quit," she sighed. "No hard feelings. I can't compete with what you can make at a restaurant in the summer," she added, watching the server take the order at the next table. "I was so excited to work on his house that I underbid. I won't make much money. But you should take the truck and do some exploring. You could go out to Aquinnah and walk around the Gay Head Cliffs if the tide's low. It's really amazing. Just try not to look at the saggy old nudies."

Aly made a face. "Can I help you paint? It'll go a little faster. And if we finish up early, maybe we could go to Gay Head together. Plus, I'm curious to spy on Lawrence's family. You make them sound like *Bridgerton*."

"Hah! And Lawrence's mother is the queen. You're not far off there," Hannah said. "They're all off-Island for a wedding. Thanks for the offer, but this is your vacation, Aly."

"And I want to spend it with you, a brush, and a can of paint."

🐑 🐑 🐑

Lawrence's house was unlike anything Aly had ever seen. There were Victorians all over San Francisco, but nothing on this grand a scale. Painted in shades of yellow with touches of midnight blue, the house rose three stories in all its sprawling gingerbread glory. The finest of all the fine homes, it sat directly on Ocean Park overlooking Nantucket Sound. All it needed was Victorian ladies sweeping their skirts up the stairs to settle on the wicker porch chairs for their lemonade and tea cakes.

Aly pointed to the round turret with an ice-cream-cone roof that anchored one corner of the house. "Is that the tower you climbed to find your prince?" she teased.

"I hadn't thought of it that way," Hannah snorted. "Yup, that's Lawrence's bedroom. It's got an amazing view."

"What's amazing is that you painted this whole place," Aly said, looking at what appeared to be miles of painted clapboard and elaborate wooden trim. She picked up a pile of tarps. "Where should I put these?"

"The porch. I need to finish that up today."

Aly dropped off the tarps and looked up at the intricate woodwork. "Is that a comet up there?" she asked, pointing to the carving above the door.

"Halley's Comet," Hannah said. "When it showed up, the original owner had a carpenter make that piece to commemorate it. The sun, moon, and stars are there too. The house is called Constellation Cottage."

"Hardly what I'd call a cottage!" Aly exclaimed. "It's gorgeous."

"A ton of work to keep it up," Hannah said, her eyes drifting up to the gingerbread trim around the eaves. "Lawrence's family bought it in the '70s, but they've been coming to Oak Bluffs since the 1920s. His great-grandparents were part of the Harlem Renaissance scene with Langston Hughes and Dorothy West. Now his family hobnobs with the Obamas and Spike Lee."

As Hannah set up, she affectionately pointed out the repairs she'd made, rattling off words like frieze boards and spandrels and pediments and corbels. "And over there, I did something for me," she smiled, pointing to a cornice. "It's a starburst, like my tattoo," she said, turning her leg to show Aly the delicate tracing above her ankle.

"It's like your signature on a work of art, there in perpetuity."

Hannah paused, looking up at the starburst. "I think I'm going to be sad when I finish. I've spent so much time here, it's started to feel like my own house."

"But you'll be by to see Lawrence."

"I'm not counting on it. I'll take what I can get." She handed Aly a pair of paint-splattered coveralls and a baseball hat.

Aly stepped into the Hannah-size coveralls and rolled up the legs and sleeves. She slipped her hands into the pockets and pulled out a handwritten poem extolling Hannah's virtues. In it, Lawrence rhymed "beauty" with "booty" and "snookie" with "pookie." Good thing he was trying to make his living as an artist, not a poet.

Aly waved the note at Hannah. "Pookie?" she said, raising one eyebrow. "I think you're wrong. I think Lawrence is a smitten kitten."

Hannah rolled her eyes. "He's just teasing me." She handed Aly a brush and a bucket of dark blue paint. "Or would you rather do the yellow—to match your aura?"

"Blue's good," Aly laughed. "That was a fun party. I loved meeting Willow and the rest of your friends. They're much more interesting than the people I hang out with back home."

"Glad you enjoyed yourself. Speaking of parties, Lawrence wants me to go to his parents' Fourth of July bash."

"Why don't you?"

Hannah made a face. "I told him I'd think about it. Now, time to get to work." She pointed out where the shutters needed a second coat. "Please stop when you get bored or tired and go do something fun. There's lots of shopping in Oak Bluffs. Or you could go hang out on the Inkwell—Inkwell Beach. Or wander over to the Campground. The houses there are teeny-tiny, like fairytale houses, and painted the most delicious pastels."

"I think I can manage a day's work."

Hannah propped a ladder up on the side of the house. "Remember, it's not like working in an office."

"And thank goodness for that."

🐑 🐑 🐑

Seven hours later, Aly's shoulders ached and her fingers were cramped from holding a brush. Both her hands and coveralls were smeared blueberry-blue and egg yolk-yellow, like jam and toast had been in a breakfast fistfight with a soft-boiled egg. The shutters hadn't been too hard once she'd got the hang of how much paint to put on the brush, but it had taken forever to do the balustrades. Annoyingly, the curves and cutouts in the gingerbread kept catching the paint and making drips long after she'd thought they were perfect. She rinsed the yellow paint off her brush and stepped back to admire her work, feeling a deep sense of satisfaction she hadn't experienced in a very long time. It was a beautiful house, and she'd helped make it just a little more beautiful.

"Nice job," Hannah said, inspecting Aly's work on the balustrades. "Not a single drip. I'm impressed."

"Am I hired?"

"Absolutely," Hannah laughed. "Anytime you want. How do you want to be paid?"

Aly stretched, working the kinks out of her back and shoulders. "Free stay in your guest room?"

"Aly," Hannah glared. "I insist. Painting is hard work. Venmo? Check?"

"Buy me a nice dinner."

"That's not enough."

Hannah's cell rang, interrupting the impending argument. As she folded the tarps, Aly half-listened to the conversation—something about somebody's recycling.

"*Obrigada*, Maria. I'm just finishing up here. I'll go over and see what I can do," Hannah said and hung up.

Aly stripped off her coveralls. "What was that about?"

"A little dispute that needs to get fixed, or a Brazilian family might find themselves out on the street," Hannah said. "I'm going to drop by for a talk. Sorry, Aly. I hope it won't take long."

"No problem," Aly said. The long, hot soak in Hannah's tub could wait. "Friends of yours?"

"No, not this time," Hannah said, securing her ladder to the truck's rack.

"Then why ask you?"

"It's kind of a long story," Hannah said. "Remember when I moved here with my friend to work at the Harborview—that's the big hotel in Edgartown—after Rio?" Aly nodded. Hannah's dropping out of college to move to Brazil had not made her parents happy. "We lived with my friend's Aunt Maria and her husband. He's the guy who got me into painting and caretaking," she said, loading the paint cans into the truck. "Anyway, Maria and I became really good friends. She's amazing, sort of a mother hen."

Aly tossed in her coveralls and climbed into the passenger seat. "OK. But why is she calling you about somebody's recycling?"

"I help Maria when she hears about someone having a problem, and there's a language or cultural barrier. Nearly a quarter of the local year-rounders are Brazilian. Mostly from this one area in Brazil, Minas Gerais. I do OK in Portuguese, so I act as an unofficial mediator, I guess you'd say." Hannah said, driving past the ferry terminal. "It's tough for the families. Things are so different here." Aly was impressed, but not surprised. She could see how Hannah's empathy and no-nonsense honesty would make her a great go-between. "The problems are mostly landlord-tenant related. With housing prices being so high, a lot of locals rent out rooms so that they can afford to live here. We've got families sharing kitchens, vegetarian landlords renting out to Brazilian families who basically grill half a cow every Sunday," Hannah explained. "This time, the tenants keep putting trash in with the recycling. Their landlord is going crazy because she has to go through the recycling and re-sort everything. She's written out the rules in Portuguese using Google Translate, everything she can think of."

"You think you can fix that?" Aly asked.

"I can try."

A few minutes later, they pulled up to a modest one-story house on a small lot. A plastic kiddie bike was turned on its side in the driveway. "Why don't you wait here. Hopefully I won't be long."

Ten minutes later, Hannah walked out carrying a big plastic container. "That was easy," she said, handing Aly the container. "Recycling is free, but they charge by the barrel for trash. She thought she was saving her landlord money by washing everything and putting her 'clean' trash in with the recycling."

"That was really nice of you."

"Favors work both ways. I hire most of my workers through Maria's contacts," Hannah said, turning left onto the main road. "And the lady insisted on giving me half a homemade Brazilian pudding as a thank you. It's like flan, only way better."

Aly peeked under the lid. She had a weakness for flan. "Hannah, I'm already putting on like a pound a day. The fried clams yesterday totally didn't help."

"So, you put on two. You're on vacation, girlfriend!"

🐑 🐑 🐑

"Aha, the parking fairies have smiled upon us," Chas said as he slipped his car into a spot on Main Street in Edgartown. The day was fresh and clear, as picture perfect as the historic clapboard houses sitting prettily behind white picket fences. Whit never could understand why tourists would spend a gorgeous day shopping instead of going to the beach or fishing, but it did keep the economy rolling along.

"I wish you would get a bigger car," Whit grumbled as he unwedged himself from the Mini Cooper and climbed out. "Why are we doing this?"

"I told you already. You need a new pair of shoes for tomorrow night. You are not wearing those crummy boots. Or your flip-flops or sneakers. And I want to pick out a dress for Aly to wear," Chas replied. "But first we're having tea. I need to get to know my girlfriend—maybe even future fiancée!—better. Oh, look at these roses!" he exclaimed, stopping to examine the fat, densely-petaled yellow roses growing up a fence.

Whit sighed. "Chas, tell me you're not really going through with this. Granny Marguerite is no fool."

Chas bent to sniff the golden-yellow blossom. "I think this is a Graham Thomas. Gorgeous," he said. "Admit it, Whit. Aly's perfect. Stunning and brilliant. Just like this rose. That party was the last place I would have expected to find her," he said, linking his arm through Whit's.

"It's not going to work." This was Whit's last chance to convince Chas that the fake girlfriend was a bad idea. Or maybe, if he couldn't convince Chas, he could talk Aly out of it.

"Oh, I think it will. Lucky I took that trip to San Francisco last month. I'll Photoshop Aly into some pictures of the Golden Gate Bridge, show them to Granny, and ta-da, instant girlfriend." Chas spotted Aly standing in front of one of the Old Whaling Church's massive mast-like pillars. "Oh look, there she is. Aly!"

Aly waved back enthusiastically, looking like a shopping expedition in Edgartown was the best thing ever.

"Mmm, how are you, dear?" Chas said, giving Aly a hug and a peck on the cheek.

"Great. I got here early and had fun poking around the church," Aly said. "Hi, Whit. I'm glad you're coming too." Her indigo eyes under her straw hat were bright. She wore a cornflower-blue print sundress and strappy white sandals, and her bag matched her hat. He'd bet she liked shopping as much as Chas.

"I dragged him along," Chas answered. He looked up at the steeple, the highest structure in Edgartown. "Magnificent, isn't it? Greek Revival. If you like this, you're going to love Granny's house. Same architect. Granny'll talk your ears off about the history," Chas said. "Do you mind if I take a selfie of us? I need to drop a few pictures of you into my Instagram."

"Of course not," Aly said.

Chas pulled out his phone, and Aly leaned in to kiss his cheek, with a cute side-eye toward the camera. "Perfect. First, some tea. Or do you prefer coffee? I should know these things!"

"Tea. I don't drink coffee in the afternoon. Whit, I hope you'll be joining us?"

"I think I'll take a..."

"Yes, he's coming," Chas interrupted. "Then we need to get him some proper shoes. I checked his closet the other day. You would not believe what I found in there." He draped his arm lightly over Aly's bare shoulders. "I thought we'd go over to the Harborview and have our tea on the porch."

Chatting away, Chas and Aly strolled down the brick sidewalk, Whit trailing behind. It was beyond weird to think about his gay friend pretending to be straight. "After tea and getting him shoes, we'll go buy your dress," Chas said. "My treat. I had Debbie pull a few things for you to try."

"I'll buy my dress, Chas."

"Absolutely not. I may fail at other things, but I always return a favor."

Whit scowled at his coffee. His attempts to convince Chas and Aly to give up their plan appeared doomed to failure. Aly seemed to think this was a lark, an opportunity to hobnob with Edgartown's elite over a fancy dinner, with a new dress thrown in as a bonus. And Chas appeared blind to the risks of deceiving his grandmother. It was one thing to have her assume he was still "off sowing his wild oats" as she liked to put it, quite another to flat out lie to her. No matter that his motives were good. And even if Granny did fall for the ruse, Whit had to assume that at least one of Chas's venal family members would eventually figure out he's not in fact bi. And gleefully fill Granny in.

The Harborview Hotel was hardly Whit's scene, but Chas knew the management and was treated like Edgartown royalty, which, in a way, he was. Built in the spirit of a grand old Newport hotel, the wide porch overlooked Edgartown's justifiably much-photographed lighthouse and the sparkling harbor. Across the narrow channel that separated Martha's Vineyard from Chappaquiddick sat the Beach Club with its row of red, white, and blue peaked-roof cabanas. While Whit's family always drove up-

Island to go to the beach at Quansoo, Chas's family were members of the Chappy Beach Club, which meant they never had to carry a beach chair, pitch their own umbrella, or pack a cooler. Whit could still taste the popcorn chicken they'd consume by the bucketful as teenagers (and charge to the Parkerson account), not to mention the rum that Chas would slip into their Cokes. It was the taste of summer.

Whit munched a shortbread cookie and watched Aly and Chas chat like the best of old friends. Aly had taken off her hat; her auburn hair, loose and wavy around her face and shoulders, shimmered with gold highlights. Her pale skin with its cute scattering of freckles complemented Chas's blond Ralph Lauren-meets-Vineyard Vines look. Chas leaned over to whisper something into Aly's ear, and she laughed, low, resonant, and infectious, the kind of laugh that made you want to join in. Whit had to admit they did make an attractive—even convincing—couple.

"Now to work. We've got only two days to prepare," said Chas to Aly. Whit admired Chas's talent for making people feel comfortable, as if they'd known him forever. "Let's see, you grew up in Vermont, and your parents are professors at Middlebury. That's respectable enough. Granny has a soft spot for intellectuals. Which department?"

"Russian language and literature, respectively," Aly said and sipped her tea.

"Wonderful. Granny adores Tolstoy," Chas said. "I assume you've read *Anna Karenina*?"

"And *War and Peace*."

Whit looked up from his coffee. "Aren't Hannah's parents professors in the Russian Department at Middlebury?"

A muscle twitched in Aly's jaw. "Yes. That's how Hannah and I know each other."

Chas waved a shortbread biscuit. "You should ask Granny about her opinion of Natasha in *War and Peace*. She has very decided views," he said. "Now, let's keep going. What is your full name?"

"Alexandra Anastasia Bennett," Aly tilted her head. "Yeah, the Russian thing."

"Lovely. Very regal. Siblings—and their names?"

"I'm an only child."

"Private school?"

Aly shook her head. "My parents believed in public-school education."

"Not ideal. Granny thinks everyone should go to boarding school, like Whit and I did," Chas said. "But not fatal."

Aly looked from Whit to Chas. "You went to boarding school together?"

"Granny's idea. And a good one. I'm not sure what would've happened if he hadn't been there. You see, I was a little guy, and Whit here," Chas patted Whit's brawny forearm, "grew big way early."

"Yeah," Whit said, feeling disconcerted as Aly turned her attention to him.

"We had some real homophobes in our class. I'm to blame for Whit getting kicked out of Milton Academy. And sealing his fate as the black sheep of his family."

Aly raised her eyebrows. "So, you're the black sheep. I always wondered where that expression came from."

"I have no idea," Chas replied. "Whit? Do you know? And stop being such a grouch. You've barely said a word."

Whit sighed. "A flock of white sheep can have a black lamb. It's a recessive gene. So, they're different from the rest—they don't fit in."

"Shall we tell Aly your story?"

"No," said Whit.

"I'll tell you later, Aly. Let's just say that Whit was my knight in shining armor." Chas gave Whit's arm a little squeeze. "Back to work," he said, turning to Aly. "Let's see, hobbies. You look like a tennis player," he said, glancing under the table at Aly's legs.

"I run sometimes. No tennis."

"Too bad. Golf? Riding? Sailing? You ski, of course."

"I do. And I sail a bit. I learned on Lake Champlain."

"Excellent," Chas said. "After we shop, I'll take you around to see Daddy's boat. Would you like to go sailing someday? After, I could show you off at the Yacht Club."

Aly's blue eyes danced. "I love boats," she said, resting her fingers on his hand. "That would be amazing."

"Anything for my maybe future fiancée," he said with a glance at Whit, who scowled back. "And I'll tell Granny I'm teaching you golf. Now, what other interests do you have?"

Leaning back in his chair, Whit had to admit that Chas was right: Aly might just pass Granny's exacting standards, at least at first glance. Smart. Attractive. Personable. She and Chas had a natural ease with each other that could pass for a relationship. Still, even though he couldn't put his finger on it, he had a nagging feeling that something was off, not that it mattered. Fake girlfriend, fake story, whatever. Not his fault if the whole thing blew up in Chas's face.

Whit drained his cup of coffee, wishing he hadn't given in to Chas about the new shoes. "I'm going over to the lighthouse."

"Good idea," said Chas. "We'll join you in a bit, and you can take some pictures of us."

🐑 🐑 🐑

Jealous. Clear as day. Aly watched Whit head down the path to the little lighthouse sitting out in the harbor on a spit of land. He couldn't stand watching Chas pay attention to her. It wasn't very nice, but Aly liked making Whit jealous. That look when she touched Chas's hand. It was kind of adorable.

Aly refilled her cup from the teapot and added milk. "So, tell me Whit's black sheep story."

"Ah, our troublemaker days. He almost ended up in jail because of me." Chas settled into storytelling mode. "It was the spring of our senior year at Milton Academy. The school let Whit and me room together, thank goodness. We had transferred from Andover, but that's another story." Chas picked up his cup. "Anyhow, some of the boys in our house had it in for me from the day I arrived. One night, they burst into our room drunk as skunks, saying horrid things to me, and they wouldn't leave. Whit got fed up and threatened fisticuffs, one against three, if they didn't." He sipped his tea. "After the ringleader tore down my Robert Mapplethorpe poster—you know, the photo of the two men dancing together wearing crowns?—Whit really got mad. He gave them one more chance to get out, and when they wouldn't, he punched the ringleader right in his precious overprivileged nose. Broke it, I believe. There was blood everywhere," he said. "The other two jumped Whit. I tried to pull them off, but..." Chas shook his head. "It was awful. The headmaster was furious and ready to expel both of us. But not the others. Their parents were big shot alumni, you know," he said. "Whit took full blame for everything. I had gotten into Princeton—development admit, of course, thanks to Granny's checkbook. Whit didn't want to go to college. He wanted to travel. Getting expelled didn't matter much to him."

"Oh, Chas." She could see Whit as Chas's defender. His knight in shining armor.

"What we didn't expect was that Bloody Nose would press charges. Whit had turned eighteen, so he was charged as an adult. It was horrible. Led off the school grounds in handcuffs! His parents refused to hire a lawyer or do anything to help him. He hadn't gotten along with his father for ages. Daddy-dearest was and is an utter asshole, excuse my French. And his mother—this was after the divorce—was off with her latest lover in Europe or something," Chas said, waving a hand. "They decided a spell in jail was what Whit deserved. To teach him a lesson. His parents' blood is as cold as it is blue." He broke a cookie in half. "Whit was terrified. I didn't know what to do. I couldn't let him go to prison. I called Granny, and she made a phone call. She can be terribly persuasive, you know. She pointed out that it wasn't a good look for the school to have a student sitting in jail for assault and battery. The headmaster convinced Bloody Nose's parents to drop the charges. But the school still insisted on expelling Whit." He sighed. "Whit's parents wanted nothing to do with him—he'd besmirched the family name."

"Black sheep of the family."

"Inky-black," Chas said. "Cut off without a dime. But his grandfather set him up with a little money to travel. And Whit disappeared off the face of the earth." Chas looked wistfully down the path at Whit's retreating back. "Never called or wrote. I had no idea where he was. Until he showed up one day on St. John after Hurricane Irma. I'd been fundraising for the hurricane victims—that's one thing I'm very good at, getting money out of people—and had gone to St. John to oversee the grants. And there was Whit." He signaled the server for the check. "Granny has a house near Cruz Bay, which was badly damaged, of course. He worked on it and volunteered to help repair local folks' houses." Chas finished his tea. "Shall we go grab him before he runs away? He hates coming into town and especially hates shopping. It's his one flaw. The first thing that fits, he buys. Now, about me."

As they walked to the lighthouse, Chas provided a synopsis of his life of privilege and ease, beginning with his birth at Brigham and Women's Hospital, Mary Poppins nanny, exclusive schools, summers on the Vineyard, winters skiing in Aspen, and his brief and admittedly dilettantish foray working as a baby private banker. Aly's forehead wrinkled in concentration as she filed away the details.

"Not that I need to work," Chas said. "Not like Whit. I sound like a spoiled brat."

"Are you sure you're gay?" she joked, feeling a bit jealous herself. "I wouldn't mind marrying into that."

"Quite sure," Chas smiled. "Wealth has its benefits, but as Granny puts it, 'good friends are worth more than a mountain of diamonds'." Aly nodded, thinking of Hannah. "But I do try to give back. As I said, I'm very good at getting people—especially exceedingly rich and famous people—to part with their money or their time for a good cause. I co-chair an amazing auction here on the Island called Possible Dreams. We auction off 'dreams' to raise money for Martha's Vineyard Community Services. I just pinned down Jake Gyllenhaal for 'Pizza and a Movie with Jake.' Doesn't that sound dreamy?"

"Totally dreamy," Aly said with a laugh.

"We raised more than half a million dollars last year. It's personal for me. A few years back, I had a lover with a drug problem. I tried everything I could to help him. But he was out of control until he went into MVC's New Paths program." Chas paused to take a picture of Aly with the lighthouse in the background. "I do the tedious stuff as well. I'm on the board at both MVC and Possible Dreams. Granny did do a good job of instilling noblesse oblige in me, even if it didn't take with the rest of the family."

"Tell me about them."

"Ah, the flip side of wealth," Chas said. "Daddy's an egotistical bastard. Mummy's a dear, but she's very vague. You'll see. I have a brother and a sister, both married. Ask Elliot about golf, and you won't be able to get a word in edgewise. Kate's the same, only about tennis. She's off-Island, playing in some tournament. Both work in Daddy's private investment firm, which is simply too boring for words," Chas said with a look of disdain. "But really, the only person you need to pay attention to is Granny." Chas put his hand on Aly's arm. "If you can, drop in something about wanting children. And that you love working on charity events. That would make her very happy."

Aly looked up at the top of the lighthouse. "Hannah said the house is amazing," she said, spotting Whit and waving.

"Granny loves to give tours. I hope you like antiques?" Chas asked.

"Love them."

"Oh, you are perfect. Let's take some pictures, then we'll hit the stores."

"I have better things to do than this," Whit grumbled like a crotchety old husband to Aly's amusement. "You know my shoe size, why couldn't you just buy me a pair?"

"Because you wouldn't wear the last ones I got you. Said they hurt that huge big toe you have. You need to try them on." Chas turned to Aly and pointed to a boutique down a side street. "Let's start there."

Whit groaned like someone had stabbed him with an ice pick.

Chas turned around. "Oh, for goodness' sake, Whit. You would think we'd just tied you to the rack."

"You might as well," Whit groused. "Racks of clothes, the rack, same difference."

"Go to Edgartown Books, then. You like bookstores. Then we're taking you shoe shopping. No argument."

"It's not my fault Willa ate my good loafers."

"Well, that dog had good taste, at least. Too bad she didn't go for your ratty old sneakers. Smell must've turned her stomach."

They really were cute together, such a Mutt-and-Jeff couple. Aly could feel the deep bonds of affection, and it made her happy.

With Whit sent on his way, Chas led Aly to a tiny boutique in what must have been the smallest house in Edgartown. "Debbie!" he exclaimed. "Let me introduce you to my new friend, Aly."

The willowy saleswoman extended a hand weighted down by rings. Her hair had perfect blond streaks, the kind that look natural but take hours and hours and cost hundreds of dollars, and her sleeveless shift dress showed off tanned, toned arms. "Chas said you need to look gorgeous for dinner with his grandmother. That will be easy," she cooed. "I've already put a few things in a dressing room. Chas guessed your size. But why don't you look around first?"

Aly started browsing through a rack of summer dresses. Debbie had excellent taste. The designs were simple, and the fabrics and workmanship were top-notch. As Aly browsed, Chas and Debbie chatted about the upcoming regatta at the Yacht Club. Clearly, the shop was a rich woman's hobby, a way to justify attending fashion shows in Paris and Milan and writing off the trips as a business expense—with the added benefit of being able to buy her own clothes at wholesale prices. Aly fingered the fabric of a deep blue backless sundress and checked the price tag. She stifled a gasp.

"Oh, try that blue one on too. That would be lovely with your eyes and hair," said Debbie. "And I've got a darling wrap that would go with it in case the evening gets chilly."

Aly was at a loss. She'd agreed to let Chas buy her a dress in exchange for being his fake girlfriend, but she couldn't let him spend *that* much. But it would be rude not to try the dresses on. She'd come up with some reason why they weren't right for her.

Aly stripped in the dressing room. "I want to see them all," called Chas through the curtain. She breathed a sigh of relief when she slipped on the blue backless dress. The neckline squashed her boobs, the waist was too tight, and the length made her legs look like they belonged on a corgi. Aly scrunched her nose.

"No, that's not it," said Chas. "Next!"

The second and third dresses met a similar fate. There was something wrong, either the cut or the color. Aly could see Debbie getting worried. "We could hem up that yellow one, it fits you so well through the bodice."

"Granny despises yellow," Chas replied. "She says it reminds her of scrambled eggs. She hates scrambled eggs."

"Last one," called Aly. She slipped the final dress off its hanger. Sleeveless, ivory with just a tinge of blush. The linen had a lovely hand, heavy and soft. Aly pulled it over her head and reached around to zip up the back. "Ooo, pockets," she said, slipping her hands inside. The neckline came down in a deep vee, accentuating the swell of her breasts, and the cut slimmed her waist. Aly twirled in front of the mirror to flare out the skirt. It was elegant without being stuffy. She could dress it up or down with different jewelry and shoes. A dress she could wear almost anywhere.

Aly looked at the price tag and sighed. It was perfect. But for the price. "Let's see it," called Chas.

Aly stepped out of the dressing room.

"Oh, now that is just lovely," said Debbie. "It fits like it was made for you!"

"Turn around," said Chas.

Aly obeyed, feeling the luscious fabric swirl around her legs. "It's white. I'll just drop food on it."

"That's what dry cleaners are for," Chas said. "We'll take it."

"And it's much too expensive." Aly turned to Debbie. "I think I'll keep looking."

Chas crossed his arms. "Nonsense. Granny'll spot cheap in a second."

"We'll split it then," Aly insisted. The dress was perfect. If she ate and drank very, very carefully.

Chas handed Debbie his credit card. "Put it all on mine."

Aly pulled out her wallet. Smiling sweetly, she said to Chas, "I'm not going to dinner with your grandmother if you don't let me pay for half."

"Checkmate," Debbie said and took both cards to the register.

They found Whit reading on the front porch of the bookstore. "Success," Chas announced, holding up the shopping bag. "See, that didn't take long. You found a book?"

"You're always telling me to read something other than history," Whit said as he held up the book. The cover was a black-and-white photo of a surfcaster on a foggy beach.

Chas rolled his eyes. "Fishing? Of all the books in that store, you bought a book on fishing? There are things in life besides fishing."

"No better things."

"*Casting into the Light*," Aly said, reading the title. "What's it about?" There was something extra sexy about a big, good-looking guy with his nose in a book. She'd pegged Whit as the outdoorsy type, not a reader.

"A woman surfcaster," Whit said. "She was one of the best on the Island, male or female. Tough too."

"Aly's tough too—a tough negotiator," Chas said and held up the shopping bag again. "Now, Whit, we're going to buy you new loafers. No argument."

Whit crossed his arms. "I'll find my other pair. No one looks at my feet."

"I do. You left your loafers in that drafty old house of yours over the winter, and they got all mildewed."

"It'll wipe off."

"Too late. I cleaned them as best I could and took them to the Dumptique."

"You didn't," Whit groaned. "Without telling me?"

"I'm telling you now."

Aly smiled as she watched the couple bicker. They were too cute together. Chas tugged on Whit's arm. "Shopping! And you need a new belt too."

Glowering, Whit stood up and tucked his book under his arm. "Next time, talk to me first before you mess with my stuff," he growled.

"Easier to ask forgiveness than permission." Chas grinned and winked at Aly. "Off we go!"

🐑 🐑 🐑

Aly set a fresh cup of coffee in front of Hannah. "You sure you don't want to go to the Fourth of July parade with me?" Aly adored the excitement and positive vibes of parades, and San Francisco went over the top with theirs. Gay Pride, Chinese New Year, Carnival, St. Patrick's Day, any excuse for floats, crazy costumes, dancers, and bands.

Hannah looked up from her laptop. "I really need to get caught up on my paperwork and send out invoices. No invoices, no payment, no money," she sighed. "And I need to get ready for the party at Lawrence's house. But I'd rather be going with you and Chas tonight to see the fireworks."

"The party'll be fun. You'll see," said Aly.

Hannah made a face. "Right."

Dandelion bounded over baa-ing as Aly opened the door. "Not today, lambkins," she said, bending down to pet her wooly head. "I've got a parade to go to. We'll play later." Across the daisy-dotted field, the rest of the sheep had clustered to graze near the pond. It was hard to believe she was down to the last few days of her visit. The Island had started to feel like home. She'd filled her days painting houses with Hannah or riding her bike to the beach. Long, warm evenings were spent grilling in the backyard, drinking wine, talking, and watching the sky and the pond slide from blue to bronze to purple.

Aly was amazed at how little she missed her computer. She'd been awed by the beauty of Lucy Vincent Beach, with its gorgeous, huge boulders and dramatic sculped shapes carved by rain and ocean waves. She loved the sea air and how the breeze sent shimmering waves across the dune grasses. She could easily spend half an hour watching Dandelion graze or an osprey fish. Like magic, Martha's Vineyard was rewiring her senses and decluttering her mind.

Dear, sympathetic, sensible Hannah had helped Aly unpack her problems with Kevin, giving her perspective and good advice, telling Aly that if she was honest with herself and with Kevin and stopped trying so hard to pretend everything was perfect when it wasn't, things would work out the way they were supposed to.

Floating happily in her Vineyard bliss, Aly didn't want to think about going back to San Francisco. She dreaded talking to Kevin about their problems, dreaded telling him (and everyone else) she'd lost her job, and really dreaded starting to look for a new one. But no sense letting her worries ruin her last few days. She had the fireworks tonight, dinner at Granny's tomorrow, and Hannah had promised to take off work for Aly's last day. They'd go to the beach and make lobsters and corn on the cob for dinner.

Aly snagged the second-to-last parking spot in the library lot and cut through the old graveyard to Main Street. As she strolled, Aly checked out the lichen-covered tombstones from the 18th and 19th centuries, so many memorializing captains and seamen lost at sea. She found a spot to stand across from the Old Whaling Church and waited happily for the parade to start, remembering the excitement she'd felt as a child going to the quirky Fourth of July parade in Warren, the best and biggest in their part of Vermont. She and Hannah would dress in red, white, and blue from head to toe. They'd tie dozens of bows onto the collar of Hannah's Newfoundland, Chloe, who would sit, patient and gorgeous, like a big black bear on the sidewalk.

A short blast from a siren marked the start of the parade. Slow-moving police cars were followed by a dozen veterans marching in the uniforms of various wars, the oldest riding in a flag-festooned golf cart. Next was a float that carried a band playing a lively rendition of *America the Beautiful*, followed by a line of classic and antique convertibles—a Ford Mustang, a Mercedes, a Rolls Royce, and a giant boat of a bright red Buick—each representing one of the Island's towns. Aly got into the spirit, clapping and waving a tiny American flag on a wooden stick handed out by a local politician.

Next came a float featuring a huge papier mâché whale riding in the bed of a pickup truck. Hand-lettered signs taped to the truck's sides read, "Save the Endangered Right Whale!" "Stop Ship Strikes and Entanglements!" and "#SaveTheRightWhale." A loudspeaker played the otherworldly sounds of whale songs. Aly cheered especially loudly for that float. She adored whales and had even considered switching her major to marine biology until Hannah's mom informed her that there was no money in it and that she'd probably end up researching something like brown algae, not whales. The last thing Aly needed in her life was more economic uncertainty. Computer science made more sense. Besides, she was good at it.

As she clapped for the whale float, her mind drifted to the last trip she'd taken with Kevin, a long whale-watching weekend in Baja. But one day out on the small (and admittedly not very comfortable) panga was enough for Kevin. He found the long hours searching for whales unbearably dull, was appalled at having to pee off the back of the boat, and, when the afternoon breeze whipped up the waves, was miserable the whole bouncy, splashy, ninety-minute ride back to port. Tiny, dusty Loreto, too, failed to hold his interest once he'd eaten at its two "best" restaurants.

But Aly had been thrilled from the moment she'd boarded the tiny boat. She loved the Mars-like desert landscape of Mexico's Baja peninsula, its desolate, cactus-studded coastline, and the deserted islands rising out of the vast Sea of Cortez. They'd been searching for whales for more than an hour when Aly spotted a spout far to the south. The captain raced across the glassy-calm waters and cut the motor to wait. Like a real-life nature documentary, the blue whale surfaced again not fifty yards from them and spouted, sending a fine mist of whale snot drifting over their boat. They followed alongside as the young whale serenely rose to the surface to breathe, then, remarkably, circled back as if it were as curious about them as they were about it. Next, it dived directly under the boat, every inch of the whale's sleek, torpedo-shaped body visible through the crystalline waters. With a deeper dive and a flip of his tail, he was gone. It was a mind-blowing experience, perhaps the most remarkable hour of Aly's life.

Next in the parade, an ox cart trundled by, followed by the Camp Jabberwocky bus painted like the American flag, and an antique firetruck. The Nip 'n' Tuck Farm truck rumbled behind with a pig and goat riding in the pickup's bed, the farm crew tossing candy out to the crowd. Aly scooped up a green lollipop, unwrapped the cellophane, and popped it into her mouth. Her mouth filled with the familiar sticky artificial-lime flavor. A far cry from the gold-leaf-dusted Madagascar dark-chocolate-ginger lollipops that Kevin offered *gratis* at the end of meals at his restaurant.

But today, she'd take fake lime over any bougie lollipop, and a real small-town parade over any big-city display.

🐑 🐑 🐑

"I'm upstairs," Hannah called. "Can you help me with my zipper?"

Up in her bedroom, Hannah was struggling to zip a blue sundress with a row of fishes embroidered around the hemline. "How was the parade?" she asked, turning her back to Aly.

"Super fun. It reminded me of the ones we used to go to in Warren when we were little kids," Aly said, tugging at the zipper. "Cute dress."

"Lawrence got it for me. He guessed—correctly—that I didn't have anything to wear to the party." Hannah fussed with her shoulder straps. "But I feel like I'm wearing a costume."

"Stop it. You look great."

Hannah frowned as she stared at her feet. "I guess I have to wear my Birkenstocks."

"They're fine," said Aly. No way would Hannah's feet fit into any of her sandals. "Let me get my makeup bag, and I'll fix you up a little."

"Do you have to?"

"Yes. Don't start arguing again. I came back from Edgartown to help you get ready, and that's what I'm going to do."

With a touch of blush, mascara, and lipstick, her exuberant golden-brown hair pinned up, and some dangly gold earrings, Cinderella—uh, Hannah—looked gorgeous and ready for her debut into Oak Bluffs high society.

Hannah went into the bathroom to look in the mirror. "Wow," she called. "I don't look like me."

Aly came up behind her and hugged her. "Just a bit fancied up."

Hannah puffed out a breath. "I still don't know what I'm going to talk about with all those snooty OB types."

"OB? Are they all obstetricians?"

Hannah laughed. "No. Oak Bluffs—OB." She peered at herself in the mirror again and made a face. "Now that you've turned into a city person, you probably go to big, classy parties all the time."

That didn't sound like a compliment. "Some. Kevin's always looking for new investors for his restaurant. There's a lot of tech money floating around. Some of the parties are pretty over the top."

Truthfully, Aly much preferred a rooftop barbeque to most of the parties she and Kevin went to. Still, it was hard to turn down an invitation to an after-hours Under the Sea birthday extravaganza at the aquarium or a private black-tie event featuring John Legend at the Palace of Fine Arts.

Hannah fiddled with her strap. "Well, that's you, not me." Tires rumbled on the gravel drive as Dandelion baaa-ed the arrival of a visitor. "Lawrence must be here early. Ugh, I wish I had told him I was going to the fireworks with you and Chas. Why am I going to this party?"

"Because he wants you there," Aly said. "You'll have a great time. Don't worry."

🐑 🐑 🐑

Aly woke to the sound of footsteps running up the stairs, followed by the sound of a bedroom door closing. She turned on her bedside light, stepped into the hallway, and rapped softly on Hannah's door. "Hannah? How was the party?"

Hannah opened the door in the oversized t-shirt that she wore as pajamas. "A disaster," she groaned, sitting down on her bed. "First, I walk in, and Lawrence's mother looks at me like she doesn't recognize me. I've only been at their house almost 24/7 and met her at least a dozen times. And when she does, it's like Lawrence brought a goat to the party. The look she gave me—she didn't even try to hide it."

"She was just probably surprised."

Hannah rolled her eyes. "I wasn't a good surprise. It was like, why is our house painter here? If I had showed up with the catering staff, I bet she would've been all 'Hannah, so nice to see you!'" Hannah sighed and put a pillow in her lap. "I don't think they have any idea that we're together. His mother kept dragging him off to meet 'important people he should get to know.'"

"Lawrence didn't bring you along too?"

"She wouldn't let him. I don't know how she did it, but I ended up standing there by myself with a glass in my hand like a stupid wallflower. Lawrence would come back, and it would happen again."

"You've never been a wallflower in your life."

"And there was this woman there—she was a poet and so beautiful. She walked over to Lawrence and started talking about people they both knew and her new book, and I could tell she just wanted to eat him up. They looked so good together!"

"Of course she's interested in him. I mean, just look at Lawrence! He's gorgeous. And he's got choices. But he picked you."

"For no good reason."

"Hannah, stop that. You must've met some interesting people."

"Nobody I could talk to. Like I'm going to walk up to Oprah and say hi."

"Hannah..."

"I know, just ask people questions about themselves," Hannah said, smashing the pillow. "But I didn't know what questions to ask." She flopped back onto the bed. "The worst, I think, was when some guy asked me what I did, and I said I was a painter, and he said, oh, what galleries are you in? And I said no, I'm a house painter. He looked at me like I pumped out port-a-potties for a living." Hannah groaned. "I was so embarrassed. You know how many times I pretended to go to the bathroom so I wouldn't be standing there by myself? Six. Oh, and then I spilled coleslaw on myself. Went to wipe it off—that was bathroom visit number seven—then I got to walk around with a big wet spot on my boob. Which, of course, was when I met Lawrence's sister. She kept staring at the spot."

Aly glanced at the blue dress Hannah had tossed on a chair. The wet stain had dried, leaving a faint white circle on the bodice. "I'm sure it wasn't that bad."

"Oh yes, it was."

Aly knew that tone. Once Hannah had made up her mind about something, there was no budging it. "It was just one party, Hannah."

"The last party I'm ever going to at that house," Hannah said. "I painted it, but I'm staying where I belong."

"Don't be silly. Next time, have Lawrence give you the guest list in advance. We'll look all these people up, figure out what you can talk to them about. I'll help."

Hannah sat back up. "There's not going to be a next time. I'm not interested in those 'interesting' people," she said, looking at Aly. "I'm not like you. I don't want to turn myself into someone I'm not."

Aly blinked. "OK. Wow." But the truth slipped in like a stiletto.

Hannah turned her face and wiped away a tear. "I'm breaking up with Lawrence. I'll tell him tomorrow night."

🐑 🐑 🐑

Whit skewered a butter curl with a tiny narwhal tusk-shaped pick and put it on his plate next to the roll. He tried wiggling his toes in his new shoes. It was his own fault that they pinched. Too stubborn to try them on, he'd bought the first pair they had in his size. He sat back in his chair, nibbling on the roll as he watched Aly chat with Granny. She cast a sidelong glance at Chas, who nodded approvingly.

Granny pursed her lips. "Yes, my dear, Natasha is spirited and charming, but she has no depth," she said. "And not the least bit intelligent. A spoiled little girl, who must always be the center of attention," she added, with a wave of her hand, "A drama queen, as you might put it."

"But what about her nursing Andrei?" Aly countered. "And when Natasha made the family leave their belongings behind so that the wounded soldiers could ride in the carts?"

Another wave of the hand. "What did she get from that? Adoration from Andrei. And all those soldiers."

"But what about her and Pierre?" Aly continued, smiling. "She might have started out spoiled, but how could she not, growing up in that society? Don't you think she's changed by the time she falls in love with Pierre?"

"Oh, dear Alexandra," Granny said fondly, patting Aly's hand. "I think it's time you re-read *War and Peace*."

Aly's bright laugh started low and rose in pitch, like scales on a piano. "Maybe I will."

Spirited and charming. That fit Aly too. She had cast a spell over the table, glowing in her ivory dress against the mahogany paneled walls and dark portraits of grim-faced ancestors. Granny appeared to have been won over in minutes. And the rest of Chas's family as well. It was a masterstroke bringing a newcomer to dinner. Whit had never seen Chas's father so well behaved. His mother beamed her approval, and even his brother managed to engage in conversation about something other than his last round of golf. Chas looked proud and happy as he gazed at Aly, almost convincing Whit that the couple were in love.

Aly's indigo eyes danced in the candlelight as she and Granny moved on to debate whether Anna in *Anna Karenina* was a victim or a selfish adulteress. Chas ran a finger along Aly's lovely neck, capturing a tendril of hair, and Whit felt an unexpected pang of envy.

Chas, as always, saw everything and winked. "Whit. Look all you like, but she's mine," he said. "It'll be time for Granny's cake and gifts in a minute. You want to get your guitar, my troubadour?"

Granny tapped her fingers on the table. "I'm too old to be getting gifts. This birthday, I'm giving one," she announced and turned to Chas. "Would you be a dear and bring down my small jewelry box, the one on my dressing table?"

Whit's eyebrows lifted. Granny was famous for many things, but generosity wasn't one of them. When the box was placed in front of her, the old woman lifted the lid and rooted around until she found what she was looking for. "Something about that dress you're wearing made me think of my debutante ball," she said. "Mind you, my dress was quite a bit more elaborate. My mother made sure of that. I'll have to find a picture to show you sometime." Granny lifted a string of gleaming pearls from the box. "These were a gift from my grandmother on my debut. Let's see how they look on you."

Chas's father interrupted, "Mother, what do you think you're doing?"

"I'm doing what I want," she snapped. "And I want to see my pearls on this lovely young woman."

"Isn't that nice," said Chas's mother, tucking her blond hair behind her ear.

"I couldn't," said Aly, shooting a stricken look at Chas.

Granny held the pearls out to Chas. "Nonsense. You could. And you will. Chas. Put these on Alexandra, please. My fingers can't work the clasp anymore."

"Your wish is my command, Granny." Aly sat frozen as Chas fastened the necklace around her neck, appearing to realize that she was in deeper than she had bargained for. "Lovely indeed," he said, bestowing a gentle kiss behind her ear.

The pearls glowed in the candlelight as if lit from within. Aly touched the necklace and smiled, raising one eyebrow at Whit as if to say, "What do I do now?" Whit returned the look with a shrug, *you'll figure it out.*

Chas interrupted their unspoken dialogue with a wave of his hand. "Your guitar, Whit? It's time to sing Happy Birthday."

🐑 🐑 🐑

The after-dinner drinks were served in "the drawing room" (sherry for the ladies—a first for Aly—and scotch for the men). With the dining table laden with Waterford crystal and heavy polished silver (including finger bowls and ice cream forks), the evening had been like something out of *Downton Abbey*—in an old New England-Mayflower-ancestor sort of way.

Granny was formidable, but Aly sensed she was, like so many old folks, dreadfully bored and preferred debate to flattery. Granny loving all things Russian was a stroke of luck. After a decade of practice, it was easy for Aly to maintain the persona she'd so carefully built from the first day of her freshman year: the bucolic Vermont childhood, the professor parents in the Russian Department at Middlebury, the family's Newfoundland dogs, the lovely farm in the hills near Middlebury. All a lie, but an innocent one. And one that Kevin still believed. Hannah knew, of course, and understood, telling Aly years ago that if she'd had Aly's disaster of a mother, she'd probably have done the same thing.

Aly could see why Chas was a favorite. He was bright, funny, and attentive. With a bit of prodding, Granny launched into a retelling of her somewhat scandalous debut involving an empty bottle of whisky, a forgotten pair of underpants, and someone else's (soon-to-be-ex) fiancé.

Aly had felt Whit's eyes on her all evening. Curiosity, probably, to see how she'd do, tinged with an edge of jealousy. To her surprise, he appeared entirely at ease in his navy blazer with a table set with finger bowls and crystal. Perhaps Chas and Whit weren't such an odd couple. And Whit's command performance on the guitar was even more captivating in the intimacy of the drawing room. As in the old Grange Hall, Whit charmed, laying it on thick as he flirted shamelessly with Granny. Aly loved watching the lines on her face soften as the decades melted away, allowing glimpses of the beautiful, charming, willful young woman Granny must have been.

And when he turned his attention to Aly, choosing to play *The Boatman*, the song in Gaelic she'd so loved, she'd felt a quiver of pleasure, the tune resonating inside her like a perfect chord. The man had good looks, talent, and charisma—and was a nice guy to boot. Chas was a very lucky guy.

Slipping away to use the bathroom, Aly glanced in the mirror. Granny's pearls glowed around her neck with an inner light. Beautiful, but she and Chas would have to find a way to return them. Aly was drying her hands on the guest towel—monogrammed linen, of course—when her cell phone buzzed.

"Hi Kevin," she said, replacing the towel on the rack. "Can I call you later? I'm out at a dinner party."

"It's kind of important." Kevin's voice sounded grim.

"OK," Aly replied, walking down the hall to the library. "Did something happen with the restaurant?" she asked, sitting down in a leather armchair.

"No."

The chair gave off the faint stale scent of cigars. "Is the cat OK?" Aly asked, growing worried. "Did somebody get in an accident?"

"Everyone is fine."

Aly drew her eyebrows together. This wasn't like Kevin to make her play Twenty Questions. "Is it something about the apartment?"

"No. Yes. Sort of."

Aly felt a wave of anxiety. Kevin really did not sound like himself. "Just tell me. Please."

"They finished fixing the bathroom but did something wrong and one of the pipes burst. Flooded the whole apartment. Poor Miso didn't want to leave the sofa; the rug was a giant wet sponge. And somehow water got into the electrical system and shorted out the whole building." Kevin blew out a puff of air. "It's a complete mess, Aly."

Aly sighed in relief. A soggy carpet wasn't the end of the world, and she'd never liked the wall-to-wall that had come with the apartment. "When did it happen?"

"Tuesday. I wasn't there. I'd gone up early to meet with the folks at Goosecross for a wine tasting. Bex got us a reservation at the French Laundry—she used to work there—so we spent the night up in Yountville."

"Bex? Your sous chef?" Bex, Ripple's sous chef, was a younger, female, tattooed version of Kevin, just as passionate and nearly as talented. Aly felt a flash of irritation that Kevin had eaten at the French Laundry, which had been on their bucket list for ages, with his sous chef, not her.

"Yeah. It was great." Kevin still sounded tense. "Anyway, they've started pulling the carpets out."

"Are there hardwood floors under there? That would be nice."

"There are, but they're ruined—warped. They come out next," said Kevin. "At least the landlord is suspending the rent until the floors are done."

"How long is that going to take?" Aly asked. "Don't tell me we have to move out."

Aly waited for an answer. "Miso and I already moved to Bex's."

"What? Why there?"

"That's the thing I have to tell you."

Aly's limbs turned to stone. "What are you saying, Kevin?"

He sighed. "I'm saying...it's...I wasn't sure, we were working together so closely. We both knew we felt—something," Kevin said. "And then that dinner...." He paused. "I'm sorry I had to tell you this way."

Aly imagined Kevin running his hand through his black hair, the habit she'd seen thousands of times. Then, nauseatingly, she saw Bex's hand in his hair, her lips pressed against his, their entwined bodies falling onto whatever she used as her bed in some shithole apartment.

Bile rose in Aly's throat. "You cheated on me—with Bex?" she choked out, feeling like she was going to throw up.

"Aly. I didn't plan for this to happen," he pleaded. "I feel awful. But I had to tell you. And about the apartment. For when you come back."

🐑 🐑 🐑

Whit could barely believe it was the same Aly who walked, zombie-like, into the drawing room. Her face was pale, nearly gray.

"Dearest, what's wrong?" Chas slurred, a drink in his hand. With Aly out of the room, Chas's father had taken the opportunity to pick a fight, combined with veiled threats about convincing the trustee of Chas's trust to cut off his income. Chas had managed to keep his cool but had pounded down a double scotch and was working on another. "You look ill."

"Just some bad news. I'd like to go home now." She managed a weak smile for Granny. "Thank you for a lovely evening. It was very nice meeting you."

Granny extended her hand. "You too, Alexandra. I hope everything is alright, and that I'll see you again soon, dear."

Chas stood up and swayed. Whit caught his arm. "I'll take Aly home," Whit said.

"Yes, good idea." Chas looked gratefully at Whit and downed the rest of his scotch. "Perhaps I shouldn't drive tonight," he said, enunciating carefully. He wobbled over to his grandmother and bent down to kiss her papery cheek. "Good night, dear Granny," he said. "I'll drop by tomorrow if you're free for tea?"

"Yes, dear, of course," she said. "You're always welcome," she added, shooting a look at Chas's parents and brother.

Outside, Chas made a show of kissing Aly goodnight in case anyone was looking out the window. "Thank you," he said, wafting scotch fumes as he gave Aly another hug. "You were perfect. Now, I will be off," he said. "I feel my bed calling me."

"You're not going home with Whit?" Aly asked.

"Why would I do that?" Chas replied. "I live right there," he said, waving an arm down Water Street. "A little cottage in a rose garden. Lovely view of the harbor. Quite adorable."

Confused, Whit asked, "Aly, did you think Chas and I were a couple?"

Chas burst out laughing. "Oh, that's a good one. Sadly, I'm without a boo right now. Our handsome Whit is, unfortunately, as hetero as they come. Ta ta," he added, giving Aly another kiss as he walked off, saying to nobody in particular. "Oh, imagine if Whit were gay!"

Shaking his head, Whit watched Chas weave his way down the brick sidewalk. What in the world had made Aly think that he and

Chas were a couple? "I'm parked up on North Summer Street. Not too far," he said, his shoes a vise around his feet. "Granny seemed to enjoy her birthday dinner."

"Yes."

Whit glanced at Aly, withdrawn into herself. They walked the remaining blocks in silence. "Here's my truck."

"Thank you for taking me home," Aly said as she opened the door and climbed in.

Whit put the truck into gear. "Some place, huh?" he said into the awkward silence. "A lot of history in those old whaling captains' houses," he added, ready to launch into the story of his Azorean great-great-whatever-it-was grandfather's rise from cabin boy to captain. Whit felt a pang of loss as he drove by his childhood home a block away. Now, it was gone forever thanks to the idiocy of his father, who'd sold the house when Whit was a teenager after his new stepmother decided she preferred New York City and the Hamptons to tiny, stodgy provincial Edgartown. Granny was right to be worried about leaving her house in good hands.

Aly, staring out the side window, didn't respond. Whit glanced over at her profile, still and drawn in the moonlight. Granny's lustrous pearls gleamed against her collarbone, accentuating the line of her neck and head. Her skin had a subtle velvety sheen. She bent forward, and Whit caught a soft scent, feminine and flowery, and a glimpse of lace peeking from the deep neckline of her dress. Tonight, Aly had indeed been stunning and brilliant, until the bad news—whatever it was—had extinguished her flame.

She closed her eyes and sighed. Whit felt a wave of something tender, an urge to fix whatever it was that had so shaken her. "Listen, I don't want to pry," he said gently as he turned onto Pease Point Way. "But are you OK?"

"I will be," Aly said and pressed her lips together. "I always am."

"If you want to talk…"

Aly cut him off. "I don't."

They rode the rest of the way to West Tisbury in silence. The moon was a fingernail sliver in the sky, and the night was pitch black but for stars and the headlights of the occasional passing car. Whit got it. He didn't go around telling just anybody his business either. Turning onto New Lane, Whit flicked on his high beams. Whatever the bad news was, Hannah would take care of it—and Aly.

Aly started texting on her phone. "Shit. I can't go to Hannah's," she said. "Lawrence is still there."

"Who's Lawrence?"

"He's...Can I go to your house, just for a little while? Hannah can come and get me later."

"Sure." Surprised by the change in plans, Whit made a three-point turn in a driveway and turned around. "Who's Lawrence?"

Aly answered the question with silence.

"OK," Whit said. "Hannah's entitled to her secrets. Hard to have any on an island this small."

Whit dodged potholes on Quansoo Road for a mile and a half and turned into his driveway. A single bare light bulb illuminated the front door. "Here we are," he said, getting out of the truck. He opened the door and flicked on the lights, seeing his place through a stranger's eyes. Paintings of sailing ships in heavy frames hung on cedar-paneled walls, streaked pale from a leaky roof decades ago. A tatty tan couch offered comfort over looks, and a half-completed jigsaw puzzle lay on the dining table. In the kitchen, a wooden hutch sat next to a vintage mint-green gas stove and a refrigerator covered with magnets and photos.

"Make yourself at home." With a sigh of relief, Whit slid his feet out of the new loafers and took off his blazer and tie. "I think I have seltzer and beer in the fridge. Maybe a Coke hiding in the back," he said, unbuttoning the collar of his shirt.

"Do you have anything stronger?" Aly said, sitting down on the sofa.

"Let me see," Whit said, opening the lower door of the hutch and rummaging around. "About an inch of gin, some scotch, vodka. No mixers, sorry."

"Vodka, please. A double. No ice."

Whit raised his eyebrows and hoped Aly wasn't planning on getting smashed. "OK."

Whit handed Aly her drink, opened a beer for himself, and sat in an armchair. "You and Granny seemed to hit it off."

A pause before Aly spoke as if she had to bring herself back from somewhere far away. "She's a sweet old lady."

"Hardly. But she liked you. Take it as a compliment."

Aly sipped her vodka, her eyes averted, looking miserable and lovely in her white dress. An awkward minute passed. Whit drank his beer, wondering if he should keep trying to make chitchat, or go to bed and leave her alone to brood.

"Can I get you anything else? A snack or something?" Whit asked.

"No, I'm fine," Aly replied. "No. I'm not fine." She closed her eyes and wiped a tear from her cheek. "Not fine at all." Aly downed the rest of her vodka in a single gulp and started to cry. First a hiccup, then the full waterworks, her shoulders shaking as she wiped the tears from her face with both hands.

Whit jumped up and brought her a paper napkin. "I don't have any Kleenex."

"Thanks," Aly choked out.

Whit sat down on the sofa next to Aly and patted her hand. She turned and buried her face in his shirt, ratcheting up her tears from silent crying to full-blown sobs. He wrapped an arm around her shoulders, sympathy expanding in his chest. What could be her bad news—did someone die? Cancer? An accident? Whit hated to see anyone go through pain, whatever the cause.

"Shh, shh, it'll be OK," he said, stroking her back and her hair, so soft, breathing in her scent. Jasmine, maybe, mixed with something earthier. Aly wrapped her arms around Whit's neck, pressing her breasts against his chest. His body, operating on a different wavelength, reacted. *Oh, shit, this is not the time or place for that*, he scolded himself.

Aly's sobs intensified. Her whole body shook as if her insides were being torn apart by sorrow. Whit hugged her closer, willing both her sadness and his ardor to lessen. "Shh. Shh," he hushed.

"Why did this happen to me?" Aly moaned. Whit continued to stroke her back. She looked up at him, her mascara smeared into dark raccoon eyes, and buried her face again into his wet shirt. "How will I find a new place to live?" she sobbed.

Place to live? Aly's tragedy was her apartment lease? Something to be upset about, he supposed, but this upset? Whatever the reason, Aly was truly unhappy, and there was nothing he could do except offer up his shirt as a giant handkerchief.

He glanced at his watch. And hoped that Hannah would come—and soon.

🐑 🐑 🐑

Hannah set down her mug of morning coffee and rested her chin in her hand, empathy oozing out of wide brown eyes. "So, what do you want to do now? Besides offering to dry clean Whit's shirt?"

"Oh my God, I'm so embarrassed. Yes," Aly said.

"It's fine. That was a joke. Whit won't care."

A wad of used tissues sat in front of Aly's untouched breakfast. Her eyelids felt like sandpaper, her nose was red and raw, her throat tight and choked. Even the corners of her mouth hurt. She leaned back in her chair and looked out the window. Outside, the bright sun thumbed its nose at her mood, lighting the sheep in the grassy field brilliant white and making sharp spangles of light on the pond. She had no idea how to answer Hannah's question: the black, sad cloud in her brain had taken away her power to think. She had no place to live. No job. No boyfriend.

"Well. One thing is easy." Hannah patted Aly's hand. "You're going to stay here as long as you like. Take your time. Figure things out, Dandelion'll be happy. Me too," she smiled. "Or go back and fight that kitchen hussy for Kevin. How are you in a knife fight?"

Aly imagined herself facing off against Bex in Ripple's kitchen, razor-sharp chef's knife in her hand. She managed a weak smile. "Bad. I'd lose."

Hannah patted her hand. "He doesn't deserve you."

"No," Aly said as a fresh wave of self-pity washed over her. "It's my fault."

Hannah glared at Aly. "Stop that. Now you're just being stupid."

Aly put her head on the table. "I really tried. I did."

"Tried how?" Hannah asked.

Aly picked up her head and sighed. She leaned back and closed her eyes. "Tried to be the perfect girlfriend."

"That's even stupider," said Hannah fiercely. "If you're with the right person, you don't have to try. That's why it wasn't going to work out with Lawrence. I wasn't about to become someone he could take to all his parties, with a closetful of cute sundresses and the perfect party chatter."

Aly opened her eyes. "Oh, geez, Hannah. I can't believe I forgot. Did you break up? How are you?"

"Sad. But OK. Lawrence was pretty upset, but he'll get over it. Me too. Like I said, it was a fun summer fling. Nothing more."

Aly didn't believe her. "I'm sorry."

"Don't worry about me," Hannah said, getting up to refill their coffee mugs. She sat down and stirred some sugar into her coffee. "All this happening? Maybe the universe is sending you a message that it's time to make a change. The whole world is out there, Aly." She squeezed her hand. "Everything'll work itself out. Maybe not how you expect. But it will."

🐑 🐑 🐑

Oh, to be a sheep, Aly thought, no cheating ex-boyfriend, no job worries, content so long as there was a dry place to sleep and something to eat. "Good grass, Dandelion?" The lamb lifted her head at her name, her soft ears pivoting, and walked over to graze next to Aly, nibbling delicately at the green blades, a steady, wooly lawnmower. Dandelion's gentle presence, sweet with lanolin and fresh-cut grass, dulled the sharp daggers of pain. A comfort sheep.

Aly lifted an arm just to watch it fall, heavy as stone, back across her stomach. It was as if the pull of gravity had doubled, pinning her to the faded cushion of the chaise. She was tired, so tired, of her hamster brain spinning in endless circles, alternating crying jags with hours of dark, hopeless funk. Sleep alone dropped the curtain on the show being performed in her head, featuring Kevin, Aly, and a knife-wielding Bex. Sometimes, Kevin played the innocent, caught in a snare by his conniving sous chef. Other times, he played a deceiver, masterfully lying to hide his secret double life. Day after day, night after night, Aly had dredged up every mention of Bex, every clue she'd missed—and came up with nothing. If not quite perfect, everything had been more than fine between her and Kevin. They both loved exploring San Francisco, finding little immigrant mom-and-pop restaurants with authentic, exotic food. Their groups of friends overlapped, then merged. He was proud of her career success, and she of his. And the sex, if a bit routine at times, was more than good. Sure, she complained that Kevin worked too hard, and he could be critical of her (justifiably, most of the time), but they never really *fought*.

Ugh. Aly shifted on the chaise, and an empty bag of peanut butter-filled pretzels fell to the grass. One hundred and thirty calories per serving, ten servings per package. Hah. One serving, thirteen hundred ultra-processed calories of fat and salt that she should never have eaten. Aly could feel the salt puffing her ankles and her fat cells inflating. She picked up her phone and scrolled through Instagram, but it made her even more depressed to see the beautiful pictures of her happy friends having fun in fabulous places. TikTok, on the other hand, numbed her brain with attention-deficit-designed videos of adorable corgi-potato puppies and cooking hacks and make-up tips and viral dance moves and a strangely compelling video of a Japanese teapot being made by hand. Numbed, at least, until her cell battery drained to zero. Aly looked at her watch and sighed. Still hours before she'd let herself drink the first of many glasses of wine that would blur the edges of the evening. What difference did it make after her life—her close-to-perfect life—just got flushed down the crapper?

A light breeze rustled the leaves on the lichen-encrusted branches of the old pear tree. The blue sky taunted her, nagging her to *go for a run, it's such a beautiful day, or at least take a walk on the beach. Help Hannah paint. Start looking for a new job. Do* something. Aly's muscles were turning as spongy as Dandelion's wool from lying around day after day in the shade of what she decided, after hours of staring up into the branches, was a very nice tree. She sat up, put her feet on the ground, and considered her options. She couldn't face starting the hunt for a new job, not yet. Running was out. Even walking held no appeal. Aly should clean up the kitchen as she'd promised Hannah. But crusty fried egg dishes? Yuck.

Beau ran over and dropped a tennis ball at Aly's feet. She looked at the hopeful dog and flopped against the cushion. At least she had company: a sweet Velcro sheep and a handsome, ball-obsessed dog. "Later, Beau. Maybe later."

🐑 🐑 🐑

"Aly, wake up."

"What?" Aly said, struggling to open her eyes from her nap on the chaise. "Hannah? You're home early."

"I'm home because you aren't answering your phone."

"Oh. Right. The battery died," Aly said. "I meant to plug it in."

"Get up. Whit is expecting you on his boat in 20 minutes. I'll drop you off in Menemsha. His friend Jak fractured his wrist, so Whit's pulling his lobster pots. He needs help."

"Can't you go?"

Hannah puffed out her cheeks and glared at Aly. "I have to get back to work. And I've got a landlord-tenant mediation thing later in Vineyard Haven. Barking puppy. I may have to line up a dog trainer." Hannah tilted her head. "You need to get out of the house."

"I was out of the house, remember? I went to the store," she said, holding up the empty pretzel bag.

"That was three days ago." Hannah put her fists on her hips. "Come on, Aly. I get that you need some 'me time,' but this is ridiculous. And Whit needs help."

"He must have lots of friends he can ask."

Her memory of that night at Whit's was a messy blur. She remembered the texture of Whit's white shirt, soaked through with tears, his broad chest, the feel of his arms wrapped around her, his soothing voice. She'd meant to apologize to him but hadn't. What had she said that night? Did she say anything about Kevin leaving her? She was so ashamed. Aly had never lost control like that, not with a near-perfect stranger. The truth was she was embarrassed to see him.

"All his friends are working. You're not."

"What about Chas?" Aly said, knowing that was not the answer. Lobster Thermidor and champagne, yes—lobster pots and stinky bait, no.

"Aly. Get. Up. Put on some clothes you don't mind getting wet and dirty. Now."

Aly groaned. "OK, OK. Don't be so bossy." Hannah would nag and cajole until Aly caved. She'd go out on Whit's boat. She owed him an apology. And to reimburse him for his dry-cleaning bill.

"And bring back lobsters for dinner. You're cooking."

As they drove to the dock, Aly groused about not knowing anything about fishing for lobsters. She grew suspicious that Whit didn't need help; this was Hannah's ruse to get Aly up off her rear end and out. But this boat trip "to help Whit" wouldn't make a whit of difference to what happened to her. Nothing would, except to rewind the clock back to before Kevin slept with his sous chef.

Hannah dropped Aly off at the boat with a beep of her horn. "Don't forget the lobsters."

"Right."

"Welcome to *Noepe*," Whit said and extended a hand to help Aly onboard. His grip on her forearm was strong and secure. "Nice afternoon to be going out."

Whit wore a blue t-shirt, loose around his biceps and trim torso, and Carhartt canvas shorts with a rip in the hem. His Larsen's Fish Market cap had faded from red to pink, and his rubber boots looked as if they'd spent some time at the bottom of the sea. It was hard to recognize him as the same person dressed in the blue blazer and crisp white shirt that she'd ruined with her tears and smears of mascara.

"Hannah said you need some help today," Aly said, even more certain that Whit was doing Hannah a favor. Which made him a very nice guy.

He flashed her that cute, lopsided grin. "We'll be off in a minute."

Aly looked around. The morning sun caught the shaggy edges of the weathered, gray-shingled fishing shacks that ringed Menemsha harbor, quaint and postcard-pretty, as the lightest of breezes pushed cotton ball clouds across a deep blue sky. Whit's boat shone clean and white in the bright July light. Hannah could be right. Maybe getting out on the water would help pull her out of her funk. Aly had always loved boats. She dreamed of riding on ferries in Hong Kong, long-tailed boats in Thailand, dahabiyas on the Nile, sailboats in the Greek Islands, barges on the canals in Europe, whale-watching boats anywhere, she wanted to go on them all. Kevin occasionally (and grudgingly) put up with her passion for all things that floated, but he'd made it clear that he'd rather keep his feet on dry land. Back when they traveled. Back before the restaurant. Back when everything was the way it was supposed to be.

"This is a pretty boat," Aly said, settling herself in one of the swivel fishing chairs in the stern. She adjusted the visor on her baseball cap and put on her sunglasses.

Whit looked around his boat with pride.

"I want to apologize for the other night. And pay for dry cleaning your shirt."

"Washed and ironed already. And no need to apologize," Whit said. "You ever pulled a lobster pot before?" Aly shook her head. "Nothing to it. Trap does all the work. We just haul it up and take the lobsters out."

After helping Whit with the lines, Aly resumed her spot in the stern. *Noepe* motored out of the small harbor, past the rusty fishing vessels lining Dutcher Dock, past the gleaming motor yachts and sailboats on their moorings, and out through the narrow breakwater.

Once past the breakwater, Whit pushed the throttle forward, and the boat picked up speed, bouncing lightly through the waves. Despite herself, Aly was enjoying the breeze that tugged at her hat and the pull of the engines speeding the *Noepe* across the water. Of course, she knew Martha's Vineyard was an island, but being on a boat made it seem more real. Far ahead, she could pick out Woods Hole on the Cape, nine miles away at the end of a long string of islands. To the right, starboard side, trees hid huge vacation homes tucked discreetly into the landscape.

"Nice houses, if you've got an extra ten million bucks," Whit shouted over the sound of the motor.

Aly left her fishing chair to join Whit in the wheelhouse. "Want to take the wheel for a bit?" he asked.

"Sure."

Whit slowed the boat and changed places with Aly. "Just keep it steady," he said. "Push the throttle—that's the lever with the black knob—forward to speed up and back to slow down."

Aly slowly pushed the knob away from her and the boat picked up speed. Like riding a bike, it all came back. She turned the wheel a bit one way, then the other to test the boat's responsiveness, and straightened course again. *Noepe* handled like the dependable fishing boat she was. Secure, sturdy, and unpretentious with a strong, graceful build. Like Whit, she thought.

Whit leaned over to correct their course a few degrees. Aly's arm tingled where his bare skin rested against hers, and she could feel her heart speed up in her chest. She breathed in his clean scent, mixed with the salt air and a touch of fishy funk from the boat. Or maybe it was his boots.

Whit stepped away and leaned against the console, leaving Aly alone at the wheel. "The pots are set off Makonikey. Won't take too long to get there." He looked over at her. "You doing OK now? You were pretty upset the other night."

Aly slowly nodded her head. "Better," she answered. She blew out a puff of breath. "I'm really sorry I made such a scene. I got some bad news, and I don't know, I took it hard."

"I know. I was there," Whit joked.

He put his arms behind his head. "Me, I'm like a turtle with *Noepe*. I've always got a place to live. Go where I want when I want. No worries about apartment leases."

"You can live on your boat?"

"I've got a bunk up in the bow, kitchen, head, shower, the works. I built everything myself—a labor of love. Go take a look if you want."

Aly relinquished the wheel, opened the hatch cover, and stepped down the ladder-like stairs into a snug cabin. While the outside of the boat was purely utilitarian, the inside was a cozy den. The ceiling glowed with wood set in a herringbone pattern, and the brass lamps and latches gleamed gold. Admiring the exquisite craftsmanship, Aly poked into nooks and cubbies designed to store everything you'd need to live aboard, secured against sliding when the seas got rough. She ran a hand over the wood, buttery smooth, and pulled on a brass ring set into the cabinet. Out slid a cutting board with its knife nestled into a carved notch. Another brass ring opened a drawer designed to fit bottles of wine—good wine, Aly noted with surprise, a Barolo and a Tuscan Brunello. A latched cabinet held a few boxes of dry pasta, canned Italian tomatoes, olives, and tuna. Another held a small set of nested skillets and saucepans.

Curious, Aly lay down on the bunk. It was cozy and womblike with soft pillows below and the wood ceiling above. She listened to the water against the hull and realized she'd never spent a night on a boat. What would it be like to be a turtle with your home on your back, sitting watching the sunset over the water, making a simple pasta, and sipping fine wine? Just go wherever you want, whenever you want.

"Everything OK down there?" Whit called from above. "We're getting close."

"Coming," Aly said, reluctantly getting up from the bunk. She climbed the ladder back to the deck. "Wow. The woodwork is amazing."

"Thanks. I took my time. Got to make every inch count," Whit said. "I figured I'd be living aboard *Noepe* quite a bit when I'm not here."

"Do you?"

"Not as much as I thought. I'm here summers, and I lucked into a little place—almost a beach shack, where I stay winters in St. John," Whit said. "But it's pretty, all covered with purple bougainvillea, and I can snorkel off the beach. I've even got my own nutmeg tree. Just a rental, but I know the owner. Nice lady. She's a writer—and very rich."

"Not too shabby," Aly said, envying Whit his lifestyle. "Chas said you went to St. John to help with the recovery after the big hurricane."

"Irma. It almost wiped St. John off the map. Lots of work in construction, if you didn't mind living in a place with a tarp for a roof. I did that for a while and saved enough money to buy *Noepe* and fix her up."

"She's a lovely boat," Aly said. Maybe it was the wind and the water, but she felt better than she had in days. "A friend of mine has a fishing boat in San Francisco that he keeps at the marina on Treasure Island. He bought it after his tech company IPO'd. Initial public offering—when a company goes public, and all the founders make a bazillion dollars?"

"I know what an IPO is."

"Oh. Right," Aly said, hoping she hadn't offended Whit. "His boat is absolutely huge with all this radar and sonar stuff. I think he wanted to show the other tech bros how much money he'd made. But he has to hire a captain to take it out."

"Guy should learn to run his boat," Whit said, shaking his head. "Great fishing in the Bay Area—Chinook salmon, halibut, stripers. Tough tides, though. You need to know what you're doing. But it's a bit far for me to take *Noepe*," he chuckled. Throttling down, Whit said, "We should start looking for Jak's buoys. They're yellow and blue."

Aly began scanning the water. "Is that one?" she asked, pointing to the left.

"Good eye," Whit replied. "I'll get us close. The gaff hook is hanging there," he said, indicating the aluminum pole clipped to the inside of the hull.

Whit let the engine idle, keeping the boat alongside the marker. "Go right under the buoy and grab the line when I come alongside." Aly reached out with the gaff to hook the rope. "Easy, easy. There you go. You got it."

Whit pulled out what looked like an old bathmat and spread it over the side. "No sense dinging up the gunwale when we pull the crusty things up," he explained. "*Noepe* used to be a lobster boat, but I removed the winch. We'll have to pull the pots up by hand. Just hang on."

Aly could feel the line tugging as the boat began to drift in the current. Whit pulled two pairs of blue rubber gloves and some metal tools from a canvas bag.

"Ready," Aly said, excited despite herself.

"I'll haul this one up." Whit slipped on his rubber gloves and began to bring in the line, pulling seaweed off as he went. Yards of rope piled up on the deck. With a grunt, Whit pulled the rectangular metal mesh trap up over the side. "Here, help me get it on deck."

Aly put on her gloves and grabbed one end. She and Whit set the trap down on the deck. It was dripping water and covered with brownish gunk. Several lobsters and a fish wriggled inside.

"Looks like a couple of nice big bugs. Let's see if they're keepers." Whit pulled more seaweed off the trap and unlatched the top. "The lobsters go into the kitchen, here, to get the bait bag," he said, pointing to various parts of the traps. "When they try to leave, they go through this mesh funnel into what they call the parlor and can't get out."

"Like a bad dinner party."

Whit guffawed. "Yeah." He reached in and pulled out a prehistoric-looking fish with giant fins and whacked it on the deck. "Sea robin. Junk fish. We can use it to bait the traps," he said as he tossed the dead fish into a big white cooler. "They'll go after fresh but prefer their fish a little stinky."

"Ew."

"Grab one of those lobsters—just pick it up around the middle—and I'll get the gauge." Whit paused. "Oh, wait. You're a city girl. And squeamish."

"Fish and lobsters are different from sticking your arm inside a sheep," Aly said. With a deep breath, she grabbed a lobster and pulled it out. The crustacean thrashed and snapped its claws, and Aly dropped it. "Ah," she yelled. "It tried to bite me!"

"It's a lobster, what do you expect?" Whit laughed. "That's why you have gloves on."

The lobster skittered across the deck, claws held up like a boxer's. Whit stood with his arms crossed, watching with an amused glint in his eye. "Better catch it. We've got nineteen more traps to pull."

The lobster backed away, waving its claws every time Aly got close. "You could help by distracting it, or something." Whit took off a glove and waggled it in front of the lobster as Aly moved in from behind. "Got it!"

Whit took the wriggling lobster and flipped it over. "Male. See how this here is hard," he said, running a finger down the center of the tail. He turned the lobster back over and laid a metal gauge across its back. "You measure from the eye socket to the end of the body here. Three and a quarter inches is the minimum. All right, we've got a keeper," Whit said, tossing the lobster into the cooler.

More confidently, Aly reached in to pull out the second lobster and turned it over. Whit stood over her shoulder and reached around to touch the underside of the lobster. His forearm was tanned and muscular. A gorgeous whale, heavily inked in the abstract Maori-style, peeked out from beneath the sleeve of his t-shirt. *Whoa girl*, Aly thought to herself as her heart began to race again. She sensed the heat of his skin beneath his shirt, the breadth of his chest. If she leaned back, it would be like leaning against a tree or a mountain. Or maybe one of the big granite boulders at

Lucy Vincent Beach, sun-warmed, brawny, with the sea washing around it.

"Too bad, she's an egger," Whit said. "See how this here is soft? And she's got a notch in her tail? That means another lobsterman has marked her as a breeding female."

"Throw her back?" Aly asked, face flushed, the lobster still in her hand.

Splashes of water had darkened patches on his faded blue t-shirt, and crystals of salt speckled his skin. The sea spray had tousled his hair into gorgeous waves, the kind women spend hours and big bucks on hair products to achieve. Whit smiled that melting, lopsided smile that crinkled the corners of his warm gold-brown eyes.

"Afraid so," he said.

A flash of desire set Aly's insides wobbling. Not in a bad way, but like pieces were being shifted inside, tumbled end over end. This was the real Whit, this man in his boat. And this real Whit was really, disconcertingly, sexy.

"Toss that one over the side, and I'll show you how to tie on a new bait bag."

🐑 🐑 🐑

Over the years, Whit had had every kind on his boat, but Aly was a natural. She moved around the boat as if she'd been born to it. Her enthusiasm for the messy, smelly, physical job of lobstering was the last thing he'd expected. He'd taken Aly with him grudgingly, as a favor to Hannah. He'd pegged Aly as a city girl, irrationally upset about a lost apartment lease, content to live her life sipping overpriced lattes at trendy coffee shops while staring at a computer screen. But that didn't fit the sunburned, admittedly attractive woman wrestling a rubber band around the snapping claw of a feisty lobster.

"You know, when you flex your arm, your whale swims," Aly said. "Where did you get that? It's an amazing design."

"New Zealand," he said as the lobster thrashed in his gloved hand. "I worked on a whale-watching boat for a while. One of the few places where you can see sperm whales."

"I thought you did sheep?"

"Those too. I've done a lot of things. Some I liked better than others," Whit said, adding fresh bait to the trap and tossing it overboard. He started the engine and moved over so Aly could take the wheel. As he moved past, the breeze lifted her hair, burnished copper in the sunshine, and brushed it against his neck. He felt a quiver inside. "How long are you staying on the Island?" Whit asked, feeling his heart speed up.

"A little while longer, at least. Things back in San Francisco are...complicated." Whit watched her profile grow sad and wished he hadn't asked. "So, what's the story? How did you end up on a whale-watching boat?"

"Long story. I was bartending in Timaru—that's along the coast, south of Christchurch—when a juvenile sperm whale beached himself. We had to get him back into the ocean." Whit said, hoping the story would distract Aly's attention from her sadness.

Aly's deep blue eyes grew huge. "How? They're huge."

"It wasn't easy. We got a sling around him and roped that to a fishing boat," Whit said. "We missed the first high tide, so we tried digging a trench in the sand. We had only one more shot." Whit ran a hand through his hair, remembering the frantic tension of the volunteers and the whale-stranding experts. "I was on the team charged with digging the trench near the head. At one point, I looked into the whale's eye. And the whale looked back. I could see his intelligence—the whale knew I was trying to help him." The connection had been powerful, otherworldly. "The trench worked, and we managed to refloat him on the next tide. It was probably the most intense experience of my life."

"You got the tattoo."

"And the job on the whale-watching boat."

The rest of the story, the weird part, Whit kept to himself. A couple of months earlier, when he was still working on the sheep station, his buddy's cousin had come by. The cousin, his friend swore, was a Tohunga Matakite: he could see the future. So, there they were, sitting on the porch watching the stars and getting royally pissed on Speight's, when the cousin said, "Pain in the arse, being a matakite. Whit, mate, you got whales," he slurred. "They're in your past, in your blood, in your future." The cousin slugged down the rest of his beer and belched. "Whales calm the waves, guide you on the right path," he added unhelpfully, closed his eyes, and fell asleep.

Whit had stared at the guy in disbelief. Of all the things to bring up on a 4,000-acre sheep ranch in the middle of New Zealand. Whales were in Whit's blood, all the way back to the 18th century. He forgot about what the guy had said until whales started showing up in his dreams, renewing the wanderlust that had sent Whit to the coast and the mind-blowing experience with the beached whale. Which, he figured, fulfilled the beer-swilling Tohunga Matakite's prophecy. If that's what it was.

"There are some whales around here," Whit said. "Humpbacks mostly. Right whales are around, but they're really rare—only a few hundred left in the world." Aly nodded. "We had a juvenile wash up dead here not long ago. A female. A rope from a lobster pot from Maine had wrapped itself around her tail. You see this on the trap?" he asked, holding up a plastic link. "It's designed to break away if a whale gets caught up in the line. The lobstermen lose the trap, of course, and the lobsters." Whit pulled a noxious bag of fish bits out of a cooler and tied it inside the trap. Aly scrunched her nose against the smell. "You can spot whales now and then around here, but the best whale watching is north of Cape Cod in the Stellwagen Bank."

Aly's blue eyes lit up. "Could you take *Noepe* there?"

"I could, but it's pretty far. It would take, I don't know, five or six hours," Whit said. "Maybe more. And a lot of gas."

Aly looked disappointed. "Too far for a day trip, then."

"You could do it as an overnight. Stop in Hyannis or Chatham for lunch, get a mooring in P-town—Provincetown, at the tip of Cape Cod—and set out to the Bank in the morning."

Whit shocked himself by imagining Aly stretched out on his bunk down in the cabin, watching him make dinner on his tiny, gimbaled stove. It was a very pleasant, if disconcerting, vision. Other than female clients (who didn't count), no woman had been on his boat since Petra. False, lying, untrustworthy Petra.

The last thing Whit wanted to do was go back down the rabbit hole of obsessing about Petra. "You could do some fishing along the way, even see a great white shark. It's a hot spot for them around Chatham." He tied the new bait bag in place. "See? It goes here. You can do the next bag." He tipped the trap over the side.

"People think we have lots of sharks here since they filmed *Jaws* on MV—you know that Martha's Vineyard was Amity Island, right? But the chances of seeing a great white around here are pretty low. There's a huge seal population off the Cape. So that's where they mainly hang out."

"Poor seals," Aly said. "I see them at the beach all the time. They're so cute with those big eyes and long whiskers. Beau gets all excited. He's sure it's another dog."

"Sea dogs," smiled Whit, enjoying the easy conversation. "They eat the fish I'm trying to catch, but that's ok." He started the boat and pulled up to the next buoy. "I saw some humpbacks off the beach this year."

"You're kidding! Where?"

"Right off South Beach. First time I'd ever seen them from shore," Whit said.

"I love whales," Aly sighed. "But not whaling. I can't believe it's still going on. Scientific research, hah."

"I'm with you there," Whit said, idling the engine. "Did you know *Moby Dick* was based on a real story about the whaleship *Essex*. Tashtego, the harpooner, was a Wampanoag from Aquinnah."

Aly smiled. "I tried to read Moby Dick once, ages ago. But I got bogged down and gave up." She caught the trap line with the gaff hook. "What happened to the real *Essex*?" she asked, appearing genuinely interested. "Did a whale really sink it?"

"It did," Whit said, moving next to Aly to help her haul up the trap. "The ship was plagued with bad luck omens. They were out on the whaling grounds in the South Pacific when a big bull sperm whale rammed the ship. According to the first mate, the whale came at them again at 'twice his normal speed with tenfold fury and vengeance.' Smashed in the bow and sank the ship." Whit pulled seaweed off the trap. "They were thousands of miles from shore. The crew escaped on the whaleboats, but it was pretty gruesome—dehydration, starvation, and cannibalism. It took three months before they were rescued. Eight of twenty made it."

Aly shuddered. "Horrible. But you can't blame the whale."

"Agreed. I'd be mighty pissed off with a harpoon in my side," Whit said, more than happy to talk about whales and whaling. His bookcase was filled with books on the topic, *Moby Dick*, *In the Heart of the Sea*, *Leviathan*, *Whaling Captains of Color*, and *The Whale*.

Aly opened the trap, pulled out a tiny lobster, and tossed it back into the water. "Now you've got pods of orcas sinking sailboats off Spain and Portugal. And they teach each other. Revenge of the whales," she grinned.

"Fascinating history, barbaric practice, now and then. Today they use sonar and grenade harpoons," Whit said, noticing how wind and salt air had set Aly's auburn hair into a mass of messy ringlets. "The whales have no chance against that."

"Japan and Norway claim they're catching whales for science. Bullshit." Aly's lips tightened. "It makes me so angry that we can't stop it."

"True," he said. "How'd a Vermont girl get interested in whales?"

"It's kind of embarrassing."

"Come on. Out with it," he grinned.

"OK. The *Baby Beluga* song."

Whit started to sing, "Baby beluga in the deep…"

"Oh my gosh, stop," Aly laughed. "You're going to give me an earworm." Whit enjoyed teasing her. With a devilish look, he sang a few more bars. "Stop, please! I made a baby whale out of a white tube sock. I used to carry it around everywhere when I was little," she said. "Ridiculous, I know."

Kind of adorable, he thought. "I used to carry a stuffed lion. His name was Brushgame, no idea why."

"Brushgame. That's cute," Aly said, pulling out another lobster, holding the measuring gauge against the lobster's carapace. "This one's a keeper. Where's that banding thingy?" Whit handed it over. "Oh, just stop that," she scolded the lobster as he snapped his claws. "OK. Got him," Aly said, proudly handing the conquered crustacean to Whit. "Your turn. Did you know beluga whales used to swim in Lake Champlain?"

"Say what?"

"It was tens of thousands of years ago—back when Lake Champlain was the Champlain Sea," Aly said. "Some railway workers in the mid-1800s found a fossilized skeleton of a beluga whale. They named her Charlotte, and she hangs in the museum at the University of Vermont."

"I did not know that."

"Sorry. I kind of geek out on whales."

"You ever see a beluga?"

Aly shook her head. "I was planning a trip to Alaska, but my boyfr..." Aly stopped. "I really want to. And I will. Someday."

"Belugas in the wild are on my bucket list too," said Whit. "As is going up to Alaska. That's one place I've never been."

"I thought you'd been everywhere."

"Not quite. Yet."

🐑 🐑 🐑

As *Noepe* neared the breakwater in Menemsha, Whit took over the helm. He'd liked seeing Aly running his boat. And talking to her about whales. He was awkward around a lot of women, not sure what to talk about. (Not Hannah, of course, she was like a sister. A sister he got along with.) He'd never gone for the type of women who looked as if they'd spent two hours and had used dozens of beauty products to achieve a flawless face and perfect hair, wafting perfume as they teetered around on heels in suggestive outfits, chatting about nothing that Whit knew or cared about. For Whit, there was nothing sexier than a woman with tan, toned legs in shorts, salt spray-tousled hair, smelling of sunscreen—and a tad of bait.

There was something special about Aly. He'd seen it that night at Granny's before the bad news. She had spirit, paired with a playful enthusiasm that made him feel the same way. Chas was always telling him to have more fun. This afternoon with Aly, he was.

Whit maneuvered the boat into its slip. Chas stood on the dock with his hands on his hips.

"Oh my goodness, girl! What has Whit done to you?" Chas exclaimed, taking in Aly's windblown hair and muck-smeared t-shirt. Sunburn reddened her arms from the wrist up, and a brownish-green smudge dirtied her cheek.

"We went lobstering," Aly said, brushing some specks from her t-shirt.

Whit cut the engine. "What are you doing in Menemsha, Chas?"

"Looking for Aly. I was worried because she," he fixed Aly with a disapproving look, "has not been returning my calls. Then I find out from Hannah that you've got her out on the boat," he said with mock jealousy. "Another man! I should be furious!"

"I meant to call you back," Aly said.

Chas pursed his lips. "Forgiven," he said. "Hannah said you weren't feeling well. But you're better now?"

"Being out on the water was good for me."

Whit had to agree. Aly's ocean-blue eyes were alight, and a smile played at the corners of her mouth. "Aly gave me a good idea. I could take clients on two-day trips up to Cape Cod with an overnight in Provincetown. Fishing, sharks, whale-watching, sightseeing."

"You're assuming people want to spend two whole days on your stinkpot with you," said Chas. "Good luck with that."

"Aly would." Whit glanced over at her, and she nodded. "You're just grumpy because we didn't invite you to go lobstering."

"I am not," said Chas. "I had a wonderful luncheon at the Yacht Club with Granny."

"Grab that end of the cooler, Aly, and we'll show him our catch. Give us a hand, Chas."

With Chas's help, Whit and Aly hoisted the heavy cooler up and onto the gunwale and then to the dock. Chas made a big show of wiping his hands. "Granny is dying to have you over for tea, Aly. I told her you were leaving soon."

"I've decided to stay a bit longer. I'd love to have tea with your grandmother. But," Aly hesitated, "I'm not sure we should keep this fake girlfriend thing up."

"I've never seen Granny so happy," Chas said. He took Aly's hand. "We're doing this for her. And I still owe you a trip on Daddy's sailboat. It'll be much more civilized than this." He ran his eyes over Whit's boat. A stinky fishy ooze from the bait bags ran in rivulets across the deck, mixed with the blood from the chopped-up sea robin and bits of brownish scum from the lobster pots. "I mean, really, Whit, what were you thinking?"

Whit grabbed a bucket, filled it with water, and began to sluice the deck. "It's a fishing boat, Chas. You get fish guts on fishing boats."

"Hardly the place for my future fiancée," Chas said, patting Aly's arm. "Oh, just look at your sunburn! I can't believe you let him talk you into this!"

"It was Hannah," Aly said.

"In cahoots with Whit again." He turned to Whit. "I'm picking up the champagne for tonight. We're doing the lobsters at your place."

"We are?"

"On your deck—I love that golden evening light across the pond," Chas said. "So, pick out four nice lobsters for us. I'm buying, of course. Or, even better, eight. You can never have enough lobster!" He took Aly's arm. "I'll drive you home—you must be dying to have a hot shower! Whit can clean up his messy old boat."

🐑 🐑 🐑

Aly slipped into the passenger seat of Chas's immaculate car, hoping she'd adequately cleaned the muck off her legs and shorts. Chas was right. A long, hot outdoor shower would be heaven. Hannah's big claw-foot tub was lovely, but showering under the open sky had been a revelation. Standing not quite square to the house, the shower was made from cedar tree posts and weathered boards, with a pair of plumbers' valves to control the water and a daisy-head showerhead that gushed instead of dribbled. Blue sky, warm water, a fresh breeze, and Aly's favorite soap made for sheer shower perfection.

"You're not going to tell me you enjoyed yourself on Whit's boat?" Chas asked.

"I didn't think I would, but I had a great time. So much fun."

"Seriously?"

Aly examined her pink arm. It was stupid of her not to have used more sunscreen. "Seriously. I love boats. And being out on the water."

"What did you and Whit find to talk about?"

"Lobsters. And whales. Sharks too, a bit." She smiled and sighed. As always, Hannah knew what was best for her. Being out on the water had—as Hannah had intended—eased Aly out of her funk. The sea air had blown her mind clear of self-pity and, blessedly, stopped the hamster wheel in her brain. For the first time since Kevin's call, Aly felt like her old self. She and Whit had worked well as a team pulling the traps onto the boat. Once the ice had broken, Whit started teasing her—gently, for sure—about her city ways, which made her even more determined to show him she could match him lobster for lobster, bait bag for bait bag.

Chas glanced over at her. "Ah. I see how it is. You aren't the first to get a crush on our handsome Whit Dias."

"What?"

"He's a heartbreaker, that one. Warning, though. Whit has built some serious barricades since his last relationship," Chas said, shaking his head. "Her name was Petra, and she dumped him for her rich Eurotrash ex-boyfriend. Whit had thought she was 'the one.' If you manage to breach that fortress, for his sake—and mine—please don't break his heart."

🐑 🐑 🐑

Aly had forgotten how much she loved lobster. Just hot, boiled lobster dipped in warm, lemon-y, melted butter, not gussied up in some fancy, complicated recipe. She dunked a chunk of claw meat into the cup of butter and popped it, dripping, into her mouth. The meat was sweet, rich, and utterly delicious. "Ummm."

"The lady likes her lobster," Whit said with a grin.

"Glad I got you out, Aly?" Hannah said, cracking a claw.

"As always, you know what's best for me."

"True."

Aly took a sip of champagne, enjoying the fizzy tingle on her tongue. She leaned back in her chair, anticipating her next bite. The long, late rays of the sun set the clouds glowing tangerine and gold, and a pale-blue iridescence glazed the surface of the pond, just a stone's throw from Whit's deck. Never could Aly have imagined she'd be sitting here, eating a lobster she had pulled from the sea just hours earlier, reveling in a gorgeous view of Tisbury Great Pond—and the gorgeous man she'd gone lobstering with.

Was Chas right? Was she getting a crush on Whit, so soon after being dumped by Kevin?

Chas used a seafood pick to extract a morsel of lobster from the tip of the pincher claw. "I've just had the most wonderful idea, Aly. I'll go back with you to San Francisco!"

"To take more photos to show your grandmother?" Aly asked as she pulled off a spindly leg. She popped it into her mouth to strip out the tiny bit of meat with her teeth, like cleaning out a straw. "I'm not sure when I'm going back. It depends on when, uh, my project gets rescheduled," she added, glancing over at Hannah.

"My calendar is quite open," said Chas, dipping a bite of lobster into melted butter. "I'll help find us our new apartment."

Whit gave him an incredulous look. "Say what?"

"I love, *love* looking at real estate," Chas said, waving a claw and ignoring Whit. "That is, if you'd like the occasional roommate?" Chas reached over and patted her arm. "Whit told me you lost your apartment lease. You need to find a new place. And I've always wanted to have a crash pad in San Francisco. It'll be rock-solid proof to Granny that we're serious!"

Whit banged on a claw with a mallet. "That's crazy, Chas."

"So, what do you think, Aly?" Chas asked. "At least two bedrooms, and I definitely want a view of the bay."

"But the rents in SF…."

"Rent, schment," Chas interrupted. "Don't you worry about that."

Aly turned the idea over in her mind. If she split the rent with Chas, she could afford a really nice place. A second bedroom would be awesome. And when Chas wasn't visiting, she could use it as a home office or as a guest room. A flock of geese flew overhead, honking their approval of the idea.

Her imagination colored her old apartment dank gray with a fuzzy, moldy carpet. To hell with Kevin. And the apartment. He could have it and move in with that sneaky, skanky little sous chef if he wanted. The flash of anger felt good. Why shouldn't she be angry? She had every reason to be royally pissed off.

Whit slowly shook his head. "One dinner—even a couple of weeks—of pretending you and Aly are an item is one thing, but get real, Chas. You need an apartment in San Francisco like a hole in the head."

"Thanks for your opinion, dear Whit, but I quite disagree. Two birds with one stone—solid evidence for Granny and greener pastures for me. Maybe I'll even find the man I want to marry." Chas dipped a bite of lobster into his butter. "Besides, if you're nice, Aly and I might invite you to visit and stay with us." He turned to Aly. "Now, where to look. What are the hot neighborhoods these days?"

"The Mission's got a great vibe. You'd like Pacific Heights; it has amazing views. Castro has some really nice houses and a lot of gay bars, but no views."

"Love the Mission. We should definitely look there. And Pacific Heights." Chas rattled off all the requirements for the ideal (and likely impossible to find) San Francisco apartment, feature by feature. A roof deck for morning yoga and barbequing with friends. Large bathrooms with both a deep tub for soaking and a spacious shower. With a shock, Aly realized she was imagining not Chas but Whit lounging in the dream apartment. Whit reading a book in front of the fireplace as the fog rolled in and across the bay. Opening a bottle of wine from their built-in wine fridge to go with their dinner in a kitchen that was cute and cozy, with just enough space for two. Waking, in a four-poster bed, his hair mussed and tousled, he'd entice her with that sexy lopsided smile to climb back in. It was a pleasant little fantasy.

"Now, Victorian or a newer building?" Chas asked as Aly imagined Whit, shirtless, opening the French doors to their balcony to let in a fresh breeze. "Hello? Are you there, Aly?"

"Oh. Yes. Either, I suppose," Aly said, flustered.

"Well, you start thinking about what you want, and I'll start looking online. What fun!" Chas sat back, looking pleased with himself. "Aly claims she had fun lobstering today, but I don't believe her."

"I really did," Aly said as she wiped butter from her chin with a paper napkin. "I never knew what I'd find inside the trap." She explained how traps worked and how they caught a lot more than just lobsters. As she talked, she realized that Whit hadn't interrupted her. Not once. Even though he knew far more about the topic than she did. But he just sat there smiling and eating his lobster, letting her tell the tale about pulling up a trap that had seven lobsters, a sculpin, and a horseshoe crab. "They were all crammed in the parlor like a bad party that they couldn't leave," Aly laughed.

"As you can see, by the third trap, Aly had turned pro lobsterman. Lobsterwoman. Lobsterperson. Whatever," Whit said proudly, pulling the body off his next lobster. "You want to go out again?" he asked, fixing his cat's eye gold eyes on Aly in a way that made her feel all jingly inside.

"Anytime," she replied. Aly watched Whit use his finger to scoop up an astoundingly unappealing glob of gray-green goo from the body of his lobster and eat it. "Uh, what did you just eat?"

"I call it lobster pâté. Officially, it's tomalley—liver and pancreas. Try it," he said, holding out his shell.

Under Whit's watchful eye, she dipped her finger into the goop and scooped up a dab. It was vaguely gelatinous and looked totally nasty, but Aly gathered her courage and licked it from her finger. The stuff was light, rich, and almost buttery, redolent of lobster and the sea.

She tried a bigger glob. "It's not like anything I've ever eaten before. I like it—I think. But I like the tail meat better." She thought of Kevin, how he would have done that weird open-mouth thing to taste the flavor. Repulsed by the memory, she reminded herself she would never have to watch Kevin eat again.

"Speaking of things you've never eaten before, have you tried lobster ice cream?" asked Chas.

Aly laughed. "You're making that up." It felt good to laugh. No wonder Hannah wanted to get her off her butt and out of the house.

"They sell it at Ben & Bill's in Oak Bluffs," Hannah said, tossing an empty tail into the shell bowl. "Lawren…" Hannah caught herself and pressed her lips together. "Someone bought me a cone once. Not bad. But next time, I'm ordering buttercrunch."

"I'd try lobster ice cream," said Aly, noticing the attractive angle of Whit's jaw.

"Me too. It's a date," Whit said. He refilled their glasses. "Want to hear a lobster joke?"

"No! No! Not one of your jokes, Whit," Chas said.

"Too bad." Whit took a sip of champagne. "Sam Clam and Larry Lobster were the best of friends, until they departed this world together in a tragic clambake accident, right there on Quansoo beach," he began. His eyes twinkled, and his voice was resonant and deep. "Larry was the nicest of lobsters, so he went to heaven. Sam, on the other hand, was a very bad clam, and he went to hell." Aly wriggled in anticipation. She had a secret weakness for bad jokes, and Whit had the knack of telling a story well. "Larry missed Sam terribly and went to hell for a visit. He found Sam running a disco there, and the friends had a great time catching up. But when Larry tried to come back to heaven, St. Peter blocked the gate. 'Didn't you forget something?' St. Peter asked."

"Please, someone stop him before he gets to the punchline," moaned Chas.

"Larry waved a claw over his head and checked his back. 'I don't think so. I've got my halo and my wings.' 'But what about your harp?' St. Peter asked." Whit glanced at Aly out of the corner of his eye. "Then poor Larry said, 'Oh no! I left my harp in Sam Clam's disco!'"

Aly laughed. She chortled and snorted and was finally overcome by giggles. The joke had cracked open something inside, a wonderful, bright release of happiness. "Whit! That's a terrible joke," she sputtered.

"Told you," Chas said.

"I think you're wrong, Chas. Aly likes my jokes," Whit said.

Hannah looked confused. "I don't get it."

"My harp in Sam Clam's disco—my heart in San Francisco?" Aly took a sip of champagne, but the giggles hit again, and she snorted it out of her nose. She started hiccupping, and tears streamed from her eyes. Whit patted Aly on the back. "Oh, oh," she said, desperately trying to pull herself together. Whit kept patting, and Aly took a deep breath. "OK. I'm better."

"Good. Because I've got another for you, Aly," Whit teased. "One day, a man was walking his pet lobster along the dock…"

🐑 🐑 🐑

A deer bounded across the road in the headlights, and Hannah jammed on the brakes. Two more does and a fawn followed and disappeared into the trees.

"That was close," Aly said, her heart pounding. She glanced over at Hannah. Something wasn't right. "Are you OK?" Aly asked. "That was really thoughtless of me and Chas, all that talk about expensive apartments."

Hannah's lips were set in a straight line, and her eyes fixed on the road ahead. Hannah was quiet only when she was feeling really bad. And Aly had to knock gently until Hannah opened the door. Then it came to Aly. "Oh, shit. Lawrence. You're not OK, are you?"

Hannah kept staring straight ahead, but Aly could see the tears in her eyes. "Lobster ice cream," she said. "That was our first real date."

Aly took a deep breath. "Oh, Hannah. So it wasn't as easy as you thought."

"Yeah. Pretty much."

"I guess I've been feeling too sorry for myself to notice." Truthfully, Aly had almost forgotten about Hannah and Lawrence's breakup as she wallowed in self-pity and bags of peanut-butter-filled pretzels. Some friend she was.

"You had enough to deal with," Hannah said. "I don't want to pile my crap on you too."

"Don't be ridiculous, Hannah. Tell me what's going on. Please."

The dashboard light lit the tears in Hannah's eyes. "I thought it would be OK, that I'd be sad for a while, and he'd be sad, maybe, but fine. But I'm not. And he's really not."

"What do you mean?"

"I mean he's not doing OK, mental health-wise, it sounds like." Hannah gripped the steering wheel. "I got a call from his sister this afternoon. Remember, the one who was so snooty? She said he's not leaving his room. Or hardly eating. I guess the family finally figured out that we'd been dating. Or maybe they think we're good friends," she said. "They're worried. The sister asked me to talk to him."

"Are you going to?"

"I don't know." She glanced at Aly with anguish in her eyes. "I want to help him, of course. But I'm not sure it would be good for me. I didn't think breaking up would be so hard."

Aly reached over and patted Hannah's shoulder. "Have you talked to Lawrence since you broke up?"

Hannah shook her head. "At first, he sent me texts and called a lot, so I told him I needed space. I finally blocked him. Maybe I shouldn't have. Then he started writing."

"Emails?"

"No, letters. Like writing on paper in an envelope. I haven't opened them. Seeing his handwriting was hard enough."

🐑 🐑 🐑

Aly looked up after reading the last letter. "Wow," she said. Aly folded the thin blue paper and slipped it back into the envelope.

The first letter was easy to read. Lawrence was sure that Hannah just needed a little break; she'd been working too hard. He got it. He would wait, take things at her speed. The next, written two days later, was an ode to Hannah. *I despaired of ever finding someone with whom I can be myself, not Lawrence Hughes, the painter, scion of the Hughes family (hah), the only son, the 'golden boy' as my mother loves to say. Then I met you.* He wrote about how Hannah had opened his eyes to see how easily he had fallen into doing what others expected of him, without realizing he could choose another way to live. *You are my rock, Hannah,* he wrote, *my anchor, my truest friend, my lover, my soul mate.*

In the third, Lawrence sounded uncertain. He asked if he could come by the house, just to talk. To apologize. *I'm so sorry,* he wrote. *I took you for granted. I should've picked up on the clues that you felt so out of place in my family's scene. And I'm sorry for whatever else I did that made you want to leave.*

Then a gap of days. The fourth letter was different. In it, Aly could tell that Lawrence was slipping.

This wasn't like Aly's heartache. Lawrence seemed like he was sliding into a pit with no bottom. He begged Hannah in the last letter to be his friend. He understood if she didn't want to be his lover, but he couldn't imagine being in a world without knowing she was there to talk to. *The world has no color. I can't paint. I can't sleep.*

Aly read it twice. She'd seen guys say anything—things they didn't mean—to get their girlfriend back. But the last letter was desperate, not manipulative.

"Hannah, does Lawrence have any history of depression?"

Hannah nodded. "In college. He has a prescription. Oh god, I hope he didn't stop taking his meds."

Aly got up and turned on the kettle for tea. Hannah looked so forlorn. Smaller, as if sadness had shrunk her from a size twelve to a six. Aly poured the hot water into two mugs. "Herbal OK with you?" Hannah nodded. Aly brought the mugs to the table.

"There's honey in the cabinet if you want it."

Aly brought the honey to the table and stirred in a spoonful. "If he weren't the famous painter Lawrence Hughes, would you have split up with him? What if he was just a normal guy? A super-hot, very sweet guy," Aly said, fishing out the teabag with her spoon.

"But he's who he is, Aly, you see that. And this is me," she said, tugging at her lobster-butter-and-house-paint-splattered t-shirt. Hannah took a deep breath. "I love him. That's why I had to break up with him."

"Uh, that's kind of nuts," Aly said. "Is that what you told him?"

Hannah twisted her lips. "I told him—I don't know what I said—something dumb like it's me, not him. I didn't want to tell him the real reason. He'd try to talk me out of it."

"Does Lawrence care about being famous and going to fancy parties and all that?"

Hannah stirred honey into her mug. "No. He doesn't. But he has to. That's who he is."

"Is he?"

"Aly, get real. It's not like he can—or would—give up everything to live on dinky Martha's Vineyard with a housepainter," Hannah said with a stubborn shake of her head.

"What about Amy Schumer and her chef? She moved to 'dinky Martha's Vineyard' for love."

"That's different."

"Is it?" Aly said, pulling out the second letter, the one about Hannah, and pushed it in front of her.

Hannah picked up the letter and started to read slowly, too slowly. Concentration set a vertical line between her eyebrows. Aly had forgotten how bad Hannah's dyslexia was.

"I can read it to you. His handwriting isn't the best."

Hannah looked up, grateful, and pushed the letter back to Aly. Her eyes filled with tears as she listened to Aly read. "Shit."

Reaching for her friend's hand, Aly asked, "Do you miss him? Do you still want to be with him?"

Hannah nodded.

"Do you really think that you couldn't make it work if you both tried? Lawrence says he wants a life that he chooses, where he can be himself. Which is with you." She squeezed Hannah's hand. "No promises that it'll work out. But it's not fair to deny him a say. You think *you* know what's best for him. But what if you're wrong?"

"But I'm not. That party…"

"Doesn't matter. But." Aly hesitated. "But there's Lawrence's mental health. You don't know what you might be getting yourself into."

The light had come back into Hannah's eyes. "And I won't know. Unless I find out."

🐑 🐑 🐑

The faded gray paint peeled off under Aly's blade in one, long, satisfying strip. Hannah's new job was a simple one, just a bit of prep and a fresh coat of paint on the trim and doors of a modest, cedar-shingled summer cottage overlooking a sliver of Menemsha Pond. Aly found that she didn't really mind the tedious prep work (which Hannah disliked), working her knife through the layers to the solid wood underneath, then smoothing with sandpaper.

Scraping and sanding left Aly with lots of time to think. About Kevin. Clean, healing flashes of anger now poked through her unhappiness when she thought of him. She asked herself the same question she'd asked Hannah. Did she miss him? Did she want to be with him? Was she really that upset about losing Kevin, or was it losing the world she'd so carefully constructed with and around him? Aly's blade jammed into a particularly stubborn glob of old paint. Was Hannah right? she asked herself as she twisted her knife. Had she turned herself into someone she wasn't? It was like looking for answers in the old Magic 8 Ball she and Hannah had played with when they were kids: *Reply hazy, try again.*

Aly had no better luck when she thought about looking for a new job. Putting aside her distress about starting the process, the answer to *what do I want?* was an amorphous, directionless blob: fulfilling work, collegial coworkers, good pay.

Then there was Whit. Had he asked her out on a date to get ice cream? For the first time, Aly realized she could go on dates. The idea was a bit terrifying, but it was exciting too. She rolled the appealing thought in her brain, putting Whit on the cover of a bodice-ripper romance novel and, giggling quietly to herself, proceeding to tear his shirt off. Why not see where things go? At worst, it wouldn't work out. At best, she'd have some fun. In either case, she'd be moving beyond Kevin, and that would be a good thing.

"Hey Aly," Hannah called, interrupting Aly's thoughts. "Let's wrap up for the day. I've got to take Beau to the vet for his checkup. Then I've got an interview later for a painting job in Abel's Hill."

Back at the house, Aly took a glass of iced tea out to the backyard. Dandelion bleated, *I missed you,* and ran up to be petted. The lamb looked at her adoringly as Aly dug her fingers into her soft coat and rubbed Dandelion's favorite spot between her front legs. "You are a sweetie, aren't you? Do you like your new pen? Are you finding some yummy new grass?" Aly had decided Dandelion needed more space and had doubled the lamb's enclosure with garden stakes and plastic mesh. Dandelion would have nothing to do with the other sheep—and the feeling was mutual. As a bottle-fed lamb, she never became attached to the flock. In her little lamb brain, she was a dog like Beau. Still, Aly's efforts to teach her "come" ended in failure.

Dandelion's and Beau's uncomplicated, affectionate company had been immensely comforting when Aly was lolling around in the sticky morass of post-breakup self-pity and sadness. She hadn't had a pet of her own since the unfortunate passing of her hamster, Rexy. Miso, Kevin's cat, didn't count. He barely tolerated her petting him, which wasn't fair since she was the one who usually fed him and cleaned his litter box. But when Dandelion looked at her with her big brown sheep eyes, it was pure love. And Aly felt her heart opening in return.

"I'm thinking of heading down to the beach, but I should do laundry," she said to the lamb. "What do you think?"

"Ba-a-a," Dandelion replied.

"That's what I thought too," giving the lamb a gentle bop on her nose. "Beach it is. I'll do laundry tonight." She gave the lamb's velvety ears a rub. "Now you be good while I'm gone."

Two hours later, Aly pedaled back home after a swim, a very nice beach nap, and a visit from her friend the seal. (Maybe it was another seal, but she liked to think it was the same one each time.) She leaned her bike against the house, rinsed the sand from her feet, and went inside to get a clean bath towel. After a long, lovely outdoor shower, she dressed and thought about checking emails—it had been days since she'd opened her laptop—but picked up a copy of the *MV Times* instead. A paper-paper, of all things. She hadn't intended to take a break from screens and still carried her cell phone for calls and texts, but the compulsion (addiction, probably) to scroll through the news apps and look at what everyone was up to on Instagram had disappeared. Aly felt untethered. Free. And she liked it.

Aly was heading back outside when her cell rang. "Hi Jo," she answered. "Good to hear from you!"

Aly could hear the squeak of Hannah's mom's wooden office chair. "So, how are things going?"

"Oh, fine, I just got back from the beach."

"California has lovely beaches, doesn't it."

"I'm on Martha's Vineyard. Hannah didn't tell you?"

"We haven't talked in a while," Jo said. The chair gave another squeak. "You're visiting her? Is Kevin with you too?"

"Not this trip." Aly didn't feel like getting into all that, not now. "I've been having a great time. The Island is absolutely beautiful in the summer."

"How long are you staying?"

"I'm not sure." Aly briefly considered making up something about telecommuting, but she couldn't lie to Jo. "I'm between jobs right now. Spire got acquired, and my team was let go in late June."

"Why didn't you tell me? How awful!"

"It happens. I can job hunt from here," Aly said, even though she hadn't even started. "But why don't you come visit? I'm planning on being here a while longer, and I'd love to see you." Aly could use Jo's perspective and advice on her job hunt. And it would be good for Hannah and Jo to spend some time together on Hannah's turf.

"That's a wonderful idea, Aly. Maybe I will."

Back outside with her newspaper, Aly sat on the chaise and looked around, surprised that the lamb hadn't run up baa-ing as she usually did. "Dandelion?" she called. "Are you asleep somewhere?" She checked under a big clump of beach plum bushes where Beau and Dandelion liked to nap. No lamb. "You have to be somewhere." She scanned the area that she'd fenced off. How could a half-grown sheep just disappear? Could Hannah have come by and picked her up? With a racing heart, Aly made a full circuit of the enclosure, part of her brain still hopeful she'd somehow overlooked her, knowing there was no way she could have. A jab of fear when she reached where the fencing met the side of the house. There, the plastic mesh hung loose from the top of the stake.

Dandelion had escaped.

Alone and bored, maybe Dandelion decided to go exploring. Trying to calm herself, Aly ran around the outside of the house, calling and looking behind trees and bushes, hoping to see the familiar white shape. She tried Hannah. No answer. Could Dandelion have tried to follow Aly to the beach? She put on her flipflops and hopped back onto her bike, realizing halfway that there was no way she could have missed seeing a lost sheep on the open sandplain. Dandelion had a collar but no tag. If someone found her, what would they do? Who would they call? The woods and fields went on for miles in this part of the Island. If Dandelion had wandered off, she could be lost for days.

Aly's heart literally hurt, thinking of Dandelion, lost and scared. Maybe she'd come back on her own, like a dog, but Aly doubted it. She took out her phone and texted Hannah again. She'd never been so glad to see the reply bubble pop up. *Calm down,* typed Hannah, *I'm on my way back. She's probably off munching on a patch of dandelions somewhere. Beau'll find her.*

Of course, Beau. Wonderful, talented Beau.

Like the brilliant dog he was, Beau sized up the situation in seconds, sniffing the tuft of Dandelion wool before dashing out of the gap that the lamb had made in Aly's substandard fencing. He ran in a wide, looping circle, doing a visual search with his keen eyes, stopping to listen for the lamb's bleats every thirty seconds or so before continuing his circuit. When that failed, Beau ran back to the fence gap, put his nose to the ground, and began tracking Dandelion by scent, zigzagging left and right, tracing her meandering path in the direction of the woods. In the meantime, Hannah called animal control in West Tisbury and as many neighbors as she knew to ask them to keep a lookout.

Anxiety had turned to wonder as Aly watched the border collie work. "See? Beau'll find her," Hannah said as they trailed him into the woods. "We'll get her back before she turns into Baarack the sheep. Remember him?"

"Who?" said Aly, twisting Dandelion's leash in her hand.

"That sheep in Australia that was lost for like five or six years? When they found him, he had grown so much fleece that he looked like he was wearing a giant boulder. The poor guy could barely walk."

Beau regained the lamb's scent again and set off down a deer trail. Aly and Hannah pushed through the underbrush, over a stream, out of the woods, across another field, and along a dirt road. At last, Beau set off into a sprint down a long driveway to where Dandelion stood, unconcernedly munching zinnias in the front yard of a modest home off Thumb Point Road.

Aly nearly collapsed from relief, wrapping her arms around the lamb, who continued to eat. "Naughty, naughty, Dandelion," Aly scolded with tears in her eyes. "I love you, you naughty little sheep."

🐑 🐑 🐑

"I'm full as a tick," Hannah said, holding the door of the bowling alley open for Aly. "You were smart to just get the salad."

"Yeah, but I think I ate half of your fries," Aly said. "Glad Dandelion gave us an excuse to celebrate."

"She won't be escaping again with that new tether and the fence you built. That would hold a herd of cattle." Hannah dropped the box with the rest of her fried chicken onto the back seat of her truck.

"I hope so. Oh, I almost forgot. I was talking to your mom, and I think she might come visit."

"You were talking to my mom? Did you invite her here?"

"I guess so. She called yesterday."

"You invited her, you get to entertain her," Hannah said, rolling her eyes.

"Hannah."

"I know, I should make more of an effort. But she's probably just coming to see you anyway," Hannah sighed. "Changing the topic—do you mind if we take a little detour? I'd like to drop in on Lawrence."

"Of course not. How's he doing?"

"Better," Hannah said. "I don't know about the 'us' part of things, but I'll see."

After parting ways at the Union Chapel, Aly decided to continue down Circuit Avenue and poke her head into a few stores. With all its gingerbread finery, Oak Bluffs had a very different vibe from prim-and-proper Edgartown. Like a younger, rowdier sibling, OB attracted tourists with its lively beach-town feel—lots of t-shirt shops, an arcade and a historic carousel, and the best bar scene on the Island.

Aly was watching the candy maker knead fudge in the window of Murdick's when she felt a tap on her shoulder. She turned. There stood Whit, large as life. Which, at six-two, was quite large. Dang, that man had a killer smile, she thought as her heart sped up. Aly had half-expected him to get in touch after the lobster dinner. When he didn't, she'd been disappointed, but not devastated. The trip on *Noepe* had put her on an even keel, and for that she was grateful.

"Hey there, lobster girl. I'm glad I ran into you." Whit's lopsided smile widened. "How about that ice cream cone I promised you? I meant to call, but I, uh…." He shifted his weight. "I guess I got busy."

Aly crossed her arms and raised one eyebrow. "And you promised to take me out on your boat again," she said, realizing with a shock that she was flirting.

"Sorry about that too. Jak got his cousin to pull his pots for him." Whit scratched his chin where he'd missed a bit of beard shaving. "You're shopping for fudge?"

"Tempting, but no. Hannah and I had dinner at the bowling alley. She's uh," Aly paused, remembering Hannah's friends still didn't know about Lawrence. "Um, visiting an old friend. I'm just wandering around for a bit."

"So, what do you think? Ben & Bill's is just across the street." Whit put his hand on Aly's shoulder. The brush of his rough fingertips set off a pleasantly exciting tingle. "I always make good on my promises."

Aly waited in the ice cream line to order while Whit got sour jellybeans from the candy side. "My favorite," he said, shaking the bag as he rejoined her in the ice cream line. "A man's got to have a few vices."

"Hardly a vice," Aly laughed, happy for Whit's comfortable company.

They headed over to Ocean Park with cones in hand. Looking like a postcard, the vast expanse of green was crowned by a small Victorian bandstand. Families and groups of teens strolled or sat on blankets as a chocolate lab terrorized the resident flock of geese. Across Seaview Avenue, a lumbering ferry, painted gold by the setting sun, docked at the pier.

Aly leaned back on the bench and licked a circle around her cone to keep it from dripping. Her tongue picked up a tiny, cold morsel of lobster, such an un-ice-cream-like thing to find in an ice cream cone.

"I hope little Bo Peep hasn't lost her sheep again," Whit said, handing Aly a napkin. "You and Dandelion made Islanders Talk—that's our local listserve-slash-gossip rag." He wiped a drip of ice cream off his chin. "You could've called me. I would've helped look."

"It was awful. I was so worried." Aly glanced at Whit out of the corner of her eye, not sure if this was a date or Whit just making good on his promise. "But at least Dandelion came back with her tail."

"Her tail?"

"You know, in the nursery rhyme, when Bo Peep's sheep wander off, they lose their tails," Aly said. "Bo falls asleep, wakes up with no sheep, and goes to find them. Which she does, but without their tails. But if she had 'left them alone, and they'd come home, bringing their tails behind them.'"

"So, the moral is don't fall asleep on the job?"

Aly caught another drip with her tongue. "Or... searching for something gets you in more trouble than waiting for it to come to you." She leaned back on the bench. Ice cream, a warm summer evening, and the company of a fine-looking guy on a maybe-date. Not bad, Aly thought, as a girl walked by and gave Whit an appraising look. Not bad at all.

Whit licked his dripping cone, and Aly felt herself melting too. "At least it's more cheerful than 'Ring Around the Rosie,'" he said.

"Isn't that one about the Black Death?" Aly asked, watching Whit. His lips were curved, almost sculpted, and very sexy.

Whit held out his cone. "Want to trade for my buttercrunch?"

"I like mine, but it's weird when you run into the lobster," Aly said, swapping cones. "Like *really* weird." Being there with Whit was like being out on his boat, as if he carried the feeling of skimming the waves and fresh sea air with him.

He licked her cone and made a face. "You're right. The lobster in this is just weird. Now, we've taken care of Bo Peep. Who's up next?"

"'Baa Baa Black Sheep?'" Aly said, crunching into a piece of buttercrunch toffee.

Gesturing with his cone, Whit recited the poem in a ridiculous British accent. He seemed to be enjoying the silliness as much as Aly. "Guess what that's about," he asked.

Aly thought, distracted by the way the muscles in Whit's arms and shoulders stretched his t-shirt. "Uh, generosity?"

"Nope. The medieval wool tax. The master and the dame were the royalty. They took two-thirds, leaving one-third for everyone else."

Whit began to lick the ice cream out of his cone. Shockingly, Aly's imagination replaced his cone with her breast. *Whoa girl, where did that come from?* "I didn't know that," she said, bringing her brain back under control.

"I've got another one—'Mary Had a Little Lamb.' Or maybe that should be 'Aly had a little lamb,'" Whit said, looking into Aly's eyes and smiling his magnetic smile. "The way Dandelion follows you around."

"But Dandelion's fleece is more cream-colored than white as snow," Aly said, returning his smile. She was sure—pretty sure—that something was happening between them. Something that maybe she wanted, and maybe he did too.

"Could be she needs a bath."

Aly's apparently unhinged mind placed her and Whit together in Hannah's huge old-fashioned tub, foamy bubbles obscuring their nakedness as Aly leaned back against Whit's broad chest. *Oh geez, did that lobster ice cream have an aphrodisiac in it too?*

She bit into her cone, and it collapsed, dripping melted buttercrunch ice cream down Aly's chin, her chest, and the front of her sundress. As she fumbled for her napkin, Whit reached over with his and wiped her face. She caught his eyes, unguarded, and saw his pupils grow wide and dark.

"Oops," she said.

"I hate when that happens." Whit's eyes moved down to the drips on the bare skin of Aly's chest and stopped.

"I've got it," she said, taking the napkin from his hand and cleaning herself up as best she could with the soggy napkin. Aly looked up. She wasn't making it up. Whatever she was feeling, Whit was feeling too.

"Not your fault," he said in a husky voice.

The warm, melty feeling rose inside her again. "You've got some ice cream on your chin too," Aly said, reaching over to wipe the spot. With her finger, Aly slowly traced Whit's sticky-sweet lips, leaned in, and kissed him.

🐑 🐑 🐑

Whoosh. Aly's kiss was like a match lighting a gas flame. Whit felt it zip through his body, priming his nerve endings as his heart raced and his breath grew shallow. Her lips were soft and full, pillows hiding a teasing tongue. Aly's hands, sticky from her ice cream cone, slid around his neck as she leaned in to press her chest—more softness—against his. Whit brought her closer, his hands stroking the warm, bare skin of her shoulders and neck.

Here he was, a grown man, making out on a park bench like a horny teenager. Ridiculous. And exactly right.

Aly pulled away and looked into his face. "Oh my," she said, her eyes wide, a fathomless ocean blue. She looked as stunned as Whit felt.

"Oh wow," he replied.

Aly nestled against Whit's shoulder and rested her hand on his leg. He inhaled the smell of her hair, clean and flowery, the curls tickling his nose, and tried to ignore her fingers on his thigh.

They sat in silence. At last, Aly asked, "What do you want to do?"

What Whit wanted to do was to kiss Aly again and a whole lot more that would involve fewer clothes and more privacy than a bench in Ocean Park. He sat, tongue-tied, beyond aroused, searching for the right thing to say.

Aly shifted around to face him. Her lips, reddened by their kiss, were irresistible. She traced the muscle of his bicep, slipping a finger underneath the sleeve of his t-shirt. "We're not very private here," she said, reading his mind.

"Do you want to come to my place, um…" Whit's mind was whirling. This could be a very good idea, or a very bad one, and he was in no state to judge.

Aly leaned forward, brushed her lips across his cheek, and whispered in Whit's ear, "Yes."

🐑 🐑 🐑

The sky grew purple, then pink. A mist lay over Tisbury Great Pond, diffusing the colors into a soft palette. The sun rose higher, turning the pink to a rosy gold, then a bright sliver broke through, shooting a ray of sunlight across Aly's pillow. She opened her eyes, disoriented by the light and unable for a moment to place where she was. And why she was naked.

Oh. No.

Oh. Yes.

Aly rolled over and propped herself onto her elbow. Whit lay asleep on his back in a jumble of sheets. Dense dark lashes rested against his cheek, and stubble shadowed his face. Sleeping, he looked innocent—and vulnerable. Vulnerable to attack. Which pretty much described what she'd done last night.

Her eyes drifted lower, first to the muscles of his chest and upper arms, the skin paler than his forearms, to the whale tattoo, and to the line of black hair that ran from his belly button to the edge of the sheet. The drive from Oak Bluffs to Whit's house had been exquisite torture. They'd made mindless small talk, Aly asking about Whit's fishing charters to (unsuccessfully) keep her mind off what was coming next. She'd remembered to text Hannah, telling her she'd run into Whit and was going over to his place.

Aly remembered Whit's look of surprise as she pulled off his shirt as soon as the front door shut behind them. *What are you doing?* he'd asked. *Taking off your clothes, of course.* He'd groaned when she reached for his belt buckle, his breath coming shallow and quick as her hands stripped him gloriously naked. Then it was his turn. He'd reached out to gently wrap a curl of her hair around his finger. Lowering his face to hers, Whit's slow, gentle kisses were exquisite torture, first her lips, then behind her ear, tracing a butterfly path down her neck. *Are you sure?* he'd asked, as Aly, impatient, tugged on her zipper. *Very sure,* she'd replied as the ice cream-stained sundress fell to the floor.

Whit had taken her by the hand to his bedroom, his eyes still questioning. Aly ran her hands across Whit's chest, his back, his buttocks, the muscles firm beneath her fingers. She was in a hurry; Whit was not. *Do you like this?* he'd whispered, as his fingers and tongue sought to learn her body, every nerve ending primed, seeking his touch. Aly's urgency passed as she slowed to his rhythm, and, finally, once exquisite waves had pulsed through Aly, he'd finally let himself go with a soft, primal cry.

As she gazed at Whit's sleeping form, so different in every way from Kevin's, a wave of desire tightened her nipples, and a damp warmth rose between her thighs. Then her sleepy brain processed what she had done.

She'd cheated on Kevin.

No, Aly corrected herself. She hadn't.

The beam of morning light moved by millimeters across the bed. Aly watched Whit's eyes flicker under his eyelids as her thoughts of Kevin sped two thousand miles away. All Aly wanted right now was in this bed, and it was hers for the taking.

Whit yawned and opened his eyes. "Hi there," he said, his lips curving into a sleepy, lopsided smile.

"Hi," Aly replied as her hand slipped beneath the sheet.

Hannah stood blinking in shock with her hand on the coffeemaker. "You did what?"

"I slept with Whit," Aly replied, sipping her coffee. She touched her cheek, still feeling Whit's rough stubble grazing her face. She felt loose and aglow, inside and out. She had no idea what had come over her. All she knew was that when they'd kissed, *something* had happened. A something Aly had never experienced before. Not with Kevin nor with any other guy. She felt Whit's fingers tracing the line of her fading sunburn from the rubber gloves. *Lobster-burn*, he'd whispered, before turning her arm over to butterfly-kiss the inside of her wrist.

"But..." Hannah stuttered, interrupting Aly's pleasant train of thought. "When you said you were going over to Whit's, I figured you two had opened a bottle of wine or something and you crashed in his guest room, not in his bed!" Hannah's eyes had widened so much they seemed ready to pop from her head.

"Believe me, it wasn't what I was expecting when he asked me if I wanted to get ice cream."

"OK. I get that." Hannah turned her coffee mug around in her hand and looked up at Aly. "Revenge sex for what Kevin did to you?"

Aly thought for a minute. She hadn't been thinking about Kevin at all, only Whit. "I don't think so. I can't really explain what happened."

"Rebound, then?"

Aly blew out a puff of air. "Could be."

Hannah paused as if weighing her next words. "Be careful. Both of you. Whit's not a sleep-around kind of guy," she said, shooting Aly a warning look. "And you still need to deal with Kevin. At least talk to him. Are you sure this is it? I mean, you guys were living together for what, two years? What if he finds out he made a huge mistake? You don't want to go making a bigger one."

"I don't want to think about Kevin right now." And she didn't. The hurt had started to scab over, and she didn't want to pick at it.

Hannah sighed. "OK. I understand."

Aly stared at the coffee in her mug. Hannah's honesty had its downside too. She had the annoying habit of telling Aly what she needed to hear, not what she wanted to hear.

"Now what? Was this a one-night stand thing, or are you seeing Whit now?"

"I don't know."

※ ※ ※

Whit tipped the green wood-and-canvas Old Town canoe onto its side, swept out the dried leaves, and pushed it down the slope to the pond. He stepped in as his grandfather had taught him—hands on the rails and center of gravity low—and settled himself inside.

Late in the day, Tisbury Great Pond was in a gentle mood. Its surface held the deep blue sky, pleated by ripples off the canoe's bow, like silk dragged by a finger across a tabletop. The pond had always calmed him, taking him back to the best days of his childhood. Crabbing, fishing, digging for steamers. Watching ospreys plummet from the sky to catch fish. Hours and hours spent talking—or not talking at all. Just Whit and his Grandpop.

Whit set course to the south where, a mile away, a line of dunes delineated where the pond met the sea. As his body found the familiar rhythm of paddling—dip, stroke, angle to correct course, repeat—Whit tried to wrap his head around the fact of waking to find Aly in his bed. He felt…devoured, as if he'd been a big old blueberry pie in a pie-eating contest and Aly the winning contestant.

Or maybe it had been the other way around.

Whit shifted his weight carefully on the busted cane seat. Random hookups were not his scene. The sex had been incredible, but Aly? Why her? He shook his head. Pheromones? Hormones? Just plain horny? Whit shook his head. He'd felt things building between them as they were eating their ice cream. But that kiss had been like a cork flying from a bottle of champagne, pouring passion through his veins. Whit chuckled to himself. He'd certainly popped his cork and more than once.

It had flashed through his mind that *maybe this is not a good idea; maybe she is not the right girl.* But by that point, they were back at his house, his boxers were hitting the ground, Aly's hands and lips were everywhere, and desire snuffed that notion like the bad idea it thought it was.

Whit beached the canoe on the sandy shoreline. There was only one motorboat, a wooden Book-A-Boat skiff, left on the beach. He pulled the canoe onto the beach and grabbed his towel. What now? Whit asked himself as he walked across the sand to the ocean. He'd woken to Aly's hands running over his body, an extremely pleasant and unexpected surprise. Afterward, he'd found himself awkward and tongue-tied, making her bacon and eggs. What happened sat like a big sexy elephant in the corner of the room as they talked about their plans for the day. She needed to go help Hannah with her painting job in Menemsha. He had a late-morning fishing charter to prepare for. At Hannah's, Aly gave him a quick kiss and said, "See you around," and that was it. Except that he felt as if he'd been dosed with a magical-happiness good-feeling tonic.

But Aly was only a visitor. He didn't even know how long she planned to stay on the Island. And she was totally wrong for him. Aly lived in San Francisco, where her real career—in tech, not as a housepainter—was. Hanging out on the Vineyard was fun for a couple of weeks, but she belonged in the city with her five thousand-a-month-or-something apartment and sophisticated friends who could taste the difference in terroir between a pinot noir from Washington State and one from California.

A small, sand-colored doodle-dog—goldendoodle? Labradoodle?—ran up to him and dropped a tennis ball at his feet. Whit bent and ran a hand over the soft, slightly portly body, making the dog wag his tail like mad. Sure, he'd had a good time with Aly that day lobstering on his boat. They both liked whales. And sheep. Otherwise, however, they had nothing—nada, zip—in common.

"Duffy, come!" called a deeply tanned couple from their beach chairs.

Whit tossed the sandy, wet ball toward the couple. Barking happily, the dog raced down the beach.

On the other hand, what was wrong with a summer fling? Why not enjoy himself for a change? It wasn't as if he were going to fall madly in love with Aly or anything. She wasn't Petra. He wouldn't make that mistake again. Maybe this was the next best step for him, dating-wise, to just go out a few times with an attractive, interesting woman. Have some fun. And he had more than enjoyed this morning's "lovely fluff-the-pillows" as Chas would have put it. The good feeling welled up inside again as he thought about Aly. And what would Chas think? Whit's cell phone rang, as if Whit had telepathically transmitted his question to Edgartown.

He slipped his phone out of the Ziploc bag. "I told you Aly would be perfect. I just saw Granny, and I haven't seen her so happy in years," Chas bubbled. "She adores Aly and can't wait for their date for tea tomorrow."

"Chas, I slept with your girlfriend."

Chas gasped. "Excellent!"

"Excellent?"

"Of course. I was hoping you might. You take care of the sex, I'll do the rest," Chas said gleefully. "I assume you two had a fabulous romp together?"

Whit let out a puff of breath. "Chas…"

"As talented with the rod as the reel, eh?" Chas laughed at his own joke. "No need to be sheepish about your sexual prowess. I'm sure you made Aly very happy. And it'll be a perfect way to get you out to visit us in San Francisco. I wasn't sure you two would hit it off after what you put her through on that boat of yours, but I'm absolutely delighted! Got a call coming in. It's about the auction. I'll call you later!"

Whit started to slide the cell back into the bag and paused. Instead, he pulled up Aly's number and typed, *hey, do you have dinner plans tomorrow?* Aly responded, *nope—no plans.* He typed *great, pick you up at seven.*

Whit dropped his towel at the edge of the ocean and peeled off his t-shirt, inhaling the marine air, the scent of seaweed and salt. The waves were mellow, no danger of rip currents. He waded in thigh deep, turning sideways as the wash of the breakers bashed against his legs, always more powerful than they looked. The ocean still carried its New England chill, and Whit felt his privates shrink in anticipation. He took a deep breath and dove into the next wave, gasping as the shock of the cold water stunned him. Swimming out beyond the break, Whit floated on his back and stared at the sky.

Good idea or bad, he'd just asked Aly out.

🐑 🐑 🐑

Daylight revealed the edges of genteel shabbiness at Granny's. The arms of the Chesterfield sofa were ever so slightly frayed, and the gleaming sterling-silver teapot had a small ding in the side. Chas's explanation was old money, Yankee thrift. Granny had no interest in replacing anything until it was totally worn out.

Granny, too, was looking her age. Her hair was set in glossy white waves, and her body was trim in a nautical striped sweater. But the afternoon light exposed the wrinkles that cobwebbed her face, and her eyes under their heavy lids were watery and tired. Still, she sat ramrod straight and regal as a queen on her throne.

Lifting her delicate teacup, Aly sipped her tea with a smile on her lips. A visit with Granny, then a date with Whit. His text had answered Hannah's question: it wasn't just a one-night stand.

Aly had told Chas again how uncomfortable she was with continuing their ruse. But Chas was adamant that no one was being hurt, least of all Granny, and that her happiness was his goal. So, Aly played along. In preparation for their tea, she had read over the plot and character summaries in the Wikipedia articles on *Anna Karenina* and *War and Peace* to refresh her memory in case Granny wanted to pick up the conversation where they had left off. But the old woman was in a cantankerous mood and didn't feel like discussing literature.

"My son Elliot is an idiot. His wife too. And Kate with her tennis? Phff," the old lady snorted. "The only one with any brains—or personality—in the family is Chas, but he doesn't have an ounce of initiative or ambition. What are you going to do about that?"

"Well," Aly stalled, fingering the pearls, which she'd tried, unsuccessfully, to return to Granny. No matter what, she was giving the pearls back to Chas when she left the Vineyard. "He does have all his charity work," Aly said. "Organizing Possible Dreams takes a lot of time. Career-wise, maybe he just hasn't found his passion yet," she added weakly, straightening a cuff. The pale blue shirt—another gift from Chas, purchased to hide the unsightly remnants of her sunburn—was the finest cotton she'd ever felt, smooth and lustrous as silk. If Chas were a real boyfriend, she'd let him buy all her clothes.

"Passion? Oh, he has a passion. It's to make sure he inherits this house and as much of my money as he can." Granny pursed her lips and glared at Aly.

The conversation had moved onto dangerous ground. Aly wondered if Granny had seen through their charade and was mischaracterizing Chas's motivation as greed. She could see how it could look that way. But he had plenty of money to buy any house he wanted, one that would suit his lifestyle better. Aly believed Chas truly wanted to make Granny happy, to keep the house just the way it was—a lovely venue for charity events, preserved for future generations—and out of the hands of his siblings who saw the house in terms of dollar signs.

She bit her lip as she considered how to reply. "I think he wants what you want," Aly said truthfully.

It was time to change the topic. She looked around the room. They were having tea in the front parlor. The antique furniture looked museum quality and, Aly would guess, original to the house. The large windows looking onto the street were hung with elaborately swagged and tasseled drapery in faded blue-silk damask, and portraits of sailing ships in heavy gilt frames crowded the walls.

"Your house has such a fascinating history. Chas was telling me that his great-great-something grandfather bought it from a whaling captain's widow after her husband didn't come back from the South Pacific," Aly said, reaching for one of the tiny butter and cucumber tea sandwiches.

"Our family made their money in railroads, not whale oil," Granny said, trying to lift the teapot with her knotted fingers. An emerald ring, the biggest Aly had ever seen, flashed green in a beam of sunlight. "Damn arthritis. Old-age-itis," she groused. "Maybe that's what I should do. Leave this place to the historical society. But I don't trust them after they leased out the old chandler's place to that real estate company."

"Here, let me help with that," Aly said, taking the teapot and refreshing their cups as she considered her options. Time to change the topic again. "I'm so sorry you aren't feeling well."

"Don't get old," Granny snapped. She sighed and looked at Aly. "Dear Aly. So young and lovely. Here I invited you for tea to get to know you better, and instead I'm sitting here grumbling like the grumpy old lady I am." She sipped her tea. "Are you sure you want to get an apartment together with Chas? That's quite a big step. In my generation, an unmarried couple would never live together. It would've been a scandal. But times change. Or so I'm told."

"We want to get a two-bedroom so we can have guests. And if things don't work out for the two of us—not that I'm expecting that, not at all—one of us could keep the apartment and get a roommate."

"Sensible girl. I like that," Granny said. "And I like your ambition. My niece Emily is visiting. Have you met her yet?" Aly shook her head. "Anyway, she was telling me how challenging it is for a young woman to succeed in that newfangled computer business."

"I was lucky."

"I don't believe in luck," Granny said. "Hard work, smarts, and a tough hide. That's my guess."

"Some of that too," Aly conceded.

Granny rapped on the table with her silver spoon. "Now. With everything you have going for you, what could you possibly see in my grandson?"

Aly took a sip of tea. "Well, he's charming and funny. And handsome. Chas makes me laugh."

"And the sex?" Granny asked, looking at her hard.

Aly paused. This was not the direction she'd expected the conversation to go in. "Well," Aly said, blushing at the memory of her evening with Whit, the pile of clothes left inside his front door as they stripped each other naked.

Granny guffawed with laughter. "Haha, I won't press you, dear girl. As modest as you are lovely. Now, back to that hussy Anna Karenina!"

Attached to her new tether, Dandelion baa-ed and gently butted Whit's thigh as he walked up the front walk at Hannah's. "Hey there, aren't you getting to be a big girl," Whit said, patting the lamb's head. Distracting (but pleasant) memories of the innocent ice cream-date-gone-erotic had played in his mind all day. Chas was convinced that dating Aly was a good idea. Whit hoped he was right.

"Hi, Whit," Aly said, opening the screen door. She wore a short white skirt that showed off her legs. "So, where are we going?"

Whit caught a glimpse of her breasts as she bent over to pat Dandelion. A wave of awkward horniness washed over him, so familiar from adolescence, so inappropriate in an adult. "Um, I had a couple of ideas. The new Mexican place in Vineyard Haven is good. Or, if you wanted to do a beach picnic to watch the sunset, I put lobster salad and some other stuff in a cooler."

Aly's eyes lit up. "Let's go to the beach. I've got corn salad I can bring, and a bunch of chicken wings." She ran into the house and came back out with a canvas bag and a fleece pullover. "I brought the chocolates I got at the farmer's market too," she said, slipping on her flip-flops.

Whit backed the truck out of the driveway. He wasn't used to knowing someone, well, *intimately*, before knowing-knowing them. Back in St. John, Petra had worked as his deckhand before they'd started sleeping together. Of course, he'd only thought he knew her. And he'd paid the price.

Whit turned and glanced at Aly. She had the window down, and her hair, loose around her shoulders, caught the breeze. Nothing wrong with a little summer fling, so long as he kept things light and easy, he thought, wishing his brain would keep her clothes on. Just go on a few dates and have some fun. He turned on the radio to WMVY, trying to think of something to say.

"Dandelion was looking good," he said finally. "Have you and Hannah thought about entering her in the fair?"

"The fair?"

"The Ag Fair—Agricultural Fair. It's held at that huge barn on Panhandle Road starting the third Thursday in August," Whit said.

"It's a real county fair with rides and food and competitions for best cake and biggest sunflower. That kind of thing."

"We can enter Dandelion? Like to win a prize?"

"More bragging rights than money."

Whit glanced at Aly, watching as her full lips stretched into a lovely smile. "I could get her all beautiful. Fleece as white as snow and all that. What'll she be judged on?"

"Health, wool, muscle tone, temperament, I'd guess. We can pick up a fair book at the Ag Hall," he said. "And I heard that they've got a new event this year—a costume contest for people and their animals."

"Like, I could dress Dandelion up as Bo Peep, and I could be her sheep?"

"Sounds like a winner to me," he smiled, imagining Dandelion in a shepherdess outfit and Aly wrapped in wooly fleece.

"That would be so much fun to do. If I'm here, that is." A shadow fell across Aly's face. "But maybe I will be." She fiddled with her silver bracelet. "This isn't really a vacation. I got let go at work." Whit glanced over. "It's OK. I'm in tech. Lots of jobs," she added brightly.

So, Aly had lost her apartment and her job. No wonder she'd been so upset the night of Granny's dinner party. "One benefit of being self-employed," Whit said. "I can't fire myself. But Hannah'll keep you on as long as you want."

"True. But painting houses isn't exactly advancing my career," Aly said with a sigh. *Johnny* by Sarah Jarosz came on the radio. "Oh, I love this song."

"Me too," Whit said and started to sing along. Aly leaned back and moved her hand to rest on Whit's thigh. He flinched at her touch.

"Sorry," Aly said, lifting her hand. "Keep going. I love your voice."

"No, it's OK. You surprised me." Somewhat sheepishly, Whit resumed singing, a test of his self-control, with Aly's hand on his thigh.

The song ended, and the DJ began his report on the standby lines for ferries in Woods Hole and Vineyard Haven. "What do you think that song's about?" Aly asked.

"Wanderlust. Inertia. Johnny's traveled the world only to find himself back where he started, on the back porch, drinking red wine, thinking about time, waiting for the stars to align. Sort of like me."

Aly slid her fingers up a few inches, and Whit wiggled in his seat. "Maybe they have," she said.

🐑 🐑 🐑

"Now, once you pass this little pond here on the right, then you start looking for the parking lot on the left," Whit said. "This is one of the town beaches." Aly had fought to push the thought of job hunting out of her mind. She was on a date and didn't want to think about anything other than the beautiful evening, handsome Whit, and the pleasures undoubtedly waiting for her later in his bed.

Whit pulled into the lot next to a faded maroon Subaru. The dented hood was tied shut with a hanger. Peeling stickers for Larsen's Fish Market, the Hot Tin Roof, and WMVY covered the bumper. "That's a good old Island car," he said.

"Island car?" Aly asked, climbing out of Whit's truck.

"A car you wouldn't—or shouldn't—drive anywhere but here. The Vineyard is like an old-age home for cars," Whit said. "If you want a car, my friends Frank and Laura are going to leave theirs at my place for August while they house-and-cat sit for friends in Brooklyn. I'm sure they wouldn't mind you borrowing it."

"Really? That would be great," she said, excited by the idea of having her own wheels.

"Lexie—that's Frank's car—is a Lexus he inherited from his grandmother," Whit said. "She's got a few personality quirks. Like a sunroof that opens when it feels like it and sideview mirrors that like to look around when you're driving," he said, pulling a soft-sided cooler, beach bag, and long, narrow canvas case with a strap from the back seat of the truck.

"She sounds perfect," Aly said, picking up the beach bag. "What's that?"

"My travel guitar. Thought I'd serenade you at the beach."

"Yay, music too," Aly said happily. They started down the path through the trees. "Where has your guitar traveled?"

"Lots of places. Years ago, when I was younger," Whit said. "Japan, Vietnam, Thailand—I almost stayed in Krabi—Bali, and New Zealand. Came in handy when I ran low on money. I could always play for beers."

"I wish I could've done that." Even with her college scholarship, Aly had loans to pay off. Growing up the way she had, financial security came first.

Whit knew half the people they passed, stopping to chat and pat their dogs. They stopped to take off their shoes where the path turned to sand. "Almost there," Whit said, as they climbed the slatted boardwalk up the side of the dune.

They paused at the top and looked around. Below them, the beach spread out in a broad sandy crescent, bounded at each end by cliffs. Here, on the north shore of the Island, the water was calm and clear, no surf like the ocean beaches. To the left, a pond shimmered beyond the dune grass. As they walked to the shoreline, a black-and-white dog zoomed past them chasing a ball, followed by a barking black ball of fluff.

"Pretty nice, huh?" Whit asked, pleased by the delighted look on Aly's face.

They walked to the shoreline, bordered by an edge of smooth granite beach stones scattered by the tide. "What's up with all the private beaches?" Aly asked, enjoying the feel of the still-warm sand under her toes.

Whit adjusted the cooler. "An old law from the 1600s gives property owners rights down to the low water mark. The idea was to encourage investment in wharves and boatyards, but we ended up with private beaches," he said. "But you can walk across a private beach if you're fishing. Some people carry a rod, in case they're stopped. But the hard part is even getting to the beaches—they're all behind locked gates."

"That's crazy," Aly said, shaking her head.

"Not to the folks who are paying up to half a mil for their beach lots. People have tried, but they're never going to change the law with that much money involved. Sort of ironic, Nantucket has a reputation of being much stuffier than the Vineyard—and it is—but their beaches are all public. And you can go topless there, by law."

"Topless? That doesn't sound like Nantucket," Aly said, stepping over a stream of water the color of Coca-Cola from the natural tannins. "What about here?"

"Nobody would care. It's kind of gone out of style, though. You still see a few naked geezers on Jungle Beach—Lucy Vincent—over by Chilmark Pond, and there are always nudies up at Gay Head. Mostly old hippies."

Aly indulged herself in the pleasant vision of Whit naked on the beach. "Hannah said I should do the walk around the cliffs. I've been to the top—she and I went for the sunset once. I had no idea that the Island just drops off at the end like that. And the colors, wow."

Whit picked up a flat rock and skipped it along the top of the water. "According to Wampanoag legend, the colors came from Moshup, the giant who formed Martha's Vineyard when he dragged his foot through the mud and separated the island of Noepe—Martha's Vineyard—from the mainland. Moshup was so huge that he ate whole whales that he bashed against the cliffs. The red in the clay is said to be the blood of the whales. The black is from his cooking fires, and the white is the whale bones. Nantucket was formed when Moshup dumped his pipe ashes into the ocean."

"Nantucket was a giant's ashtray?"

"That's how the legend goes. If you've ever been there, it kind of fits," Whit chuckled. Aly liked his laugh, easy and comfortable. She loved how he loved the Vineyard, knew its stories and history. She felt completely relaxed in his presence, saying whatever came to mind without thinking about it.

The evening was warm and calm, with barely a breeze to ruffle the water. Aly bent her head and scanned the beach as they walked along. An unusual shape caught her eye, and she picked it up. "Look, a heart-shaped rock!" she exclaimed, showing Whit.

"They're hard to find. And that's a nice one. You should keep it."

Aly slipped the rock into her pocket. Finding it felt like a sign. She squeezed Whit's arm, firm and warm. "Let me find a stone for you."

There, in the backwash of the water, glistened an oval stone, black and bisected by a wide quartz ring. "Look at this one," she said, handing it to Whit.

"If the ring runs all the way around, it's a lucky stone. You trace the ring and make a wish," he said, running a fingertip around the rock. "I know what I'm wishing for," he said with a sexy lift of one eyebrow.

Aly reached her hands around Whit's neck and pressed her body against his. "Me too."

🐑 🐑 🐑

Watching Aly lick the sticky-sweet chicken glaze from her fingers had been almost unbearably erotic. *Down boy*, he told himself, *plenty of time for that later*. If his wish on the lucky stone came true. "You should finish the wings. And the corn salad too," Aly said, handing Whit the Tupperware container.

"Twist my arm. Hannah made that?" Whit asked. The food was about the best he'd eaten in a long while: the salad, smoky with grilled corn, and the wings covered in some kind of delicious Asian glaze.

"Nope. I did," Aly said, chewing a bit of lobster. "I've been trying to help with the cooking, though Hannah's not as stressed about work since she hired two new kids. Anyway, most things I make come out pretty good. I think I must've learned by osmosis watching," she hesitated. "Watching other people cook."

"Lucky Hannah."

The setting sun bathed the beach and Aly with a glowing, golden light. Her hours in the sun had freckled her nose and cheeks and gilded her hair, loose in soft waves and curls, with red-gold highlights. Aly leaned back on her elbows on the tatty old cotton bedspread Whit used as a beach blanket, raised her eyebrows, and sighed.

"So good," she said, looking out across the water. "Look at the colors now. What would you call that, right along the horizon? It's too pink to be orange."

Whit pulled his eyes away from Aly and turned toward the sky. "Hmm. Coral, maybe?"

"Now it's turning purple." She held out her jelly jar for more wine, and Whit obliged. He fished the box of chocolates from Aly's bag. "Want some?"

"One tiny piece," she smiled. "I'm stuffed. You shouldn't have let me eat all that lobster."

"That was on purpose," Whit teased. "I like what lobster does to you. That ice cream only had tiny chunks. I wanted to see what would happen if you ate more."

Aly sat up and slid next to Whit. "This," she said, leaning over and kissing him. Her lips tasted of wine, and her tongue did amazing, tantalizing things that nearly made him crazy.

"Hey, it's my turn to seduce you," he said, trying to keep his voice under control.

She rolled up her sweatshirt as a pillow and stretched out. "Seduce away."

Whit unzipped his guitar case and pulled out the travel guitar. The slender instrument with its fan-shaped body showed years of hard use. He thought about what he'd play as he tuned the strings. "Do you want to go way back? Some James Taylor?" Aly nodded, and Whit picked the intro to *Sweet Baby James*. "The song was written as a lullaby for James Taylor's nephew—his namesake."

How long had it been since he'd last serenaded a woman? Aly closed her eyes, and her lips started to move with the chorus. "Join me?" he asked. A shadow passed over her face. He was nearing the end of the song when Aly took a deep breath and started to sing. Her voice was low, for a woman, and lovely. She kept her eyes closed as she sang harmony in perfect pitch. In the fading light and with Aly's voice in his ears, Whit was exactly where he wanted to be.

🐑 🐑 🐑

Clouds streaked the sky and painted the water with brush strokes of orange and magenta as the bright gold disc of the sun dropped below the horizon. Still holding the day's warmth, the night air hugged Aly. She felt herself open up, like joining her voice to Whit's had broken a shell around something deep inside, releasing a wonderful, bright feeling of joy that had been hidden and forgotten.

"You have a beautiful voice," Whit said.

"I don't sing much anymore. I used to love to."

"You could join me on stage next time I play at the Ritz."

"Uh, no, thank you," Aly said, shaking her head. Performing in front of a crowd was not in the cards, not ever again. That last time she'd sung—other than in the shower, in the car, or to Dandelion—was at a karaoke bar with Kevin and a bunch of restaurant people. It was late, she was a bit drunk, and she'd chosen a song at random. (What had she been thinking? What had made her pick an Adele song?) It had not gone well. Kevin had teased her for weeks. It had taken the joy out of singing.

"Think about it. It's a great little bar. Mostly locals, but we get all types in the summer. Even city girls," Whit teased. His sexy, irresistible grin spread across his face. "Take a chance. You never know what you can do until you try."

Until you try. She tried to imagine herself under the spotlight next to Whit, but the Adele song disaster had left her tender and hurt. "Maybe. Where did you get your guitar? I've never seen a little one like that before."

Whit pulled the strap over his head and handed it to her. "My Grandpop gave it to me after the worst Christmas of my life. My father had filled my stocking with cigarette butts. It was my only 'gift.' I had to sit there and watch my brother and sister open all their presents," Whit said, slowly shaking his head. "I was sixteen."

"Your father did what?"

"I'd been smoking. I know. It's a disgusting habit. But it was a thing for a while in my school. I'd been hiding the butts in my room, and Dad found them. And I'd let my grades tank that semester, among other things," Whit said, tracing a circle on Aly's arm. "But Grandpop understood me. He knew I'd be a traveler."

"To get away from your father?" Aly asked, resting her head against Whit's shoulder. At least her mom had always tried to make Christmas nice, even if her gifts came from Goodwill.

"In part. It was a long time ago. Besides, it got me started playing guitar," he said, wrapping an arm around Aly. "Worked great for seducing girls."

"Did it though?" Aly said, leaning back to tickle the underside of Whit's chin.

The barest edge of purple delineated the horizon, and the first stars sparkled, their twins mirrored in the calm water. Far down the beach, the last groups of sunset watchers packed their chairs. The night air was warm and still. Aly breathed in Whit's smell, salty and masculine, and closed her eyes, nearly purring with contentment.

"Hey there, Aly-cat. No sleeping," Whit said, kissing the top of her head. "You want to go swimming? I brought towels."

"I don't have my bathing suit," Aly said, happy where she was.

"Sure you do. You've got your birthday suit."

"Someone might come by."

"What if they do?" he said, standing up. Bereft of her backrest, Aly rolled down flat on her back. Whit stretched out his hand. "You won't regret it. I promise."

"OK. OK," Aly said, as he pulled her to her feet.

Aly watched Whit strip off his clothes and drop them onto the sand: first his t-shirt, exposing his broad chest, then his shorts and boxers, exposing pale skin that glowed faintly in the moonlight.

"Hey! You too," said Whit, a naked Adonis, stepping forward to tug at Aly's top.

"I got distracted," Aly said with a smile as she unbuttoned her shirt. Whit watched with rapt attention as she unhooked her bra and let it fall to the sand. He reached out to brush his thumb across Aly's nipples. She trembled as a warm ripple of pleasure shocked her senses.

"Are you cold?" he asked, cupping one of her breasts in his hand as his other hand slid inside her skirt to the curve of her buttocks. Aly tugged at her waistband. "Here, let me help," Whit said, pulling off her skirt and panties in a single motion. He stepped back. "Aly, you are beautiful."

"You are too." A slight puff of air against naked skin. Aly slid back into Whit's arms, pressing against his warmth.

They walked hand-in-hand into the sea. The calm surface reflected the stars and the quarter-moon in wavering dots and lines. On a cliff at the end of the cove, light from a single house stood sentinel, the curve of the beach empty and dark.

"You know what this light is called?" Whit asked as they walked out to deeper water, calves, then knees, then thighs.

"Dusk?" Aly asked. "Oooh, that's cold," she said, rising on her toes as a swell brought the water up to her hips.

"Nautical twilight," Whit said. "When you can see both the horizon and the stars. It's the time when a sailor can set a course by the stars. The French, being more romantic, call nautical twilight *l'heure bleue*—the blue hour."

"*L'heure bleue.* That's beautiful."

Whit's bare chest glowed faintly in the moonlight. "Time to take the plunge," Whit said as he released her hand. He dove into the water, popping up with seal-wet hair.

Timidly, Aly bent her knees to bring the water up to her shoulders, gasping slightly at the shock of the sea against her bare skin, so cool after the warmth of Whit's hands. Kicking, she floated on her back and looked up at the stars. Her breasts broke the surface of the water, twin pale buoys in the near-dark.

"I like your floaties," Whit said, swimming over. He slid his arms underneath Aly's back and cradled her to his chest, as if teaching her to float. "Like a beacon to a lost sailor. He bent his head to take the tip of one breast in his mouth, rolling it over with his tongue as if it were a candy. Aly's heart began to race. "Mmm, salty," Whit said, lifting his head. "And delicious."

"Oh my god," Aly moaned as Whit's hand slid between her legs, his thumb seeking its task. A nimbus of heat radiated as pleasure rose and swelled, as she floated, senseless to all but Whit's mouth, his hand, as her breath grew shallow and fast.

"Whit," she gasped, atoms split apart in a bright hot explosion, shuddering wave after wave. Aly melted and disappeared, then gradually reformed anew.

Whit gently kissed her parted lips. "And you didn't want to go skinny-dipping."

🐑 🐑 🐑

Thinking about Whit made for a pleasant diversion while Aly did her chores around the house. After finishing Hannah's laundry, Aly filled a water bottle, slathered on some sunscreen, and grabbed a can of bug spray. Outside, Beau and Dandelion backed away as she sprayed her legs and shoes. "I know it smells bad. But I don't want ticks—or Lyme disease. Stupid ticks are the only thing I don't like about the Vineyard. Ready to go for a walk?"

Beau woofed. He knew "walk" and approved.

With Dandelion and Beau trailing behind her, Aly headed toward the north pasture, pausing as the flock of sheep trotted to the fence, hopeful that she'd brought some grain as a treat. Dandelion, refusing to acknowledge her relatives, hung back with Beau.

"Come on, Dandelion. At least say hello. Your mom is in there somewhere with your siblings." The lamb backed away, and Aly could swear she saw her shake her wooly head no.

When no treats were forthcoming, the flock of sheep wandered away, moving together to graze like a team of synchronized lawnmowers. Followed by the dog and lamb, Aly headed down a trail into the woods. Hannah had told her that it was an ancient way, one of the centuries-old footpaths that crisscrossed the Island. She took her time wandering among the oaks, dim and cool, looking up at the leaves rustling in the breeze, thinking pleasant thoughts about Whit, reliving every moment of their magical evening.

After about ten minutes, the path opened to a field dotted with huge granite boulders. Erratics, she knew from a geology course taken years before, left when the glaciers retreated in the last ice age. The field was bordered on all four sides by an old stone wall, splotched and furred with gray-green lichen, tumbled here and there where trees had taken root. A farmer's field once. Or a pasture for sheep.

As she walked through the field, Aly noticed a spray of tiny berries on an otherwise undistinguished bush, a few pale green, some ripening to purple, others a dark, inky blue. She pulled one off. A wild blueberry, only a fraction of the size of a grocery store berry. She popped it into her mouth. It was sweet and tart and delicious, as if all the flavor of a bigger berry had been compressed to a miniature size.

She dug a plastic bag from her backpack and began picking. On some bushes, the sprays of berries were so thick and ripe she could pick five, six, seven with a gentle tug of her fingers. Others were still half green, promises for the future. With the sun warming her shoulders and a light breeze blowing, she felt as if she'd been transported back in time, the silence interrupted only by the occasional shadow of a plane high overhead. An hour passed unnoticed as she fell into the rhythm of picking, moving from bush to bush as Beau napped and Dandelion grazed in the long grass.

It was bliss: the simplicity of gathering the unexpected gifts of nature. A hidden corner of paradise, just waiting for her to find it. Baa-ing, Dandelion bounded over to nuzzle her leg. She bent and ran her fingers along the lamb's ears, savoring their velvety warmth and melting into the gentle gaze of the lamb's brown, innocent eyes as she looked up at Aly. As she picked, Aly began to sing *Strawberry Fields Forever* by the Beatles, changing strawberry to blueberry. Dandelion began to leap and cavort to the sound of Aly's voice. "I don't like singing in front of people," she laughed. "But you, silly little thing, are a great audience," she said, getting out her phone to record the lamb's dance moves.

Once her bag was full, Aly set it down and walked over to check out a flat-topped boulder the size of a baby elephant in the center of the clearing. She climbed up and lay back on the warm, sunbaked granite, lacing her fingers behind her head. Up in the deep-blue sky, puffy white clouds floated by. Sheep clouds, her favorite. She closed her eyes, feeling the warmth of the granite against her back. Then a strange vibration came, she would swear, from the rock, and so faint that she could be making it up. Oddly comforting, she relaxed into the sensation as it moved into her body. After a while, the feeling floated away like dandelion fluff on the breeze.

Opening her eyes, Aly sat up on the boulder. What the bejabbers was that? She put her palm on the stone. Nothing. But something inside Aly had changed, as if the vibration had recalibrated the atoms in her body, joining her to the natural world in a way she'd never felt before. She felt different. Lighter. Happier. *Connected*. She looked down at her hand on the rough granite, flecks of mica and quartz glinting in the sun. It was as if the boulder had sent her a message: rocks, trees, wind; we are real.

A gust swept across the glade, rustling the leaves of one tree then the next and lifting strands of her hair as it passed by, as if acknowledging that she had correctly interpreted the meaning of what was maybe the strangest experience of her life. How many hours had she spent staring at a screen, letting the pixels mesmerize and seduce her? How many times had she chosen to stay in her apartment in San Francisco, in that life that wasn't real, flopped on the sofa, and staring at her phone instead of getting out into the world? No image of a tree, no matter how realistic, can come close to feeling the tenderness of a spring leaf, inhaling its fresh, green scent. Or feeling the round smoothness of a tiny blueberry and tasting the burst of surprisingly intense blueberry-ness. Or witnessing the pure joy of a lamb bounding across a field, the wind making waves across the grass.

How much of life had she missed already?

🐑 🐑 🐑

The big glass bowl brimmed with tiny wild blueberries. Aly leaned back on the sofa, still perplexed by her experience in that old, old field.

Hannah, paint splattered as usual, banged through the door and flopped down next to Aly. "Ooo, wild blueberries," she said, reaching into the bowl. "That must have taken you hours. You should make jam. I love wild blueberry jam." She popped a few berries in her mouth. "That is, if I don't eat them all."

"I don't know how," Aly said as she imagined a wild blueberry jam disaster, blueberry goop splattered all over the kitchen, improperly sealed jars giving people botulism. Or she could take Whit's advice: *you never know what you can do until you try*. A tidy row of wild blueberry jam jars with cute hand-lettered labels replaced the disaster scenarios.

"It's not hard, just a little messy. There's a jam category in the fair—registration's starting. I'm entering Beau in the dog show. You should enter Dandelion." Hannah reached for the bowl. "I should save some of these for Lawrence."

"Any news? How's he doing?"

"Really well, I think. He's going to try painting in the hayloft. It's really nice up there. Tons of space and a big window."

"Anything else…?"

Hannah smiled. "And I think maybe he was right about us. We'll see."

"I'm glad," Aly said, confident that Hannah and Lawrence would figure things out.

"These are addictive," Hannah said, reaching for more blueberries. "Where did you find the bushes?"

"I took that path you told me about to the old north field—you know, the one with the big boulders and the stone walls?"

"That was part of the original Luce homestead in the late 1600s," Hannah said, picking a stem off a blueberry. "I bet there have been blueberry bushes there forever. It's a special place." She took another handful from the bowl, eating them one by one. "Willow, my woo-woo friend, you've met her. She makes those fabric bags and pillows you like at the Chilmark Flea Market? Anyway, Willow says she's figured out where the ley lines are on the Island, and that's the one place where they cross."

"The what lines?"

"Ley lines. L-E-Y, I think. They're like power lines of natural and spiritual energy that run around the earth. Or so Willow says. And she says the intersection is super intense," Hannah said. "She gets permission from the owners to do her Reiki healings there sometimes. That big flat boulder is where the lines cross. Supposedly."

Aly felt the hairs on the back of her neck. "Oh. Wow."

Hannah looked up from the bowl. "What?"

"Um. I was up on that boulder, and I think I felt something. Kind of like a vibration."

"Cool. I'll have to tell Willow. She'll say that the old rock was trying to tell you something." Hannah ate another few berries. "Now I'm sounding woo-woo too, but I think the Vineyard's got magical powers. Transformative, even. At least it feels that way to me. Not everyone feels it. But you're lucky if you do."

🐑 🐑 🐑

Whit opened the fridge and handed Aly a big hunk of Parmesan. "I cheat sometimes with the pre-grated stuff, but it really is better with fresh," he said and turned on the water to fill a stock pot. Perched on a stool in his kitchen, Aly looked like she belonged there, bright, eager eyes and sexy as hell in a white tank top and jeans. Just the thought of her coming over for dinner buoyed his mood like a balloon rising into the clouds.

"I'll warn you," Aly said, turning the chunk of cheese into a pile of fluffy shreds. "My vodka pasta standards are pretty darn high. There's a family-run place back home—Nonna's—that makes the best pasta. It's totally a throwback to the 1960s, about as untrendy as you can get."

"With the red and white tablecloths and a tiny Italian grandmother in the kitchen rolling out the gnocchi by hand?"

"Exactly!" laughed Aly. "Nonna'll come out of the back when it's not busy to chat. I love her." Aly put the shredded parmesan in a blue bowl. "She's to blame for my not cooking pasta. I could never make it as well as she does."

"I can teach you," Whit said. "And next time I'll get out my pasta roller, and we'll make noodles together."

"I bet you've used that line to seduce lots of girls," Aly said and smiled.

Whit's mind flashed to a memory of Petra in his tiny kitchen in St. John, draping fettuccine to dry on every available surface. Now probably wasn't the time to bring her up, but he wanted Aly to know.

"Not really. But I should tell you, there was one woman in St. John…"

"Chas told me. And I don't care," Aly interrupted. "But I do want to know where you learned to make noodles from scratch."

"Italy," Whit said, happy to let the topic pass. "I told you. I'm serious about my pasta." He poured more wine into their glasses. He'd picked out a special bottle, hoping to impress her.

"Is there anywhere you've not been?" Aly asked. "I'd love to go to Rome and stay for a month or two. Or three." She swirled and sipped her wine. "Nothing better than good wine like this, pasta, and a handsome chef," she said with a flirtatious look. "What else do you make?"

"Bolognese, when I have time. Carbonara, puttanesca. I think my favorite is clam linguini."

"*Linguine alle vongole*, yum. I tried going carb-free for a diet once," Aly said, turning the cheese edgewise against the grater. "I didn't make it a week before I broke down and went to Nonna's for her *spaghetti cacio e pepe*."

"I make that too," Whit said. "Next time, I'll do that. Unless you'd rather have pasta with clams?"

"Ooo, hard decision," Aly said. "Clams, please."

"You got it." Whit leaned over and kissed the top of her head. Just being near her made his nerve endings tingle in a most pleasant way. "My friend Robby has a secret clamming spot on Quitsa Pond."

"I'd love to do that," Aly said, wriggling in her seat.

"It's a date." As Whit took a stick of butter from the refrigerator, he added clamming to the mental list of things he wanted to do with Aly. Outside of bed, that was. "And maybe someday, if you're lucky, I'll even teach you the ravioli dance."

Aly laughed, bringing brightness and light to the room. "What's a ravioli dance?"

"I can't give away all my secrets."

"OK. What'll I have to do to get it out of you?" Aly said, moving around behind Whit and poking a finger into his armpit. "Tickle torture? Or this?" she asked, slipping her other hand down along his zipper.

"You can try, but you'll get no secrets out of me." Whit turned around, captured Aly's hands, and kissed her, tasting wine on her irresistibly soft lips. Reluctantly, he pulled back, planting a kiss on the tip of her nose. "You're distracting me. You want a cooking lesson?"

"I do. And then I want you to teach me that song in Gaelic. *The Boatman*."

"You sure? That's a hard one to learn."

"You doubt me?"

"Never," Whit laughed. "But your cooking lesson first. We start with a big glob of butter like this," he demonstrated, putting a chunk in the pan. Aly leaned closer and he felt her breast, warm and supple against his arm. "Then add a few shakes of red pepper flakes," he added, trying to focus on his cooking. "More if you like it spicy. Give it a stir and let that cook on low for a few minutes." He handed her the wooden spoon. "Then we'll add the tomatoes—you use the whole ones from Italy, not diced—and the vodka. Heavy cream and parmesan at the end. You can be in charge."

Sipping his wine, Whit watched Aly stir the pan as the butter melted and sizzled. He realized he was feeling happier than he had in a long time. It wasn't just the sex, as awesome as that was. Being with Aly was like strumming the perfect chord, both hearing and feeling the strings vibrating in the air in harmony. He'd been wrong about her. All the city trappings were just a veneer, as easy to strip off as her clothes at the beach. Underneath was the real Aly, who was genuine and warm and smart and curious. He felt different with her, as if he'd walked out from under a cloud into a bright sunny day.

To hell with taking it slow.

Aly couldn't help but contrast Whit's cooking—a glob of this, a few shakes of that, fishing around in the pantry for the rigatoni and only finding half-boxes of spaghetti and penne—with Kevin's *mise en place* approach, which had every ingredient premeasured, weighed, and waiting in little white bowls lined up on the counter. Whit explained he cooked by instinct and taste. He couldn't make the same dish exactly the same way twice, even if he tried.

Aly opened the can of tomatoes. "You know, I bet you could live off the land here. Dig for clams, pick blueberries, trap lobsters," she said as her imagination put the two of them in a rustic cabin that would be romantic for about as long as the coffee and chocolate held out.

"Don't forget fish, mussels, crabs, oysters—and if you want to hunt, deer and rabbits. And grow your own veggies."

Aly slid her arm around Whit's waist, inhaling the world's sexiest aroma: simmering tomatoes, fresh basil, and her guy. "Of course, that's what the Native Americans did forever. I was reading in the newspaper about the Wampanoag community out in Aquinnah."

"Of course, the tribal lands are a fraction of what they had been. No surprise there."

"The British came."

"And stayed. Can't blame them for wanting to."

It wasn't just the sex. Aly leaned against Whit, immeasurably happy and relaxed in his company. "Go on. I like learning about the Island."

Whit kissed the top of her head. "Sure. Descendants of the original colonists still live here, which I think is pretty cool. The first guys in the mid-1600s, the Mayhews, were arguably—for their time—not so bad." He glanced at Aly as if to make sure she wasn't getting bored. "But European diseases wiped out something like ninety percent of the Wampanoag population. And the settlers cut down almost all the trees for sheep pastures. There were so many sheep on the Island that the British stole more than ten thousand when they raided the Island during the Revolutionary War."

"Ten thousand!" Aly tried to imagine ten thousand Dandelions being herded onto ships. "Chas told me you were a big history buff."

"Hard not to be, when your neighbors are Mayhews and Manters and Allens and Belains. It's a small Island with a long history." He rooted around in his liquor cabinet and pulled out a bottle of Smirnoff. "Now we add about half a cup of vodka to the tomatoes."

Aly poured the liquor into the pot and stirred it. "What's your family's history?" she asked as the sauce bubbled gently.

"It goes way back on my father's side to the whaling days," Whit said. "And I've got a tiny bit of Wampanoag from the Chappaquiddick Tribe on my great-grandmother's side. Or so I've been told. I tried to do some genealogical research, but I couldn't find much of anything." He sipped his wine. "My great-great-something grandfather came from the Azores as a deckhand on a whaling ship and worked his way up to captain. I look like him, supposedly."

"Seriously?" With a tiny bit of prodding, Whit launched into the tale of Joseph Dias and his adventures on the South Seas, the grand house he built in Edgartown to win the hand of his Quaker sweetheart, Diana Coffin. "Classic immigrant story—only hundreds of years ago."

"What happened to your house?"

Whit's face tightened. He stirred the pasta sauce. "My father and stepmother sold it when I was at boarding school. Not my favorite topic."

Black sheep, Aly thought, remembering the story Chas had told her about Whit getting kicked out of school. Poor guy. No wonder he wanted to go off and travel with no home to come back to. His expression told her that now was not the time to pry.

"That could be a new boat tour—Island history-by-water. You could talk about Wampanoags as you go around Gay Head—that story you told me about how the cliffs got their colors?—and whaling in Edgartown. And sheep, of course. I can design a fantastic website for you. A few pictures of you looking all handsome on *Noepe*, add that you'll sing some old sea shanties, and you'll have bookings galore."

🐑🐑🐑

Aly had finally found her balance.

With her feet planted on her paddleboard, back straight, and knees slightly bent, Aly dipped her paddle into Tisbury Great Pond and cut through the surface of the water, leaving a trail of ripples like the wake of a tiny boat. She'd been playing it safe, keeping close to shore, but today she set off toward the middle of the pond. The overcast sky had cleared late, and the pond was all hers.

It had been a steep and wet learning curve. The old Aly probably would not even try to paddleboard, especially after the unmitigated disaster that was her college roommate's attempt to teach her to surf. But the pond had called to her, tempting her with the idea of skimming across its shimmering surface. Aly wanted this for herself alone. No one else.

She'd found the paddleboard in a stack of dusty, abandoned kayaks, surfboards, rowing shells, boogie boards, and canoes that the owners of the property had discarded in favor of newer models. Aly named her board Paddle O'Leary for no other reason than it amused her. Her first attempt at paddleboarding had sent her windmilling with a giant splash into the pond, five feet from shore. After that rocky start, she tried a gradual approach until she got a feel for the board and the paddle, first paddling from a sitting position, then kneeling. Then came the standing-and-wobbling-and-sometimes-falling-off stage. Inelegant, but progress. Today, with the pond silvered blue like smooth, iridescent glass, she got it.

Aly had fallen in love with Tisbury Great Pond, the way it reflected the sky's moods on calm days and had its own when the wind blew, grouchy with whitecaps and chop. She loved the horizontal lines of the landscape, narrow bright green for the fields, a darker irregular band of oak trees, and a slash of pale sand to the south beneath the vast arc of the sky. Some days, the pond played mirror, so exact in its reflection that but for gravity, Aly couldn't tell up from down. This afternoon was one of those days, she thought, as she paddled over one cloud, then another. Her sense of calm grew as she glided across the water, her strokes even and strong, balanced, in control. And happy. A coming-from-inside kind of happy, as calm and balanced as the board. It wasn't a I-must-be-happy-because-I-have-everything-I-want kind of happy. It was different. A toes-to-the-tip-of-her-nose happy. Genuine. Content. Satisfied. The kind of happy she wished she could share with the whole world.

And with Whit.

🐑 🐑 🐑

Aly felt like a spy on a secret mission. Silently, she pulled her paddleboard up next to Whit's old canoe and crept up the path from the pond to the house. Aly peeked up over the deck and through the screen of the sliding door. A pair of bare feet stuck out from the arm of the sofa. A gentle snore broke the silence. Aha! She'd capture her target unawares, using ninja stealth and surprise, and overpower him despite his size and strength.

The target was still sleeping. Whit's mouth hung open slightly, and his face was shadowed with stubble. Those thick eyelashes Aly so adored rested on his cheeks, and his hair, mussed by the pillow, stuck out from his head in messy, dark waves. He was wearing an old t-shirt and a pair of well-worn work shorts. This pair had a rip at the hem, displaying an enticing strip of thigh. Aly was still amazed at the physicality of Whit. The lumberjack type, she'd first thought when she'd met him, all muscles and broad torso narrowing deliciously into his hips and strong legs. There was simply more of him than there was of other people. And that was a very good thing.

Whit murmured in his sleep as Aly planned her attack on her defenseless prey. She could go for that bit of bare tummy between the bottom of his t-shirt and the top of his shorts. Or move in with a full-frontal strike. Then there were the feet. Whit's ridiculously ticklish feet.

She moved into position to hide behind the arm of the sofa. With one finger, she touched the arch of Whit's foot. He twitched as if shaking off a fly. Then she went for the other foot, then both at once. Whit growled and rolled over on his side, pulling his feet away. She crawled around to the front of the couch. As she watched Whit sleep, Aly thought about the fates that had brought her to this Island (and conspired to make her stay) and to this guy. This ticklish, sexy, genuinely kind and giving guy.

With a tremor of excitement, the realization burst upon her. She had fallen in love. The idea caught her breath, set her mind spinning. Aly rolled it around her head, testing it. Was it love, or just infatuation? But her heart told the truth.

Eyes glowing, Aly planted a gentle kiss on his lips.

🐑 🐑 🐑

Beau barked happily as he ran in circles around Hannah's legs. Dandelion bounded behind, baa-ing her head off in her excitement to be out of her pen. "You ready for sheep day?" Hannah asked, closing the gate behind Aly.

"Yup," Aly replied, her heart as light as the lamb's step and her mood as buoyant as the clouds in the blue sky. She bent to stroke Dandelion's ears, feeling lamb-love (and Whit-love) wrap around her like a fuzzy blanket. She was smitten, more than she thought possible, with the fuzzy little creature. And Whit too.

"The sheep look like they don't like getting their hooves trimmed, but they don't really mind much. It's for their own good," Hannah said. "After we're done, I need to go to Vineyard Haven. I got another call from Maria."

"What is it this time?" Aly asked. The sunlight filtering through the dim barn caught dust motes floating in the air, and the hay's bucolic smell was reassuringly warm and comforting.

"A boss-employee dispute. The restaurant manager put Paulo on Sundays. He's a dishwasher, just a kid. That means he'll miss church and his weekly family barbeque, which is a big deal. He's all upset but won't say anything. Too afraid he'll be fired," she sighed. "I kind of know Paulo's boss, so I'll talk to him."

"It's wonderful you do that."

"No biggie. Speaking of wonderful," Hannah whispered with a look of pride. "Our famous painter is up there." She pointed to the hayloft-cum-studio.

A chair scraped the floor above their heads. "I heard you," Lawrence said, peering down from the landing.

"Can I see it?" Hannah asked. Lawrence's paintings were spectacular. Landscapes that weren't landscapes so much as feelings that expressed a sense of place through color and light.

"Nope. Not until it's done."

"If you get bored, we'll be out with the sheep in the south pasture. Hoof-trimming day!"

"Uh, no, thanks!"

"Artists. Heads in the clouds," Hannah said, shaking her head fondly. "We get to spend our day on the ground with many little sheep hooves. Lawrence has been encouraging me to experiment more with my wood sculptures. But I just don't have the time. Not until winter. Here. You can carry this," Hannah said, handing Aly an aluminum rectangle with short legs, strung with bungee cords.

"What's this?" Aly asked.

Hannah checked the sharpness of a pair of shears. "Lounge chair for the sheep. You'll see. Now, where is that drenching syringe? Oh, here it is," she said, pulling an oversized syringe with a ball at the end of a long metal tube. "Beau takes care of rounding up the woolies, and we do the rest." Hannah opened the gate to the pasture, and Beau and Dandelion ran in. "We'll start with Dandelion. She still doesn't like hanging out with the others. I doubt she ever will." She propped the metal contraption up against the fence, its two bent legs hooked over the rail. "OK, lambkins. You're up first."

Eying the chair, Dandelion made a dash for it but was cut off by Beau. Hannah grabbed her collar, lifting her so she flopped back into the web of bungee cords, splayed on her back with her legs sticking out like toothpicks in a marshmallow. "Poor Dandelion," Aly laughed as she recorded a video of the lamb waving her legs in the air.

"I know. It's a bit undignified," Hannah said. "And just look at your dirty armpits." She opened the bottle and carefully drew liquid dewormer into the syringe. "We tuck this into the corner of her mouth," she said, slowly pressing the plunger. "I used to give them pills, but they spit them out at me. There. Done," she said and put the syringe away. "What are you going to do with all the videos and pictures you're always taking of Dandelion?"

"Nothing, probably. I just don't want to forget what Dandelion was like as a lamb. She's growing up so fast."

"That she is," Hannah agreed, rubbing the lamb's round tummy. "OK, girl. Now time for your feet."

Hannah lifted one cloven hoof. "You have to keep the hooves trimmed so they don't grow over. See how that edge is curling a bit? We trim that flat. But not too close or we'll get into the quick." Aly reached out to touch Dandelion's foot. It felt like a cross between a fingernail and leather.

Aly held her breath as Hannah sprayed the shears with alcohol, then, securing the hoof in her left hand, confidently trimmed the curling edge, the base of the hoof, and then the top, first one toe, then the other. "See how the color is paler? If you get to pale pink, you've trimmed enough. She ran her finger over the hoof. "Nice and even. Aly, your clippers are in the bag."

"My clippers?" Aly had tried to clip Miso's kitty claws once and ended up with hands and wrists that looked like she'd worn barbed wire gloves. She'd sworn never to pick up clippers again. Dandelion looked up as if to say *just get it over with and let me out of this chair*. Aly doused the clippers with alcohol and took a deep breath.

"Start with that bit there," Hannah said, reaching out to touch a curling edge. "You'll be done in two shakes of a lamb's tail."

"Hah," said Aly. Dandelion, deciding that the chair really wasn't so bad, had closed her eyes for a nap. Timidly, Aly snipped a bit of hoof. It was like cutting through leather, but softer.

"Keep going. Get that whole side piece off, then the top and the bottom. We want it nice and flat."

It took Aly at least ten times as long as Hannah, but she felt her confidence grow with each successful snip. They tipped Dandelion from her lounge chair onto her newly trimmed feet.

She took a few tentative steps, as if she were wearing a pair of heels, then bounded off.

"OK, Beau. Time for our next customer." With a whistle and arm motion from Hannah, Beau was off like a flash.

"Never imagined I'd be doing this," Aly said.

"And shopping at the Dumptique like the rest of us."

Aly looked down at her outfit, a pair of jeans and an old pair of Blundstone boots she'd lucked into at the local freecycle. She was far from the polished, citified Aly who'd arrived on the Island just a few weeks before with a suitcase full of vacation clothes, chosen to please Kevin's sense of style. "I like being comfortable."

"Glad you finally figured that out," Hannah said. "Let's keep going. We've got lots of sheep to do."

Beau drove Sheep Number Two, a huge, unhappy ewe, toward the hoof-trimming team. Eyes rolling in distress, she battled being hoisted into the aluminum contraption.

"I appreciate the help with the sheep," Hannah said. "But I don't think you're going to make a career of this. Have you started job hunting?"

The question rolled over Aly like a black cloud. "Not yet. Soon. I can do most of it from here online and on Zoom."

"I guess there's no rush. It must be nice to get a big fat check when you're laid off." Hannah said as she loaded the syringe and slipped the medicine into the sheep's mouth. "This is awkward, and I hate to ask. But could you help with the rent?" Looking up at Aly, she added, "It's not much, by Vineyard standards, since I'm the caretaker, but I got some bad news this morning."

"Of course I can help." Aly was an idiot for not thinking to have offered before. "What bad news?"

"Remember that big job in Edgartown I had lined up for the rest of the summer? The owners decided they want to put it off until the fall. They don't want painters crawling all over the house while they're there." The ewe wriggled as Hannah grabbed her hoof and started to clip. "It means I'll have to fire the kids I just hired." She shook her head. "I turned down other jobs for that one. But it is what it is. Some things are good—me and Lawrence—some things not so good," she said. "And that's not the only bad news. Mom called. She's coming for the weekend."

Hannah frowned. "I guess I'll have time to take her around. But she'd have more fun being with you."

"That's not true."

"Come on, Aly," Hannah said, with a bitter twist to the corner of her mouth. "You've always had more in common with her. She hasn't approved of my 'life choices' since I dropped out of college. You know that."

"But Hannah..." Aly objected.

Hannah flashed Aly a look that meant I'm done with this, and Aly shut up. "What's the latest with your apartment—and Kevin?"

Aly took a deep breath. "I haven't talked to him."

Hannah looked up. "Shouldn't you?"

She could just text Kevin, words on a screen, not even talk to him. But a little whiny voice, like a stubborn three-year-old, rang in her head, *I don't wanna, you can't make me.*

"You don't want to. I get it, Aly," Hannah said, reading Aly's mind as always. "Does Whit know about him?"

"No."

"You should tell him," Hannah said. "And I sound like a broken record, but maybe it's time to face real life."

🐑 🐑 🐑

Aly rocked back and forth in the wicker rocking chair, enjoying the view of Ocean Park and Nantucket Sound from Lawrence's front porch. Parents cheered on a small boy running across the grass trailing a seagull-shaped kite as a trio of beachgoers lugging chairs and an umbrella headed down the sidewalk toward the Inkwell, Oak Bluffs' popular beach. OB had a very different vibe from up-Island, lively beach town versus bucolic countryside. Aly loved both, but for her, West Tisbury felt more like home.

"Here's your iced tea," Lawrence said, handing her a frosty glass and settling into a rocking chair.

"OK, here's the plan," Aly said. Lawrence had happily agreed to help Aly canvas potential clients for Hannah's painting services. "You start with the houses here since you know the neighbors, and I'll go over to the Campground. Tomorrow, we'll hit Edgartown."

"Worth a try. Hannah's really stressed out."

"I know." Aly handed Lawrence a stack of the flyers she'd designed on her laptop the night before. Hannah's new website could use a few more testimonials and pictures, but the before-and-after photos of Lawrence's house—and some pictures Hannah had taken of the wooden gingerbread trim she'd made with her scroll saw—were evidence enough of the quality of her work. Even though she'd used all of Hannah's printer ink, Aly was especially pleased with how the flyer came out. It featured a flattering picture of Hannah smiling from the top of a ladder at Lawrence's house and another photo of Hannah's new employees, Isabel and Karolina, looking cute as they painted a window together. Aly had designed the logo, a cartoon Hannah holding a paintbrush, superimposed over the outline of Martha's Vineyard.

They finished their iced tea and headed out with their flyers. Aly loved the Campground, named from when it was a Methodist meeting place and attendees stayed in tents. Gradually, the tents were replaced in the mid-to-late 19th century by adorable Victorian dollhouse-like homes boasting intricate gingerbread trim. Surely, a few could use a fresh coat of paint. It didn't take Aly long to spot one, a tiny house with a porch swing and peeling purple and white trim. No one answered that door, so she slipped a flyer underneath. Same at the next two places she tried, but at the end of the path, she spotted a house done up in shades of blue that could use Hannah's services. A white-haired woman sat in a wicker chair on the porch reading a book.

"Sorry to bother you, but would you be interested in a flyer for my friend's painting company?"

"Painting, you say? Come up here." Aly handed her a flyer. "Is that the house on Ocean Park with the turret?" the woman asked, peering closely at the picture.

"That's Constellation Cottage. Hannah did all the painting. And she does woodworking too. She copied and replaced the damaged gingerbread there."

"Humph," she said, looking up at the porch trim. "Blueberry Cottage could use a new coat of paint. But could she have the job finished by Grand Illumination? It's August 14 this year."

"I think so. I'll ask. What's Grand Illumination?"

"You've never been? Oh, it's a magical evening. All the houses put up lanterns for one night. And only one night. Mine are old silk ones from China that were my grandmother's. Very fragile, very beautiful," she said. "I wouldn't mind having this place spiffed up for that. And having a young person here to hang my lanterns for me. But I don't want to be woken up at 7:00 a.m. by some strange man scraping my bedroom window and staring at me."

"No men, just Hannah and her assistants—they're both girls. They can start whenever it suits you best."

"And she does a good job?"

"Very."

The woman studied the flyer. "Have her call me."

🐑 🐑 🐑

Hops hung heavy and green on the pergola shading the patio at Bad Martha's Brewery. The late afternoon after-beach bar crowd trickled in as Whit unpacked his amp and microphone. The open-air brewpub was one of his favorite venues: good beer, good customers, good vibes.

"Careful with that," he grinned as Aly walked out with a flight of five beers on a small wooden tray.

"Oh, I've got it."

"Over here, Aly," Chas called. She set the beer tray onto the table and slid onto the bench next to Chas. He whispered something in her ear. With a pang of irrational jealousy, Whit watched Aly lean over and give Chas a big kiss on the lips as he snapped a selfie. Then she looked over at Whit and smiled, and his heart swelled with happiness. When he played, he played her favorite songs, playing only for her.

On his break, Whit came over to the table and flopped down next to Aly. "Hey there, troubadour," Chas said, "You know, you're supposed to look at the other customers when you sing, not just Aly. Especially the girls who look like they haven't had a date for a while. That's how you get tips."

"How do you know I'm not a big tipper?" Aly teased, squeezing Whit's forearm. "The type that drops a C-note or two into the tip jar? Or would you rather take your tips in kind back home?"

Chas fanned his face with his beer coaster. "Oh my goodness! This is worse than I thought."

Whit ignored him. "If you want, you could come up and sing with me in the next set?"

"Aly sings?" Chas asked.

"She does. Perfect pitch—and lovely harmonies."

Chas's eyes widened. "Yet another talent. We'll have to tell Granny. She'll be delighted."

Aly's cell phone buzzed. She picked it up, typed a few words, then put it back in her bag.

"Who was that?" Chas asked.

"My old boss. No idea what she wants. I'll call her later."

Whit had almost let himself forget that Aly had another life, one in San Francisco. One she'd go back to, eventually. He shook off the thought. What mattered was that she was here now. And wanted to be with him.

"So, what do you think?" Whit asked, taking a sip from one of Aly's beers. "We could do *Sweet Baby James* together."

"Maybe some other time," she laughed. "I love singing, but my public performances have always been a disaster." She turned to Chas. "You see, I was cast in the lead role as a singing sunflower in second grade…"

Whit leaned back in his chair, enjoying the tale of Aly's first—and last—experience on the big stage: first, there was the jealous daisy who pulled off Aly's petals, next, forgetting the lyrics to *The Sun Song*, and then, the final humiliation, the kid who was playing rain left a puddle under Aly's feet that looked as if she'd peed her pants. Aly made him laugh. He felt relaxed and happy when he was with her: she made the sky bluer and the sun brighter. Aly, his love.

🐑 🐑 🐑

With a groan, Aly put down her scraper and stretched to relieve her cramped hand. The owner of Blueberry Cottage had met with Hannah, inspected the painting on Lawrence's house, and not only hired Hannah, but also told everyone in the Campground (and she appeared to know everyone) about Hannah, leading to enough jobs for the summer and more. Plus, several days work doing nothing but putting up and taking down lanterns for Grand Illumination Night.

As a result of her promotional successes, Aly was redrafted for the painting team. Compared with stripping paint from the straight pieces of trim on the last house, getting old paint off curves and curlicues made for slow going.

"Hannah," she called. "How did you manage to scrape all the gingerbread on Lawrence's house without losing your mind?"

Hannah extracted an earbud and said, "I had a bigger team for that job. Other than that, I'd say patience. And good playlists." She switched over to a small chisel to get to the inside of a cutout. "A lot of painters get stoned, but that makes them work really slow. You hear that, girls? No weed on the job."

"Yes, Hannah," they replied in unison and went back to chattering in Portuguese.

Aly retrieved her scraper. "What time tomorrow are we picking up your mom?"

"Her boat arrives in Vineyard Haven at 6:00. I thought we'd pick up some fish for dinner and eat at home. Then you get to take a couple of days off to play tour guide."

"Why don't you do that, and I'll keep working here?"

"No thanks," Hannah spotted Lawrence walking down the path with paper bags and waved. "Here comes our lunch."

"Are you going to introduce Lawrence to your mom?"

"I'm figuring that out."

"Figuring what out?" Lawrence asked, dropping the bags from Tigerhawk Kitchen on the front porch. He walked over to Hannah's ladder and kissed what he could reach, which was the back of Hannah's knee. Isabel and Karolina giggled.

Hannah reached down and patted the top of his head. "Whether to introduce you to my mother."

"Of course you are. Are you embarrassed to be dating me?"

Hannah climbed down the ladder, wrapped her hands around Lawrence's neck, and gave him a proper kiss. "But I could introduce her to Larry."

Lawrence's eyes widened. "I'm Larry? And what does Larry do?"

"He might be a house painter." Hannah picked up a clean brush and tickled his neck. "She won't ask any questions about that."

Lawrence laughed. "Whatever you want."

"Why do you want to hide who Lawrence is?" Aly asked, her mouth watering as she took out a fried-chicken sandwich.

Hannah made a face. "It would be weird. Mom would get all, I don't know, impressed." She turned to Lawrence. "You don't mind, do you?"

"Not at all," he said. "If she likes Larry, someday we'll introduce her to Lawrence." He kissed Hannah's nose. "When you're ready."

🐑 🐑 🐑

Aly and Hannah waited as the ferry delicately maneuvered its bulk alongside the dock, looking like a huge white bathtub floating upside down.

"I'm glad you're here to keep my mom distracted," Hannah said. She'd grown increasingly anxious about her mother's visit, scrubbing the house and truck spotlessly clean and making a list of places her mother might like to visit with Aly. Aly teased Hannah that it wasn't like the Queen was coming to visit, it was just her mom.

"It's still not fair that I get to play while you work," Aly said.

"Don't be silly. You deserve to do some sightseeing too," Hannah said.

The massive doors at the front of the vessel swung open, and cars began rolling out as a metal footbridge was pushed into place against the side. "There's Mom, in the white hat," said Hannah, pointing to Jo among the crowd of foot passengers carrying duffels and dragging rolling suitcases, a few with dogs on leashes. "Here we go."

Unlike Hannah, Aly had been eagerly anticipating Jo's visit. She looked exactly as Aly remembered, short and huggable with pink cheeks, bright hazel eyes behind gold-wire-rimmed glasses, and frizzy gray-brown hair pulled back into a sensible rubber band bun. Aly could see no signs of Jo's March accident but for a pale pink scar on her chin.

"Hannah! Wonderful to see you! And Aly, it's been much too long!" she exclaimed, hugging both of them in turn.

"It has," Aly said, returning the hug. "You look great."

"Your father sends his love. I tried to convince him to come, but he's obsessed with finishing his article on Dostoevsky's 'ideal man,'" Jo said. "Besides, it'll be more fun with just us girls."

"Sure," Hannah said, not sounding convinced. She picked up her mother's suitcase. "I thought we could stop and buy some fish for dinner, unless you'd rather go out?"

"Fish sounds perfect. Aly, can you get a recipe from your chef?" Jo asked, taking Aly's arm. "I imagine you've become quite the cook living with Kevin."

"Um, his recipes are really complicated," Aly said, glancing at Hannah. "Do you like grilled swordfish? We have some leftover green sauce from the Fish House that's delicious on sword."

Back at the house, Beau and Dandelion stood waiting at the gate, barking and baa-ing, a furry and wooly greeting committee. Beau's entire rear half started to wag when he smelled the bag of fish. "Hello, Beau," Jo said, opening the gate. "And this must be the lamb you helped bottle-feed, Aly. What was her name? Daisy?"

"Dandelion," said Hannah.

"How cute. And look at your adorable house, Hannah."

"You've never been here before?" Aly asked.

"I've always meant to come, but, you know, things come up. But with you here visiting, it was time to make the trip."

Hannah rolled her eyes at Aly. "Let me show you your room," Hannah said. "You get the guest bedroom. Aly's going to stay over at a friend's house while you're here."

"That's too bad. I thought we'd all be staying here together."

"Sorry to disappoint you, Mom."

Aly opened a nice California Chenin Blanc, poured three glasses, and set out a third chair so they could sit together in the yard and enjoy the sunset over the pond. The view was as pretty as any Allen Whiting landscape. The oaks, shaped by the prevailing ocean winds, looked like oversized Japanese bonsai trees, the tall meadow grasses swayed gently in the breeze, and the pond shimmered and reflected the colors of the sky.

Planning Jo's visit, Aly realized she'd begun to feel like a local—well, a washashore, to be more accurate. She had her favorite farm stands (Flat Point Farm for eggs, Mermaid Farm for tomatoes and yogurt, Grey Barn & Farm for sourdough bread and pastries); her favorite beaches (Quansoo for ocean beach, Menemsha for sunset); and fish markets (Larsen's for fish, Menemsha Fish Market for chowder and bisque); and of course, Tisbury Great Pond was the loveliest spot on the Island. Maybe, as Hannah said, the Island did have magically transformative powers. Aly felt as if she were a different person—more truly herself. In a deep, fundamental way, she felt connected to the stunningly beautiful landscapes. And she was surrounded by real friends who "got" her, friends not just because they had the same employer, lived on the same block, or ran in the same crowd. And she had Dandelion, the sweet lamb who had stolen part of her heart. And Whit, who'd taken the rest.

"Well, this is such a lovely view," Jo said once they'd settled into the chairs. "I guess being a caretaker has its perks. But before I forget, Hannah, I wanted to thank you again for coming to the hospital after I fell. And for installing the rails and fixing that little table I broke. You've gotten quite handy," she said in a way that didn't quite sound like a compliment.

"No problem, Mom."

"Now, Aly, tell me all about your job hunt—and that handsome chef of yours," Jo said. "He must be missing you like crazy. I follow him on Instagram. His restaurant looks like it's quite the hit."

"You're on Instagram, Mom?" Hannah asked.

"Of course. Isn't everyone?"

Aly took a big swallow of wine. "We broke up. He cheated on me."

"Oh, Aly," Jo said. "That's terrible. I'm so sorry."

"I'm doing OK," Aly said. "I'll tell you about it later."

"I understand," Jo said with a sympathetic look. "Too nice a night to get into all that. But tell me what you've been up to here on Martha's Vineyard."

Hannah walked away to set up the grill. Aly chatted about the beaches, lobstering, and teaching herself to paddleboard, trying to bring Hannah (who remained uncharacteristically grouchy) into the conversation.

"What's going on?" Aly asked when Jo went inside to use the bathroom. "You're hardly talking at all."

"How did Mom know that you'd lost your job?" Hannah asked.

"I told her the last time she called."

Hannah picked up her wineglass and refilled it. "How often do you talk?"

"I don't know. Maybe once a month or so? She likes to check in and see how I'm doing."

A flash of pain crossed Hannah's face. "I didn't know that." She put the wine bottle back in the refrigerator. "I asked Mom to stop criticizing my life choices a few years ago. I guess she figured we didn't have anything to talk about. So, we don't, much."

"That's sad, Hannah," Aly said. "But she wanted to visit. That's a good sign."

"If you say so."

🐑 🐑 🐑

The passenger door of the ancient Lexus opened with a loud creak. "This is Lexie. She's an Island car," Aly explained to Jo. She'd developed an affection for the old clunker; it got her from point A to point B without complaint. Lexie's "Island stripes" from veering into the brush when passing cars on the Vineyard's narrow one-lane dirt roads meant Aly didn't need to worry about getting scratches in the paint, another thing that Kevin was paranoid about. "That means a car you wouldn't drive anywhere but here." Lexie, in response, decided to open her sunroof. "Sorry about that," Aly said, closing it. "She does that sometimes. Not great if it's raining."

Jo sat down and fished around in her bag for her tube of sunscreen. "I imagine you have a nice car in San Francisco."

Aly didn't have her own car, and she hated driving Kevin's, an immaculate black Tesla Model 3. "I don't really need one in the city."

"I am so looking forward to spending the whole day with you. What's the plan?"

"I thought we'd start in Edgartown. The houses and gardens there are so pretty, I think you'll really like them," Aly said, starting the car. "There's a little lighthouse we can visit and good shopping too." She pulled out onto the dirt road. "After that, we'll go to Oak Bluffs and meet Hannah for lunch. In the afternoon, we can come back here and rest up, then go to the beach—Hannah borrowed a beach key. She'll try to finish early and join us."

"Sounds wonderful. And tomorrow?"

"It's Saturday, so there's the big farmer's market in West Tisbury. And the Chilmark Flea Market. Then we could go poke around Menemsha—it's a really cute little fishing village. There are a couple of galleries there that I like." And if they were lucky, Whit would be there. Aly hoped Jo would like him. How could she not?

"I'd love to do a little shopping," said Jo. "It's been so long since we did that together! I'm sure you know all the cute stores." She pulled a pair of sunglasses out of her bag. "I am sorry about your chef. He sounded perfect for you."

"I thought he was too. But he wasn't."

"How so? Or do you not want to talk about it?"

"It's OK. I don't mind telling you," Aly paused. "You know Kevin's a perfectionist."

"Not surprising in a chef."

"I guess not," Aly said. "He was so amazing when we first started dating. So romantic and charming and attentive, I don't know. He seemed to love everything about me. Then as time went on, he didn't."

"I think that happens in all relationships, to some degree."

"I suppose so. Then the restaurant started taking over our lives, and he got more and more stressed."

"And took it out on you?"

"Not directly. He never yelled at me. Most chefs are screamers. Kevin's not. He's too tightly wound. I really tried hard to be understanding. But I don't know. He got more controlling. More critical. Everything had to be just the way he wanted. Including me," Aly said. "I tried to change who I was. For him." She thought of Whit, how he let her be herself. "I only realized that recently. But that didn't make the breakup any easier."

Jo patted her arm. "Couples have gotten over worse things, including infidelity, with therapy. You put a lot into that relationship, Aly. I could tell you were happy."

Aly shook her head. "I think I talked myself into thinking that I was happy. But being on the Island, away from him and San Francisco, made everything clear," she said. "It's over. For good. And I've started seeing a friend of Hannah's. He's a really nice guy. A fisherman—he runs charters out of Menemsha. And a musician. And very good looking."

"A good-looking fisherman," Jo said, raising an eyebrow. "And a musician. Hmm."

"I hope that we'll catch him tomorrow at the dock. I want you to meet him. And see his boat. It's beautiful. He did all the work himself."

"He sounds handy." She placed her hand on Aly's forearm. "I'm sure I don't need to tell you this. Please be careful with rebound relationships. It's easy to get in too deep, too fast. Remember, there are lots of fish in the sea. You don't have to catch the fisherman."

But Aly had. And she wasn't going to toss him back.

🐑 🐑 🐑

Aly was troubled by Jo's comment, and as they walked up North Water Street in Edgartown toward the lighthouse, she wondered whether Jo could be right. She'd never felt like she did with Whit. Not with Kevin. Not with anyone else. But was it really love and not a rebound?

"Oh, look at that house," Jo said, stopping at the white picket fence in front of Granny's home, which looked as stately and grand as the old lady who owned it. "Isn't it lovely? And the garden with all those late roses and lace-cap hydrangeas. Just beautiful."

"That's the Captain Finley House. It's owned by my friend Chas's grandmother." She had an idea: Granny had insisted that Aly drop by anytime she was in Edgartown, no need to call first. "If you want, we could drop by to see if she's home. Granny adores showing off her house."

"I'd love to see the inside, if you don't think it's an imposition," Jo said, her eyes lighting up.

"Aly, sweetheart!" Chas exclaimed, answering the door. He gave Aly a big, affectionate kiss on her cheek. "What a wonderful surprise."

"I hope you and Granny don't mind. I'm playing tour guide for Hannah's mom, Jo, for a couple of days," Aly said. Jo waved from the end of the brick walk. "I thought she might like to see the house, and that Granny might enjoy meeting her. You know, the Russian lit thing."

"Right, of course," Chas said. "Hannah's parents and yours are colleagues together at Middlebury."

With a jab of panic, Aly realized her mistake. Granny still thought Chas was dating the respectable daughter of a pair of professors. She would naturally ask Jo about Aly's parents. Chas didn't know the truth. No one did, except for Hannah and Jo.

"Yes," Aly said, anxiety rising. "But maybe now's not the best time," she said, desperately backpedaling. "We have quite a few things we wanted to do today."

If they stayed, her white lie about her parents would be exposed in the most humiliating way. She could imagine the looks of confusion passing between Chas and Jo. Not to mention Granny's disappointment. Not only that, she didn't want to expose the ruse that she was dating Chas, who was not the fisherman boyfriend Aly had told Jo about. What a mess. She was an idiot. She should have just pointed out Granny's house and kept walking. What was wrong with her?

"Another day, maybe. I'll call first," Aly said.

"But you're both here now," he said, opening the door wide, thus cutting off Aly's escape route. He motioned to Jo, encouraging her to come up the walk. Aly's brain failed to come up with an option to somehow keep her cats in the bag. She was doomed. "I'm happy to show you around the house," Chas said. "But I'm afraid Granny's toddled off to Boston for a few days for some doctor's appointments. Nothing serious, just her usual round of checkups. Can I get you both something to drink?"

Aly's anxiety receded. Chas wasn't like Granny; caught up in his docent role, he wouldn't ask Jo about Aly's parents. Or mention anything about the ruse of their dating each other. But, she realized, she'd cut it close. Too close.

Chas began the tour in the entryway, pointing out the paintings and architectural details, embellished with tidbits of family history. "We put a new kitchen and master bedroom addition off the back in the 1980s, but the rest of the house is original."

"As beautiful on the inside as the outside," Jo said. "Look at the paneling. Gorgeous. And the crown molding. Are those whales carved up there?"

"Sperm whales, to be exact," said Chas.

"Amazing," Jo said. "And your family bought this house from a whaling captain's widow?"

"Indeed, in 1870, with the ill-gotten gains from swindling investors in a railroad that was never built. If you want a tale of a heroic whaling captain, you'll have to ask our Whit."

🐑 🐑 🐑

Aly heaved a sigh of relief, glad that the rest of the visit to Edgartown went without incident. Jo adored the lighthouse with its views of the harbor, the tiny three-car ferry that ran between Edgartown and Chappaquiddick, and the excellent (if expensive) boutiques. As they shopped, Jo peppered Aly with questions about her life in San Francisco, carefully stepping around the topic of Kevin. But Aly had been unsettled by her close call at Granny's doorstep, how easily the truth about her parents could've been exposed. She'd dodged a bullet this time, but what about next?

"You're going to love the Campground and Oak Bluffs," Aly said, explaining the history of OB's vibrant, well-heeled Black summer community as they drove up Beach Road. "But the Obamas decided to buy on Edgartown Great Pond. For security reasons, I think," Aly said as they walked to Blueberry Cottage.

"Hi, Mom," Hannah said, climbing down a ladder. She wiped pale-blue paint off her hands with a rag. "Are you and Aly having a nice day?"

"Wonderful day. Aly showed me all around Edgartown, and we got a tour of your friend Chas's grandmother's house," Jo said. "Oh, and we did some shopping. Aly found the cutest top. And I found one for you."

Hannah groaned. "I don't need anything."

"Well, just try it on. For me," Jo said. "Aly lets me spoil her. Why not you?"

They both sounded exactly like they had when Hannah and Aly were in high school, Jo always trying to get Hannah to wear "nice" outfits, Hannah rebelling by wearing her thrift shop finds. At least

Aly was able to steer Jo's choice for Hannah today toward something she might possibly wear.

Lawrence came around from the side of the house wearing painter's coveralls with a scraper in his hand. "Verisimilitude," he whispered to Aly. "The owner's OK with my pretending to be a painter for a couple of hours. But scraping is giving me a cramp in my hand."

"I know," Aly whispered back. "Careful that you don't get a blister. That really hurts."

Hannah gave Lawrence a nervous smile. "Let me introduce the rest of the crew, Mom," she said. "That's Isabel and Karolina up on the ladders." The girls waved. "And this is Larry."

"Nice to meet you," Lawrence said, extending his hand.

"Same here," Jo said, her jaw literally dropping as she took in his movie-star good looks. "So. You're a painter."

"I am," he replied, winking at Hannah. "I've loved painting since I can remember. My parents said I couldn't make a living at it, but look at me," he added, holding his paint-smeared hands wide. Aly suppressed a giggle. Lawrence's last painting had sold for six figures, a fact she suspected Hannah was blissfully ignorant of. "You should have Hannah take you by Constellation Cottage—that was our big project this spring."

"Good idea," said Aly, regaining her composure. "We can walk by after lunch."

"Larry and I have been, uh, dating a bit this summer," Hannah said.

"And spring," Lawrence added. "More than a bit," he smiled, slinging an arm around Hannah's shoulders.

"Really," Jo said. Her eyebrows shot up as she looked from her daughter to Lawrence and back again.

"So. That's that," Hannah said, looking relieved to have the introduction over. "Let's go get lunch. What are you in the mood for, Mom?"

🐑 🐑 🐑

A grayish morning drizzle didn't deter August visitors from the farmers' market. Aly followed the line of cars that extended as far back as Panhandle Road, wrapping around the perimeter of Ag

Hall, a spacious post-and-beam barn set on several acres just outside the tiny village center of West Tisbury.

"This is where they'll hold the big fair later this month," Aly said. "It's a real county fair—exhibits and games and food and music and rides. Even a women's skillet toss! I'm going to enter Dandelion in the ewe lamb category." Aly imagined herself sharing a warm funnel cake dusted with powdered sugar (her secret weakness) with Whit as they admired Dandelion's blue ribbon. Maybe she'd even win Best in Show. "And maybe showmanship too. That's like a dog show, only with sheep. Or maybe the costume contest. Hannah's entering Beau in the dog obedience competition and one of her lamps in woodcrafts," Aly said, pulling into a parking space. "You know, the one in the living room?"

"Hannah's always been artsy-crafty."

"She's been working on ideas for other designs too—pendant lights, mobiles, standing lamps. I love how the wood lampshade glows when you turn on the light," Aly said. "And if she makes enough over the winter, her friend Willow said she'd sell them at the Chilmark Flea Market." Thus far, Aly's efforts to interest Jo in Hannah's life had fallen flat, but the weekend wasn't over yet. "This evening, we'll have her show you her workshop out in the barn." She grabbed the shopping bags from the back seat of the car. "Should we get some corn for dinner?"

With the sound of a bluegrass trio in the background, Aly and Jo browsed among the stands and filled their bags with ears of fresh-picked corn—the only summer vegetable that Hannah didn't grow—from Morning Glory Farm, fat FV Martha Rose scallops, Flat Point Farm goat milk soaps (and a cute little felted lamb for Aly), local Chilmark honey, a gooey Eidolon cheese, Salt Rock chocolates, and a jar of West Tisbury Traffic Jam (mixed berry, Aly's favorite) from Linda Alley at New Lane Sundries. A box of the tiniest potatoes Aly had ever seen, and a Vietnamese egg roll to snack on, and they were almost done.

"You were right. This is a very nice farmer's market," Jo said, as they strolled across the market to their last stop, the flower stand.

"It's fun to chat with the vendors. The Vineyard is full of all sorts of interesting, creative people. Some grew up here, and others moved to the Island after careers somewhere else," Aly said. "Lots of writers, filmmakers, and young entrepreneurs. And the food scene is amazing. I thought we had the best bread, cheese, and chocolate in San Francisco, but not anymore."

They paused to admire the flower vendor's display: mixed bouquets in a rainbow of shades, from pastel to bright, and buckets of daylilies, hydrangeas, and sunflowers. Jo reached out to touch a petal on a snapdragon. "It sounds like you've been having a lovely vacation, but have you thought about when you're going back home? And how is the job hunt?"

Jo's words cast a pall over the bright colors. Aly had almost forgotten to call her old boss back. Elisa informed her she was leaving Spire and had started conversations with a startup. She couldn't give Aly any details yet, but there might be a job there for her too. Aly had thanked her, but then Whit had come by to take her out for tacos and margaritas, and she'd promptly put the conversation out of her mind.

"Well, hiring picks up next month, in September," Aly said, not wanting to admit that she'd done exactly nothing about finding a new position. Unless she could count that phone call. She didn't want to look for a job. Or to think about moving back to California. Or to have anything about her life change.

"Dear," Jo said, "after all you've worked for and achieved, you can't let yourself get distracted. Once you're off track, it can be hard to get back on. I'll be honest. I've been worried about you since you told me you'd lost your job and had come here. It's natural to want to run away and lick your wounds. And to hook up with the first attractive guy you meet. But don't let the Vineyard seduce you into thinking that you can stay and make candles or chocolates or become a house painter like Hannah." She picked out a zinnia and twirled it between her fingers. "It's like the people who go on vacation to France and decide they want to drop everything and become winemakers. Or the next Van Gogh. A lovely fantasy." She put the flower back and placed her hand on Aly's arm. "It's beautiful here. I'll grant you that. But you need to think about your future. I can see how losing your job—and your problems with Kevin—have knocked you off your pins. But you can't run away from your real life."

"This is real, Jo," Aly said.

"It is. But it's not for you."

Her words split Aly's world in two. How could everything Jo said be right when it felt so wrong?

Jo continued, "I can't do anything to help Hannah. But I can help you. Have you updated your resume?" Aly shook her head. "Let's work on that after dinner. It'll be like when you were applying to colleges," she smiled. "Or will I have to bribe you with chocolate chip cookies?"

A memory of sitting with Jo at the kitchen table with a plate of warm cookies, spinning Aly's mostly unremarkable high-school activities (Science Club, Model UN, her truly mediocre performance on the lacrosse team) and summer jobs into impressive accomplishments, drafting and redrafting her college essays until they sparkled like diamonds.

"It's OK. I can do it myself."

"Promise?"

"I promise," Aly replied automatically, her heart sinking. "I did hear the other day from my old boss. She might have a job prospect for me."

"Excellent. Stay on top of that. But I'm sure I don't need to lecture you about the importance of networking. And with your experience, you'll have your pick of jobs," Jo said. "I don't know if I ever told you how proud I am of you. You moved across the country, put yourself through college, launched yourself into a career that is not the easiest—especially for a woman—and succeeded. But remember when you were looking at colleges and thought you liked Hampshire? What a mistake that would've been!" she said, selecting a bouquet in shades of white and lavender. "I want what's best for you, Aly. Always have, always will."

"I know, Jo. And thank you."

🐑 🐑 🐑

Dandelion nosed up under Aly's hand for a pat, pushing Aly's fingers off the keyboard. "Hey! Stop distracting me," she said, stroking the lamb's ears. "Don't you see I'm working here? Or trying to." High above Aly, a thin layer of clouds rippled and overlapped like fish scales in the sky. Mackerel sky, Whit had told her once. Aly took in a deep breath of fresh air and looked out at the pond in the distance.

As a surprise, she had started designing a website for Whit's business, featuring (of course) pictures of Whit looking irresistibly attractive on *Noepe*. She'd added tabs for fishing charters, sunset cruises, and a few new ideas: a musical cruise with a sea shanty theme featuring Whit on guitar, an around-the-Island history tour, day trips to Cuttyhunk and the Elisabeth Islands, and an overnight trip up the Cape to see whales and sharks. But she still needed more pictures and video: it was time to talk Whit into letting her tag along with him on a charter or two. Aly sat back in her chair, thinking. She wanted the website to come alive. Nothing as complex as the 4-D effects she was working on at Spire, but something interactive. Maybe a fish—or a whale—to swim through the pages spouting fun facts about the Vineyard?

Reluctantly, she closed the mockup of Whit's website and, as she'd promised Jo, dug up her old resume. Not that it was much help, being so out of date. Aly was grateful that Jo didn't bring up job hunting again. Or Whit. But Jo's advice sat inside Aly, eating away at her certainty that spending the summer on Martha's Vineyard was good for her. Jo had always been right before: about college, about Aly's major, and about steering her into the job at Spire instead of taking the offer at Salesforce. Was her life on the Island just a vacation fantasy? Life wasn't a rom-com movie, after all.

She typed in "Spire" under Experience and her dates of employment (had she really been there seven years?), heaved a sigh, and closed the document. At least she could tell Jo she'd been working on it. She'd finish it...later.

Aly's cell rang. "Hey, you doing anything?" Whit asked. "Or are you still on tour guide duty? My late afternoon charter just cancelled. And sorry I was out when you stopped by the dock with Hannah's mom."

The sound of Whit's warm, deep voice lifted Aly's spirits. "I was about to take a walk with Dandelion and Beau, but I'm off the rest of the day. I convinced Hannah that she should spend some time with her mom—just the two of them—before Jo leaves tomorrow," she said. "I even got them a dinner reservation at the Outermost Inn."

No matter what Aly tried, when the three of them were together, conversations kept veering back to Aly and topics that Hannah didn't know or care about. One-on-one, Aly hoped, Hannah and her mom would really talk. Aly's goal was to have Jo see how happy Hannah was with the life she'd made for herself on the Island—and be happy for her.

"It won't be fancy-restaurant caliber, but I could make us pasta for dinner," Whit said.

"Twist my arm."

Half an hour later, Aly was on Whit's deck staring out at Tisbury Great Pond. As if someone had pulled a plug, the level of the pond had dropped six feet lower than it had been the day before, leaving a bathtub ring halfway up the marsh grasses.

"Whit? What happened to the pond?" she called.

"They opened the Cut this morning."

"They did what?"

Whit joined Aly outside. "Opened the Cut. See, there?" He pointed to a gap in the dunes. "They literally cut through the beach with a backhoe to drain the pond."

He wrapped his arms around Aly, and she leaned into the secure comfort of his chest. Lumberjack arms. Not her type, she smiled, remembering when they'd first met. Now, it seemed, so long ago. No way this was a rebound. What Aly felt was real. Just because Jo was right about some things didn't mean she was right about Whit.

"It's good for the pond," Whit continued. "The sea water flushes out the nitrogen buildup. And the oysters and the shellfish like it a bit salty." He gave her a squeeze. "Let's go down and see it. I'll throw in a line, maybe catch us a bluefish."

"Sure." Jo's comment about all the fish in the sea echoed in Aly's head. She had caught the fisherman, and he was a keeper.

"I'll go get my gear ready," Whit said, kissing the top of her head.

Aly pulled a cooler out from the pantry closet. "When did they start doing that? Opening the pond?" Aly asked, opening the refrigerator and peering inside.

"It goes back to colonial times, though they think the Wampanoag may have cut openings too. And it's not just Tisbury Great Pond—it's all the great ponds," he added, pulling out his tackle box. "They open naturally if the water gets high enough, especially if there's a big storm."

Where the pond had once lapped up to the marsh grasses at the end of Whit's yard was now a steep four-foot drop-off. Whit gave Aly a hand as she clambered down to the newly exposed shoreline. "They try to keep the date of the opening a secret," he said. "But it's usually around a full moon high tide."

"Why's it secret?" Aly asked, slinging the cooler's strap over her shoulder.

"Safety. If everyone knew, we'd get a huge crowd—teenagers, not to mention all the crazy yahoos who don't believe it when you tell them how dangerous it is," Whit said. "The Cut starts small—just the width of the backhoe shovel—but it widens within a few hours, and the water starts raging. It's like a flash flood. Last summer, some idiot was swimming and got caught in the current. Went right through and got swept way out into the ocean on the rip. Could've died. Luckily, he was OK, but it scared the hell out of everyone," Whit said. "But once the Cut settles down, it's fun to float from the pond to the ocean and vice versa on the tides. Not today, but tomorrow will be safe."

"How long does it stay open like that?"

"No telling. Weeks usually. Sometimes months."

As they walked along, the pebbles gradually changed to hard sand. "If you see any beached oysters, toss them back into the water," Whit said. "There's always a lot around here near the oyster floats. There's one." He picked up a juvenile oyster and flung it into the pond. "Not their fault that they get left high and dry."

Aly lifted a big crusty fellow with three tiny oysters stuck to its shell. "Look at this one," she said, showing it to Whit before chucking it back into the pond. "Guess they can't get themselves back to the water."

"Nope. No legs," said Whit. "Come October, it'll be time to scoop them up and eat them. Best oysters in the world," he added, bending down to rescue another beached oyster. "It's beautiful here in the fall. No crowds. Nicest time of the year, I think."

A shadow darkened Aly's mood. Come October, where would she be? Back in San Francisco at a new job, staring at a screen? Her "real life," Jo had told her. The thought depressed her. And what about Whit? She watched him, bending to rescue a baby oyster, and a tsunami of emotion rose within her. Would it be a mistake to stay on the Vineyard? To stay with Whit? What would happen when he left for St. John? A long-distance relationship wasn't ideal, but they could try. Like strands of seaweed caught in the surf, her feelings about Whit, about California, and about her career, mixed and tumbled and tangled in her head.

"You missed one there," Whit said, picking up an oyster at Aly's feet. He kissed her knee on the way up, and Aly felt a shimmer of lust, which was not going to help her figure things out. Not in the least. But she had plenty of time. They'd work it out. Somehow.

The shoreline along the row of dunes had been transformed. Where once the water had lapped up against the dune grass, there were sweeping, wide-open expanses of sand. Vast, flat sandbars rimmed the pond like islands, abstract curves in shades of tan and warm gray dotted with flocks of white seagulls. Crab Creek, which connected Tisbury Great Pond to Black Point Pond, its smaller sibling to the west, had shrunk to a serpentine squiggle barely knee deep.

"I can't believe how different everything looks," Aly said, holding her flip-flops in one hand as she waded through the creek.

They walked across the beach toward the Cut, where a twenty-yard-wide channel of rushing water had carved steep, twelve-foot-high cliffs through the sand. "Don't get too close," Whit warned. "It looks like it's still draining. See how the edge is caving in?" As he spoke, a foot of sandy cliff slid into the churning flow.

Aly stared, mesmerized, at the water rushing through the Cut. "Oh look, there goes a crab," she said, as the crustacean, flailing, was sucked out to sea.

"Not just crabs. Lots of baitfish too." Whit pointed to a wide delta of lighter water in the ocean. "After they get sucked out, they usually stay schooled up for a while. That brings in the bluefish. Let's see if we get lucky and catch ourselves a nice big one."

Aly spread out the beach blanket on the sand and stretched out to watch Whit fish. In one sweeping, fluid motion, he cast the lure far into the delta formed by the pond water. The movement was beautifully effortless, like the swooping dive of a shorebird. Aly sat down, opened a beer, and rested back on her elbows. All doubts fled her mind as she settled into a state of pure bliss. Jo was wrong. Aly was exactly where she belonged. This was her real life now. She thought back to the visit at Granny's. How easily her white lie about her parents could have unraveled. Underneath, the truth about who she was had started to itch like a too-small wool sweater, one that fit comfortably in San Francisco but was too hot and scratchy to wear here. It was time to tell Whit.

"Any bites?" she called.

"Patience, Aly," he called as he reeled in the line. "You can't expect to get a fish on your first cast."

"Why not?" She watched him cast a few more times and stood up to join him at the edge of the surf. Aly put up her hands like a megaphone. "Here, fishy fishy," she called.

"I don't think that helps," he laughed.

"It might. You never know." She turned back to face the sea. "Fishy fishy," she called again. "We want to catch you for our dinner dishy!"

Whit cast again, the lure flying impossibly far, landing with a distant splash. "Well, I'll be darned," he said, pulling the line tight, then furiously reeling. "I think I got one!"

🐑 🐑 🐑

Whit placed the plate in front of Aly with a flourish. "Spaghetti alla puttanesca—with-a the bluefish-a," he announced in a cheesy Italian accent. "My own recipe." He was pleased with this dish, a swirl of pasta topped with a spicy red fish sauce.

"Smells wonderful," Aly said, bending her head. A curl of hair fell enticingly against her cheek, and Whit, his heart swelling, reached down to tuck it behind her ear. A gorgeous evening surfcasting on the beach, freshly caught bluefish for dinner, a bottle of good wine—and Aly. Life didn't get better than this.

Whit refilled their glasses and sat down. "A lot of people say they don't like bluefish, but they've never eaten it really fresh." Whit watched as Aly took her first bite. "What do you think?"

"Mmm," she said. "Fantastic."

"I can't believe I haven't made bluefish for you before," he said, twirling pasta around his fork. "A lot of clients change their minds about keeping their fish, and I end up with a whole mess of filets to give away." He skewered a forkful of fish and took a bite. The tomato-y, garlic-y sauce was spicy and bold, with the acid pop of the capers and olives, enhancing the juicy mild fish. It was (if he said so himself) delicious.

"It's too bad you were out when I was in Menemsha yesterday. I wanted to introduce you to Hannah's mom."

"Back-to-back clients yesterday—not that I mind—including a last-minute sunset charter," he explained. "Two couples, pounding gin and tonics the whole time. I was worried about getting them off at the dock. At least they tipped well." He dipped a piece of bread in the sauce. "It's very nice of you to take Hannah's mom around, by the way."

"It's no problem. Jo and I are really close." Aly sipped her wine. "But I almost blew the cover on me and Chas with Granny. I'd stopped by the house on our way to the lighthouse to see if Granny would show us the interior. I'd forgotten that I'd told Jo I was dating you." She twirled pasta on her fork. "Luckily, Granny was off in Boston. But it's time to 'fess up to Granny. We've got to convince Chas. We should try to come up with a way to tell her that won't reflect poorly on him."

"The truth usually works," Whit said. "Granny's quite fond of you. I'll bet you no one in Chas's family has even read *War and Peace*, let alone sat around and discussed it intelligently with her."

"I'm fond of her too." Aly blew out a puff of air. "And you were right. I should never have agreed to play along. Even if Chas's motives were good."

"I have a suspicion she's already figured it out and is just stringing you two along. She's a sharp old bird."

Aly shook her head. "I don't think so. I tried to give back the pearls, and she wouldn't take them. If she knew, she wouldn't have let me keep them, would she?"

"My guess is it's some other game she's playing," Whit said. "She adores Chas but can be a bit spiteful toward the rest of the family. Or maybe she just wants you to have the pearls. You look beautiful in them."

"It doesn't feel right to keep them," Aly sighed.

"Then give them to Chas. He got you into this mess."

Aly washed the dirty dishes as Whit carried their wineglasses out to the deck. The nearly full moon reflected brilliantly in the still water. It cast an unearthly bluish light over the pond and trees and fields, so bright that he could see individual leaves fluttering in the warm breeze. Whit set the glasses down and stood at the rail looking out. To think he'd even considered renting the camp to vacationers. What a mistake that would've been.

Aly joined him a moment later. "You're so lucky to live here."

"I was just thinking that," he said, lowering himself onto the loveseat. He patted the cushion next to him.

"It was nice spending time with Hannah's mom, but I'm ready to be done playing tour guide." Aly snuggled under Whit's arm. "I told you she was like a mother to me when I was a kid, right?"

"I think so," Whit said. "What about your mom? Are the two of you close too?"

Whit felt Aly's body stiffen and wished he hadn't said anything. "Sorry I asked. I don't get along very well with my mother." Whit tried to remember the last time he'd talked to her. Could it have been Christmas? He hoped she was happy, living in France or Italy, or wherever she was.

Aly stared out at the moonlight on the pond. "There's something I need to tell you." She finished her glass and stood up. "I think I need more wine."

Heart sinking, Whit's mind spun through the possibilities. Aly had decided it was time to leave the Island and go back to San Francisco. Maybe Hannah's mom had made her realize that. He felt his insides tighten into a sick knot as he braced himself for the bad news. It was inevitable that she'd go back to California. The only real question was when.

Aly returned and sat down with a full glass of wine. Whit watched a rush of emotions cross her face in the moonlight. "It's about my mother," she said at last.

Whit's gut unclenched with relief as he waited for her to explain. And waited. Whatever this was about, it was a very big deal for Aly. "You don't have to tell me anything you don't want to. I'm sorry I asked."

She looked at Whit and pressed her lips together. "I do want to tell you. Jo wasn't just like a mother to me. I've been, well, kind of pretending that she *was* my mother. For a very long time."

"Pretending?"

"I tell people that my parents were professors at Middlebury. But my real mom was a high school dropout—she had me when she was a senior in high school." Aly stared out at the moonlight on the pond. "She had a drinking problem. And a holding-down-a-job problem. She didn't get along with her own mother. We got kicked out of my grandmother's house when I was little. I basically had to raise myself. I got pretty good at making Kraft macaroni and cheese and hot dogs." She snuggled into Whit's side. "As I got older, we started to fight. A lot. She blamed me for everything wrong with her life—her dead-end jobs, our crummy trailer, even her loser boyfriends." The tension seemed to leave Aly's body as she talked. "I don't mean to make her sound evil, she wasn't. But she was pretty bitter. And the alcohol didn't help. Things got so bad in high school that I moved in with Hannah's family. They made it seem like it was no big deal, but it was. Hannah's parents made sure I took AP classes and studied for the SATs. They took me to visit colleges, paid my application fees, and bought me all the stuff I needed for my freshman dorm. They even took me to college, just like real parents. My mom wouldn't—couldn't—have done any of that."

"You're lucky."

"I am." She sipped her wine. "Jo had given me a photo of all of us out on the lake on their boat. My first year roommate assumed they were my parents, so I let her. And everyone else too. I was all the way out in California. I wanted to, I don't know, make a fresh start."

"What about your father?"

"No idea who he was." Aly leaned her head back against the cushion. "Mom never told me. Maybe she didn't know, maybe he was some college boy at Middlebury. I still don't know why she had me. Except that once I was born, she wished she hadn't."

Whit squeezed her hand. "I'm sorry." It felt inadequate, but he didn't know what else to say. He saw a tear run down her cheek and gently wiped it away with a fingertip. His childhood had been its own kind of shitshow, but he'd never once thought that he was unwanted. Whit thought about his appallingly wealthy and narcissistic family. To one degree or another, all people rewrite their past. "None of that was your fault."

"I know that. I saw a really great therapist when I was in college. I get that my mom could love me and resent me at the same time. And how hard it must've been for her as a teenage mother on her own, then later to see me with all the opportunities she never had."

"She's still in Vermont?"

Aly shook her head. "Before I left for college, she moved to Texas with her dirtbag boyfriend. It was clear I wasn't invited—not that I wanted to go. I guess she still lives there. I don't know."

"We're not who our parents are, thank God. I don't care who your mom was," Whit said and gave Aly a gentle kiss. "It's you I want to be with."

🐑 🐑 🐑

The passenger line for the ferry began to move. "Safe travels," Aly said, hugging Jo. "It was great seeing you."

"I'm so glad I came. It was a wonderful visit. Aly was the best tour guide," Jo said to Hannah. "I still can't get over how beautiful it is here. All the beaches and the adorable little towns. And such good food. Thank you both so much." She wrapped both Aly and Hannah in a hug. "You come visit us in Vermont, Aly. It's been too long. And don't be surprised if I show up on your doorstep in San Francisco someday!"

Hannah handed her mother her rollaboard. "Thanks for coming, Mom."

"Glad to see you looking so well. I hope we'll see you at Thanksgiving this year?"

"We'll see. I may be hosting Friendsgiving again here."

"Well, think about it," Jo said and joined the stream of passengers walking up the ramp to the ferry. She stopped and turned at the top to give Aly and Hannah a final goodbye wave.

"I'm glad that's over," Hannah said as they walked back to the parking lot.

"Oh, Hannah. Dinner with your mom didn't go well?"

"Nope. All she wanted to talk about was you," Hannah said. "And nag me about finishing my degree so I can start my 'real career' like you. Hah." She turned to Aly. "I did what you said. I tried to talk to her about my wood crafting and mediation stuff, but she wasn't interested. I was even going to tell her who Lawrence really is."

"I'm so sorry."

"Not your fault—she won't accept that I'm satisfied with my life here. I guess she never will," Hannah said, shaking her head. "You two connect in a way that she and I don't. She came to see you, not me."

"Hannah. Your mom loves you."

"Of course she does. And I love her. That's not what I'm talking about. Mom and I have nothing in common. Except maybe you," Hannah said. "I'll always be a disappointment to her. Whatever," she sighed. "But she had a nice time. That's what matters. And now things can go back to normal. What did you and Whit do last night?"

"We went down to check out the Cut. That was pretty amazing. And Whit caught a big bluefish," Aly said. "Speaking of mothers, I told Whit about mine. It was harder than I thought, but I'm glad I did. He doesn't care."

"Why should he? But how'd she come up in conversation?"

"Well, we were talking about your mom, and he asked me about mine," Aly said. "I don't want to hide anything from him. You know that day I took your mom to Edgartown and stopped by Granny's house? I almost got caught in a lie."

"About dating Chas? You guys really need to come clean about that."

"That one too. But no—that my parents are professors at Middlebury. Your parents. You know," Aly said, and looked at her watch. "Oh, hey. Can you wait a minute? I want to stop by the bookstore to see if they have a book I want. It's a beach read set here on the Island about a goatscaper and a rich city girl. Chas's recommendation."

"I'll go pick us up an apple fritter at the Black Dog Bakery. I'm in need of comfort carbs."

After her bookstore visit, Aly opened the passenger door and climbed in. "They just sold the last copy of the book I wanted," she said, clipping her seat belt. "But I got one for Whit," she added, pulling *Whaling Wives of Martha's Vineyard* from her bag to show to Hannah. "He's going to love this. Hey, did I tell you he's taking me clamming later today?"

Hannah handed Aly the bakery bag, started the truck, and pulled out of the parking lot and into the ferry traffic at the Five Corners intersection, drumming her fingers on the steering wheel as she waited for the car ahead of her at the stop sign to figure out how to make a left turn.

Aly pulled off a chunk of apple fritter. "Well, with your mom gone, you'll get to see more of Lawrence. And I can go back on your painting crew." Hannah didn't respond. Aly looked over. Hannah's face was stony, her lips pressed tightly together. "Are you still thinking about that dinner with your mom? I'm really sorry it didn't work out." She waited, watching Hannah's hands tighten on the wheel. "Come on, Hannah. Talk to me."

"It's not the dinner," Hannah finally said. "I've been thinking about what you said. About you 'borrowing' my parents."

"OK," Aly said, drawing her eyebrows together. "What about it?"

Hannah frowned. "I mean, I knew that's what you told people in college. But you never stopped? Wow."

"I didn't really think about it," Aly said, taken aback. "Habit, I guess."

"Kevin must've known."

Aly shook her head. "I told him—and the rest of my friends—that my parents had passed away. Kevin never pressed for details. I guess it was easier that way." Aly paused, realizing the only person she'd ever told about her real mother was Whit.

"That's weird, Aly," Hannah said, finally getting through the intersection. "And it feels wrong. Not just the lying. So maybe it's irrational, but I'm, like, really upset." Hannah ran a hand through her hair. "And the way you and my mom have stayed close all these years? It got me thinking again that Mom wished you had been her daughter instead of me." She blew out a puff of air. "You had straight As, near-perfect SAT scores, and got admitted to Berkeley. Me, I could barely read."

"That's ancient history, Hannah. It doesn't matter. Not anymore."

Hannah cut Aly a hard, cold look.

"It does to me."

Hannah barely spoke a word to Aly the rest of the way home, dropping her off at the house with a curt "Maybe you'll want to stay at Whit's again tonight" before driving off to meet Lawrence. Aly sat down on the grass and pulled Dandelion into her lap. She felt awful that Hannah was upset, but she didn't know what she could say to make things better. Hopefully, Lawrence would talk some sense into Hannah, and everything would go back to the way it was.

"How about a walk?" Aly asked the lamb. "We could see if there are still some blueberries on the bushes. Hannah would like that."

Aly changed into long pants tucked into socks for tick-proofing, added a spritz of bug spray, and, with the dog and lamb for company, headed out and across the fields. Reaching the old homestead, she walked over to the boulder. Spreading her arms, she hugged it, resting her cheek against the gray granite surface. She felt nothing but the rough, hard stone, no vibration, no tingling. The rock, having sent its message, chose to keep its silence.

The July flush of blueberries had passed, and Aly found fewer ripe berries. Most had been eaten by birds or were on their way to becoming teeny-tiny blueberry raisins. Still, the rhythm of picking cast its spell, with only the sound of Dandelion's grazing to break the silence. A happy childhood memory, buried deep, came to the surface. Aly was little, and her mother had taken her blueberry picking at one of those pick-your-own roadside farms. The berries there were big and fat, the supermarket kind. Even though they weren't supposed to, she and her mom had eaten as many as they wanted as they picked, probably so she wouldn't have to pay much. Her mom had been laughing and so pretty: blond and smiling, making a game of seeing how many berries they could hold between their lips, blueberry teeth, before gobbling them up.

Aly's mind wandered further into her childhood, picking out the few good memories with her mother like ripe berries. Swimming in chilly Lake Champlain, then stretching out their towels to warm up on the pretty black stone beaches. A visit to Shelburne Farms to visit the goats and chickens and sheep with one of the few nice boyfriends, the kind who would stick around for a few months. Picnics on the quad at Middlebury College, eating leftovers from the dining hall when her mom worked in food service and was still young and pretty enough to be mistaken for a student.

Aly's teenage mother had been a child with a child. Her mom loved her as much as she could. There was no fault, no blame. For them both, just an unlucky roll of the dice.

Her container slowly filled, inch by inch. Aly crouched to tie her shoelace and noticed more blueberry bushes. Barely reaching her knee, they were laden with late berries, even tinier, darker, and shinier than those on the big bushes. This time, she would make blueberry jam, maybe adding a bit of lemon and a touch of cinnamon, like a blueberry pie. She knew she could do it. All she had to do was try.

🐑 🐑 🐑

The morning sunshine had given way to clouds. Back home, Aly filled the glass bowl with blueberries and tried calling Hannah, but Lawrence had answered Hannah's phone, shaking Aly's confidence that Hannah was getting over being upset. After refilling Beau's water bowl, Aly folded the laundry that had been in the dryer and packed her overnight bag to take to Whit's. It didn't make any sense. If Hannah had been OK with Aly's little white lie—really, that's all it was—back when she was in college, why did she care so much now? Whit understood. He didn't think it was a big deal. Why should Hannah?

She drove to Whit's and unpacked her clothes, putting them into the bottom drawer—now her drawer—in the bedroom dresser. Climbing onto the kitchen stepstool, she pulled down the big strainer insert that went inside the pasta pot, cheered up by the idea of the afternoon's outing to dig clams with Whit. Hopefully, they'd find enough to make both stuffies—stuffed clams—and pasta with white clam sauce. And she'd make a wild blueberry tart for dessert.

The tires of Whit's truck crunched in the drive. "Ready to go?" he called to Aly from the truck window. "Tide's coming in. We should get a move on."

Aly slipped on her flip-flops and hopped into the truck. "Will this work to hold the clams?" she asked, holding up the strainer.

"A bit big, but sure. Robby's bringing a couple of extra pairs of dishwasher gloves. They help keep your fingers from getting cut up." Whit was in a talkative mood, telling Aly about the day's charter with a family from DC that went south when the two kids' lines crossed and both lost their fish, starting an argument that lasted the rest of the four-hour trip. "Long day. I'm ready for some peace and quiet. Here's the turn," he said, making a right onto an unmarked dirt road and bumping down to a small parking area on the far corner of Nashaquitsa Pond.

Bare-chested and deeply tanned, Whit's drummer friend Robby was already out digging in thigh-high water. "Hey guys," he called. "Grab some gloves and come out. I've got a good spot here."

"Oysters are the easiest shellfish to get; they just sit on top of the sand," Robby explained as they waded out. "Steamers—soft shell clams—are the hardest since they dig themselves deep if they sense you coming after them. Bay scallops swim away. But quahogs don't move; they just sit there a few inches under the sand."

Aly regretted not having put on her bathing suit under her clothes. While Whit's long arms meant he could dig without getting his torso wet, Aly had to roll up a sleeve and plunge her shoulder underwater to reach down into the sand.

"If you don't want to get so wet, you can also dig with your feet," Robby said. "And if you hit a clam, call Mr. Long-arms over to get it for you."

As Whit and Robby chatted about mutual friends in the local music scene, Aly changed to the foot technique, finding two rocks and one empty shell before locating a clam. She felt peaceful there, staring across the pond at the boats bobbing on their moorings as her feet dug around in the sand. If talking to Lawrence didn't help with Hannah, maybe Whit could try—or tell her what to do. That thought made her feel better.

Her toes wrapped around a smooth, roundish shape. "Here's another, I think," she called to Whit. "Can I borrow your arm again?"

Aly's cell phone buzzed in her pocket. She pulled it from its Ziploc bag, careful not to drop it in the pond. Shit. The message was from JC, Kevin's best friend. *Hey Aly, I hope you're doing OK,* she read. *Hi JC,* she wrote back. *What's up?* She watched the bubble dots turn into words. *I know what happened, and I'm sorry. But Kevin needs to talk to you. He says he can't reach you. Please call him.* Aly stared at the phone. She'd blocked Kevin, of course. She didn't want to talk to him. Finally, she typed, *I'll think about it. Gotta go.* Quickly, she turned her phone off as if it would give her a disease and slid it back into its bag.

She didn't have to talk to Kevin just because he wanted to talk to her. Or do what he wanted. Ever again. Still, the message lingered like the taste of a bad oyster. She'd gotten over Kevin. He needed to get over her.

A dozen big, fat quahogs later, Aly was back at Whit's, lighting the candles on the table as Whit ladled out the spaghetti alle vongole. "Voilà," he announced, placing a bowl in front of her.

She breathed in the briny, buttery, lemon-y aroma and sighed with pleasure. "Turns out, my idea to send Hannah and her mom out for dinner together was an utter failure," Aly said, digging into the pasta. "It's like we're back in high school, with her mom telling her she should be more like me. Jo still thinks Hannah should finish college and start a 'real career.'" Aly twirled the spaghetti with her fork. "It's so frustrating. Hannah's made a really good life for herself here. She's happy. Why can't her mom see that?"

Whit refilled their glasses. "Think about it, Aly. Hannah's mom is an academic surrounded by a bunch of overprivileged, overachieving Middlebury students. That's going to shape—I'd say, warp—her idea of success."

"I guess so." The pasta tasted as good as it smelled. Not that she could tell the difference between a clam she'd dug herself and one she'd bought at Larsen's. "But worst of all, now Hannah's all upset with me too."

"Why? You did Hannah a big favor taking her mom around."

"I said something about 'borrowing' her parents, and she totally tilted."

"She didn't know about that?"

"A long time ago," Aly said, jabbing a piece of clam. "She was fine with it then. But now, she's all mad or hurt or something." She rolled her eyes. "I feel terrible, but she's being ridiculous. It was a little white lie. Nothing to do with her. And hardly even a lie. They were my parents in all the ways that mattered. But now

Hannah is all upset, saying she feels like her mom wishes that I were her daughter instead of her."

Whit paused and looked at her. "That's not ridiculous, Aly. That's some therapy-grade stuff you're talking about. You of all people should know what it's like to feel that you weren't wanted by your mom."

"No comparison, Whit, to the shitshow I had growing up," Aly said, starting to feel annoyed.

"And finding out that you've been 'borrowing' her parents your whole adult life? I can see how that would upset her." Whit broke off a piece of bread and dipped it into the sauce. "I don't know her mom, but Hannah could be right about Jo's wishing that you were her daughter. Whether or not you intended to, you put Hannah in the shade. Still do."

"So, you're saying it's my fault."

"You tell me. Are you sure you didn't play a role?"

"A role? Back in high school, Hannah was glad I was around to get her parents off her back. Thrilled, in fact."

Whit leaned back, frustratingly calm and reasonable, as if she were a child who had to be taken step by step through a complicated math problem. "But I assume," he added, "that you were fine stepping into the spotlight?"

"I didn't ask for it. I owed it to Jo to succeed after everything she did for me. Which she absolutely did not have to do. I was a guest in their house, remember. Not family," Aly said, her annoyance ballooning into anger. "I didn't grow up like you and Hannah with dinner on the table at six every night and no worries that you were going to get evicted or find your mom in jail for drunk driving. Or that you'd wake up with some gross guy your mother had picked up in a bar in his underwear in your kitchen."

"I get that, Aly." Whit reached across the table for her hand, which Aly moved to her lap. "But the flip side is the impact on Hannah," he said. "I'm not saying you meant to hurt her, but it sounds like you did by stepping in—from Hannah's perspective—as the daughter her parents wished they'd had. Just because an injury is old and buried deep doesn't mean it's healed. I imagine seeing you and Jo together dug all that up."

"Whit, I just spent three days trying to get Hannah and her mom to talk to each other. Not that it worked, but I should get some credit for trying, shouldn't I? I can't believe you're on Hannah's side."

"I can't believe you don't see it."

Aly knew she was being a drama queen, but she didn't care. She'd had enough. Leaving her half-eaten dinner on the table, she stood up, went to the bedroom, and pulled out her overnight bag. With a sigh, Whit pushed back from the table. Leaning against the doorjamb, he watched her pack.

"What are you doing?"

Aly narrowed her eyes. She didn't get mad often, but when she did, it was a hot flame that burned inside, one that reasonable words could not extinguish. "What does it look like? I'm leaving."

🐑 🐑 🐑

Aly was straightening the blue-striped seersucker bedspread when Chas knocked on the door of the guest bedroom. "Come in," she said, giving the pillow a final fluff.

"Good morning. I've made you a cappuccino," Chas said, handing her a cup.

"Wonderful," she said, taking a sip as the scent of coffee and cinnamon filled her nose. "Thank you again for letting me stay here. And coming to pick me up last night."

Aly had stomped off from her fight with Whit fuming. What did he want her to do? Apologize to Hannah for meeting Jo's expectations, for doing well in school, and earning a six-figure salary in San Francisco? For borrowing her parents? Hannah had been perfectly fine with that—and knew it had zero to do with her. Chas had been begging her for weeks to come for a visit and stay a few days in town. Given the way Whit was acting, Aly was happy to take him up on it.

"I'm delighted to have you. I'm just sorry about the circumstances," Chas said, walking over to the window. "I almost lost that view of Edgartown Harbor. The place across the street wanted to put on a hideous big addition and a pool house."

Aly joined Chas at the window. Clad in immaculate white clapboard and topped with a widow's walk, the neighbor's stately Greek Revival house was lovely, graciously and generously proportioned with large windows, black-painted shutters, and an impressive portico. "But that house is already huge," she said.

Chas nodded. "It's a shame. The new money coming in just doesn't appreciate the history and architecture here in Edgartown," he huffed. "Fortunately, the construction required a zoning variance. And the architect had completely ignored the historic commission's guidelines. The neighbors and I sent them back to the drawing board. Permanently, I hope." He sipped his cappuccino. "This morning, I thought we'd drop in on Granny. She's been dying to see you. This evening, it's the Regatta Ball at the yacht club. I need to make an appearance, but if you'd rather, we could eat at a restaurant."

"Regatta Ball? It sounds fancy! But I didn't pack a ball gown," she said and smiled.

"No ball gowns in the summer! It's cocktail attire. Think navy blazers and Lily Pulitzer, but we can put you in something more flattering than that. I'd love to take you shopping again," Chas said. "Unless you'd like to swing by Hannah's to pick up your ivory dress?"

"I think Hannah would rather not see me for a couple of days. I was going to stay with Whit, but..."

"I know—it was inevitable that you and Whit would have a little lovers' quarrel at some point. He sees things in black and white, right and wrong. You and I, we see gray, like our little ruse."

"About that," Aly said, "don't you think we should 'fess up?"

"When the time is right, we'll break up. And I'll tell Granny that I'm gay. I promise." Chas looked at Aly. "But back to dear Whit. He can be stubborn and pig-headed—and, unfortunately, often right. But he'll come around. I'm sure Hannah will too." He looked at Aly. "I won't press for details, but you know I'm here if you want to talk. And not that you've asked for my advice, but anytime I've found myself in a tiff with someone, dear Granny would always trot out that old adage about 'walking a mile in someone's shoes.' In the case of Whit and his smelly sneakers, that's a rather appalling thought," he chuckled. "I'll make us an omelet for breakfast. Why don't you go pick some flowers for Granny. We'll head out after we eat."

"Sounds perfect."

"Almost ready, my Cinderella, for the ball?" Chas called from the living room. "I hope you don't mind. This is the ideal opportunity to show you off."

"Not at all. Just give me a minute," Aly said, the beginnings of social anxiety nibbling at the edges of her confidence. She finished pinning up her hair and added a touch more lipstick. After trying on what seemed like every dress in Edgartown, they'd settled on a demure navy halter dress with white piping and a nautical vibe. "I've forgotten how to do makeup." She put on Granny's pearls as a finishing touch and spun in a circle for Chas in the living room. "Will this do?"

Chas, natty in a pale-blue blazer and paisley ascot (of all things), raised his eyebrows approvingly. "Indeed, it will. Quite flattering."

"You sure I shouldn't have bought that lime green and hot pink Lily Pulitzer with the ruffled sleeves?"

Chas rolled his eyes. "That was ghastly. I can't believe you let the salesperson convince you to try that one on. A G&T before we go? Or a glass of wine? Or my specialty, a Chum Bucket?"

Aly laughed. "Chum Bucket?"

"My own creation. Gin, Campari, green Chartreuse, maraschino liqueur, and lime. It's quite delicious."

"Sold. One Chum Bucket, please."

Settled on the loveseat on Chas's side porch with their drinks, they looked over his rose garden toward the harbor. Chas filled Aly in on the history of the club (established in 1905 to bring together those interested in "yachting, sailboat racing, seamanship, and competition in the highest Corinthian spirit"—that is, gentlemanly sportsmanship), its activities (regattas, sailing programs for kids and teens, tennis at the club's courts near Eel Pond), and its role in Edgartown society (to facilitate the social lives of the Edgartown elite).

"There will be a lot of eyes on you. We're a rather exclusive little group, and we don't see a lot of newcomers. But don't worry. I won't abandon you. And you've already earned Granny's stamp of approval. She will have told everyone about you."

Despite Chas's assurances and the Chum Bucket, Aly's anxiety level had climbed. Weeks of hanging out in the comfortably casual company of Hannah and Whit had left her feeling unprepared for social interaction with "the elite."

"Just ask about sailing, tennis, or both, and you'll be just fine," Chas said and finished his drink. "Ready to go? No pumpkin carriage needed. We can walk."

Jutting out into the harbor on its own pier, the Edgartown Yacht Club sat anchored at the end of Main Street like a docked ship. Tastefully modest in scale, the clubhouse took advantage of its premier location with large windows on three sides, offering a 270-degree view of the harbor. Inside, walls paneled in polished teak gleamed like the inside of a yacht. Above the windows, yacht club burgees brought color to the room, and mounted half-hull ship models and giant paintings of schooners under full sail added to the appropriately nautical décor. A local band, the Dukes of Circuit Avenue, promised a lively time once the G&Ts had loosened up the crowd.

The club members were as buffed and polished as their yachts: clean-shaven men in navy blazers with gold buttons and sailing-motif ties, the women with their tan, tennis-toned arms and legs in brightly preppy print dresses, their sleek blond hair coiffed in a neat bob or shining updo. Aly tucked in one of her escaping curls, wishing she'd taken the time to tame her hair into a tidier French twist.

Chas leaned over and whispered in Aly's ear, "I know. It's like a giant pack of golden retrievers. And about as bright, some of them."

"That's not very nice," Aly smiled and sipped her cocktail, poured strong by the bartender. She'd have to pace herself if she wanted to make it through the evening.

"It's true. Purebred and pedigreed, just like me. Ready to enter the fray?"

Aly braced herself for an evening of chitchat with perfect strangers. She paused to admire a glass cabinet full of polished silver trophies and asked, "Do you ever race?"

"Not since I was a wee tyke. Not that I cared much about winning. But it was quite fun to sail my little Opti around Cape Poge Bay," Chas said, pointing out a framed photo of small, somewhat bathtub-shaped sailboats tacking around a buoy. "Have you seen them? Quite adorable. Like a flock of little ducklings sailing through the harbor. Whit was always the better sailor, of course." He looked around the room. "Oh, there's Granny holding court over there in the corner. We should go pay our respects. Then we can hit the seafood buffet. You must be starving."

Sitting upright in her chair, Granny waved them over with an imperious hand. "Chas—and Aly. I was just telling Donna here all about you."

"Bragging about you, to be more accurate," said the woman, with perfectly curated blond hair and a creaseless face. She was unfortunately and unattractively attired in the same ruffled pink-and-green monstrosity that Aly had tried on earlier.

The woman opened her pale-blue eyes wide. "A degree from Berkeley. You must be a smart girl," she said in a way that didn't sound like a compliment. "Fascinating. Never expected our Chas to have to go so far afield as California to find," she paused with a sidelong glance at Granny, "a girlfriend. So, Newport Yacht Club—or San Francisco?"

"Neither, actually. I only sail a little—Sunfish, mostly. But I enjoy sailing."

"Aly's from the East Coast. Vermont, to be exact," Granny said, defending Aly against criticism. "Her parents are professors in the Russian Department at Middlebury. I'm sure we can lure her back East. The young people do like to go off for a bit of adventure, but they always come home."

"Not my Julia. She wouldn't consider living anywhere but Boston," the woman said with a nearly imperceptible turn of her shoulders that indicated un-yacht-clubbed Aly was no longer of interest. "Did I tell you that she and James just bought the sweetest little house in Back Bay? I wanted them to buy on Beacon Hill near us, of course, but they would have their own way."

Taking her arm, Chas said their farewells to Granny and led Aly toward the buffet table, pretty much overflowing with seafood: oysters and clams on the half-shell, enormous cocktail shrimp, stone crab claws, and tiny lobster rolls. Chas's Cinderella comment was more apropos than he knew. She was an imposter, a low-class girl pretending to be a princess. Coming out of Granny's mouth, the white lie about her parents scraped raw where it once sat like a cozy blanket over the truth. Not only had she deceived Granny and Chas, but the lie had torn an ugly rift with Hannah—and Whit.

She yearned to be with Whit on his deck, watching the pond as he serenaded her on his guitar, learning the lyrics to the songs in his repertoire so she could sing along. Or in Hannah's backyard, playing with Dandelion as she chatted with Hannah after a long day of painting houses. Aly wasn't like Chas, seemingly comfortable anywhere with anyone. She had finally found the place in the world where she felt truly herself and happy. And she had gone and messed everything up.

🐑 🐑 🐑

Chas's kitchen table had been converted into Auction Central. Aly picked up a paddle and neatly inked "27" with a black Sharpie on both sides and added it to the stack. Twenty-seven down, 182 to go.

"You're doing me a huge favor," said Chas from his laptop. "I can't believe Kaila ordered auction paddles without numbers. That's what you get for relying on interns! And I still haven't heard back from the assistants for Meg Ryan, Jake Gyllenhaal, *or* Emily Blunt," he added, running a hand through his blond hair. "I really don't like to put an item up for auction unless it's been confirmed by the people who run their schedules. Why do I put myself through this every year?"

"Because it's for a good cause?"

"Of course. One of the best. And most of our celebs are quite wonderful. Seth Meyers is hosting again, and this year, both David Letterman and Larry David got right back to me," Chas said. "I do hope that Floaty-Boaty Picnic with Amy Schumer and Chris Fischer does well. Brilliant idea of yours, by the way, to move that onto Whit's boat. We haven't offered anything like that before. And it was very generous of Lawrence to donate a painting *and* a studio tour." He stood up and stretched. "I'm feeling a tad peckish. Shall I go get us some lunch from Rosewater Market? I love their cauliflower Reuben."

After Chas left, Aly uncapped her marker and went back to work on the number-the-paddle project. The evening at the Yacht Club had been a tedious exercise in small talk about sailing and tennis. It was about as far as you could get from the sparkling conversations that would take place at the dinners Chas was auctioning off. All evening, Aly's thoughts kept returning to Whit, wishing she were with him instead of politely listening to the latest infraction of the tennis-whites-only rule (pink socks) and wondering whether he was missing her as much as she missed him.

And then there was Hannah. What a stupid, stupid fight.

Aly got up and poured herself a glass of iced tea. Hannah was hurting, and that wasn't OK. And Whit. He'd taken Hannah's side. Could he be right? Was Aly to blame for how Hannah felt? Picking up paddle thirty-four, she decided to take Chas's advice, replaying the memories from her childhood, only this time through Hannah's eyes. She watched herself come into Hannah's home and become the focus of Jo's attention, eagerly bringing every good grade and test score to Jo seeking her praise. Aly had been like a dog pushing its head under its owner's hand to be petted, doing everything she could to win Jo's approval. The dinner table conversations night after night for literally years focused on the pros and cons of the colleges Aly might apply to, as Hannah sat silent. Staying at home while Jo and Aly took trips all around the country to visit schools—Tufts, Williams, UChicago, UNC, William & Mary, Carnegie Mellon, University of Virginia, Berkeley, Stanford.

Through Hannah's eyes, Aly saw the love flowing like a river diverted from Hannah to Aly, and like Hannah, Aly reached the sad conclusion that Jo had wished that Aly had been her real daughter. And Aly, too needy, too oblivious, and too self-absorbed, hadn't seen it.

Whit was right. Aly hadn't been a passive participant. She had, through her actions—intentional or not—usurped Hannah's place in her mother's affections. With a shock of dismay, Aly realized that she'd been the root cause of Hannah's estrangement from her mom. And still was. How it must have hurt Hannah to learn that Jo was still cheering for Aly and her San Francisco life, applauding her successes, putting in sharp relief what a failure (in Jo's eyes) Hannah had been. It was deeply wrong to have injured Hannah, who had never been anything but the best of friends to Aly, then and now.

Aly put down her Sharpie, feeling sick at heart. But there was more. Jo's advice was more than advice. It was control, shaping Aly into "the perfect daughter." Aly had let it happen. More than that, she had *wanted* it. Even if it meant pushing Hannah aside. How messed up was that?

But it made sense: Achieving Jo's goals was a way to keep herself safe and secure and loved. It wasn't that Aly was weak or dumb or amoral. It was a reaction to the trauma of the unstable life with her real mother. Aly leaned back in her chair, floored to realize that Kevin offered her the same thing: love and security in exchange for being the girlfriend he wanted. And in the process, Aly let herself be convinced—brainwashed—that whatever Jo and Kevin wanted was what she wanted for herself.

🐑 🐑 🐑

Aly pushed the bowl of wild blueberries across the kitchen table closer to Hannah. "I'm so sorry. I never meant to hurt you. But I did."

Hannah took a few berries and popped them in her mouth. "I'll be honest, Mom's visit plus learning you're still 'borrowing' my parents dug up a lot of old feelings and resentments. But I talked it over with Lawrence. I'm feeling OK now."

"But what I did, after your family was so generous to take me in, being so needy and selfish…"

"Was totally understandable, given where you were coming from with your mom," said Hannah. "When you moved in, it was like getting the sister I never had. And my parents got the smarty-pants daughter they wanted. You needed my mom; she needed you to feel like a success as a mother, and I stepped out of the way. I don't resent you for that."

"But Hannah…" Aly's revelation about her role in Hannah's estrangement from her mother had tilted Aly's world.

"Let me finish. My mom acted in her own self-interest. You see her as this magic fairy godmother, but she's not. Lawrence's mom is the same. His success means she gets to brag and trot him out at her cocktail parties," Hannah said. "My mom is too narrow-minded to see that there are other paths in life other than the one she set you on. That's not your fault. Sure, I was jealous, but you made her happy. I could never do that."

"This can't be how things end up between you two."

"I'm a disappointment to her and always will be," Hannah said. "It's how she is. And I'm OK with it. I love her, and she loves me. But that doesn't mean she's proud of me."

"Maybe you should invite your parents here for Thanksgiving?" Aly asked, grasping for some straw of possible reconciliation. "Don't you always host a big Friendsgiving thing?"

"Right. Like they'd ever come." Hannah glanced at her watch. "We should get going. That house isn't going to paint itself."

🐑 🐑 🐑

Aly's world had righted itself. Generous Hannah held no grudge, and when Aly had shown up on *Noepe*, apologetic and contrite, Whit had forgiven her with a kiss. The final push to finish painting Blueberry Cottage was done, and Grand Illumination, with its glowing lanterns, was as magical as promised (despite the crowds that reminded Aly of New York City sidewalks at rush hour). But what Aly was most excited about came next on the summer calendar, the annual Martha's Vineyard Agricultural Society Livestock Show and Fair.

The sheep showmanship event was on Saturday afternoon. Aly had woken that morning a bundle of nerves. Arriving early, she distracted herself by wandering around the Fair, first with a visit to the animal barn, where Dandelion seemed more than content in her stall next to the baby pigs, and to the fiber tent, where she watched a woman spin a pile of clean, carded wool into thick yarn, which she tried to convince Aly wasn't so hard once you got the hang of it. (Next year's project: Dandelion-wool knitted scarves?) The exhibits in the Ag Hall were amazing: the handmade quilts hanging from the rafters, the photographs and paintings, and the most exquisitely carved hawk she'd ever seen. No surprise that a blue ribbon hung from Hannah's lamp, stunningly crafted as it was from strips of translucent wood woven and twisted with mathematical precision into a geometric shape that echoed nature's Fibonacci spirals. As she wandered among the exhibits, Aly began to make plans for next year. Maybe she could enter Jo's

Cinna-Love Buns in adult baking—or a flower arrangement in the antique chamber pot Hannah used for ripening avocados in the "Container not originally used for flowers" category?

"There you are," Whit said, coming from behind Aly as she admired a life-sized crocheted woman in a kerchief with crocheted chicken in her lap. "That's Nancy Luce, the famous chicken lady of West Tisbury."

Aly reached up on her toes to kiss Whit. "That must have taken someone months and months to make."

"Winters are long here. Ready for the fried dough you keep talking about?"

Aly glanced at her watch. "Sure. Then I'll have to get ready for my event. I'm so nervous!"

Whit put his arm around her shoulder. "You'll do great. Don't worry."

Twenty minutes later, the fried dough they'd shared, which had tasted deliciously bad for her as she'd remembered—hot, crispy, and chewy, with powdered sugar melting into the surface in sweet little mountains—now sat in her belly like a hard lump, rendered indigestible by anxiety. Gathering her courage, she entered the show ring with Dandelion. The lamb was perfection: fleece washed (with Woolite to preserve the lanolin) and brushed; hooves trimmed and polished; ears, armpits, and rear end cleaned; a dab of Vaseline on her nose; and a pink ribbon around her neck.

Aly had been practicing sheep showmanship (learned from YouTube videos) on and off for weeks. Dandelion was a star at walking, harnessless, with Aly's hand under her chin to guide her, and standing for the judge with her four feet square, like the legs of a table. The third element, bracing, which was supposed to showcase the sheep's musculature, hadn't been going so well. Rather than push against Aly's knee, Dandelion tended to hop backwards. That they'd have to fake. Following the instructions in the fair booklet, Aly had memorized the sheep facts she might be asked: Breed: Corriedale; terminology for male and female sheep: ram and ewe; Dandelion's weight: 29 pounds; her diet: grass, clover, and other pasture plants; her sire and dam: Rambo and Maisy; and her date of birth: March 16.

Aly checked out the other entrants, a bit taken aback that none of the other participants appeared older than fourteen—the 4-H kids would be stiff competition. In the barn judging, Dandelion had taken a disappointing third place behind the lambs from Whiting Farm and Slough Farm. Showmanship was their last chance to redeem themselves and win a coveted blue ribbon. (She'd bailed on the Mary-had-a-little-lamb costume contest idea when she realized how many cotton balls she'd need to make herself a credible sheep costume. And her sewing skills weren't up to stitching a lamb-size shepherdess outfit.) Beau, however, had killed it in Saturday's dog show, winning not only the Best-in-Breed competition but Obedience as well.

Whit, Hannah, and Lawrence sat in the stands to watch Aly's performance. The judge, a lanky farmer with a weather-beaten face and broad southeastern Massachusetts accent, instructed the handlers to walk their lambs around the ring. Head held high, Dandelion strolled on her dainty hooves like a runway model, and Aly relaxed.

"Now stop and set your lambs," the judge instructed. Holding one hand under Dandelion's chin, Aly bent over to move her hind legs and then her front legs into position, nice and square with her weight balanced. So far, so good. "What we're looking for here," the judge explained to the audience, "is both the presenter's skill in showing the lamb to its best advantage as well as the lamb itself: musculature, frame, soundness, and wool."

The judge approached Aly and Dandelion, casting a critical eye over the lamb. "Nice lamb. What's under the wool?"

Aly gasped. "Under the wool?"

"Just kidding. It's a joke. A little barnyard humor," said the judge. "Now, please brace."

Aly moved her knee to rest it against Dandelion's chest. The lamb hopped back several steps and bumped into the preteen handler behind her. Startled, Dandelion leapt into the air and began to bound around the ring. Like a chain reaction, the other lambs took off too, and soon the ring was full of shouting kids chasing their lambs.

The judge shook his head. "Control your sheep," he said, barely suppressing a grin.

Aly could hear the laughter from the watching crowd. This was worse than she could possibly have imagined. She tried to corner Dandelion, but the ring had no corners, and before she knew it,

Dandelion had found a gap by the gate, squeezed through, and dashed under the stands.

"Lamb on the loose!" called a woman in the audience.

Aly fumbled to unlatch the gate where Whit stood waiting. "No blue ribbon today, I guess," he grinned.

Aly was not amused. "Come on, did you see where she went?"

"That way," Whit said, pointing to the Ag Hall. "Don't worry, Hannah and Lawrence went after her. They'll catch her—or somebody will."

As they jogged past the fiber tent, Aly caught a glimpse of white disappearing into the crowd amid laughter and distant shouts of "Did you see that?" and "Was that a sheep?" She grabbed Whit's arm. "There she is. Come on, let's go!"

They sped up to a run. From somewhere near the food booth, Aly heard Hannah shouting, "Dandelion, come here, now!" The lamb might think she was a dog, but she didn't respond like one. Aly regretted giving up on teaching Dandelion "come." Now, the entire fair was a playground for a giant game of keep away.

"Your sheep's over here," she heard someone shout from the amusement area.

"Grab her if you can," Aly yelled back, and she and Whit changed direction, dodging fairgoers as they ran past the carousel and the kiddie games. They stopped in front of the Ferris wheel and looked around. No sign of Dandelion.

Aly's phone rang. "Any luck?" asked Hannah.

"Not yet," said Aly as the flow of people moved around her.

"I almost had her, but she ducked between the pie stand and Bobby B's. Lawrence is headed over to the stage area, and I'm keeping an eye out here. I had no idea she was so fast—or slippery!"

"We're over by the rides. Should I have Whit go get Beau? Oh! Wait! I think I see her!" Aly shrieked as she spotted a quick-moving flash of white heading toward the Ag Hall. She knew she looked like a crazy person running through the crowd yelling "Dandelion! Cookies!" but she didn't care. Shouts and laughter told Aly that Dandelion had run inside the hall. There, surrounded by a smiling crowd, stood Dandelion, contentedly munching the blue-ribbon-winning dahlia.

"Lady, is this your lamb?"

🐑 🐑 🐑

Like a swan among the motor yachts and enormous fishing boats, the Hinckley Daysailer was a lovely thing, forty-two feet of polished wood with a glossy navy-blue hull. Whit watched Aly climb from the tender onto *Stella Blue*. In her white shorts and striped t-shirt, she looked as if she'd been born to the yachting life.

The billowing sails filled, and they were underway. Aly leaned against the varnished teak of the cockpit and gazed up the mast. "*Stella Blue* is such a pretty sailboat," she said. "I love the way the hull swoops up in the stern."

"My father likes his pretty toys," Chas said. "Pretty boats, pretty women. Of course, I like pretty things too," he added, with a wistful look at Lawrence. "It really is too bad you're not gay."

Hannah squeezed Lawrence's knee. "I'm good with that," she smiled, looking decidedly un-nautical in an Up Island Automotive t-shirt splattered with yellow paint. "Where are we going?"

"Nice wind today, so I thought I'd take us to Cuttyhunk. What do you think, First Mate Whit, shall we put *Stella Blue* through her paces?"

"That's a fair haul, Captain Chas," replied Whit, whose mood was as fine as the weather. He deserved a day off from work. They all did. And what better way to spend it?

"Let's see how it goes," said Chas. "You can get us a mooring in Menemsha if we don't feel like sailing all the way back, right?"

"It's August, Chas."

"Well, then we'll just move your stinky old tub out of the way, and we'll tie up in your slip. Now, set a course for Cuttyhunk."

"Aye aye, Captain."

Stella Blue sailed swiftly from the harbor on a stiff southwest breeze, leaving the Edgartown lighthouse and the Chappaquiddick Beach Club's striped beach cabanas behind. Sails set, Whit sat down next to Aly. Her eyes, deep blue like the sea, glowed with pleasure. She'd stripped off her t-shirt and shorts down to her flowered bikini and looked sexy as hell. The fates had a funny sense of humor, throwing her—city girl, so wrong for him in so many ways—in his path. Aly put her hand on Whit's thigh, sending tingles in all sorts of inappropriate places. He was stupidly, ridiculously, smitten. And stupidly, ridiculously happy.

Chas polished his sunglasses. "First mate, could you bring up the oranges? I can't have the crew getting scurvy."

"I'll get them," said Aly, and stood up. "I wanted to look around the cabin anyway."

"I'll go with you and give you the tour. I'll show you how the head works," said Whit, getting an idea.

"No need. I've used a marine toilet before."

"Let me show you anyway, just in case." Whit followed Aly belowdecks and shut the cabin door.

🐑 🐑 🐑

"You make me crazy, you know," Whit said and bent his head to nuzzle Aly's neck. Her insides quivered with pleasure. "I thought about throwing the rest of them overboard so I could get you alone, but then I figured that this would be easier."

Whit's hands tugged on the strings of Aly's bikini top. "So, you're not going to give me a tour?"

"We can do that later," he murmured, as her top fell to the floor. His hands slid up to cup her breasts, thumbs circling her nipples, triggering waves of pleasure. "Here's the bunk. Let's see how comfortable it is." Aly lay back, shivering with anticipation as Whit stripped off her bikini bottom.

"Oranges!" called Chas." I feel scurvy coming on! My gums! My teeth!"

"Tell Chas to go away," said Whit, his voice muffled by Aly's body.

"We'll be up in a minute," Aly called back, trying to keep her voice normal as Whit's fingers and tongue and lips did unimaginably wonderful things. "Whit's, uh," she gasped. "Still showing me around."

"I know what you're doing down there," called Chas. "For goodness' sake," he muttered, rapping on the door. "This isn't some cheesy motel, Whit."

Whit lifted his head. "Almost finished with my tour," he called.

Tracing a circle, then probing, Whit sucked Aly down to where there was no thought, no sight, no sound, nothing but sensation as wave after wave after wave crashed through her. She stuffed her mouth with a pillow to muffle her cries as a warm, golden glow, like a honey-sweet sunbeam, spread from her core to the tips of her fingers and her toes.

"I think I'm done," Whit grinned, looking very pleased with himself.

"Oh my god," Aly murmured. She was breathless, flattened, melted into the bunk. "I don't know if I can move."

He leaned down to add one more kiss on the tip of each breast, another exquisite tingle of pleasure. "Happy to be of service."

With a shout of "hard-a-lee" from the top deck, the sailboat changed direction and rolled abruptly from port to starboard, pitching Aly off the bunk and onto the floor. Whit burst out laughing and put out a hand to help her up from the polished wood floor. "I think that's a hint that Chas wants his fruit."

"I was not expecting that," Aly giggled as she put on her bikini.

"Hey, Captain, you didn't need to jibe," Whit said, climbing the steps from the cabin. Aly followed, bearing a bag of oranges and a sheepish expression.

Chas gave them a prim look. "Naughty, naughty," he said. "Not my fault you weren't ready. I'm teaching Lawrence how to sail." He turned back to his student. "On this tack, we want to be on a close reach. Now grab that line and winch it in more." Lawrence pulled on the rope, politely ignoring Chas's admiring looks at his biceps as the boat picked up speed, heeling against the wind. "Lawrence said he'd introduce me to his cousin. Any family resemblance?" he added hopefully.

"Some," Lawrence replied. "I'm sure Aly has friends she can introduce you to in San Francisco. Hannah said you're going to be roomies."

A cloud passed over Aly's eyes at the mention of San Francisco. Would her San Francisco friends still be her friends, or would they take Kevin's side in the split? She pushed the unhappy thought away.

"You OK with tech types? I know restaurant people too."

"A sexy sommelier?" Chas asked. "I'd like that."

Whit leaned back and scanned Vineyard Sound. "Chas, you're way off course."

"Minor change in plans," Chas said. "You can tie off that line now, Lawrence."

"We're heading to Menemsha," Lawrence grinned, wrapping the rope around the cleat in a neat clove hitch. "While you were below, we elected Hannah Commodore of the Fleet for the day."

"I've issued my first order—lobster rolls for lunch," Hannah said.

"Aye aye. But don't eat too much. I've arranged a special surprise for us in Cuttyhunk," Chas said, relinquishing the wheel to Whit.

Leaning back on the cushioned seat, Aly listened to the wind in the sails and the water splashing against the hull. While the rest of the crew relaxed, Whit stood at the helm with his hands on the wheel, legs spread and braced, eyes focused on the horizon. Dress him in a tricorn hat, brass button jacket, and breeches, and he would have made a dashing schooner captain, breaking hearts in every port.

"Ready for a joke?" asked Whit.

"No," groaned Chas.

"Guess I'll have to go over your head," said Whit. "Commodore Hannah-Banana?"

"Yes, please."

"Ready?" Whit smiled and winked at Aly. "A pirate and a sailor were sitting together at a bar. The sailor looked at the pirate's peg leg and asked, 'How did you get that?' The pirate said, 'Aye, I wrestled a shark and lost me leg.' The sailor pointed to the pirate's hook and asked, 'How did you get that?' The pirate said: 'Aye, I fought Red Beard's crew and lost me hand.' The sailor pointed to the pirate's eye patch and asked, 'How did you get that?' The pirate said, 'Aye, a bird pooped in me eye.' The sailor said, 'That's not much of a story.' 'Aye,' the pirate replied. 'It was me first day with the hook.'"

Chas rolled his eyes as the rest of the crew burst out laughing.

"Oh, Whit, that's terrible!" Aly said.

"What? You don't like pirate jokes?" Whit asked, with mock indignation. "Maybe you'll like my dirty ones better. Have you heard the one about Roger's jolly?"

"I need a walk after stuffing my face like that," Aly said, climbing from the inflatable dinghy that was *Stella Blue*'s tender onto the dock at Cuttyhunk Island. Chas's surprise had been the arrival of the Raw Boat, a floating raw bar with, thanks to Chas's generosity, a huge selection of clams, oysters, and cocktail shrimp. Aly, despite having eaten an entire lobster roll, had nevertheless managed to consume half a dozen of each. Sailing, seafood, friends, Whit—she'd had many wonderful days since she'd come to the Vineyard, but this was the best.

"Chas likes spoiling his friends," Whit said, securing the dinghy's line to the dock.

"Did you see Lawrence eat? I had no idea he was such a seafood fiend." Aly said, waving to the rest of the gang, who had decided to nap and digest on *Stella Blue*. "Ready to explore?"

Cuttyhunk was like a miniature-golf-course version of Martha's Vineyard. A pretty scattering of gray-shingled buildings made up the town, and golf carts took the place of cars. "Let's go up there and check out the view," said Whit, pointing to a low hill that was the highest point on the island.

Hand in hand, Aly and Whit walked up the road toward a small pond. A rainbow unicorn floatie bobbed in the middle, and a small sign that read 'Nude Beach' stood by the edge of the pond.

"Go stand there. I want to take your picture." Whit was her magic unicorn, the perfect boyfriend. He dutifully stood by the sign and grinned. "Got it," Aly said, showing him the picture. "Did you hear the Raw Bar guy say that there's only like a dozen people who live here year-round?" Aly asked. "I've always wanted to live on an island. But this one's too small."

"You're living on one now."

"I mean a tropical island. With snorkeling right off the beach." The words were out of Aly's mouth before she realized it. They'd never talked about what came next, when he'd go down to the Caribbean for the winter season and she'd go back to California.

Whit took her hand. "Like St. John?"

A pulse of pure joy ran through Aly: Whit wanted her to come to St. John. The long-distance thing wouldn't be easy, but they could make it work. If they both wanted it to.

"And we've got whales too," Whit continued. "Humpbacks winter in the Virgin Islands. I've seen them lots of times, breaching and doing that tail slap thing."

"Lobtailing." Aly imagined herself in Whit's bougainvillea-covered cottage, going out on *Noepe* to see whales, then coming home to make love in the warm jasmine-scented breezes. "I'd love that."

They'd reached the top of the hill and climbed onto the remnants of a World War II naval watchtower. They looked down onto the large, protected bay where they'd moored *Stella Blue*, a near-perfect circle. "You know, I was supposed to take Hannah to the Caribbean for her thirtieth birthday. Instead, I went to Martha's Vineyard and delivered a lamb."

Whit raised his eyebrows. "*You* delivered a lamb?"

"OK. I watched a guy stick his arm into the mucky rear end of a sheep to deliver a lamb."

"Was that the moment you decided you were going to seduce that poor, innocent fellow?" Whit asked, wrapping his hands around Aly's waist and squeezing.

"Hey," Aly giggled. "That tickles." She turned to face Whit and put her hands around his neck. "That was the moment I knew I had made a very big mistake letting Hannah talk me into coming to Martha's Vineyard in March. The guy? Not my type."

"How not your type?" Whit bent to kiss her, long and gentle. Aly felt the warm, melty-ice-cream feeling from the first time they'd kissed.

"If I had known what an amazing kisser he was, I might have reconsidered. But the rest of the package? Too tall, to start." She reached up, barely able to reach the top of his head. "Too broad and muscular," she added, putting her hands on his shoulders and squeezing. "What can I say, the lumberjack thing is just not my type. Oh, but I did like his smile. And his lips." She raised herself onto her tiptoes and returned the kiss. "What about you? Love at first sight?"

Whit burst out laughing. "Hardly." Aly stuck out her lower lip. "Sorry, sorry," he said, bringing himself under control. "Let me see. First, you looked like a drowned rat."

"It was raining," Aly pouted. "And cold. And I'd been standing out there waiting for you for hours."

"An hour and a half, tops. And you were cranky."

"Of course I was cranky. You would've been cranky too if you had been in my boots. My wet, cold, soggy boots."

"And squeamish."

Aly glared at him. "You name one girl in a thousand who would not have been grossed out when your arm went in—up to the elbow!—poor Maisy's rear end."

"True, true," he laughed. "Maybe I didn't give you a fair break. But you've won me over now, Aly Bennett."

🐑 🐑 🐑

"Yo ho ho, and a bottle of rum," Chas sang as he wobbled across the dock in Edgartown, swinging an empty rum bottle. "Rum tum tum. In my tummy tum tum."

To entertain them on the long sail back, Chas had pulled out a bottle of fine rum, a bag of pirate costumes, and had run the Jolly Roger up the mast, turning the *Stella Blue* into the most elegant pirate ship ever to sail in Vineyard Sound. Waving a plastic cutlass over his head, Chas attempted (and failed) to terrorize every vessel they met on their way. And each failure required each crew member to down a shot of rum as the penalty—except for Whit, the designated driver/helmsman.

Straggling behind and none too steady on their feet, Lawrence and Hannah lugged the cooler while sober Whit and wobbling Aly followed with the trash. Aly felt exhausted, delighted, and more than a little drunk. It had been a fine day. Maybe the best ever.

"What do ya say, me mateys? Back to me pirate lair and I'll open another cask of grog?" asked Chas.

"I'm all grogged out," said Lawrence. "I'm going to hit the ole hammock early tonight."

"What about you, Commodore Hannah-Banana?"

"Argh, I've got the early watch tomorrow," Hannah said tipsily.

"First Mate Whit-Whitless? Second Mate Aly Cutlass?"

"Bed for us too," Whit said, catching Aly as she swayed beside him.

"Bunch of lily-livered scallywags, the lot of you!" Chas complained. "Time to divvy up the plunder then!"

Aly pushed back the eyepatch that made seeing in the near dark even more of a challenge. "What plunder?" she asked, holding onto Whit's arm for stability. "We didn't board a single ship."

"True," said Chas, his gold hoop earring shining under the streetlight. "But we discovered the greatest treasure of all!"

"What's that?" asked Lawrence, adjusting the bandana Chas had tied around his head.

"Friendship, of course. More valuable than all the gold and jewels in the world."

Aly's eyes filled with sentimental, drunken tears. "You're so right!" These were her friends. True friends, worth more than anything. Dear Hannah, as real and honest and good as they come. Chas, his flippant veneer hiding a kind and generous heart. Dear, sweet, talented Lawrence, Hannah's improbably perfect match. And Whit, friend and a lover combined, best of all. "I love you guys!"

"And we love you," said Hannah, giving Aly a big, squeezy hug, nearly toppling them both over.

"To friends!" Chas lifted the empty Flor de Caña rum bottle to his lips. "Blast ye scurvy scuppers! I'm out of grog."

Aly tripped on an uneven board, and Whit swept her up into his arms. "I'm taking my share of the treasure home with me," said Whit.

"Put me down, Whit! I can walk. Pretty much," Aly giggled. "That was good rum."

"I like carrying you. Safer that way," Whit replied. "Can't have you falling off the dock."

A cool breeze came off the water, and Aly snuggled against Whit's flannel-clad chest, his big arms cradling her. She yawned, suddenly feeling sleepy. Whit was like a safe, secure, warm harbor, protecting her from all storms. Aly sighed. It wasn't just the rum. She was in love.

🐑 🐑 🐑

"Thanks for the lift, Whit. You were smart to avoid the rum-tum-tum," slurred Hannah as she and Lawrence climbed from the truck. "Did I leave the lights on?"

The drive back to West Tisbury had done nothing to help Aly sober up. Chas's fine rum had been both delicious and very strong, and she wasn't used to hard liquor. "Be right back," Aly said, fumbling with her seat belt buckle. "I need to grab some clothes."

"Then home and to bed with you," said Whit.

"Okey-dokey-artichoke-y," said Aly, leaning over to kiss Whit's stubbly cheek.

Aly sucked in her lower lip as she focused on keeping her feet on the narrow, uneven stone path. Clean underwear and an outfit for tomorrow. And a glass of water. Despite her efforts, she wobbled off the path into the petunias. She hadn't reached the world-spinning, double-vision stage of drunkenness, but she was a lot closer to it than she should be. Demon rum, indeed.

Aly opened the kitchen door. Hannah and Lawrence stood staring at a slight, black-haired man. "Kevin's here," Hannah said. "He let himself in."

Gasping, Aly grabbed the edge of the doorframe. Kevin? What? How? She shut her eyes as if he were a hologram that she could make disappear with a blink. It didn't work. He was still there. Where he shouldn't be. In Hannah's kitchen. "Oh my god."

"I figured if I told you I was coming, you'd tell me not to," he said.

Aly was nauseated. She closed her eyes. *Go away*, she wanted to yell at him. *You don't belong here.*

"Hannah, maybe we should go upstairs?" asked Lawrence.

"No. Don't," said Aly.

Kevin stared at Aly, taking in her wind-snarled hair, the pirate eyepatch pushed up on her forehead, her t-shirt blotched red from a mishap with the Raw Boat's cocktail sauce bottle. "I got in this morning. I've been trying your cell. Both your phones," he said, glancing at Hannah.

"I left mine in the charger," said Hannah.

"I blocked your number," Aly said. "A while ago."

"I figured that. That's why I'm here. I need to talk to you, Aly."

Hannah frowned. "Not now. It's late," she said, suddenly sounding sober. "You both can talk tomorrow. Where are you staying?"

Kevin's mouth twitched. "I thought I could stay here." He motioned to a suitcase and a backpack sitting in the corner of the kitchen. "It's fine. I'll call a cab."

🐑 🐑 🐑

The tables under the café's cheerful white-and-blue-striped awning were filled with happy vacationers, starting their day with a coffee and a good breakfast. After sending Whit off with the excuse that she was feeling sick (which she was, but not from the rum), Aly crashed in her own bed, blotto and miserable. She woke up the next morning, hoping that Kevin had been some sort of drunken hallucination. But he wasn't. He was here, on Martha's Vineyard, sitting across from her at the café.

"I don't want to fight. I made a mistake. I came to tell you I'm sorry. You have no idea how sorry I am," he said, his eyes imploring her to forgive him.

"So, you're sorry."

"I'm not with Bex anymore. That lasted only two weeks. I was an idiot," Kevin said. "I've been staying in an Airbnb—a nice one—until they finish the new floors in our apartment." He sipped his coffee, made a face, and put his mug down. "You've got to forgive me, Aly. I'll make it up to you. Just tell me what I need to do."

"You can't undo what happened."

"Come on, Aly. One little mistake. I admit it was a mistake. But you're willing to throw away everything we had together?"

Anger made Aly's eggshell head and heart pound together like the worst drum solo ever. She fought to keep her voice low when what she wanted to do was shriek and scream and throw her latte all over his crisp white shirt. "Little mistake? How do you have the nerve to call sleeping with your sous chef a little mistake?"

"OK. Big mistake. Call it anything you want. Just forgive me and come back. I've learned my lesson. I love you."

But I don't love you. She fought an impulse to run, get into her car, drive to Whit's, and pretend this never happened. Aly needed to send Kevin away. Now. And everything would go back to the way it was.

The server arrived with their food. "Quiche?" Kevin motioned with his hand. She set the plate in front of Kevin. "And a yogurt bowl. Enjoy."

Aly scooped up a spoonful of homemade granola. "The food's pretty good here."

Aly sensed he was shifting gears as he put on a smile. "Not as good as at Tartine Manufactory," Kevin said. "Remember their morning buns? And the porchetta and egg sandwich with the salsa verde?"

Aly could see them at their favorite brunch spot in the Mission, the open, airy café set in the corner of the famous bakery, laughing as Kevin recounted stories of the near disasters during the previous evening's dinner service. They'd always order a morning bun to share, buttery and sweet with cinnamon and candied orange. Brunching at Tartine with Kevin felt like another life. It was another life.

"The Grey Barn here has great pastries." *Stop putting it off,* she scolded herself. *Say what you need to say.*

Kevin took a small bite of his quiche. Aly had almost forgotten how picky he was about his food. He fixed her with an earnest, hopeful look. "We were really good together, Aly. We can get that back. It's time for you to come home. Please. We can do couples therapy. Whatever you want."

"No."

"No what?" Kevin asked. A flash of fear crossed his face.

"I'm staying here."

"You can't. I need you, Aly." A muscle twitched in Kevin's cheek. She felt his frustration rise. Kevin was used to getting his way. "What? You're going to keep punishing me by staying here with Hannah in that weird old house? What about your job? They're not going to let you telecommute forever."

"I got laid off."

A look of relief crossed Kevin's face. "Oh. OK," he said and ran his hand through his hair, the gesture so familiar. "Now things are making more sense. Why didn't you tell me, Aly? Why did you run away?"

Aly pressed her lips together. "I'm not here because I'm running away, Kevin. Or punishing you."

"Then what is it?"

It was surreal, sitting in this café where she and Whit had been just a week before, like watching two movies projected on the same screen. She didn't want to get into it all: Kevin's criticism, his obsession with his restaurant, his control-freak streak. She didn't want to hurt him. But she couldn't go back.

Kevin drummed his fingers on the table. "I know you were unhappy with how much time I spent at Ripple. But things have changed. Everything is running pretty smoothly now. I've got a new sous chef, Michael. He's great," Kevin said. "Did you know we got five stars in the *Chronicle*? The reviewer raved about the geoduck. That was your idea. And…"

"What happened to Bex?" Aly interrupted.

Kevin looked pained. "She quit when I moved out. I told you. It's over. Don't make something out of nothing." He reached across the table for Aly's hand. He grimaced as she snatched it away. Kevin's handsome face was haggard and tired. "Oh god. Don't tell me. Is there another guy?"

Aly bit her lip. "That's none of your business."

"There is, isn't there? Who is he?"

Aly stared at the table. She didn't want to bring up Whit. But if it would help convince him they were over as a couple, she'd tell him. She looked up. "He's a fisherman and a musician. A friend of Hannah's."

"A fisherman? Have you lost your mind, Aly?"

Aly's temper flared. "No, I have not lost my mind."

"What about us?"

"Kevin. There is no *us*."

They sat in silence. Aly could tell that Kevin wasn't going to give up. Not yet. He never did. Until he got his way. But not this time.

Aly felt someone come up behind her. "Aly, I didn't expect to see you up and out this morning!" Chas leaned over the back of Aly's chair to kiss her cheek. He smelled of fresh soap and cologne. Dapper in his blue blazer, Chas extended his hand to Kevin. "Chas Parkerson. Nice to meet you."

Kevin rose to shake his hand. At a slender five-eight with a shock of thick, black hair, he could pass at first glance for a teenager. "Kevin Wang."

Chas gave him a quizzical look and turned back to Aly. "How's the hangover? Mine was a wicked beast. Had to tame it with a Bloody. Hair of the dog."

"I'm sticking with coffee," Aly said, relieved to have the distraction of Chas's company. Then it hit her. What if Chas said something to Whit? So stupid, going out. If she'd been thinking clearly, she'd have met Kevin at the inn where he was staying. She needed to get Chas to leave. Now.

"And you're a friend of Aly's?" Chas asked Kevin.

"Old friend," Aly said quickly. "From San Francisco."

"Boyfriend," Kevin said.

Chas's eyebrows shot up. He looked at Aly. "Ex. Ex-boyfriend," she said.

"We live together," Kevin said, with a meaningful look at Aly. "Or we did."

Panic pounded in Aly's temples as she spun out what would happen next. Chas would tell Whit about running into Aly's ex unless she did first. She had meant to tell Whit about Kevin. She really did. But the time was never right. And he'd never asked.

Pursing his lips, Chas made a show of checking his watch. "Oh my, look at the time! I'll be late for brunch at Granny's. Kevin, nice to meet you. See you later, Aly-gator!"

"Chas is a good friend," Aly said. "He's one of the first people I met here. He's…"

"I don't care who he is, Aly," Kevin interrupted, "I need to know why you won't come back to San Francisco with me. Whatever it is, we can fix it. You can't just give up on us," he said, a beseeching look in his eyes.

"I'm sorry, Kevin. But no. There is no us, not anymore."

🐑 🐑 🐑

Aly was still shaking when she got back to the car. It hadn't been pretty. Kevin had started begging, pleading, and then reminding her of all the good times they'd had, the life they had built together. He'd promised to hand over more responsibility to his staff at Ripple, to work on his OCD. He refused to accept that she didn't love him, didn't want to be with him. It was awful. She felt awful.

But it was over. She'd done it.

Aly put the key in the ignition and pulled up Chas's contact info on her phone. *Please don't say anything to Whit about meeting Kevin,* she texted. *I'll explain later.* She watched the three dots as Chas typed his reply. *Not to worry. I'm the soul of discretion.*

Back at Hannah's, Aly found Lawrence stretched out on the sofa with the curtains pulled and his eyes closed. A bottle of Advil and an empty glass sat on the table next to him.

"I don't think I've had a hangover this bad since college," Lawrence said without opening his eyes. "I feel like shit."

"Sun and rum will do that to you," Aly said, flopping down in the armchair. "I'm not feeling so great myself. How's Hannah?"

"Not good. But she went to work anyway." Lawrence tried to sit up and changed his mind. "How'd it go with Kevin? I can't believe he just showed up here."

"Not well," Aly sighed. "But he's going back to California. At least, I hope he is." She leaned back against the chair. "It's my fault. Hannah's been telling me that I needed to talk to him. But I kept putting it off."

"I get that," Lawrence said. "But you did what you had to. You're a heartbreaker, Aly," he added with a weak smile.

"Thanks." She picked up his glass. "I'll get you some more water."

Aly walked into the kitchen and took a second glass from the cabinet. She turned on the tap and filled their glasses, no longer noticing the metallic flavor of the well water.

"Who got the pastries?" Aly asked, spying the box on the counter. She picked up half a chocolate croissant and took a bite.

"Whit. He stopped by to check on you," Lawrence called from the living room.

She carried the water glasses back in. "It was nice of Whit to stand in that line at the Grey Barn. I'll give him a call. I need to talk to him."

🐑 🐑 🐑

The pewter-colored sky threatened rain. Aly adjusted the blue tarp covering the makeshift lean-to she and Hannah had fashioned out of wood scraps. "Well, at least that's over with, and Kevin's gone," she told Dandelion, who was busy eating a particularly tasty-looking tuft of grass. She ran her hands along the lamb's sturdy body, pausing to scratch the lamb's favorite spots. Her fleece had grown thicker and spongier over the summer, making her look less like a lamb and more like a sheep.

"It was dumb for him to come here. It wasn't going to change anything." She looked up at the darkening sky. "It's going to rain soon. You'll be OK in your little shelter. Right?"

Aly went inside as the first fat drops of rain fell. Hannah had dragged Lawrence into town to see a movie. Aly had declined, promising herself that she'd use the rainy day to tackle her jam-making project.

She picked up her phone. Maybe she could convince Whit to come over and keep her company. But he'd barely responded to her texts and messages, and that wasn't like him. *Blueberry jam day!* she typed. *Want to come help?* She waited eagerly for his reply, watching the little dots on the screen. Surely, he wouldn't be going out fishing with clients in the rain. *Engine's been acting up. Got to figure out what's wrong.* Aly sighed in disappointment. She tapped in, *Later? Dinner? I'll cook* and waited for a reply. *Busy. Got a last-minute gig. Party in West Chop.*

Aly chewed on a fingernail. She still hadn't told him about Kevin's coming to the Island. But there was no rush to tell Whit and no reason for him to be upset. It wasn't as if she'd lied about Kevin. He'd never asked, and she'd never volunteered. Besides the woman Chas had told about, there were likely lots of ex-girlfriends lurking in Whit's past. He probably was just busy. She'd tell him about Kevin the next time she saw him. Not that it mattered now that Kevin was gone.

Aly turned on the radio to WMVY and got out her jam-making supplies: jars, sugar, pectin, a lemon, and the quarts of tiny wild blueberries she'd picked and frozen. She'd never canned before and was a bit worried about how it would come out. But if she failed, she knew Whit would laugh, pour her disaster over ice cream (or eat it with a knife and fork), and pronounce it the best he'd ever had. She couldn't imagine even thinking of trying to make jam with Kevin around to critique every step.

Her goal was a jam that wasn't too sweet, so you could really appreciate the sweet-tart flavor of fresh wild blueberries. Aly set a huge pot of water on the stove to boil and poured the frozen berries into a bowl. They were teeny-tiny, smaller than baby peas. As she sorted through the berries for stems, she thought about all the hours she'd spent with Beau and Dandelion while she picked the berries in that magical field, listening to the wind in the trees and feeling the warm sun on her shoulders as her fingers moved over the bushes. It was blissful: the Zen state of mindfulness that she'd never achieved before. And her boulder. The magical boulder that had sent its message through that weirdly wonderful experience, telling her to embrace life, real life, and not to be seduced by the fake life of pixels on a screen.

Aly pulled the empty sterilized jars and lids from the boiling water with a pair of rubber band-wrapped tongs and set them on a kitchen towel. After pouring the stemmed berries into a large saucepan, she added sugar, zest and juice from a lemon, and (her own inspiration) a tiny shake of cinnamon. She waited until the blueberries came to a boil and then added the liquid pectin. Next came the tricky part. With a tea towel-wrapped hand, she steadied the hot jars, one at a time, and ladled in the jam with the other, aiming to fill each jar precisely to a quarter inch from the top. It was a gloppy, messy process that left sticky-sweet dark blue smeared all over everything: stove, counter, tea towels, and Aly.

Aly carefully wiped the threads and top of each jar with a damp paper towel, screwed on a lid, and set the sealed jars back into the boiling water. After setting the timer, she licked the wooden spoon. The jam was bright and delicious. Most of the blueberries had held their shape, little pops of intense berry flavor.

Busy or not, tomorrow would be breakfast in bed with Whit, homemade blueberry jam on toast.

🐑 🐑 🐑

It hurt to have Aly so close. She'd arrived at the Black Dog Tavern smiling, looking pretty and carefree in her summer sundress as if this were any other date, as if nothing had happened.

"Oh, great. You got a table by the window," she said, slipping into her seat after planting a kiss on Whit's cheek.

Whit stiffened, dreading the conversation they were about to have. Like watching a movie with someone else in it, he could see himself that morning at Hannah's, a box of croissants in one hand

and orange juice for Aly's hangover in the other. He could still hear Lawrence's groggy voice saying, *Aly's not here. She's off to brunch with that guy she lived with in San Francisco. The chef.*

Whit still couldn't believe Aly had never mentioned that she'd been living with someone in California. A lie of omission was, in his book, still a lie. Petra had done the same before she took off with her ex on his yacht, discarding Whit once he'd outlived his usefulness as a tool to make her ex-boyfriend jealous. This was like his mother and her cocktail party liaisons aimed at getting his father to pay attention to her. So many affairs that made a farce out of their marriage. Or maybe Kevin wasn't really an ex, and Aly was cheating on him. Just like Petra. Not that it mattered either way.

Whit didn't play games. Or lie. And he hadn't thought that Aly did either. Or Petra. But he was wrong again. The earth had crumbled beneath Whit's feet, pitching him into a bottomless sinkhole. There in the darkness, evil creatures lived, telling him he had no right to find true love, that he was meant to be alone, that people were never what they seemed, that there were always lies hiding the truth. He was in a dark and maybe irrational place, and he could see only one way out: to break up with Aly.

Aly unwrapped the napkin from her silverware. "You'll be proud of me. I made nine jars of blueberry jam yesterday. The lids popped, just like you said. All of them."

"Congratulations."

"I can't wait for you to try it." She picked up the menu. "I like that portabella mushroom thing. But I'm kind of in a fish and chips mood." She looked up with her ocean-blue eyes, so innocent. "But it's so much food. Want to split it with me? And a salad?" she asked. "I know you've been super busy, but I've really missed you."

Whit stared out the window as a ferry pulled into the harbor, tinted orange-gold from the setting sun. He knew he had tilted, but he couldn't help how he felt. He'd trusted Aly, and now that trust was gone. And he couldn't be with someone he didn't trust.

"Aly. I can't do this."

"Can't do what?" she asked. "It's fine if you want to order for yourself."

He turned back to look at her with a fresh pang of sorrow. She'd put her hair up, and a single ringlet had escaped down her neck. He'd loved playing with her curls, tugging them to watch them spring back.

Aly reached across the table for Whit's hand, and he flinched. "What's going on?" she asked, searching his face. She paused and cocked her head. "Chas told you about Kevin showing up, didn't he? I asked him not to say anything."

Because she wanted to keep deceiving me. "Not Chas. Lawrence." Whit's hands clenched under the table. "Chas knows? Am I the last one here to find out about this guy?"

Aly took a deep breath. "I was going to tell you myself as soon as I saw you. I had no idea he was coming here. It's the last thing I wanted." She fiddled with her napkin. "But he's gone. It's not important. He doesn't have anything to do with us."

"You're having a live-in boyfriend in San Francisco wasn't important? If that's not important, then what is, Aly?"

Aly looked surprised. "I didn't take you for the jealous type." The server interrupted to take their order. She sipped her water. "I'm sorry. I should've told you about Kevin before. I guess I didn't because I didn't want to think about him. It's over."

"Out of sight, out of mind. Well, that's a great philosophy of life."

Aly's eyebrows drew together. "I didn't lie. I just didn't want to talk about him."

It wouldn't help, but Whit needed to know. "Were you with him when you came to Martha's Vineyard? How long had you been living together?"

Aly leaned back in her chair and crossed her arms. "I don't see how this helps anything."

"Please tell me, Aly."

Aly sighed. She turned her head to look out at the harbor. "Yes, I had been living with him when I left San Francisco to come here. We'd moved in together two and a half years ago."

Whit's shoulders slumped. "OK." This wasn't just some short-term boyfriend. This was the guy she was probably thinking she'd marry. *Just as well I found out now,* he told himself. *I should've known better. I'm just a magnet for women with no moral* compass. And this wasn't the first thing Aly had lied about. I should have put the pieces together before.

"I'd broken up with him before you and I got together, if that was what you were going to ask next," she said with a frown. "Do you want to know what he did to me?"

"Does it matter, Aly?"

"Yes, it does." Aly's eyes flashed. "He cheated on me with someone he worked with in his restaurant. Moved in with her even. And there were other things he did to me too. Things I didn't realize until I got here and was away from him."

Whit took a deep breath as a new, deeper level of hurt opened up. So that's how it was. He was handy, and oh so willing to jump into bed with her. "I was revenge sex."

"No. I mean, not intentionally," Aly fumbled. "That's not why I'm with you." She twisted her napkin. "If you care so much about my ex-boyfriends, why didn't you ask?"

"I don't know," Whit admitted.

"I never asked about your exes because, frankly, I don't care. I knew someone in St. John broke your heart, but it wouldn't have made any difference if I hadn't known."

"But the lying, Aly. Look at the facts. It sure seemed easy for you to lie to Granny. I could never do that. And that thing about Hannah's parents? What was that? And now you've lied about Kevin. It's a pattern, Aly. How can you not see that?" Her face had grown pale. "I don't feel like I can trust you. And I can't be with someone I can't trust." Whit took a breath. "Who are you, Aly? Do you even know? Because I don't."

Aly stared into his eyes, pleading. "I want to keep seeing you. It's not just the sex. I…"

Whit shook his head. This was a mistake, meeting her for dinner. He'd made up his mind. Nothing Aly had said—could say—would make a difference. "We had a good time together. Let's leave it at that."

Bewilderment crossed Aly's face. "You can't mean that."

"Maybe it's time for you to get that apartment with Chas in San Francisco and move on with your life." Whit couldn't bear sitting across from her. He stood up to leave. "Your real life."

PART 3 – FALL

Aly passed a sleeping man wrapped in a dirty gray blanket and tried to convince herself that it had been a dog turd that she had just narrowly missed. After the verdant green of Martha's Vineyard with its farms and fields and quaint, tidy, gray-shingled buildings, San Francisco seemed dirty and noisy. Too much cement, too many people. And too much poop.

Aly paused at the end of the road where the grade became so steep that the street turned into a flight of stairs. Below, downtown San Francisco, its skyline, bay, and bridges, were as familiar and breathtakingly beautiful as ever. A city of contrasts: homelessness cheek-by-jowl with nearly inconceivable wealth, multi-million dollar homes on grimy streets. Through a break in the clouds, Spire's silver skyscraper building gleamed like a trophy won by someone else.

Aly shifted her shoulder bag, glanced at her watch, and started down the stairs. Where she was heading was definitely less glamorous: a run-down warehouse that had been converted into a tech incubator. Based on the number of toothbrushes in the shared bathroom, she suspected that many (if not most) of the tenants were illegally living in their offices. Understandable, given the rents in San Francisco. And kind of depressing.

It had taken a week for Aly to realize that Whit was serious. A week of third-wheeling in the house with Hannah and Lawrence, listening to them chatter like an old married couple, trying to block out the sounds of their lovemaking with a pillow over her head. Aly was waiting for Whit to stop being ridiculous. At first, she'd confidently written off the scene in the Black Dog Tavern as a fit of jealousy. Kind of sweet, she'd thought. But finally, Chas, having pleaded her case with Whit, sat her down and delivered the verdict. It was over.

It wasn't like when she'd found out about Kevin's cheating. Through her sobs, Aly blamed herself for not mentioning her ex before. Then she blamed Whit for having never asked. She would have told him about Kevin if he had. She hadn't cared about the lovers in Whit's past, so why did he care about hers?

She missed Whit. She missed the breadth of his chest, solid and warm, and how he would reach out for her in his sleep and, with a soft hum of contentment, draw her close. She missed his lopsided smile, the crinkles around his eyes, pale crow's feet against his tanned skin. She missed the way he watched her as if no one else in the room mattered. How he really listened to her. As if what she said was interesting and important. She missed how he'd assume she could do anything, giving her the confidence to try. She missed the evenings on his deck when he would pull out his guitar and sing, his voice as gorgeous as the rest of him, and she would join him for the joy of hearing their voices weave and intertwine, the harmonies perfect and effortless. She even missed his terrible, awful jokes. Whit was true and fine and honest. And now he was gone.

Aly felt herself come unmoored, like a boat slipping its line, drifting into dark waters. She cried in the shower, at breakfast, driving to the supermarket. Hannah and Lawrence were patient, rolling their eyes (Aly was sure) at what a hot mess she'd become. Then came the call from her old boss at Spire. Her Stanford roommate's startup had gotten its angel round of financing and was flush with cash. They needed someone with a background in 4-D web design, and she'd be perfect. It seemed like a sign. Jo was right, as always. It was time to restart her real life, her career. Whit didn't want her. Hannah didn't need her now that Isabel and Karolina were working for her. And Dandelion was just a sheep, after all.

Aly didn't have a single good reason to stay on the Island. Except that it felt wrong to leave.

She ran down a second flight of stairs, and the street turned back into a steep road again, packed full of cars parked with their wheels turned into the curb to keep from rolling down the hill. The truth was she'd been feeling like a stranger in her own city. It was new, this lingering doubt that San Francisco, for all its wonderful qualities, wasn't the be-all-and-end-all. At least for her. She missed looking out the wavy glass windows of Hannah's antique house at fresh green fields dotted with sheep, Tisbury Great Pond shimmering in the distance. Aly missed the unscheduled life, dropping in on friends for an impromptu barbecue or to boil a pot of lobsters rather than planning two weeks out. She missed Dandelion, who always greeted her with little baas of joy whenever she returned, and the serene hours in the chaise, reading and watching the lamb graze on the grass under Beau's watchful gaze. She missed riding her bike to pick up meat and eggs from the farmstand at Flat Point Farm and cheese and bread at the Grey Barn, and picking ripe tomatoes and vegetables from Hannah's garden. Aly missed the blissful feeling she got every time she took her paddleboard onto the pond. She missed waking to the sound of geese honking in the early morning fog, and she ached to roll over in bed to gaze at Whit as he slept, that deep, deep sleep that she so envied.

She missed Whit with a pain that wasn't fading.

But Aly was thankful that in San Francisco there was nothing to remind her of Whit. Hannah stayed in touch, of course, and sent Dandelion-of-the-Week texts, and Chas called nearly every day to check in on her and the apartment hunt. Neither mentioned Whit.

Time, distance, and the distractions of a new job were working. A little. She and Whit had been a summer fling, Aly told herself for the umpteenth time. Fun. And done. She was back where she was supposed to be. In the best city in the world. She'd lucked into a job that allowed her to pay the appalling rent on her Airbnb. And as much as she missed the Vineyard, there was a vibrancy to city life: the cable cars rumbling up and down the steep hills, a festival or parade almost every weekend, the diversity of people and neighborhoods, new restaurants and shops to check out. No longer bound by the edges of a twenty-mile-long island, she could get into a car and head out for a weekend of wine-tasting in Sonoma or camping in Yosemite. She could drive along the stunningly beautiful coastline north to Point Reyes or south to

Santa Cruz or Monterey, or head inland to Lake Tahoe to go paddleboarding across the seemingly mile-deep, crystal-clear water. She'd been away on a lovely, long vacation, she told herself, but San Francisco was home.

Aly should be happy. She *would* be happy. In time. This was the life she'd always wanted.

The perfect life.

🐑 🐑 🐑

Kevin. He wanted to see her. And she'd agreed. Aly felt her stomach clench. Their friends begged her to give him a second chance. At least meet him for dinner. They had probably told Kevin that she and Whit had broken up. Aly suspected self-interest: if she and Kevin were a couple again, her friends (were they her friends? Or were they his?) wouldn't have to take sides, which made their social lives easier. Even Hannah agreed she should see him. *You need to talk things out. The guy deserves that. I'm not saying you should get back together. But if there's something there—or nothing there—anymore, then you'll know for sure.*

Aly tied a scarf around her neck, looked at her reflection in the mirror, and switched it for a gold necklace. She ran a brush through her hair, appreciating its smooth swing from a blow-out from the new salon around the corner. Maybe it was time to tame her curls for good and get a Korean straight perm at that place that Adrienne and Peggy raved about. On the Vineyard, none of this mattered. But she was back in the city now.

She was meeting Kevin at the new Peruvian restaurant around the corner from her apartment. Punctual as ever, Kevin was waiting for her at their table. He had a fresh haircut, crisp button-down shirt, and a nervous look. "Kevin, you're looking well," she said, as her insides gave a flip. But it was not in a good butterflies-in-the-stomach way. "Having the hottest new restaurant in town agrees with you."

Kevin flashed her his boyish grin. "It does." Aly sat down. She could see the wheels turning. He was trying to tamp down the impulse to talk obsessively about Ripple. "I like your hair that way. Really pretty."

"Thanks."

Aly covered up the awkward silence by reading the menu. Impatient, Kevin waved down a young, ponytailed server. "Could you bring the wine list?" He turned to Aly. "They should have some good Argentinian wines here." He reached out and put his hand over hers. She waited for the old tingle. His fingers felt only familiar, comfortable. Kevin looked around at the décor, bare brick walls hung with bright Peruvian textiles and tropical plants in retro macrame plant holders. "By the way, it was pure genius—your idea, remember—to put up that wallpaper with the blue ripple pattern. I thought it might be too loud, but it really pops in the Instagram photos."

Aly had been following the restaurant on social media. "What's up with the parchment paper cones?"

Kevin brightened. "I put those over the plates to capture the aromas and add an element of drama, like lifting a silver dome. What I didn't realize is that the customers would put them on," he chuckled. The "in" thing was to post a picture of yourself wearing the cone as a party hat against the Hokusai-wave-inspired walls, #ripplepartyhat. Aly got it. There was something joyous and silly about posing with a paper cone on your head. "You should come to Ripple for dinner. I know somebody there who might be able to get you a reservation," he smiled. Ripple, Aly knew, was booked within 10 minutes of the reservation line opening a month in advance. "Bring some friends. You can sit at the chef's table." He took a sip of water. "I've told you before, but it's true. I couldn't have done it—opened Ripple—without you. I mean it. Really."

Aly caught a glimpse of what had made her fall in love with Kevin. He worked hard, too hard, but he always let her know he loved her and how important it was to have her in his life. But everything had changed. At least for her.

The server came back to the table. "I'll order for us," said Kevin, picking up his menu.

"That's OK. I'll order for myself." She scanned the menu. "Um, the *ceviche verde* to start and the *lomo saltado*. And I'd like a pisco sour."

"Are you sure you don't want to try the *escabeche o pescado*? I've heard that's very good here."

Aly bristled. She'd had too many meals where she ate only what Kevin wanted to try. "I'm in the mood for steak. But I'll have a bite of yours."

Over cocktails, Kevin launched into a passionate description of the new dishes he'd created for Ripple, the farmer he'd convinced to grow the prized Japanese matsutake mushrooms for the restaurant, and the possible opening of a second Ripple in Sonoma. Kevin's enthusiasm and passion were at full strength. But this time, it didn't light Aly up. The desire and pride she'd felt, as if his passions and success were echoed in her, was gone.

"I've been doing all the talking," Kevin said as their first courses arrived. "How are things going with you? How's the new job?"

Aly tasted her *ceviche*. "Good so far. The company is designing a robot that'll do most of your household chores for you. I'm working with Elisa, my old boss from Spire, so that's great. But most of the guys there—and they are all guys—are robotics nerds, which is a whole new level of nerd-dom," she said, rolling her eyes. "My part of the project is on hold, so they have me doing some other stuff." Aly's heart wasn't in it. It wasn't like being in her old job at Spire. Forced to spend her days staring at a screen, she struggled to focus and stay on task, which was new for her—and worrisome.

"And on weekends?"

"Catching up with friends mostly," Aly said. "But I forgot how much people like to talk about their bonuses and when their company might IPO." Fortunately, she had Chas's visit to look forward to. "I think I'll go to the aquarium on Saturday. They have a new exhibit I'd like to see." Shoot, would he think she was inviting him to come with her?

"You always did love that aquarium. But I like my fish on a plate." Kevin put a bite of cod on his fork and inspected it before putting it in his mouth. Aly waited for him to do his weird retronasal open-mouth tasting thing, but he didn't. "Work should be finished on the apartment in a couple of weeks, three at the most. I was hoping, maybe…"

Aly completed the sentence in her head. *I'm hoping you'll move back in with me.* "How's Miso?" she interrupted. She didn't want him to ask, even though she knew what the answer had to be.

"Still a lazy beast. He's been lonely since you left," Kevin said. "I'm thinking about getting him a kitten for company. I stopped by the ASPCA the other day. There's a new litter of gray kittens that'll be ready for adoption soon."

Aly knew what Kevin was up to. She'd been begging him all spring to go to the ASPCA to look at the kittens. He knew that she had a soft spot for Russian Blues. "Are you sure you want a kitten? You said Miso used to climb on the curtains and shred everything."

"Of course. Kittens will be kittens. A few shredded curtains are worth having a soft, furry little beast purring on your lap. Don't you think?" Kevin twisted his napkin. "I want to ask you something." Tiny beads of perspiration stood out on his upper lip.

Aly looked around, desperate to avoid the question. But she had to face it. She took a deep breath. "Kevin, I'm sorry, but no. My answer is no."

🐑 🐑 🐑

Whit closed the engine cover and groaned. Whatever was wrong with *Noepe*'s motor was beyond his skill set to fix, and now, at the end of the season, the boatyards on the Island would be swamped with summer people who wanted their pleasure boats pulled from the water and winterized. If he couldn't get her fixed, he'd have to start cancelling not just today's clients but future charters too. With the Striped Bass and Bluefish Derby going on, he risked losing nearly a quarter of his revenue. Not to mention the dozens of very pissed off people who'd be unlikely to book him again.

He tossed his tools back into his metal toolbox, cracked open a beer, and frowned. Over the past weeks, it seemed as if everything had gone to hell in a handbasket. First, that call from the marina in St. John, telling him that the dock repairs had gone way over budget, so they were doubling his slip fees. Then the new leak in his house. The roofer would patch it for now, but the whole roof needed replacement. On top of all that, he'd been told that Petra had married her Eurotrash boyfriend in a million-dollar, glitterati-studded affair in Cannes. Not that he'd ever want her back. Still, the news left Whit feeling even more depressed.

Then there was Aly. Whit saw her, felt her, everywhere. And each memory drove a fresh spike into his heart. Like a porcupine's quill covered in tiny barbs, it went deeper and deeper, increasingly painful. He'd go to town, and he'd see her licking an ice cream cone with a look in her eye that made an innocent cone seem as wicked as an X-rated movie. In his bed with her curls spread across the pillow, she was a sleeping beauty, her tiny snores lulling him to sleep. It had gotten so bad, he'd decided to bunk in *Noepe* until, in theory, time would exorcise the ghosts from his bedroom.

He saw her next to him on his deck, drinking wine and savoring gooey ripened cheese as the setting sun lit the pond in shades of apricot and rosy pink. Watching her indigo eyes light up when she'd talk about friends, or blueberries, or Dandelion, or whatever happened to bring delight to her that day. On her paddleboard, showing off her new skills as he paddled alongside in his canoe until the wake from a passing motorboat toppled her, hollering blue curses as she splashed into the pond. He missed her with an ache that should have been fading by now, but was not. Each quill stayed embedded, leaving him miserable and both wishing and not wishing that he'd never met her, let her into his heart. When he'd split up with Petra in St. John—well, after she left him to go back to her ex-boyfriend—the pain had been mixed with unexpected relief. This time was different. And it wasn't getting better.

And now, *Noepe's* motor.

Whit closed his eyes. Time to focus on the important problem. Could he get towed to a boatyard on the Cape? Beg, borrow, or steal some other fishing boat?

He watched Chas park the Mooch illegally in front of the dock. He was not in the mood for Chas to start lecturing him about Aly again, if that was why he was there.

Chas leaned against a piling. "Hey, handsome. I thought you'd be out catching fishies?"

"Boat's broken," Whit said and glared at the motor. "I've got to call around. See if I can beg someone to take a look at it." He ran his hand through his hair. "And you can't park there. Don't blame me if you get a ticket."

Chas's eyes gleamed. "Oh, I'll get your stinky motor fixed for you."

"Sure you will."

"Surely I will."

Whit raised an eyebrow, relieved the topic was not going to be Aly. "How?"

"Well, when I was at the Port Hunter in Edgartown last night," Chas said, "I met the most adorable coastie. That's the nickname for a member of the U.S. Coast Guard. Isn't that cute? His name is Tanner. He's very handsome, and he's stationed here in Menemsha," he added. "That's why I'm here. I'm taking him out to dinner at the Homeport. Among other talents, Tanner's a mechanic. I'm sure I can talk him into looking at the motor on your smelly old tub here."

"*Noepe's* not smelly. That's coming from lobster pots on the dock," Whit said. "How do you know he's a good mechanic?"

"Boat, docks, pots. It's all smelly," Chas said. "And to answer your question, let's just say he's *very* skilled with his hands." Chas pulled out his phone. "I'll text him now and have him meet me here." He hit send. "See? Told you. Now, do you have anything to drink on board? I'm parched," he said, stepping from the dock onto the boat.

"I'll look," Whit said, feeling a glimmer of hope that *Noepe* could be fixed before he had to cancel any more charters. "And thanks."

Chas made himself comfortable in one of the fishing chairs as Whit climbed into the cabin. "Beer would be great," he called. "That's what Tanner likes."

Whit climbed up carrying two cans and handed one to Chas. "Coors Light OK? That's all I have."

Chas popped the top and took a sip. "Now, I have to tell you about Tanner. He's from Georgia. Just wait until you hear his accent. It's like a tall, cool glass of sweet iced tea. And that's not all."

Stoically, Whit sat through endless minutes of Chas's descriptions of the wonderfulness of his new lover. "Now. Enough of my love life. Have you called Aly yet?"

Whit blew out a puff of irritation. "No, and I'm not going to. I told you before, I'm tired of you bringing her up," he said. "We broke up. She went back to San Francisco. It's over."

"Broke up, schmoke up. Lover's quarrel," Chas said. "Bicoastal isn't ideal, but it's workable." He propped up his feet and leaned back. "You know, I've got an idea. I'm going to SF soon to look at apartments. You should come too. Take a couple of days' break from this stinky, broken-down old tub. We'll surprise her."

"That is an outstandingly bad idea, Chas," Whit said, glaring at his friend. "Even if I didn't have to work. I bet it took less than 48 hours for Aly to get back together with that chef guy," he said bitterly. "Did you know they had been living together for years? I was just someone to have some fun with while she let him dangle."

"And you know this how?"

"I just know. That's how," Whit said. "Besides, it was the same for me too. Summer fling and all that. Just a bit of fun. Done. Over. Finito."

Chas pressed his lips together. "You are a real blockhead, Whit Dias."

Whit glared at his best friend. "The topic's off the table."

"She's not Petra, you know. You're blind if you can't see that. Aly's something special, Whit," Chas said, looking serious. "And what the two of you had together was special. I could see it even if you couldn't. I'd never seen you so happy. It's like you had all this joyfulness locked inside you—news to me, by the way—and she figured out how to open the door. And you made her happy too. The way she'd look at you…" He shook his head. "If you cared about who she was dating before you, you should've asked. Aly would have told you. This," he said with a wave of his hand. "This fit of pique—or jealousy, or whatever it is—is ridiculous. You're not being rational."

"I am being rational. Finally," Whit said, crossing his arms. He was getting supremely annoyed. "It wasn't ever going to work out. I've told you all this before. Her life is in California. It's where she belongs. Enough. OK? Just leave me alone."

"Alone. You think you're better off alone. Well, you're not," Chas said, in a rare flash of temper. "I get you have trust issues. Petra lied and cheated on you. Your mother lied and cheated on your father. Aly's not Petra, and she's not your mother." He set his beer down. "I watched you hide in that stupid shell of yours— your lone-wolf mode, or whatever it is—until you met Aly. You know she's different. And what the two of you had was different and real and special. You don't want to admit it to yourself."

"Give it up, Chas," Whit growled.

Chas glared at Whit. "Fine. Be miserable. See if I care."

🐑 🐑 🐑

Aly propped the pillow behind her back and picked up her phone. Her studio Airbnb was tiny and soulless, and the leather bar on the street corner was kind of creepy. But she could walk to work, and the coffee shop across the street made excellent cortados and pastries.

Hey Hannah, she typed. *How's everything going? I miss you.* She looked out the window at her sliver of a view across the bay and waited for a reply. *We miss you too! Oh, hey, I forgot to send the Dandelion of the Week. Just a sec,* Hannah texted. A video popped up on Aly's phone. *Got to run. Talk soon!*

Aly played the clip that Hannah sent over and over. She loved seeing the lamb leaping with pure joy, as if her hooves were springs, and bounding over to nudge Beau to play. It brought back a tiny wave of bliss. With a little effort, she could imagine the breeze rustling through the leaves, smell the fresh salt air, and feel her fingers sink into Dandelion's soft, thick fleece. Missing Hannah and Dandelion and with nothing better to do, Aly opened her laptop and searched the folder where she'd been saving pictures and videos of Dandelion and Beau. She scrolled through them, starting with Dandelion as a tiny newborn that dreary March day. As she watched the videos, she felt herself relaxing: meditation via baby lamb.

For Hannah, Aly assembled a short video collage of Dandelion, making sure to have lots of clips of Beau too. Next came picking the right music, something upbeat and happy. Aly labeled the video "Happiness: Dandelion-the-Lamb" and sent it. For fun, she created a social media profile for Dandelion on Instagram and Facebook (username She_eepish) and posted the video there and on YouTube. If watching the lamb play made her feel good, maybe it would make others happy too.

Aly woke up the next morning and, out of curiosity, clicked on Dandelion's profile. The video was going viral with 1,969 likes and 277 comments on Instagram alone, most begging for more videos.

And the numbers were growing every minute. *Hey Hannah*, she texted, *want to help make Dandelion an internet star?*

🐑 🐑 🐑

Absentmindedly, Aly ate as she worked on Dandelion's new Instagram postings. Reheated in the microwave, the leftover *lomo saltado* wasn't nearly as good as it had been in the restaurant, but at least she wasn't sitting across from Kevin. And wouldn't ever have to again. With Hannah's download of pictures and videos (and promises to film more), Aly had tons of material for Dandelion's growing celebrity. The only downside to her project had been the gut punch she'd felt when she'd come across a picture of Whit. But the Ex-Terminator ex-boyfriend/ex-girlfriend photo-eliminator app took care of that problem in seconds.

Aly's imagination had taken off. She loved watching videos that put her inside another place, another life. And what better way than sharing Martha's Vineyard, Dandelion, and Beau with the world? The first video had already garnered fans from around the globe, people seeking to connect with something simple, pure, and natural (and adorable). Aly put together another burst-of-happiness video of Dandelion leaping around the field, a calming one of Dandelion grazing, a best-friends video of Dandelion and Beau cuddling and playing together, a silly Pedicure Day video of Dandelion having her hooves trimmed, and a video of Beau demonstrating his border-collie herding skills. Maybe she should ask Lawrence to film Hannah taking Dandelion around to see the sights of Martha's Vineyard, a sheep-themed travelogue with overdubbed narration from Dandelion's perspective?

She ought to build a website for Dandelion too, with pictures and videos. Maybe it could sell local sheep-themed products, like those wonderful Flat Point Farm felt-wrapped soaps, or partner with the Allen Farm Sheep & Wool Company. If Hannah was interested, they could offer both real-life and interactive "live" podcast visits with Dandelion: a "cream tea with sheep" out in the field with the pond sparkling in the background; an educational visit for kids; even lamb-focused mindfulness (agra-meditation?) or sheep yoga? Hannah's goat-yoga friend, Sky, could help with that. Aly was getting more and more excited. If only she could be there to help!

With a library of six videos to upload over the week, it was time to take a break. Aly rinsed her dish in the sink and put it in the tiny dishwasher, feeling better than she had in weeks. She'd been invited to join her ex-colleagues at a dive bar in Dogpatch, but a boozy evening in a noisy bar held little appeal. After texting her regrets, she changed into her pajama bottoms and a t-shirt and began to scroll through the Best-of-Netflix lists. Or she could watch another rerun of *Sex and the City*, her current retro junk-TV indulgence. She readjusted the pillows on her bed, which definitely was not seeing as much action as Carrie's or Samantha's. None at all, in fact. Which was OK. Deciding on another evening with Carrie and friends, Aly leaned back with a splash of good scotch on the rocks and a piece of hazelnut milk chocolate, her favorite TV-at-home combination. Woo-hoo, she smiled to herself, Saturday night in the big city.

🐑 🐑 🐑

The polished-brass doors of the elevator opened with a chime. Aly stood up from the chair where she'd been waiting and waved. Chas, nattily attired in slim trousers, crisp white shirt, and blazer with a pocket square, crossed the hotel lobby with a broad smile.

"Aly, my dear, you look stunning. I barely recognize you!" Chas said, bestowing a European-style double-kiss on Aly's cheeks. "Being back in the city agrees with you."

"Thanks. The Vineyard had turned me into a bit of a slob." Aly brushed back her sleek, newly straightened hair. She'd paired her favorite black pants with a snug taupe cashmere sweater that showed off her figure, down five pounds since leaving lobster rolls, Whit's pasta feasts, and Hannah's butter-in-everything treats behind. Aly had spent time (and money) on her makeup: foundation flawless, eyes emphasized with subtle black mascara, brows carefully shaped, lips a deep rose.

"The Vineyard look. Ah, but that emphasized your natural loveliness." Chas tilted his head as he further assessed Aly's looks. "This is sophisticated and quite gorgeous. Still, I do miss your Island glow."

Aly laughed. "San Francisco fog. No one glows in Northern California without bronzer. You're looking handsome."

"I never know who I might meet."

Aly pushed open the door to the street. "You're sure you're up for going out after flying all day?"

"Absolutely. I'm not planning to waste a minute of my trip here. Where are you taking me?"

"I thought we'd start with a drink at a little place I know. Sort of a speakeasy vibe," she said, taking his arm. "You don't order a drink, you give the bartender a song or a poem or an idea, and he'll create a one-of-a-kind cocktail, just for you. I took a friend who wrote a novel with goats in it, and he made a drink with fermented goat milk liquor from Nepal. It was surprisingly good."

"Bespoke cocktails. What fun!" Chas and Aly walked toward SoMa. "You haven't missed much on the Vineyard. The Possible Dreams auction was fabulous. I wish you could've stayed for that. Granny has been asking for you. Hannah and Lawrence are still disgustingly adorable lovebirds. A nearly world-famous artist and a house painter. Who'd have thought that was a recipe for true love?"

Even though the Island had never been truly her home, seeing Chas triggered a pang of homesickness. "I was sure Hannah would end up with a farmer or carpenter," Aly said. "She called last week. They've invited Lawrence's family over for dinner, and Hannah is in a tizzy. But his sister is in her corner. She gets that Hannah is good for him."

The topic of Whit hung in the air like a giant inflatable elephant-shaped balloon. Once, she'd asked Hannah about Whit, but Hannah refused to say more than he was "fine." Aly did and didn't want to ask about him. But what could Chas say that would help? Did she need to know that Whit was happy? Or miserable? It wouldn't change anything. "It must be much quieter there now."

"The fall is lovely. No crowds, perfect weather. Although we had an exceptionally nice summer. You were lucky."

Aly steered Chas down an alley to an unmarked door. The room was small and dark with thick red velvet curtains and a wall of what must have been more than a hundred bottles of booze. Standing behind the mahogany and brass bar stood Aly's favorite bartender, bow-tied, with a smile under his impressive handlebar mustache. Chas and Aly took two of the four seats. "We beat the crowds, I see," Aly said to the bartender.

"Hello, love. Lucky you did." He leaned over the bar to give Aly a whiskery kiss. "It's been a while. Who's your friend?" he asked, subtly eyeing Chas.

"This is Chas. He's visiting me from the East Coast."

"Martha's Vineyard, to be precise," Chas said. "That is quite the marvelous 'stache."

"Thank you," said the bartender, smoothing the ends of his moustache. "Pleasure meeting you. I'm Kyle, your mixologist." He leaned forward against the bar toward Chas and smiled. "This is how it works, Chas. You give me an idea, some inspiration—it can be anything, and I mean anything—and I make you a cocktail. But if you order a gin and tonic or whatever it is you drink on Martha's Vineyard," he growled with mock ferocity. "Out you go."

"I think I've got it," Chas said. "Ladies first."

"OK. First, let me show you something." Aly played the video she'd made of Dandelion cavorting in the grass. "Can you make me that?"

"Let me see," Chas said, reaching for the phone. "My goodness, look at how many views you have!"

"It's only the beginning. Hannah and I are going to make Dandelion an internet influencer. Maybe," she said and laughed.

Kyle twirled the ends of his mustache. "Let's see. White and frothy, yes. Playful. Sweet, but not too sweet. Ah, yes. I have an idea. You're OK with an egg white?" Aly nodded. "This will give us nice in-a-grassy-field notes," he said, selecting a bottle of the Botanist gin and, after a pause, a bottle of green Fontbonne liqueur. "This is a bit more delicate than Chartreuse." After adding ice to a shaker, he added a measure of gin, one splash each of Fontbonne and *crème de violette* (for a floral note), half-and-half, lemon juice, sugar, and, with a deft flourish, cracked an egg one-handed and dropped in the white.

After several minutes of vigorous shaking, he poured Aly's drink, fluffy and white, into an old-fashioned, cup-shaped Nick and Nora glass, and added a tiny sprig of basil. "Your Frolicking Lamb," he said, presenting the cocktail to Aly. She took a sip. It was delicious: sweet and tart, frothy and creamy, like drinking a fresh, flower-dappled meadow.

"Wonderful," she said. If Kevin were here, he'd be trying to weasel the recipe out for the restaurant: so pretty and unique, so Instagrammable. Kevin. He'd called again. And texted. Obviously, the message hadn't gotten through. Aly dreaded talking to him again, but he needed to understand that it was over, for good.

Kyle rinsed his shaker. "I only wish I had a fresh clover for a garnish. Then it would be perfect."

"That looks a bit like a Ramos Gin Fizz crossed with an Aviation," said Chas, reaching over to try a sip. "Very nice."

"You know your cocktails," replied the bartender, looking impressed. "Now, what shall I get for you, tall, blond, and handsome?"

"I'm looking for the perfect apartment," Chas said.

"Here, in San Francisco?"

"Where else?"

"That's very rare, very expensive. Can you afford it?"

"I can."

"Excellent." Kyle opened an upper cabinet and started rummaging around. "I'm looking for that too."

"The perfect apartment or someone who lives in one?"

Kyle smiled. "Both. May I join you?" he asked, pulling out two dusty glasses. "My shift is almost over."

"Of course, my treat," said Chas.

Kyle washed and dried the glasses. "Rumor goes that these glasses survived the earthquake and fire of 1906, from a bar called the Saloon, our namesake. Quite the heroic effort—the sailors and firemen ran a hose from the bay. You see, prostitutes lived on the upper floors." Kyle twisted the ends of his moustache as he perused his bottles. "If I had three days, I'd make you a California Milk Punch. It dates back to the Gold Rush. Jamaican rum, cloves, coriander, cinnamon, lemon, pineapple, brandy—and, of course, milk. You let it steep, then strain it. Rich, spicy, and boozy," he said, sending Chas a look.

"Oooh. I like the sound of that. Maybe I'll have to come back," Chas flirted. Aly rolled her eyes. Chas was going to love San Francisco.

"Ah. Inspiration!" Kyle said, pulling a vial of gold flakes and three bottles from the top shelf. He dropped a square, perfect ice cube into each glass, a measure from each of the bottles, and two drops from an apothecary bottle labeled "XXX." "My very most secret ingredient. Some swear it's an aphrodisiac." Kyle stirred the drink, sprinkled it with a few gold flakes, and handed one to Chas.

"To the perfect apartment," said Kyle, raising his drink.

Their glasses clinked. "To finding exactly what you want."

🐑 🐑 🐑

Aly opened the heavy wooden door to Nonna's for Chas. "You won't find this on any Best of San Francisco list, but it's my favorite restaurant," Aly said. "My old apartment was around the corner."

"This is perfect. Carbo loading for the rest of the evening to keep up my energy!"

"Is there somewhere you wanted to go after this?" Aly asked uneasily as they sat down at their table. Clubbing had never been her scene, if that's what Chas had in mind. A big meal at Nonna's put her to sleep, and she was counting on jet lag to do the same for him.

"I've got a date," he said, showing Aly a cocktail napkin with a phone number scribbled on it.

"With Kyle-the-bartender?"

Chas grinned. "I'm going to his place to mix up a little 'California milk punch.' You can see why I want an apartment here. Best dating scene anywhere." Chas said and crunched a skinny breadstick. "Though I did manage to find a local hottie on the Vineyard. Only took me all summer. He's in the U.S. Coast Guard. Nothing serious, Tanner's the type to have a sailor in every port."

"Sounds like you're not far behind." Yes, San Francisco would definitely be Chas's scene. And he'd make a fun part-time roommate to boot.

Chas opened the wine list. "Granny almost caught us one day. She dropped by my place to say hello, and I had to hide him naked in the closet. She wanted tea and kept nattering on and on for so long, the fellow nearly suffocated! But I made it up to him."

"I imagine you did," Aly smiled.

The waiter's face lit up when he recognized Aly. "Aly! Where have you been?" he exclaimed, bending over to kiss her on both cheeks. "Nonna's making cavatelli. I'll go get her. She was asking and asking why you stopped coming."

A minute later, Nonna was at their table, and Aly was in Nonna's warm embrace. "You had us worried," she scolded. "At first, I thought you were on one of your diets again, but then you were gone for such a long time. I thought you had moved away without telling us."

"I was in Massachusetts, Nonna. Martha's Vineyard. I was visiting a friend and decided to stay a while."

"Martha's Vineyard. So fancy. Did you meet Mr. President Obama?"

Aly shook her head. "No such luck."

Nonna kissed Aly on her cheek. "You come back, and the two of us will talk. I want to hear everything about your summer. Now, you and your friend, you have a nice dinner," she said and bustled back off to the kitchen.

"Would you like to order some drinks? Some wine, perhaps, to start?" said the waiter.

"A bottle of the Brunello," Chas said, pointing to the most expensive bottle on the list. "My treat, Aly."

"*Buono*," the waiter said with a smile. "Fantastic choice. I will bring the *vino subito*, right away. Would you like to order now?"

"I'm starving," said Chas. "Aly, dear, please order for both of us. Calories be damned."

Seeing the dishes on the menu that she and Whit had cooked together—vodka pasta, *pasta puttanesca*, *spaghetti alle vongole*—had pierced her heart. She couldn't do it, not yet. Instead, Aly ordered the cavatelli with pesto, lasagna, and some appetizers and handed their menus to the waiter.

Chas reached for another breadstick. "But we haven't talked about you yet. Are you happy being back? I imagine you don't miss us at all, living in this fabulous city."

"I miss you all," Aly said. "Coming back was a shock. I was like the country mouse wandering around, staring up at the tall buildings. But San Francisco, well, it's home," she said, hoping she sounded more convincing than she felt.

"Martha's Vineyard will always be your home, too, you know. I could tell you'd fallen in love with it."

Aly felt an almost painful tug of longing for both the Island—and Whit. "I did. It's a magical place."

"Ah. Here comes the wine." Chas went through the ritual of tasting the wine before nodding, "Delicious. That's going to open beautifully." He turned to Aly. "Now that the cute teddy bear of a bartender isn't here to distract me, I have to ask you an important question. Did you get back together with your chef?"

Aly shook her head. "My friends talked me into having dinner with him the other night. He wants us to get back together. But when you're over someone—and I am so over him—you're done." The waiter brought the appetizers to the table. "We were happy together once," Aly said, cutting off a piece of mortadella. "Or at least I thought we were. But no way am I moving back in with him."

"That's good news. For both of us."

"But living out of a suitcase is getting old. I'm ready to get settled into my own place."

"That's why I'm here. To pick out an apartment with my fiancée."

Aly's eyes widened. "Please don't tell me you haven't told Granny about us. You promised, remember?"

"I meant to," Chas said, looking sheepish. "I really did. But before I could say anything, she brought out her jewelry box and started showing me diamond rings for when the right moment comes. The only way I could talk her out of giving me one of her rings was to tell her I was having one made for you. You should have seen how happy Granny was. I couldn't break her heart."

"Oh, Chas," Aly sighed.

"It will be for just a little while longer." Chas pulled a small box out of his jacket pocket and opened it. "Aly, will you please pretend to marry me?"

Inside was a cushion-cut sapphire in a setting of delicate, hand-hammered yellow gold. Chas handed it to her, and she turned it over in her fingers, watching the stone flash blue fire in the candlelight. "The sapphire is from a ring an ex-lover gave me. I wasn't ever going to wear it again," Chas said. "I came up with the design for the setting. The jeweler wanted me to go Lady Di with a circle of diamonds, but this seemed more 'you.' I had to guess your size."

"But...." Aly was speechless. It was lovely, exactly the kind of ring she would have picked out. Simple and unique, and the stone was stunning, a rich cobalt blue. "I can't believe you actually had a ring made. Why?"

"Because I wanted to. I hated having that beautiful sapphire sitting in a drawer. I was never going to wear it. But you can. Please say yes."

Reluctantly, Aly put it back in the box. "It's beautiful. But my answer is no."

"I was afraid you might say that." He pushed the box back across the table. "But the ring is yours. A token of my affection."

"You should save it and make it into a different ring—someday—for your real fiancé."

"A stone from a ring another man gave me? That would be very bad juju."

"A gift for your mother, then? Or sister?"

Chas gave her a look. He opened the box and handed her the ring. "I'm not usually a stubborn man, but I'm afraid I'm going to have to insist. Please keep it, Aly."

"Only until you decide you want the stone back." Aly took the ring and tried putting it on her right hand, but it wouldn't go over her knuckle. She slipped it on the ring finger of her left hand, a perfect fit.

Chas beamed. "I won't."

"I guess this means you didn't give Granny back her pearls either?"

"I'm afraid not," he said, dipping a piece of bread in olive oil. "Well, this takes care of how I'll tell Granny. I'll say you turned me down. I guess we should break up too."

Aly looked up from cutting into the burrata. "But that's still deceiving her. You need to come clean, Chas, and tell her that you're gay."

Chas stared into his wineglass and sighed dramatically. "I know."

"Whit's one hundred percent sure that Granny already knows and is just stringing you along," she said, pleased with how casually she was able to say his name, despite the pain inside.

"I hope Whit's right. I truly hate disappointing her," Chas said. "Speaking of Whit, he'd love this place. Back in our troublemaker days, we'd play hooky, and he'd drag me to this little hole-in-the-wall Italian place in Boston's North End. Then again, the spaghetti they served in the dining hall was inedible. That boy does like his pasta like no one else I know."

"He does," Aly said with a pang. She saw Whit in the kitchen, the steam from the pasta pot curling his dark hair, the aroma of garlic and tomatoes filling the air. Across the table, he'd be glowing with pride as she loaded her plate with a second helping. She twisted the napkin in her lap. The longing to see him, to be with him, tugged her heart from her chest. Just get over him, Aly scolded herself. Enough is enough. No matter that she hadn't meant to, she'd messed up, and she couldn't fix it.

"How's he doing?" she asked, trying to sound casual.

Chas sighed. "He's miserable. I can't talk to him. Believe me, Aly, I've tried."

🐑 🐑 🐑

Aly sipped her decaf cappuccino. Miserable, Chas had said. Irrational. And stubborn. Whit wasn't getting over Aly any more than she was getting over him. She gazed at the sapphire ring. Even if she called, he probably wouldn't answer. What good would it do anyway? Heartache always fades. Sometimes it just takes a while.

Her cell phone pinged. Why was Hannah sending her a link from the Woods Hole Oceanographic Institution? She clicked on it, and her eyes widened. WHOI Creative Studio was looking for a Senior Web Designer. *This is what you do, right? You should apply.* Aly shook her head. *Yeah, but I live here. And I have a job already,* Aly typed back. *You didn't read it—100 percent remote if you want! Willow's ex-boyfriend's brother works there. I'm sending you his contact. It's perfect!!! Got to go. Love, H.*

"Aly, *mia cara*," came a gravelly voice from behind her. "What happened to your friend?"

Aly turned in her chair. "Nonna," she said, standing up to hug and kiss the old woman, two cheeks, Italian style. "He had a date."

Nonna patted Aly's cheek. "How about I come right back, and we can have a girl talk."

Nonna returned instantly, carrying a plate heaped with miniature cannoli. "Your favorite. With the chocolate chips and pistachios," she said, setting the plate on the table and sitting down. "Ah. It feels good to sit."

"You work too hard, Nonna," Aly said and sank her teeth into the cannoli's crisp outer shell.

"But no one else makes the gnocchi or cavatelli right. Or the cannoli," Nonna said, helping herself to a pastry. "I've tried to teach them, but what, they rush, say my way is too slow." She took a bite. "You must take your time, *mia cara*, to do things right."

"It's worth it. The cavatelli were absolutely delicious."

"Ah, my secret is to make them with ricotta and add a little lemon zest." The old woman noticed the sapphire on Aly's ring finger. Her eyes flew wide. "Oh mio Dio," she said and reached for Aly's hand. "Beautiful, beautiful! When did it happen? Where?"

"Here, Nonna," Aly smiled.

"That night, so long ago? Your chef? The one who likes my boxed *grissini* and nothing else?"

Aly shook her head and smiled. "Tonight, just now."

"But..but..." Nonna sputtered. "That boy, he is *omosessuale*, a gay boy! He's not a gay boy?"

Aly laughed at her confusion. "He is. It's not a real engagement. It's..." she hesitated. Nonna would not approve of Chas's ruse to trick Granny. "It's a gift. A very generous gift."

"You'll give your Nonna a heart attack."

Aly took another bite of her cannoli. "Kevin, the chef, and I broke up over the summer. He wants us to get back together, but it's over." Nonna listened intently, nodding her head, as Aly told the story of what had happened: the cheating, their breakup, Kevin's trip to Martha's Vineyard to convince her to come back.

"Ay, *mia cara*." Nonna leaned back and sighed. "Maybe he is so charming as you say. Maybe you thought you were happy. But you were here all the time for dinner. By yourself—so lonely!—while your chef worked." She patted Aly's hand. "But when I meet him, I can see. You talk, he talks over top of you, like what you say is not important. And the language of your body was not good. He leaned forward; you leaned back. He puts his hands on the table, you put yours in your lap. When the right man touches you, it is like you get all hot and melty inside, like warm mozzarella. It'll be a feeling like when no other man touches you." Nonna patted Aly's hand again. "I see passion in that Kevin, but it is not for you. I am sorry. And a cheater! Aly, you deserve better."

Aly took another cannoli. "I know."

"And did you see how he picks at his food? You want a man who knows how to eat, enjoys his food. Not all picky-critical. Picky-critical at food, picky-critical at life, picky-critical at girlfriend—or wife. Am I right?"

Aly nodded. "He's a perfectionist. In all things. Including wanting a perfect girlfriend."

"Oh, *mia cara*. No one is perfect! You see those two over there?" She waved her hand at a couple in their thirties in the corner, laughing as they fed one another tasty bites from their plates. "She's my niece Jessica. I probably told you about her? She brought all her young men here. Pfft. Terrible taste. Some picky-critical like that Kevin, one so selfish he never shared his food, one such a pig. One said, 'I don't eat carbs!' He was the worst!" Nonna's eyebrows flew up. "Until Ethan. And he loved my cooking, especially my spaghetti and meatballs. Such a good eater, such a nice man. Now, they are happily married."

Aly felt a pang. Whit would've passed Nonna's spaghetti-and-meatballs test with flying colors. "They're lucky."

She narrowed her eyes. "There is something you haven't told your Nonna. Maybe there's someone else?"

Aly sighed. Nonna had a remarkable ability to read minds. "His name was—is—Whit. He's a fisherman. It was a summer fling. Fun while it lasted. He made me forget about Kevin."

"And on the mattress?"

"Very hot melty mozzarella," Aly smiled. "But it can't work. Not just that he broke up with me. We're very different. He's there, and my life is here. This is where I should be. I know that."

Nonna reached over to tap Aly's forehead. "That is your head talking. What does your heart say?"

Tears pricked Aly's eyelids. Her heart? Her heart was still back in Martha's Vineyard.

With Whit.

Nonna put her hand over Aly's. "You deserve a love like I had with my Giovanni. Not just the whoosh, the flame, the passion.

Oh, we had that." Her eyes lit up. "The neighbors, we were too loud, they would complain! But this is very important, *mia cara*, my Giovanni made me feel safe and strong and *fiduciosa*—confident— like I could do anything, try anything. What I wanted, he wanted for me. Like this restaurant. We were like a perfect recipe, the ingredients together making something magical." Nonna sighed. "And he made me laugh. He loved me for who I am, even when I am not right." Nonna squeezed Aly's hand. "That Whit, how did he make you feel?"

Aly was silent. She looked down at her hands.

"That's what I thought. Now finish the cannoli or I will."

🐑 🐑 🐑

At her neighborhood coffee shop, Aly sat at a table with her laptop waiting for her cortado and nibbling on a buckwheat chocolate muffin. She played a game as she watched the customers in line place their orders: the sweaty guy in the Hoka sneakers had just run a 5K; the girl in head-to-toe lavender Lululemon was on her way to her barre class; the couple in sunglasses and sweats rolled out of bed with matching hangovers in search of caffeine after a hard night out. She missed Chas already. Unfortunately, his visit had ended without their locating an apartment that met his exacting standards. Aly got it. If he were going to shell out for a place, it should be special. Besides, hunting for an apartment was something for her to do on weekends.

Her phone rang. "Hi, Jo," she answered. "How are you? I've been meaning to call you back. But I'm free now if you want to chat. Just getting some coffee."

"Wonderful. I'm fine, but how are you? You must love being back in San Francisco. And how is your new job? I'm so pleased you get to work with your old boss."

Falling back into old habits, Aly painted a rosy-pink picture of her life, telling Jo what she wanted to hear (and Aly wanted to be true): San Francisco was as great as ever; her Airbnb apartment was small but charming; at her fascinating new job, the company's robots had almost perfected their clothes-folding skills. But with each white lie, she felt her life become more colorless and less real, as if she were describing the life of someone else. Someone happier, more successful. She should be happy. What was wrong with her?

"And," Aly said, "I'm thinking about taking a vacation next month. Maybe I'll go to Puget Sound to see the whales."

Aly could hear a lawnmower start up in the background. "You know," Jo said, "We had such a wonderful time this summer. Would you like to do a trip together? I've always wanted to go to Santa Fe. Maybe stay at a spa? I could meet you there."

Aly's vision of whales sadly swam away, replaced with art galleries and massages. "Santa Fe's really nice. I'll look into it."

"I'm glad you think it's a good idea! And that everything is going so well. You made the right choice to go back," Jo said. "But there's one thing you haven't mentioned. Have you seen Kevin?"

Aly pulled a piece off her muffin. "We had dinner last week. He wants to get back together. But it's over," she said, feeling better finally to be speaking the truth.

Jo sighed. "Oh, Aly. You invested a lot in that relationship. Couples have gotten over worse, you know. Remember, you were very happy with him."

"Kevin wants to do couples therapy. I would if I thought there was a spark to rekindle. But there isn't," Aly said. Of that, she was sure.

"Please think about counseling. There's nothing to lose. Sometimes you think the spark is out, but it just needs a puff of air and the right piece of tinder to get it going again."

Aly's certainty wobbled, a bowling pin ready to topple. Could Jo be right? Was it a mistake not to try again with Kevin? "I know you didn't approve of me dating Whit." She stopped. Just saying his name twisted her heart into a tight, painful knot. "But I learned what I need—what I deserve—from a guy."

"That's the kind of thing you take to counseling. If Kevin doesn't know what you need, he can't give it to you."

The muffin turned dry in her throat. "I'll think about it."

"Either way, I'm glad you got something out of your summer fling," Jo said, not sounding entirely satisfied with Aly's answer. "But you should be getting out as much as you can. What are you doing tonight?"

"A friend from work invited me to a party in the Berkeley Hills tonight, but I don't know if I want to go." Aly was still weighing the lure of cozy pajamas and Netflix over a long Uber ride to a party full of strangers who would probably talk only about robotics and video games.

"You should go. Have some fun. You might meet someone."

Aly sipped her coffee and sighed. She had been spending too many nights in the apartment. "You're right."

"And if things don't work out with Kevin, you might try that super-selective Ivy League dating app," Jo continued. "That would be perfect for you."

"I'll look into it."

"Promise?"

"Promise." The idea held no appeal, but it made sense.

"Good. And I'm glad you didn't fall into a trap like Hannah, dating that Lawrence. Good looking enough, but neither of them will ever get anywhere in life," Jo said. "Maybe you can talk to her. She never takes my advice. Never has, never will. Not like you."

🐑 🐑 🐑

The jellyfish floated through the water in their tank at the Aquarium of the Bay, their delicate tentacles like yards of aquatic lace. Was that Aly, thinking she was in control of her life but being pushed around by the currents, first by Jo, then by Kevin? Or was she like the oblivious prey of an octopus, letting herself be wrapped and trapped in their arms?

With a swirl of tentacles, the jellyfish drifted away, and another, with a transparent body like a bowl of glass and long, threadlike tentacles, took its place. Had she ever made any major life decisions on her own? Without taking Jo's advice?

She thought back, reviewing the big choices one by one: College? No. Major? No. Internships? No. Job? No. Breaking up with Kevin, she supposed. But she didn't have much choice in that one. And of course, she had checked with Jo before taking her job at I-Robotics.

Aly's thoughts twisted and swirled like the jellyfish's tentacles. She moved back to San Francisco because that was where Jo said she belonged. She took the first job that was offered to her, not because she truly wanted it, but out of fear of the interview process. And Jo advised her to take it. She'd agreed to give up a vacation she wanted for one she didn't, let herself be persuaded to go to a party when she'd rather stay home. She'd even agreed to consider couples therapy with Kevin. After so many years, Aly was still letting Jo make decisions for her. And, despite the rosy picture she'd painted, she wasn't happy. She still wasn't living her own life.

But it didn't have to be that way.

Her mind spinning, Aly entered the clear acrylic tunnel to the Under the Bay exhibit. Rockfish, bright orange garibaldi, and shimmering schools of anchovies swam around her as she walked through the tunnel, a magical entrance into another, watery world. Aly paused to watch a school of rays glide by slowly, elegantly rippling their wing-shaped bodies. The light refracting through the water and the mesmerizing motion of the sea creatures soothed her, making her wish she hadn't let Jo steer her away from studying marine biology. It was too late to do anything about that now. But it wasn't too late for her to take control of her life. To do what she wanted. But what was that? A garibaldi peeked around a clump of swaying sea kelp, looking like the world's largest, fattest goldfish. She could audit some classes on oceanography and cetology. Learn to scuba dive. Maybe even travel to Fiji or the Great Barrier Reef.

And apply for the job at WHOI.

🐑 🐑 🐑

Aly brewed a cup of tea and sat on the sofa. She scrolled through her messages to find Hannah's text about the opportunity at WHOI. She clicked on the posting and carefully read the job description. The responsibilities included web-based outreach about the Woods Hole Oceanographic Institution's scientific research and programs, including (to Aly's delight) its Whale Safe program. The ideal candidate should have expertise in 4-D animation web design, which is what she'd been doing at Spire. She could work in Woods Hole, a short ferry ride from Martha's Vineyard, or partially or fully telecommute. The job paid a fraction of her salary at I-Robotics, but money wasn't the most important thing. She'd be working at WHOI!

Aly's heart began to race. She wanted this job.

She could live anywhere, so long as she watched her budget: a cabin in Tahoe and ski after work, or a beach bungalow on some tropical island and snorkel at lunch. Aly had no ties. She could rent an inexpensive *appartamento* in Rome or Florence for a month and go on a pasta binge. Then, when she got tired of that, she could try the Azores or Bermuda, or couch-surf with college friends in London or Paris or Tokyo. She could spend as much or as little time as she wanted in San Francisco. Stay with Hannah on the Vineyard and commute by ferry to Woods Hole. The possibilities were endless. At that salary, Jo wouldn't understand why she'd even consider applying for the job. But Whit would, she thought with a jab to her heart.

Hannah was right. It was the perfect job.

🐑 🐑 🐑

Whit cradled his cell phone to his ear as he put a half gallon of milk in his shopping cart. "What do you think about the engine, Tanner? OK to take *Noepe* down south?" He added a box of Cheerios and joined the checkout lane.

"Not sure I would," said the voice on the phone. "Not heading into hurricane season. Easier to buy a new engine here than to find yourself stranded halfway down." Ka-ching. There went most of Whit's profits for the year. "Besides, a new engine will be more efficient. Save you a ton on fuel. I'll keep this one going through the Derby, but I'd start calling some dealers if I were you."

Whit sighed. "Yeah. Not surprised. Thanks. Really appreciate it."

Whit blinked. And blinked again. There, ahead of him in line, was Aly. No, he corrected himself, someone who looked like Aly, in jeans and Blundstone boots. But the hair was different. She turned around to pull oat milk out of the cart—Aly's brand, extra-creamy—and looked up. Ocean blue eyes met Whit's. It *was* Aly, buying groceries at Up-Island Cronig's.

An immense sapphire ring flashed on her ring finger. Whit felt a rushing, sinking feeling. Despite what Chas said, Aly must've gotten back together with the chef. And they were engaged. She'd picked up right where she'd left off. Not like him, still mucking around in a morass of regrets.

"Whit. Hi," Aly said, eyes wide. She didn't seem happy to see him.

"You're back," Whit sputtered. Stupid thing to say.

"Only for a couple of days."

He caught a whiff of her shampoo, and his heart did a flip. Her hair had changed, all sleek and citified, but not her scent, that camellia or honeysuckle or whatever it was that brought back the feel of her, soft and warm in his bed, a tangle of curls spread across the pillow. Damn Chas (and Hannah) for not warning him Aly was back on the Island. Or maybe they thought it was better if he didn't know.

Aly put a bunch of bananas on the belt. "Did Chas tell you I'm interviewing for a job at WHOI? They've got an opening in their division that does ocean education web design. I did the other interviews over Zoom, and I'm here for the final round." She gave him a half-smile. "Fingers crossed."

"Good luck." Whit's heart both leapt and sank at the idea of Aly on the Cape, just a ferry ride away. But the ring? Her engagement? "You'd move to Woods Hole?"

"The job can be either hybrid or one hundred percent telecommuting," she said, adding a milk chocolate Lindt bar to the belt. "I could stay in San Francisco. Or live anywhere, really." She pushed her cart through. "But it's nice being back and seeing Hannah and Dandelion. Plus, Chas and I are going to meet up with Granny. We're finally going to come clean about the fake girlfriend thing. I just hope she's not mad." Aly lifted her left hand to show him the ring. "Chas wanted to keep the charade up—even had this made for me—but I talked him out of it. He insisted I keep the ring, though. I'm giving it back to Chas to have it resized for a different finger."

Whit felt as if he were a buoy popping to the surface. Aly wasn't engaged, not for real. "Granny will give you both a hard time, but I doubt she'll be angry," he said, trying to match her casual tone. *Just acquaintances, running into each other at the supermarket.* "How's San Francisco?" he asked, setting the plastic divider on the belt.

"Great," Aly said. "But I miss the Island, it's so beautiful here. And it's even nicer now with all the crowds gone. The air is so fresh. I'd almost forgotten that." She looked out the store window at the clear October sky. "I almost missed buying overpriced groceries at Cronig's," she smiled. "How are you? Hannah told me you were having boat problems."

"Yeah. I need a new motor before I head south. I'll leave in November if I get a window in the weather."

"Back down to St. John?"

"I thought about Nevis," said Whit. "But I've got a mooring in St. John. And a place to live."

"Your cottage with the bougainvillea and the nutmeg tree."

"Island card number?" interrupted the checkout clerk.

"I don't have one," replied Aly. She tapped her credit card to pay and turned back to Whit. "Hannah's probably back from the garden center," she said with a glance at her watch. "Nice to see you. And good luck with your boat."

And then she was gone.

🐑 🐑 🐑

"Game's up, dear," Granny said, rapping her silver teaspoon on the table and looking at Aly with her sharp old eyes.

Aly breathed a sigh of relief. Of course Granny knew. "I'm so sorry. I shouldn't have agreed when Chas came up with the fake girlfriend idea. I hope you aren't very mad at us."

It had taken Aly most of the morning to get over having run into Whit in the supermarket line. Seeing him had bulldozed right through the self-protective wall Aly had erected. She'd forgotten how tall he was, the breadth of his chest, his hands—so strong, yet the fingers so gentle—the way his hair curled over his ears, the warmth of his lopsided smile. Aly knew she'd probably run into Whit. But she hadn't expected it then, so soon. It had taken every ounce of her self-possession to hold it together.

Granny pursed her lips, deepening the wrinkles around her mouth. "Apology accepted."

Aly glanced over at Chas, who looked stunned. She pulled a silk pouch out of her pocket and handed it to the regal old woman. "I really am sorry. And here are your pearls. Thank you for letting me borrow them."

"But, but?" Chas broke in. "You've always known that Aly and I weren't a couple?"

"Of course. My goodness, dear, I've known that you're gay ever since you were a child. I do hope that poor young man in your closet didn't suffocate when I dropped by the other week," Granny said with a glint in her eye. "Oh my, the eau de sex in your place would have put my poodle in heat!" Granny rapped on the table again. "Next time you bring your fiancé to meet me, he better be a nice young man with a proper pedigree. Like that Whit. Too bad he's not gay." She picked up a cookie and waved it at Chas. "I was ever so amused that you thought you needed to bring me a girlfriend. Why did you do that, dear boy?"

"I thought it would make you happy. I know you want to have great-grandchildren running around your house someday."

"Oh, it did make me happy, but not in the way you thought. I've been enjoying your little show immensely. You're quite a fine actress, Aly dear. Have you ever done theatre?" She sipped her tea. "And of course I want you to have children, Chas, but surely you know there are all sorts of things you can do with modern medicine—egg donors, surrogates, and whatnot. It's hardly anything new."

Chas looked stunned. "But why didn't you ever say anything?"

"Oh, I wanted to see how far you would go. Why do you think I pulled out my jewelry box and started talking about engagement rings? My next step was to start planning the wedding. The backyard would make a lovely venue, especially in June when the peonies and roses are blooming." She fixed him with a stern look. "But lying to Granny is a very bad habit. Even when you mean well. That goes for you too, Aly."

"I'm very sorry, Granny," Chas said.

"Me too," Aly said, genuinely contrite.

"Well, I hope you've both learned your lesson," Granny said. "But that's not the mystery I wanted to solve this afternoon," she added. "Could you pour me some more tea, please?"

Aly lifted the teapot and refilled their cups. "What mystery?"

"My dear friend Brenda's granddaughter is a freshman at Middlebury. She wants to study Russian as her minor. I had her look in the course catalogue for the classes your parents teach. Guess what? They aren't on the faculty. Unless your parents have a different last name from yours, they've never taught there. So, who are you, dear?"

🐑 🐑 🐑

Hannah looked up from her cutting board as Chas and Aly walked in. "How did it go? Was Granny mad?"

Under Granny's questioning, Aly had blurted out everything: her teenage mother, the unknown father, the years living in a trailer park before she moved in with Hannah. Granny appeared more curious than anything else, concluding that it "was not exactly the ideal upbringing, my dear. But at least you turned out fairly well. Except for the lying. That does need to stop."

Chas slumped into a kitchen chair. "She's known all along," he said, looking stunned. "Whiskey."

"I need one too," Aly said.

The whole episode at Granny's was beyond humiliating. Aly poured two double scotches and joined Chas at the table. She took a swallow and turned to Hannah. "It was, uh, interesting."

Chas sipped his drink. "Granny never said anything. I can't believe that."

Hannah pulled a cucumber out of the refrigerator and started to slice it. "Maybe she was waiting for you to tell her."

Aly leaned back in her chair and sighed. "She was. It was all an amusing game for her. And she'd figured out that my parents weren't professors. I even had to admit that I was named after a Disney princess, not Russian royalty."

"We both got quite a severe lecture about deceiving people," Chas said. "I must say it is a relief to have everything out in the open at last. I suppose both of us learned that truth always comes out."

🐑 🐑 🐑

Aly picked up her bag and joined the line of foot passengers waiting to get off the ferry. It had been a pleasant 45-minute ride from Woods Hole back to the Island, warm enough to sit outside on the upper deck. She spotted Hannah's truck in the 10-minute lot at the ferry terminal.

"How'd it go?" Hannah asked as Aly climbed into the passenger seat.

"Good, I think. I really, *really* want this job," Aly said, clipping her seatbelt. "But they still have two other candidates to talk to in this round." She'd done her homework for her interview, and when the conversation turned to her idea for integrating real-time information from WHOI's Whale Safe program into an interactive 4-D whale's eye view of life in the sea, Aly could tell that they liked it. And her. And, thankfully, her enthusiasm about the job had calmed her anxiety about interviewing.

"Fingers crossed you get an offer," Hannah said, pulling out of the lot.

"Toes too," Aly said, looking out the window. She sighed as the stress of the interview melted away, grateful to be back on the Island.

"OK if we run a couple of errands? I need to stop at SBS to pick up some dog food for Beau. And get some eggs at Arnie's on our way home."

"Sure." Aly's heart skipped a beat when she saw a truck that looked like (but wasn't) Whit's. It had been three days since she'd run into him at Cronig's. If he had wanted to see her, he would've called. But he hadn't.

"Did I tell you they've spotted a coyote again in the State Forest? He's got plenty of wild turkeys around to eat, but the owners of the Dinghy want me to look into getting a guard llama for the sheep."

As they drove home, Hannah chatted about the pros (fierceness) and cons (spitting) of llamas as livestock guardians and made a detour down a dirt road to Flat Point Farm's you-would-never-know-it's-there-unless-someone-told-you-about-it
farmstand. Aly hopped out, said a brief hello to the chickens and the goats, and picked out a box of eggs, leaving cash in the honor-system cashbox.

A few minutes later, they were home. Hannah hoisted the dog food from the back seat, saying, "Go out back. Lawrence and I have a surprise for you."

"What?" Aly asked, walking over to the pen. Not one but two half-grown lambs came running over to greet her, bleating in tandem.

"My idea," said Lawrence, walking down the back steps from the house. "Day one of teaching Dandelion how to make friends. How'd the interview go?"

"Really well, I hope. I'll find out if I get an offer by the end of the week. Wait," Aly said, "I thought Dandelion didn't like other sheep." In the weeks Aly had been gone, Dandelion had put on both weight and wool and was looking more and more like a sheep and less like a lamb. It made Aly a little sad, seeing her little lamb grow up so fast. Dandelion nudged her new friend to play, and Aly pulled out her phone to shoot a new video for Dandelion's next post.

"She likes this one," Lawrence said as the lambs bounded off together to the far corner of the pen. "Hannah and I were talking about how to keep Dandelion warm this winter. I started to think that maybe her problem wasn't with sheep per se, but with a whole flock of sheep. You know, like when you go to a big party, and everyone else knows each other?"

"Only too well." Aly's mind flashed to a memory of the party after Whit played at the Grange, walking into a room of people and not knowing a soul except Hannah—and Whit. Whit, still oozing charisma after his performance as she'd asked him about *The Boatman*, the Gaelic song she loved so much. The one she'd learned and would never again sing with him. It felt like such a long time ago.

"The plan is to introduce Dandelion to the sheep a few at a time and to let them teach her that hanging out with other sheep is a good thing," Lawrence said, leaning against a fence post. "If all goes well, we'll eventually build up to the whole flock. Then it'll be like a party where everyone is a friend."

Aly gazed fondly at Dandelion and her new buddy. "Great idea—I hope it works."

🐑 🐑 🐑

"I've brought you a special treat," said Chas, waving a brown paper bag as he stepped onto Whit's deck. "I stopped by John's Fish Market. Only the best lobster rolls on the Island. Maybe all of New England. But not as good as those lobsters you and Aly caught. Those were superlative."

"Yeah," said Whit. Not that he needed any more reminders about Aly. He'd been trying to get her out of his head for days.

"I was quite surprised that she got into all that mucky lobster-fishing business the way she did," Chas said.

"What do you want to drink?" Whit hoped Chas's visit wasn't to nag him about Aly again. If so, lobster roll or no lobster roll, he'd send him packing.

Stomach growling, Whit set down their drinks and joined Chas out on the deck. He unfolded the white butcher paper. The split-top hot dog rolls were toasted with butter on both sides, and the huge chunks of lobster, lightly dressed with a touch of mayo, nearly overflowed the roll. "Thought I might go down to the beach later and throw a line in for a while."

"Fishing, fishing, fishing," said Chas. "Don't you ever get tired of fishing?"

"No," said Whit.

Chas took a bite. "I've changed my mind. I think now that I should buy a house or condo in San Francisco instead of renting. It's wonderful being in a place where being gay is as normal as—maybe more normal than—being straight. Aly would still have her own bedroom and bath, of course. Maybe even an in-law suite to give her a little more privacy," Chas said. He sipped his drink. "You know she's on the Island, don't you?"

"I ran into her in the checkout line at Cronig's."

"What? When? Did you make plans?"

"Of course not. And I'm not going to."

"You idiot boy," Chas said.

Whit glowered. "Watch it."

"Don't be stubborn, Whit. You know the two of you had something special together. Like I told you, I'd never seen you happy like that before. Ever," Chas said. "You were a hell of a lot more fun to hang out with too." He fixed Whit with a stare. "You're even worse than after Petra broke up with you, which I didn't think was possible."

"I'm better off by myself," Whit said, trying to keep his temper in check. His relationship—ex-relationship—with Aly was no business of Chas's. "She lied to me about that live-in boyfriend, don't forget. Respectfully, Chas, and I'm getting really tired of telling you, butt out of my love life."

"Ex-boyfriend. And she didn't lie; she just didn't tell you about him. I'm sure she had her reasons." Chas put his hands flat on the table. "So I'm supposed to sit around and watch my best friend be miserable? I'm not going to do that. And you wouldn't if the shoe were on the other foot. This is bullshit, Whit," he said, deadly serious. "She's here, right now, and she's not dating anyone."

"Enough about Aly, OK? We're not going to get back together," he said, resisting a glimmer of desperate hope.

"At least talk to her. You're just being stubborn."

Whit was truly tired of arguing. "Just drop it. Not everything ends happily ever after, like in some romance novel. She's going back to California."

"Then go with her."

"Enough, Chas."

"When Aly gets her new job, she can work and live anywhere," Chas said. "You can go anywhere too, well anywhere with water."

"This is stupid."

"It's not. If you think about it, it's quite obvious. St. John in the winter, San Francisco in the spring, the Vineyard in the summer and fall. You don't want to be in SF in the summer. Was it Mark Twain who said, 'The coldest winter I ever spent was a summer in San Francisco'? Oh, and November is perfect in San Francisco."

"And what, in your grand plan, am I supposed to do in San Francisco?"

"Do fishy-boaty things, of course. All that water around. I met a wonderful bartender who lives on a houseboat in the bay," Chas said. "He tells me that all the tech bros go out and buy boats after they make their first hundred million. And they don't know the first thing about them. He's quite sure you can find plenty of boats to play captain on." Chas ate a bite of lobster roll. "Or rent another tubby stinkpot like *Noepe* and take rich techies fishing. Or catch fish yourself and sell them to Aly's ex-boyfriend and his chef friends."

"That's an idiotic idea."

"What's idiotic is if you let Aly get away."

Taking a break from answering work emails, Aly stopped to admire her haul from the farmer's market: carnival-striped delicata squash, leaf-topped carrots, a beautiful bunch of rainbow chard, and three jars of beach plum jam to take back to San Francisco. The summer's tomatoes and corn, with the shift in seasons, had given way to hearty greens and a cornucopia of squash, as locals shopped to the background of a small country quartet picking out old-timey tunes. Like so many other things on the Island, the music reminded Aly of the first time she'd seen Whit on stage at the Grange, gorgeous and talented, charming the audience.

Aly picked up the book she'd brought to read on the plane and went outside. It was one of those warm early-October days that are like a last glimpse of summer. Over in the pen, Dandelion and two new sheep friends chased one another around, baaing and leaping. Like Whit, Dandelion, too, had moved on.

An intense feeling of nostalgia and loss washed over Aly. The Vineyard still felt like home, but it wasn't hers. Not anymore. Sighing, she stretched out on the chaise under the old pear tree to read, but her novel about an octopus failed to distract her. She looked across the field to where the pond glowed an iridescent pale blue, tranquil and soothing. She stood up and stretched. One last paddle, she decided, the perfect medicine to calm the tumult inside.

The barn gave off its familiar scent of freshly cut wood and hay, with a touch of oil paint and solvent from Lawrence's studio. On Hannah's workbench, a pile of translucent strips of wood sat next to a half-dozen projects in various stages of completion. Aly picked up one, an oval-shaped shade for a pendant light. Hannah's craftsmanship was exquisite. She had twisted each strip of wood and secured it so precisely that it barely overlapped with the next in a mesmerizing, sculptural design, a little Japanese, a little Danish modern. Aly held it up to the light. It was as beautiful as any piece in a museum. Hannah didn't have just a little bit of talent: she truly was an artist. Several high-end stores in San Francisco would probably jump at the chance to sell her work. Aly made a mental note to investigate that when she got back.

She put on her life jacket, picked up the paddle and board, and headed down the path to the shore. Wading out knee deep, she set the paddleboard on the water. Muscle memory kicked in as she climbed onto the board, first kneeling, then carefully placing one foot and then the other to stand with her feet hip-width apart over the center of the board.

Skimming across the water with the wind at her back, Aly fell into the meditative rhythm of dip, stroke, glide, dip, stroke, glide. Fall had settled on Tisbury Great Pond. The small wooden docks were nearly empty of boats, and the trees along the shoreline were fading from summer's bright, deep green to russet and ocher. The angle of the sun had shifted, marking the passage of time. Only the water, ruffled with ripples from the slight breeze, and the sky, streaked with clouds, remained the same.

In the distance, the dunes and beach formed a horizontal line separating the blue of the sky from the pond. Aly glanced at her watch. Sunset wasn't until 6:15. That would give her time to say goodbye to the ocean. She took some deep, steadying breaths and felt for her center, her balance. She cleared her mind to focus on what she had to be grateful for.

Dandelion, a sweet, joyous, gamboling lamb, had taught her the simplicity of affection, the happiness that comes from taking care of something besides yourself. And to slow down to admire the buttercups before eating them.

Hannah. Dear Hannah. She had built a life of giving and caring. An authentic life. Not a life shaped by conformity to the expectations of her parents or others. A life filled with love and friends.

And Whit. A cord drew tight inside. With Whit, Aly had discovered passion. The whoosh, the flame, as Nonna had said. And love. Whit had never tried to change her. He had given Aly the safe space where she could find herself, supported and encouraged by his strength and confidence in her. They had laughter. And singing. And lobsters. And love. Until it was time for both of them to move on.

And the pond, the Island itself, had brought her peace and healing. For that, Aly's gratitude knew no bounds.

🐑 🐑 🐑

"Come on fish, bite," Whit said to the unseen and uncooperative striped bass somewhere out there in the surf. He reeled in his line and cast again. Chas's plan for a life with Aly had taken hold of his imagination and wouldn't let go. It was ridiculous even to think about it, but he couldn't help it. He'd have no more luck with that far-fetched idea than he'd have catching a fish he'd thrown back into the sea.

Whit dug a sharpened plastic tube into the sand and inserted his rod. It was almost time to head back and get dinner going. He turned to judge the angle of the setting sun, to see if he had time for a few more casts before giving up. Not that he was feeling the least bit lucky. About fishing or anything else.

A woman's figure was silhouetted against the sun on the path at the top of the dune, a black shape against the red-orange blaze. Whit gave a half-hearted wave. This time of year, now that the derby was over, he was used to having the beach to himself and his thoughts. Sometimes, though, he wished he could leave those back at home. Whit turned back and pulled his rod from the holder. He braced his legs, left leg in front, levered his surfcasting rod behind him, and with a fluid, whiplike motion, propelled the lure into the waves and waited.

"Whit," said a voice behind him.

He turned. It was as if his imagination had conjured Aly up from the sand and the sky. His heart lurched before pounding a rapid tattoo in his chest.

"How's the fishing?" Aly asked. Whit stared, speechless, as the rod nearly jerked out of his hands. "Looks like you've caught something."

Whit began to reel in the fish, leaning back to pull the line taut, then forward as he furiously spun the handle on the reel, bringing in the line. Suddenly, the line went slack. The fish was off the hook. "The fishing's been like that. No luck. I hook them and lose them," he said, willing his heart to slow down as he put the rod back in the holder. "Not my day, I guess. It's nearly time to pack it in anyway."

The breeze picked up, blowing Aly's hair across her face. She brushed a stray strand from her lips. A surge of emotion ran through Whit. He wanted, more than anything in the world, to take two steps closer, to hold her in his arms, to feel her body pressed against his, to bend his head and kiss her lips. It pained him to stay where he was.

Aly watched the waves crest and break against the shore. "No fish for dinner, huh?"

"Nope." Heart pounding, Whit unclipped the lure and put it into his tackle box. "How did the interview go?"

"Good, I think. Fingers crossed."

He waited, hoping she would leave, release him from the torture of being close to her. "What would you be doing?" he finally asked, picking a safe topic. Whit watched Aly light up as she described the job, her enthusiasm like a warm sunbeam breaking through the clouds. He remembered what it was like to be with her, to look into her blue eyes that reflected her moods, dark with passion and bright with joy. Aly had the power to bring color to the world when he was with her. Chas was right: Aly was special.

"They might even let me go out on research vessels. How great is that? It'll be a big pay cut, but I don't care," Aly said. "How about you? Any luck with finding a new motor?"

"I ordered one. Chas's new boyfriend got mine running well enough until it arrives."

Aly turned as if to go. Then she stopped and gazed across the water, her lovely profile backlit by the setting sun as tender fingers of breeze played with her hair. After a time, she turned to him. "I'm sorry how things turned out. I should've told you about Kevin. I didn't mean to hide anything from you."

"I overreacted. No need to explain." Whit bent and slung the strap of his tackle box over his shoulder.

"I want to." She put a hand on his arm, stopping his heart. "I don't want to leave you thinking what you're thinking about me, that I lied to you on purpose."

Whit waited. Aly wasn't making this easy for him. He'd let her say her piece. Then he'd go home and go back to trying to forget her.

"I didn't want to give Kevin any real estate in my brain," Aly said. "I realize now that I was changing, finding my real self. And I couldn't do that with him in my head, telling me what to do and who I was. Or should be." She dug her toes in the sand. "I now realize that I've always let others control me, first Hannah's mom, then Kevin. With you, it was different. I made my own decisions. You treated me the way I deserve to be treated." She took her hand off his arm. The warm imprint of her fingers quickly cooled. "I should go."

He should say something, tell her he understood. Apologize for being the idiot Chas kept telling him he was.

Tell her he wanted her to stay.

Tell her he loved her.

🐑 🐑 🐑

Whit had seen her. And waved. It wasn't like she could just walk away. The paddle back to Hannah's was hard, against the wind, as if it was pushing her back to the beach—and Whit. Aly's emotions were a messy jumble, as tangled as seaweed. It would've been weird, abnormal, she told herself, to feel nothing when she saw him, a lonely figure on the empty, windswept beach, his body and fishing rod moving as one as he gracefully, effortlessly cast. But did it have to be so…so…ugh. She closed her eyes and winced. So hard.

Aly knew she couldn't leave things the way they were, with Whit thinking she was a liar. *Closure,* they'd call it. She didn't know what she was looking for. Understanding? Sure. But had she unconsciously hoped Whit would sweep her into his arms and they would go back to the way things were before?

But Whit had done nothing, said nothing. He just let her dump her emotional baggage there on the beach like a trash bag with a giant hole. Chas was wrong. Whit didn't care. Not anymore.

Aly put the paddleboard away for the last time. It was time to go home and take charge of her life, find her own happiness doing what she wanted to do, go after her own goals. New job, new hobbies, new life. But the thought of doing all that, on the other side of the continent from Whit, felt… Aly paused, searching her heart.

It felt wrong.

🐑 🐑 🐑

The Ritz was a dive bar, but in a good way. A disco ball hung over the bar, PBRs were cheap, the floor sticky, and the oak barstools were designed for durability, not comfort. The walls were plastered with old concert photos and pictures of musicians, and flags and Christmas lights decorated the ceiling. In the corner, a small area cleared of tables served as a stage, set up with a microphone, drum set, and keyboard. It was the perfect, very Vineyard place for them to kick up their heels and celebrate Aly's job offer.

The crowd was mostly locals and a scattering of tourists, easily identified by their Black Dog caps, bright clothes, and Vineyard Vines shopping bags. At the end of the bar sat a gaggle of six women wearing matching Barbie-pink "I'm with the bride" t-shirts. The seventh wore a sparkly tiara on her shiny brown hair and a "Bride" t-shirt. They were drinking martinis and appeared to be well on their way to getting trashed.

"Why do they call this the Ritz?" Aly asked Chas as they made their way to the table to join Hannah and Lawrence. "Ironic, I guess?"

"I haven't a clue," said Chas. "It's been the Ritz forever. And they've always had live music. About the only thing on the Island that hasn't changed. For better or for worse," he added, glancing around the room.

"Hey guys," Aly said as they joined Hannah and Lawrence at a small table near the stage.

Lawrence stood up and kissed Aly's cheek. "Congratulations on the job. Let me buy you a drink to celebrate. What'll it be?"

"Champagne, obviously, if they have it," said Chas.

Aly smiled. "Actually, I'd love a beer."

"Aly, I have a new plan for the apartment," said Chas as they sat down. "I've decided I want to buy instead of rent. Give myself some real roots in the city. Even start looking for some good works to apply my talents to."

"That's great," Aly said, heart sinking. "No problem. I can get my own place."

"That's not what I meant. I'm buying only if I can find something with a guest suite for you. Maybe one of those lovely, big Victorian houses with lots of room for entertaining." Chas explained. "I thought I'd go out there again next month. Besides, I need to keep looking for my Granny-standards-meeting, gay, and kid-loving potential fiancé."

"What about Kyle, the teddy-bear bartender?"

"Hmmm," said Chas. "He did mention something about attending Stevenson in Pebble Beach. Look, I think the music is going to begin soon."

The weathered-looking bartender tucked her hair behind her ears and stepped onto the stage. She took the microphone from the stand and tapped it. "Sorry to disappoint all you Bluefish fans. Johnny picked up a last-minute wedding gig off-Island. But lucky for us, I'm happy to introduce our own Whit Dias, fisherman by day, musician by night. Handsome to boot," she winked. "And we've got Robby on the drums, Frank on the bass, and Paris on the keyboard. And hey, Whit takes song requests, so we're going to have some fun tonight."

The bachelorette party at the bar squealed and clapped as Whit and the rest of the band walked on stage. Aly sat stunned. She shot a look at Chas and Hannah. Both looked pleased with themselves. "You told me Johnny Hoy was playing," she whispered to Chas as Whit adjusted the microphone.

"He was."

"You knew about this, didn't you?"

Chas merely pressed his lips together and raised an eyebrow. "They're starting."

"Evening, folks. Always glad to play for a Saturday night crowd at the Ritz," Whit said with that lopsided grin that made Aly's heart flip. It had been hard enough holding it together when she'd seen him on the beach. Aly took a deep breath. So much for celebrating. She'd been sandbagged.

Hannah waved and hooted. Whit's smile wavered when he looked over and saw Aly. She wanted to sink down to the sticky floor and disappear under the table. He didn't want her here. Recovering, Whit turned his attention to the bachelorette party at the bar. "I hope you ladies have your dancing shoes on," he said. One of the bachelorettes gave Whit a long wolf whistle. "OK," he said, "Let's get going!"

Aly leaned back as Whit launched into the first song. Hannah and Chas must've planned this. Even though she'd told them both it was over with Whit. Repeatedly.

Whit drew in the crowd with effortless charm. Aly couldn't pull her eyes away even if she tried. When he started to sing, goosebumps tingled her skin. Whit's hair, blue-black under the spotlight. The angle of his jaw, rough with stubble. The whale tattoo, which her fingertips had traced countless times, seemed to swim as Whit's muscles flexed. The timber of his voice resonated inside Aly, reminding her of all the times he had picked up his guitar to play and sing as they sat on his deck, watching Tisbury Great Pond turn shimmering blue to rosy gold with the setting sun.

Whit had discovered something in her that she hadn't realized had been trapped inside. They had sung together for the pure joy of hearing their voices twine and intertwine in the easy harmonies that felt so right. She'd rediscovered her voice with him, and for that she was grateful.

Aly closed her eyes. She felt as if Whit were strumming her heartstrings, drawing her back to him. It was beautiful. And, oh, so painful.

Whit and the band picked up the pace with some dance tunes, playing an eclectic mix of new music mixed with retro pop and a little New Orleans gypsy jazz. The drunken bachelorette party moved from the bar to the tiny dance floor. The tipsy bride-to-be planted herself directly in front of Whit, shimmying and bouncing her boobs to attract his attention, then turning herself butt-first and twerking.

Chas leaned over to Aly, "Oh my. Good thing that girl is getting married off. She rather reminds me of a female baboon in heat."

"That's not very nice."

"Well, it's true. Poor Whit, all that bouncing right in his face."

The dance floor filled up. "Come on," Hannah said, pulling Lawrence to his feet. "Let's boogie."

"Aly?" Chas asked.

"No thanks. I'm not in the mood."

Aly sipped her beer and watched Hannah laughingly trying to copy Lawrence's dance moves. She didn't have to stay. But she knew Hannah or Chas would insist on driving her home, and she didn't want to ruin their evening.

A few songs later, Hannah and Lawrence returned sweaty and breathless to the table. "That was fun," Hannah said, flopping down in her chair. "Isn't he just the best?" Hannah asked, glowing with happiness. "An artist and a dancer!"

"The best," Aly echoed.

Whit took a swig of water and looked around the crowd, his eyes pausing, unreadable, on Aly before swinging around to the bridal party. "I think it's time to see if anybody has any requests?"

"Taylor Swift! Taylor Swift!" the bachelorettes chanted.

"Hmm," Whit said, strumming on his guitar. "OK. Not my strong suit. We can try this one," he said, playing the opening chords of *You Belong with Me*. He turned to the rest of the band. "You guys good?" The band nodded. Whit turned back to the audience. "But I'll need a little help with the lyrics. Any singers out there?"

"Me, me!" bounced the bride. Whit handed her the microphone, and the band began to play. With drunken, vaguely Taylor-esque dance moves and her tiara slipping, the brunette warbled off-key, forgetting more lyrics than she remembered. Whit gamely played along, joining in and looking deep into the bride's eyes as she wailed the chorus.

A sharp pang of jealousy jabbed Aly's heart. It really was time to go. But Hannah and Lawrence were dancing again.

Whit and the bride-to-be were still singing Taylor Swift. She was clearly having a fabulous time, flirting with Whit, who appeared to be having nearly as much fun. They began *We Are Never Ever Getting Back Together*. It felt like a message.

🐑 🐑 🐑

It had been a long set, and Whit was tired of playing Taylor Swift and being pawed at by the bride. "Time to wrap things up, folks," he said to a chorus of groans. The more he tried to ignore Aly, the more he failed. Just another gig, he told himself. Pretend she isn't here. But that hadn't worked. Whit wanted, *needed,* to talk to her again. To say to her what he should've said on the beach. He was an idiot. He should have listened to her, trusted her, not let his emotional baggage mess everything up.

Most likely things would just get worse for him, and she'd walk away again, he thought. But he didn't care.

"One more song. I promised the last request to Liz behind the bar. Liz, what'll it be?" Whit asked.

"*Sweet Baby James*," shouted the bartender. "That's my favorite."

"You've got it. Love me a little James Taylor to settle down for the night," he said, strumming his guitar.

Whit gazed at Aly's table, and their eyes locked. As the tune rose in his mind, he was back on the beach that magical evening, Aly stretched out on his tatty old bedspread and glowing in the setting sun. Her voice, joining with his as if matched by the gods, as the sky turned orange and pink and purple, and the waves lapped at the shore. Was she remembering that too? He knew it was probably the worst thing in the world again, but he wanted to hear her voice, feel her near to him. One last time.

"I'd like to ask someone special to join me on stage. This song has never sounded better than when she sang it with me. Aly?"

🐑 🐑 🐑

In shock, Aly shook her head no.

"You're crazy," called a bridesmaid.

"C'mon, don't be so shy—get up there," yelled another. "Or I will!"

Chas nudged her arm. "Aly? It's not too late. Please."

Why was Whit asking her to sing with him? Didn't he know how much it would hurt? Was it possible? Could he still want her as much as she wanted him? The bachelorettes whooped and hollered as she set her glass on the table and stood up. There was only one way to find out.

Her life. Her choice.

"Yay, Aly!" Hannah hooted as Aly joined Whit on the stage.

"You don't have to do this," he whispered in her ear.

She felt the heat of Whit's skin through his shirt, breathed in his smell of sweat and salt and the sea. "I want to." And she did, more than anything else.

Whit signaled to the band that they should sit this one out and adjusted the capo on his guitar. "Ready?"

Aly nodded. Whit began to play, leaning in to share the microphone. Their lips, so close. She felt a nimbus, like a current of energy, surround them as they sang together. The room grew quiet as their voices rose in perfect harmony. The crowd fell away, leaving the two of them in the spotlight, making music.

The song ended with riotous applause. "One more," Aly whispered in his ear. She leaned into the microphone. "And this one's my favorite. It's in Gaelic, but it's about a boatman and his love, separated by the sea. I hope I remember all the lyrics." In a clear, confident voice, she began singing a cappella. The room hushed. After the first verse, Whit joined her, their voices weaving and twining together like threads made of notes as they sang of their longing for one another. This was what she wanted. This man, this life.

The song ended. Whit put his arm around Aly, and she leaned into him. Where she belonged. A pause, as if he too was unwilling to break the spell. Finally, Whit pulled himself together enough to say, "That's it, folks. Drive safely. Don't forget to settle your bar tab. And please tip generously."

Whit turned to Aly. "Will you wait for me?"

Aly turned and looked at him, aglow. "Yes."

🐑 🐑 🐑

A cool breeze blew through the parking lot behind the Ritz. "I didn't know you'd be there," Whit said.

"I didn't know you'd be playing."

"If you had, would you've come?"

"Probably not."

Aly took a step closer, and she was in Whit's arms.

🐑 🐑 🐑

"Wake up, sleepyhead. Want to go fishing?" Whit asked, offering Aly a cup of coffee.

Feeling as content as a cat full of cream, Aly sat up and let the sheet slide to her waist. Whit's eyes grew wide, and Aly gave him a sexy wink. It felt inevitable, and right, that she was back in his bed. Like their first kiss on the park bench, sticky-sweet with ice cream, the kiss by the side of Whit's truck in the Ritz's parking lot had filled Aly with joy and desire, mixed with a sense of rightness, as if the gods had been working behind the scenes, smiling at their success. And after their lovemaking—and, oh, what lovemaking that was—they'd stayed up nearly all night talking, both admitting that they'd been wrong, saying how desperately they'd missed each other, sharing everything that they'd learned about themselves and each other since they'd parted, letting their love move them past the pain. No lies, no mistrust. Just two souls as bare as their bodies.

"Fishing? You're kidding, right?" Aly asked. "I can think of something else to do instead," she said, patting the empty place in the bed.

"Plenty of time for that," Whit said. "I'm feeling lucky."

Aly set her coffee cup on the bedside table, stretched her arms overhead, feeling happy from the tips of her fingers to her toes. A beam of sunshine broke through the clouds, illuminating Whit, a fishing-obsessed Greek god. "What if I'm bad at it and mess up your reel or something?"

"Then I'll show you how to untangle it, and you'll try again," Whit said, bending over to kiss her hair. "If you like pulling lobsters out of stinky traps, you're going to love surfcasting. And if you don't, it's still a nice day for a beach walk. But it's up to you. I like your idea too," he said, letting his fingers slide down her shoulder.

A vision of the two of them surfcasting together, their lines making a graceful arc on a beautifully desolate beach, replaced the tangled and knotted line. Excitement swelled inside Aly. Whit was Nonna's question answered. He made her feel safe and strong and confident. She could do anything so long as he was at her side.

And very hot melty mozzarella. "How about we compromise? We can do both?"

"Perfect solution." Whit sat on the bed and nuzzled Aly's neck. "Besides, I need to find out if you can fish if we're going to be together."

"Together?"

"It's no use, Aly. I've tried, but I can't get you out of my head. And my heart. I love you, Aly Bennett, and I want you in my life."

Aly's mind spun cartwheels. "But, how? Your boat? St. John?"

"Chas, for once, is as brilliant as he thinks he is. With your new job, we can live wherever we want. San Francisco, here, St. John. Anywhere."

Whit explained Chas's plan. Aly saw their life together. The bougainvillea-covered cottage overlooking turquoise Caribbean waters, lounging in beach chairs with fruity rum drinks topped with freshly grated nutmeg. The brisk breeze filling billowing sails as she and Whit race the fog under the Golden Gate Bridge. And after, a pasta dinner in the warm embrace of Nonna's restaurant. And beaching, fishing, lobstering, and making music together on marvelous Martha's Vineyard, near all the people she loved most in the world.

With the man she loved.

"That is a brilliant idea."

"Depending on how you do fishing, maybe I'll train you to be my first mate."

"Co-captain."

Whit's irresistible, lopsided smile spread across his face. "Co-captain it is. Ready to catch us some fish, Captain Aly?"

CODA – SUMMER

Aly carefully lowered Whit's guitar case over *Noepe's* gunwale and into the cockpit. Beer, wine, soda, and seltzer? Check. Charcuterie tray with local cheeses, smoked bluefish, and vegetables? Check. Guitar? Check. All they were missing were their "guests," and they were ready to go.

"You sure people are going to want to pay to hear me blather on about Vineyard history and sing a couple of songs?" Whit had seemed nervous all day, which was odd given that this was only a practice run of his new boat tour, and the guests would be Chas, Hannah, and Lawrence.

"Absolutely. Just you wait and see. You have so much interesting stuff to talk about—nautical history, the whaling era, Wampanoag lore, wrecks, fishing," she said, pulling a lime seltzer from the cooler. "Plus, I've been talking it up on Dandelion's social-media pages. Tons of likes and shares." She settled into one of the fishing chairs. "Do you think Dandelion would like the boat? We could do a trip focused on the history of sheep farming on the Island, maybe talk that cute couple over at Allen Farm into coming along?"

Whit laughed. "Love your imagination and enthusiasm, Aly, but I think that a cruise with a freaked-out bleating sheep is not going to be a big seller."

"Hmm. Probably not," she admitted and sipped her seltzer. "But I've got two more bookings for Cream Tea with Dandelion.

Thank goodness the owners of the Dinghy loved the idea. They've been signing up their houseguests. Hannah's been teaching Dandelion how to drink from a teacup. It's really cute." Aly rubbed sunscreen onto her nose. "And the first sheep yoga class is already full. Plus, someone called about renting Dandelion and another sheep for their wedding. They want us to dress one up with a little top hat and bow tie as the groom and the other as the bride with a veil. How adorable is that?"

"Adorable," repeated Whit. "So long as they don't try to eat the bridal bouquet."

Aly spotted Chas's car pulling up. "Hey, here they come. Oh! Good Lord. Look at Chas."

Chas walked down the dock wearing an orange Black Dog bucket hat, a Hawaiian print shirt, and lemon-yellow plaid shorts. He completed his outfit with an immense striped beach bag and drugstore flip-flops. "Oh, you must be Captain Whit," Chas said. "I can't wait to learn who Martha is. And where *is* her vineyard? I've been searching my map, and I can't find it!"

Whit rolled his eyes in reply.

"We decided who gets to be who," Hannah said. "Chas is the tacky tourist who won't shut up with stupid questions. I'm the old lady with balance and hearing issues," she said, taking Whit's hand and pretending to fall into the boat. "And Lawrence is the whiny kid who didn't want to come and gets seasick."

"Bleh," responded Lawrence, handing Aly his empty chocolate frappe cup. "I don't feel so good."

"You guys are too much," Aly said, overjoyed to be with her friends again. "I love St. John, I love San Francisco, but it's great to be back."

The gang tired of their role-playing after a long (but very amusing) half hour, which allowed Whit to polish his patter and Aly to show off her piloting skills. Chas propped his feet on the cooler. "So, Whit. You let Aly do all your work now?"

"I like running the boat," said Aly from the helm. "I'm studying for my captain's license. We might even get a smaller boat for me in St. John and start offering snorkeling tours. Did I tell you we're doing whale-watching trips now too? I've gotten really good at spotting them."

"All that and your job?" asked Lawrence.

"I start work early and end at 3:00, leaving me plenty of free time," Aly said. Whit unwrapped the charcuterie platter. "What's new with you guys?"

"Well, I've got a new boo," Chas said, reaching over for a slice of salami. "And I think I'm in love."

Hannah reached over to pat Chas on the shoulder. "Whoa, congratulations. Your San Francisco bartender?"

"Kyle wasn't looking to settle down. But Aubrey is."

"Why haven't I heard about him?" asked Whit, looking offended. "I'm your best buddy."

Chas leaned back against the cushion. "We didn't want to get all those gossipy tongues wagging in Edgartown until we were sure. He's a film producer and a trust fund baby, like me. I met him flying back from San Francisco when the flight attendant spilled my drink on his lap. We got to talking and the next thing you know, we're on a plane together to Martha's Vineyard," he said with a moony expression. "He fell in love with the Island—and me. I can't wait for you all to meet him. I'm taking him over to Granny's tomorrow."

"I'm sure she'll approve," said Aly. "Does he like Russian literature?"

Chas laughed. "I've never asked." He turned to Hannah and Lawrence. "How about you two? Any news?"

"Lawrence sold another painting at the Granary Gallery," said Hannah.

"But more exciting, we've launched Hannah's new business," Lawrence said. "We gave my sister one of Hannah's table lamps for Christmas. Her best friend, who's a big-shot interior decorator, liked it so much she borrowed it for this year's Kips Bay Decorator Show House."

"I'd never even heard of Kips Bay. Now, I've got so many orders, I've had to cut back on my painting jobs," Hannah said with a laugh. "And I've got a waiting list. You won't believe what Lawrence makes me charge!"

Lawrence beamed at Hannah. "Supply and demand, baby."

Aly's heart swelled with pride. "Put us on the list too. We'll want one for Chas's new house in San Francisco."

"Absolutely." Hannah opened a beer. "I forgot to tell you, Aly. My mom called this morning. She wants to come back again this summer, this time for a whole week. She's insisting on meeting Lawrence's parents, now that she knows who he is," she said, rolling her eyes.

"Come on, Hannah," said Lawrence. "You know you two are getting along better since she and your father came for Thanksgiving. I think Maria hosting that big Brazilian barbeque in your honor helped."

"*Churrasco*," said Hannah. "It was so nice of Maria, and Mom and Dad had such fun. I still can't believe they wanted to come."

"Well, I'm glad they did," Aly said. "Your mom still thinks I made a mistake taking the WHOI job. And moving in with Whit. But, whatever."

"Not a mistake—at least, I hope not," said Whit, with an odd quaver in his voice. "Chas, would you take over the wheel? I need Aly."

"For what?" Aly asked.

Whit fumbled in his pocket and dropped to one knee. Aly's eyes widened in disbelief. Could this really be happening? Right here? Right now?

"Yes!" Chas shouted. "She says, yes!"

"Let him ask her!" cried Hannah and Lawrence in unison.

Whit's hands shook as he opened the small box. "I love you more, more… more than all the fish in the sea. Aly, will you marry me?"

Speechless, Aly took out the sapphire ring and let Whit slip it onto her finger. She threw herself into Whit's arms as Hannah and Lawrence whooped and hollered. It felt unreal. And very, very right. "Yes," she finally said after covering him with kisses. "A million times, yes!"

"It's about time, Whit," said Chas. "I gave you that ring months ago."

"Just waiting for the right moment," Whit said, grinning ear to ear. Aly pressed herself against him, smiling the biggest smile her face could hold. "We don't have any champagne. But maybe we can toast with this?" Whit asked, opening the beer cooler. Hannah handed out five cold cans of Narragansett.

"My favorite," said Aly.

"A toast," said Chas, raising his beer. "To the perfect couple, with best wishes for all the happiness in the world. Now, you two," he said, turning to Whit and Aly. "You need to pick a date for the wedding!"

The setting sun lit the Gay Head Cliffs with brilliant golds and oranges as if flames were burning from within the clay. In a state of blissful joy, Aly listened with half an ear as Chas chattered away about dresses and caterers and flowers and venues and music. She squeezed Whit's hand, and the sapphire flashed blue on her finger. Whit couldn't have picked a more perfect time and place to propose, surrounded by the people she loved and who loved her and Whit. "How about we put Chas in charge of planning the wedding?"

"I'd be honored," said Chas.

"You'd better not try to put me in some ghastly flowered bridesmaid dress," Hannah said. She held up Whit's guitar case. "Hey, Whit. You forgot to sing us a sea shanty. You'll have to refund our money."

"Up to my beautiful fiancée," said Whit. Aly's cheeks pinked as happiness welled inside her. *Fiancée*.

"I'd love to hear you sing," said Aly.

"You've got it," Whit said, pulling out his guitar. "So long as you join me. How about the *Wellerman* song? I'll need you all to keep the beat for me. Like this." They all joined in, pounding a steady four-beat tempo with their feet. "I might change the lyrics a bit in honor of the occasion." Strumming and stomping, Whit began to sing in his rich, clear tenor voice:

> *There once was a ship that put to sea*
> *The name of the ship was the Aly-drinks-tea*
> *The winds blew up and the bow dipped down*
> *Blow my bully boy blow*
> *Soon may my Aly-love come*
> *To bring us sugar and tea and rum*
> *One day when the fishing is done*
> *We'll take our leave and go*

- THE END

BONUS– A FEW RECIPES!

SWEET
Cinna-Love Buns with Maple-Cream Cheese Frosting

PASTA
Nonna's Spaghetti and Meatballs
Vodka Pasta
Spaghetti alle Vongole
Pasta Puttanesca with Bluefish
Ricotta Cavatelli with Basil Pesto

SAVORY
Ken's Oxtail Ragoût
Beach Picnic Sweet and Sticky Wings
Lovers' Lobster Salad (or Lobster Rolls)
Fresh Grilled Corn Salad

JAMS AND JELLIES:
Wild Blueberry Jam

COCKTAILS
Chum Bucket
Frolicking Lamb

SWEET

CINNA-LOVE BUNS WITH MAPLE-CREAM CHEESE FROSTING
(9 rolls)

Dough:
2 cups all-purpose flour, plus more as needed
2 tablespoons white sugar
2 teaspoons baking powder
1 teaspoon table salt
3 tablespoons unsalted butter, softened
2/3 cup milk
2 tablespoons melted butter

Filling:
½ cup brown sugar, firmly packed
1 tablespoon ground cinnamon

Cream Cheese Frosting:
¾ cup confectioners' sugar, sifted
3 ounces cream cheese, softened
3 tablespoons unsalted butter, softened
1 tablespoons maple syrup
½ teaspoon vanilla extract

Preheat the oven to 400 degrees F. Butter an 8-inch square baking dish.

Whisk flour, white sugar, baking powder, and salt together in a large bowl. Work the 3 tablespoons of softened butter into the flour mixture with your fingers until butter is combined (like coarse crumbs). Add milk and mix just until a soft dough forms. Turn dough out onto a well-floured work surface and shape into a 10-inch square. Brush the surface of the dough with the 2 tablespoons of melted butter.

In a small bowl, whisk the brown sugar and cinnamon together. Sprinkle cinnamon sugar over the dough all the way to the edges on 3 sides, leaving a 1-inch edge (to seal) on one side. Roll dough up to form a log; cut log into 9 rolls about 1-inch wide; place rolls, cut-side up, in the prepared baking dish.

Bake until rolls are puffed and lightly golden, 20 to 25 minutes. While the rolls bake, beat the confectioners' sugar, cream cheese, softened butter, maple syrup, and vanilla extract together in a bowl with a mixer (or by hand) until frosting is smooth.

Let cool slightly and top warm cinnamon rolls with cream cheese frosting.

PASTA

NONNA'S SPAGHETTI AND MEATBALLS
(*Serves 10-12*)

4 pounds ground sirloin ("use good meat")
4 eggs
5 hamburger rolls ("no seeds on top")
1 cup grated parmesan cheese (plus more for serving)
2 teaspoons sugar
4 (28-ounce) cans crushed tomatoes ("not the one with the basil")
2 (6 oz) cans tomato paste
1 onion, finely diced
2 (16-ounce) boxes spaghetti
Olive oil

Preheat the oven to 350 degrees.

In a food processor fitted with a metal blade, pulse the rolls to make breadcrumbs. Add enough warm water to "make a sloppy mixture" the texture of cooked oatmeal. (Grandma would bake the breadcrumbs first, but you don't have to.)

Put the ground beef in a large bowl. Add the eggs, cheese, some salt and pepper, and the breadcrumb mixture and combine with your hands ("mix with your hands, little by little; make sure you can still form them into balls, but they're still pretty mushy"). Don't overmix.

Shape the meatballs (a bit bigger than a golf ball), and place on an oiled cookie sheet (about 35-40 meatballs). Bake until just grayish/brownish (about 15 minutes), flip onto the other side, and bake for another 10 minutes. (Grandma would brown them in an electric skillet.)

While the meatballs are baking, make the tomato sauce. In a saucepan large enough to hold the sauce and meatballs, heat the olive oil sauté the finely diced onion over medium heat until translucent. Add the crushed tomatoes and two cans of water. Bring to a simmer, and stir in the tomato paste, sugar, and salt and pepper.

Add the baked meatballs to the pan of tomato sauce. Simmer on low for 2-3 hours, gently stirring from time to time —meatballs will finish cooking in the sauce. (The meatballs will be done in about 30 minutes, but Grandma simmered them for hours.)

Serve over cooked spaghetti with more parmesan. Mangia!

(With thanks to Elisa Speranza, also Tracey Chalifour and Cindy Drislane who observed Grandma and took great notes.)

VODKA PASTA
(serves 4 as a main course)

1 16-ounce box rigatoni
4 tablespoons unsalted butter
A few shakes of red pepper flakes (about ¼ teaspoon)
1 large (28 ounce) can peeled plum tomatoes
½ cup vodka
½ to 1 cup heavy cream
1 cup freshly grated parmesan cheese, plus more for serving

Bring a large pot of salted water to a boil for the pasta. Cook pasta per directions on the box. When done, put aside a cup of pasta water and drain pasta.

While the pasta is cooking, melt butter and red pepper flakes in a large deep skillet over medium heat. Cook, stirring, for 2 minutes. Add the can of tomatoes and their juices and cook, breaking up chunks of tomatoes into smaller pieces, until most of the liquid has cooked off.

Add vodka, stir, and cook for a minute or two to boil off the alcohol. Add heavy cream and grated parmesan and stir. Add rigatoni and stir to coat, adding a bit of the pasta water to make a creamy sauce. Serve with additional grated cheese.

SPAGHETTI ALLE VONGOLE (SPAGHETTI WITH CLAM SAUCE)
(serves 4 as a main course)

1 16-ounce box spaghetti
4 dozen well-scrubbed littleneck clams (or 1 cup chopped raw quahog clams + 1 dozen littlenecks)
3 tablespoons extra-virgin olive oil
2 tablespoons unsalted butter
4 large cloves of garlic, minced
A few shakes of red pepper flakes (about ¼ teaspoon)
3/4 cup of dry white wine (and/or white vermouth)
1 teaspoon lemon zest
½ cup chopped fresh parsley
2 tablespoons unsalted butter

Bring a large pot of salted water to a boil for the pasta. Cook pasta per directions to almost al dente (a little chewy) and drain, tossing with a bit of olive oil to prevent sticking.

In a large saucepan, add olive oil, butter, garlic, and red pepper flakes. Sauté over low heat, so that garlic doesn't brown, until garlic is soft.

Turn heat up to medium, add wine and clams, and cover. When most of the clams are open, add the cooked pasta and stir. Cover and simmer for a couple of minutes until the pasta is done. Discard any unopened clams, mix in lemon zest, parsley, and butter, and serve.

PASTA PUTTANSECA WITH BLUEFISH
(Serves 4 as a main course)

1 16-ounce box of linguini
3 tablespoons olive oil, plus more for sautéing fish
½ teaspoon red pepper flakes (or more to taste)
3-4 anchovy filets, chopped (or ¾ to 1 teaspoon anchovy paste)
5 cloves of garlic, peeled and smashed flat
1 (28-ounce) can diced tomatoes
1 (14-oz) can crushed tomatoes
½ cup pitted black olives, kalamata or oil-cured
3 tablespoon capers
Zest from ½ lemon
¼ cup thinly sliced fresh basil and/or chopped parsley
1 pound very fresh bluefish filets (skin on)

Bring a large pot of salted water to a boil for the pasta.

Heat olive oil in a large saucepan over medium heat. Add red pepper flakes, anchovy filets, and garlic and cook until garlic starts to brown. Add both cans of tomatoes, olives, capers, lemon zest, and a few grinds of black pepper. Bring sauce to a boil then reduce heat to a simmer.

While the sauce is simmering, salt and pepper the bluefish filets. Drizzle olive oil in a skillet over medium heat, add bluefish, and cook until the fish begins to flake. Remove skin, cut into bite-sized chunks and add to sauce. Turn sauce off while you cook the pasta per package directions. Drain the pasta and toss it with the sauce. Serve with basil and/or parsley on top.

RICOTTA CAVATELLI WITH BASIL PESTO
Recipe courtesy of Chef Carlos Montoya of The Maker Pasta Shop, Martha's Vineyard
(Serves 6)

Cavatelli:

1 (15-ounce) container ricotta cheese
1 egg
¼ cup milk
¼ cup chopped chives
1 lemon, zested
1 tablespoon salt
4 cups flour

Pesto:

4 cups fresh basil leaves
4 tablespoons pine nuts
4 garlic cloves
1 cup extra-virgin olive oil
1 cup freshly grated parmesan
1 teaspoon fine sea salt
½ teaspoon freshly grated black pepper

Cavatelli:

Strain ricotta over a bowl to remove excess water/moisture.

Mix the milk, strained ricotta (discard the liquid), lemon zest and egg together in a small mixing bowl. Reserve. Mix the flour, chives and salt in a large mixing bowl.

Place the flour in the middle of a work surface and create a "well" in the center of the flour. Add the liquid ingredients, (ricotta, milk, eggs). Mix the flour and the liquid ingredients gradually, drawing the flour from the inside walls of the well. A wooden spoon works very well for this stage of the process, but once the dough becomes thicker and begins to stick to the spoon, it is best to use your hands to work the dough. The flour is continually pulled from the sides of the well into the center until all of the flour has been incorporated into the dough.

Wrap the dough tight with plastic wrap and refrigerate for at least an hour before use.

When dough has rested, lightly flour a clean, smooth work surface. Using a rolling pin, roll the dough out to 1/4" thick. Cut into 1" wide strips. Dust with flour. Using a cavatelli machine, spin the dough strips through while being careful that the dough doesn't stick.

(TEB: alternatively, to shape cavatelli by hand, instead of rolling into strips, shape the dough into a ½-inch diameter rope and cut into ¾-inch pieces. Using the tines of a fork, press each piece firmly with two fingers and drag towards you to make a curl.)

Pesto:

Combine basil leaves, pine nuts, salt, pepper and garlic in a food processor and process until very finely minced. With the machine running slowly dribble in the oil and process until the mixture is smooth. Add the cheese and process very briefly, just long enough to combine. Transfer to storage container. Label. date, and refrigerator. (Or freeze)

To cook:

Bring a large pot of salted water to a boil. Cook cavatelli in batches until the pasta rises to the top, scooping out with a slotted spoon. Serve with the pesto sauce.

SAVORY

KEN'S OXTAIL (OR SHORT RIB) RAGOUT
(serves 6)

5 pounds meaty oxtails (or thick bone-in beef short ribs)
2 tablespoons vegetable oil
2 large heads garlic, halved crossways
1 medium onion, roughly chopped
2 medium carrots, roughly chopped
3 tablespoons tomato paste
2 cups dry red wine
3 tablespoons soy sauce
1 thumb-sized chunk of fresh ginger, peeled and cut into 3 chunks
3 pieces star anise
1 teaspoon dried thyme (or 4 sprigs fresh)
3 bay leaves
1 tablespoon sugar
2 cups beef broth, bouillon, or stock

Heat oven to 275 degrees. Salt and pepper meat. Heat oil in a large Dutch oven over medium-high heat. Working in batches, sear meat on all sides until deeply browned. Remove to a plate and set aside.

Reduce heat to medium. With cut edges down, lightly brown garlic and set aside with meat. Add carrots and onions and cook until vegetables are softened, 5 to 10 minutes. Add tomato paste, stir, and cook for 2-3 minutes more.

Add red wine, scraping up browned bits from the bottom. Add soy sauce, ginger, star anise, thyme, bay leaves, sugar, and broth. Return meat and garlic to the pan (in a single layer, if possible), adding additional stock (or water) to cover the meat. Bring to a boil, cover, and place in the preheated oven.

Braise until meat is tender and can be shredded with a fork, 3 to 4 hours. Remove meat to a serving platter and strain sauce. Serve with miso-butter baby potatoes (boil 2 pounds of baby potatoes until tender, drain. Return to the pan and add 4 tablespoons of unsalted butter mixed with 2 tablespoons of white miso paste. Cook stirring or shaking until the potatoes are coated). The ragout can be made ahead of time—it's even better the next day.

BEACH PICNIC SWEET AND STICKY WINGS
Recipe courtesy of Caroline Wohlgemuth
(Serves 8 as hors d'oeuvres)

4 pounds of chicken wings (drums and/or flats)
1 tablespoon vegetable oil
1 cup soy sauce
½ cup dry red wine
2/3 cup brown sugar
2 teaspoons fresh grated ginger (or ½ teaspoon dried)
3 scallions, thinly sliced
1 tablespoon sesame seeds, lightly toasted in a dry skillet

Preheat oven to 400 degrees.

Line a large roasting pan (or sheet pan) with well-greased parchment paper (or foil). Arrange chicken wings in one layer in the pan. In a small saucepan, heat soy sauce, red wine, brown sugar, and ginger until the sugar is dissolved. Pour the sauce evenly over the wings. Bake on the middle shelf of the oven for 40 minutes. Turn wings over, turn heat up to 425 degrees, and bake until the sauce is thick and sticky, 20-45 minutes more.

Transfer wings to a platter and top with scallions and sesame seeds.

LOVERS' LOBSTER SALAD (OR LOBSTER ROLLS)
(Serves 4 as a main course or 8 as an appetizer)

1 pound cooked lobster meat (from about 4 one-pound lobsters)
1 to 3 teaspoons fresh lemon juice
4 to 6 tablespoons mayonnaise (Hellman's original)
½ cup finely diced celery
Lettuce leaves, avocado, cucumber, and/or ripe tomatoes to serve (or 4 split-top hot dog buns)

Cut lobster into ¾ inch chunks. In a bowl, mix 1 teaspoon lemon juice with 4 tablespoons mayonnaise, and celery, add salt and pepper to taste and more lemon juice if desired. Mix in lobster chunks and taste again, adding more mayonnaise and/or lemon juice to taste.

Lobster salad: on each plate, arrange a bed of lettuce leaves, mound the lobster salad in the center, garnish with avocado, cucumber, and/or tomatoes.

Lobster rolls: heat a large skillet over medium-high heat. Generously butter both sides of each hot dog bun. Cook the buttered sides in the skillet until toasty brown. Fill each bun with one-quarter of the lobster salad.

FRESH GRILLED CORN SALAD
(Serves 4)

2 to 3 ears of corn
1 large ripe tomato, diced
½ cucumber, diced
1 red bell pepper, diced
½ jalapeno, minced
1 avocado, diced (optional)
3 scallions, thinly sliced
2 tablespoons rice vinegar
1 tablespoon lime juice
2 tablespoons extra virgin olive oil

Leaving the husk on, cook the corn over a hot grill until the husk is lightly charred on all sides. Let cool, peel, and cut the kernels off the cob. Mix all ingredients in a bowl, add salt and pepper to taste. (For a heartier salad, add a can of drained, rinsed black beans.)

JAMS AND JELLIES

WILD BLUEBERRY JAM
(approximately 8 half-pint jars)

10 heaping cups wild blueberries, rinsed and de-stemmed
Juice and zest from one lemon (or lime)
Shake or two of cinnamon (optional)
5 cups sugar (up to 8 cups for a sweeter jam)
1 box (2 pouches) of liquid pectin
9 half-pint (8-ounce) ball jars

When you're ready to start making jam, sterilize the jars, lids and rings in a large pot of boiling water for 5 minutes. (If using more sugar, sterilize a couple of extra jars.) Turn hot jars upside down on a clean dishcloth to drain along with the lids and rings. (It's easier if you sterilize the lids and rings in a separate small saucepan. Also, if you don't have a jar lifter, wrap rubber bands around the end of a set of tongs for extra traction lifting and lowering the jars.). Bring the water back to a boil, making sure that there will be enough water to cover the jars by 1-2 inches.

In a large, heavy saucepan (such as a Dutch oven), bring the berries, lemon juice and zest, cinnamon (if using), and sugar to a full boil over medium-high heat. Boil 5 minutes, smushing down the berries. Add 2 pouches of liquid pectin and boil 1 minute. Skim off the foam. Ladle carefully into the hot jars, leaving ¼ inch space between the jam and the top of the jar. Wipe the edge and threads clean with a damp paper towel. Cover with the lid and screw the rings on tightly.

Return jars to the boiling water for 10 minutes. Remove jars and place on a dish towel to cool. As they cool, the lids will a "pop" as they seal. Tighten rings. Check to make sure all have sealed by pressing the lid—if it springs back, it hasn't sealed. Store any unsealed jars in the refrigerator.

COCKTAILS

CHUM BUCKET
(one cocktail)

¾ oz. dry gin
¾ oz. green Chartreuse
½ oz. Campari
¾ oz. maraschino liqueur
¾ oz. fresh lime juice
Lime wedge
Maraschino cherry (Luxardo or similar)

Mix well and serve over ice. Garnish with a lime wedge and cherry.

FROLICKING LAMB
(one cocktail)

2 oz. Botanist gin
½ oz. Fontbonne (or green Chartreuse) liqueur
½ oz. crème de violette
2 oz. cold half-and-half
1 oz. lemon juice
2 teaspoons sugar
1 egg white
Basil sprig to garnish

In a large cocktail shaker, combine all ingredients (except basil) and shake vigorously without ice for 30 seconds. Add ice and shake vigorously for another 30 seconds or until well chilled. Strain and serve in a coupe (Nick & Nora) or martini glass with a basil sprig garnish.

THE SONGS

If you'd like to hear some of the songs mentioned in the book, here are my favorite versions below:

- "Miss Flora McDonald's Reel": www.youtube.com/watch?v=2TNKLraGUv0

- "Fear a' Bhàta (The Boatman)": www.youtube.com/watch?v=CoZfNtAW1Ms

- "Johnny" by Sarah Jarosz: www.youtube.com/watch?v=eu8hn0Qo-XM

- "Sweet Baby James" by James Taylor: www.youtube.com/watch?v=MXjXp6GYP6M

- "The Wellerman": www.youtube.com/watch?v=ddZKwg63bRg

ACKNOWLEDGMENTS

The biggest possible thank you to my husband and family for their support and to my beta readers—Felicia, Adrienne, Alice, Donna, Emily, Bex, Aqsa, Peggy, Linda, Melissa, and Chris—for their incredibly valuable comments, edits, and suggestions on everything from sheep showmanship to plot to paddleboarding. I'd also like to give a particular shoutout to the amazing Allison Alsup for steering the novel back on track and to my fellow Washashore writers for their boundless help and encouragement. The kind words from our local booksellers (looking at you, Mat), my friends, and readers of *Goats in Time of Love* and *Counting Chickens* provided a boost when I needed it. And I don't have enough words to thank my last-minute proofreaders—Morgan, Robin, Jennifer, Donna, Alice, Jessie, Chris, and Adrienne!

I'm also deeply grateful to the island of Martha's Vineyard for inspiring me to write *Sheepish*, with special thanks to Kaila and Ned at Allen Farm, Allen at the Whiting Farm, and Arnie at Flat Point Farm for sharing their knowledge and love of sheep—and letting me visit their adorable lambs.

P.S. to my Readers: thank you so very much for reading Sheepish—*I'd love to hear from you (email: tebauthor@gmail.com, Instagram @tb.dc.mv or Facebook @telizabethbell)! And if you have a minute, please leave a review on Amazon and/or Goodreads, post about* Sheepish *on social media—and, of course, tell your friends!*

ABOUT THE AUTHOR

T. ELIZABETH BELL swapped writing legal memos for crafting sea-breezy, toes-in-the-sand novels (*Goats in the Time of Love* and *Counting Chickens*) inspired by her love of Martha's Vineyard. A beachcomber, dog-lover, wild blueberry-and-beach plum picker and jam-maker, she also dabbles in silversmithing, glittering Mardi Gras shoes, and capturing the island's beauty through her photography (@tb.dc.mv on Instagram and @telizabethbell on Facebook).

ALSO BY T. ELIZABETH BELL

COUNTING CHICKENS

"When you hire Nest, you are hiring 24-7, personalized attention to your every need." (Marketing brochure for Nest, a Bespoke Concierge)

Back on Martha's Vineyard after a failed marriage, Remy Litchfield is struggling to launch her high-end concierge service. Her business plan is complete, down to the fresh eggs provided courtesy of her very own flock of designer chickens. What she didn't plan on was the return of her high school crush, Jake Madden, or the suggestion by her impossibly handsome and wealthy client, Eli Wolff, that he is interested in having Remy do more than his shopping.

With the help of an escaped dog and her gang of eccentric and loyal friends, Remy must find a way to balance all the demands of her new life. But will catering to the whims of her high-end clients leave time for anything else?

GOATS IN THE TIME OF LOVE

Schuyler Harrington has fallen apart: her ex-fiancé is a serial philanderer, her beloved Grams has died, and she's quit her job. Escaping her city life, Sky seeks refuge on idyllic Martha's Vineyard, her childhood summer home. She hires Nate Batchelor, local Island goatscaper and scion of one of the Island's oldest families, to clear a view of Tisbury Great Pond with his herd of unruly goats.

Nate knows better than to get involved with a summer person—and a rich one at that—but the attraction for both is instant and undeniable. Sky's new life quickly collides with her old, and she must make some tough decisions.

Runaway goats, quirky characters, and a comedy of errors set the stage in this sea-breezy novel that proves that love will find you—whether you want it to or not.

Made in the USA
Monee, IL
24 June 2025